# PRAISE FOR THE SERIES

"Hodgell has crafted an excellent and intricate fantasy, with humor and tragedy, and a capable and charming female hero. Highly recommended."

—*Library Journal*

"Jame is a fully fleshed character in a rich fantasy milieu influenced by the likes of C.L. Moore and Elizabeth Lynn"

—*Publishers' Weekly*

"Already she brings a welcome freshness and flair to a field where creativity often seems more the exception than the rule."

—*Locus*

"Hodgell's affinities lie with the complex plotting of Mervyn Peake, the dark humor of Fritz Leiber, and the gruesomely poetic detail work of Clark Ashton Smith."

—*Fantasy Magazine*

# TO RIDE A
# RATHORN

## P. C. HODGELL

Meisha Merlin Publishing, Inc.
Atlanta, GA

**To Ride A Rathorn** Copyright © 2006 by P.C. Hodgell
All maps Copyright © 2006 by P.C. Hodgell

This book is printed on an acid-free and buffered paper that meets the NISO standard ANSI/NISO Z39.48-1992, Permanence of Paper for Publications and Documents in Libraries and Archives.

## TO RIDE A RATHORN

Published by Meisha Merlin Publishing, Inc.
PO Box 7
Decatur, GA   30031

Editing by Stephen Pagel
Copyediting Beverly Hale
Interior layout by Lynn Hatcher
Cover art by Christian McGrath
Cover design by Kevin Murphy

ISBN:   Hard Cover     1-59222-102-5
ISBN 13: Hard Cover   978-1-59222-102-8

**www.MeishaMerlin.com**
First MM Publishing edition: September 2006

Printed in Canada
 0  9  8  7  6  5  4  3  2  1

# TABLE OF CONTENTS

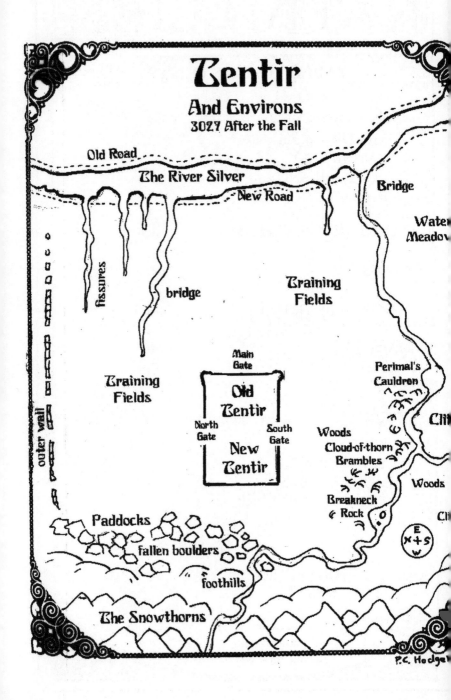

THE RIVERLAND

Restormir

Kithorn

Tagmeth

Valantir

Mount·Alban

Wilden

Tentir

Falkirr

Shadow Rock

Gothregor

Chantrie

Omiroth

Kraggen

Kestrie

25

○ keeps
⊕ ruins

THE·RIVER·SILVER

# TO RIDE A

# RATHORN

## P. C. HODGELL

# Chapter I: An Unfortunate Arrival

## 1st of Summer

## I

THE SUN'S DESCENDING rim touched the white peaks of the Snowthorns, kindling veins of fire down their shadowy slopes where traces of weirding lingered. Luminous mist, smoking out of high fissures, dimmed the setting sun. A premonitory chill of dusk rolled down toward the valley floor like the swift shadow of an eclipse. Leaves quivered as it passed and then were still. Birds stopped in mid-note. A moment of profound stillness fell over the Riverland, as if the wild valley had drawn in its breath.

Then, from up where the fringed darkness of the ironwoods met the stark heights, there came a long, wailing cry, starting high, sinking to a groan that shook snow from bough and withered the late wild flowers of spring in the upland meadows. Thus the Dark Judge greeted night after the first fair day of summer:

*All things end, light, hope, and life. Come to judgment. Come!*

On the New Road far below, a post horse clattered to a sudden stop while his rider dropped the reins and stuffed the hood of her forage jacket into her ears. It was said that anyone who heard the bleak cry of the blind Arrin-ken had no choice but to answer it. She had heard...but so had the rest of the valley. It probably wasn't a summons to her at all, the cadet named Rue told herself nervously. Surely, she had done nothing that required judgment, even at Restormir, even to Lord Caineron.

*Just following orders, sir.*

Sweat darkened her mount's flanks and he resentfully mouthed a lathered bit. They had come nearly thirty miles that day from the Scrollsmen's College at Mount Alban, a standard post run between keeps, but not so easy over a broken roadway strewn with fallen trees. They were near home now and the horse knew it, but still he hesitated, head high, ears flickering.

The earth grumbled fretfully and pebbles jittered underfoot. Rue snatched up the reins to keep her mount from bolting. The damn beast ought to know by now that he couldn't outrun an aftershock. Three days ago, a massive weirdingstrom had loosened the sinews of the earth from Kithorn to the Cataracts. The Riverland had been shaken by tremors ever since but, surely, they must end soon.

"Damn River Snake," she muttered, and spat into the water—a Merikit act of propitiation that the Kendar of her distant keep had adopted.

The hill tribes believed that all quakes were caused by vast Chaos Serpents beneath the earth who must occasionally either be fought or fed to be kept quiet. Rue found nothing strange in such an idea but had the sense—usually—not to say as much to her fellow cadets.

Memory made her wriggle in the saddle: "*Stick to facts, shortie, not singers' fancies.*"

That damned, smug Vant. Riverland Kendar thought that they were so superior, that they knew so much.

But only the night before on Summer's Eve, a Merikit princeling had descended, reluctantly, to placate the great snake that lay beneath the bed of the Silver. Rue had seen the pair of feet, neatly sheared off at the ankles, which he had left behind.

The horse jumped again as a silvery form tumbled down the bank and plopped onto the road almost under his nose. With a twist and a great wriggling of whiskers, the catfish righted itself on stubby pectoral fins and continued its river-ward trudge. *If the fish were coming back down from the hills*, thought Rue, *the worst must be over.*

She kicked her tired mount into a stiff-legged trot. The sun sank. Dusk pooled in the reeds by the River Silver, then overflowed them in a rising tide of night. Shadows seemed to muffle the clop of hooves and the jingle of tack.

They crested yet another rise, and there before them lay Tentir, the randon college.

Rue stared. All along the river's curve, the bank had fallen in, taking trees, bridge, and road with it. Parallel to the river, fissures scored the lower end of the training fields, some only yards in length, others a hundred feet or more, all half full of water reflecting the red sky like so many bloody slashes.

Farther back, much of the outer curtain wall had been thrown down. The fields within lay empty and exposed.

The college itself stood well back on the stone toes of the Snowthorns. Old Tentir, the original fortress, looked as solid as ever. It was a massive three-story high block of gray stone, slotted with dark windows above the first floor, roofed with dark blue slate. As if as an afterthought, spindly watch towers poked up from each corner. To the outer view at least, it was arguably the least imaginative structure in the Riverland. Behind it, surrounding a hollow square, was New Tentir, the college proper. While the nine major houses had once dwelt in similar barracks, changes in house size and importance over the centuries had allowed some to seize space from their smaller neighbors. When they could no longer expand outward, they had built upward. The result from this vantage point was an uneven roofline of diverse heights and pitches, rather like a snaggle-toothed jaw. At least none of the "teeth" seemed to be missing, although some roofs showed gaping holes. Rue sighed with relief: she had expected worse.

But what was that, rising from the inner courtyard? Smoke?

Rue's heart clenched. For a moment, she might have been looking down on Kithorn, the bones of its slaughtered garrison lying unclaimed and dishonored in its smoldering ruins. None of her generation had been alive then, eighty years ago, but no one in the vulnerable border keeps ever forgot that terrible story or the cruel lesson it had taught.

To the Riverland Kencyr, however, it was only an old song of events far away and long ago. After all, no hill tribe would dare to try its strength against *them*.

No. Not smoke. Dust. What in Perimal's name...?

The post horse stomped and jerked at the reins, impatient. Why were they standing here? Why indeed? From behind came the click of hooves and a murmur of voices. The main party had almost caught up.

Rue gave her mount its head. It took off at a fast, bone-jarring trot toward stable and home.

## II

INSIDE OLD TENTIR, shafts of sunset lanced down through the
high western windows and through holes in the roof. Dust motes
danced in them like flecks of dying fire. The air seemed to quiver.
A continuous rumble echoed in the near empty great hall, punctuated by the crack of a single word shouted over and over, its sense
lost in the general, muffled roar.

A Coman cadet stood at the foot of the hall, before one of the
western doors beyond which lay the barracks and training ward of
New Tentir, the randon college. His attention was fixed on the
purposeful commotion outside and his hands gripped the latch, ready
to jerk the door open. He didn't hear Rue knock on the front door
at the other end of the long hall, then pound.

The unlocked door opened a crack, grating on debris, and Rue
warily peered in, one hand on the hilt of the long knife sheathed at
her belt. A quick glance told her that the hall was empty, or nearly so.
Frowning, she pushed back the hood of her forage jacket from
straw-colored hair as rough-cut as a badly thatched roof.

"Tentir, 'ware company!" she shouted down the hall. "Somebody, come take this nag!"

A moment later she had stumbled over the threshold, butted
from behind by her horse. She caught him as he tried to shove past,
and then led him into the hall, needing all her strength to hold him in
check. In response, he laid back his ears and arched his tail. Turds
plopped, steaming, onto flagstones already littered with broken slates
from the roof, downed beams, and fallen birds' nests.

Rue glanced around as she tramped on legs stiff from riding
down the long hall that bisected Old Tentir. Disordered though it
was, the wonder of it struck her anew. All her short life, she had
dreamed of training at the randon college and now here she was, a
cadet candidate sworn to the Highlord himself.

*But for how long*, whispered fear in the back of her mind, *given the
events of the past week*. Rue set her jaw. Here she was and here she
would stay. *Don't think of failure*, she told herself. *Don't think. Look.*

In the galleries of the second and third floors, rank on rank of
silver collars seemed to float against the darkening walls. Suspended

from each shining ring were the plaques that recorded the career of its owner—in what class graduated, what ranks and stations held, what honors won in which battles and in which slain: white edged for the debacle in the White Hills when Ganth Gray Lord had been overthrown, blue for the Cataracts early last winter when his son Torisen had stopped the Waster Horde, black for the misery of Urakarn in the Southern Wastes, from which so few had returned, and on, and on.

Along the lower walls hung the banners of the nine major Kencyr houses whom most of the randon served. Leaping flame, stooping hawk, and snarling wolf on the south wall: Brandan, Edirr, and Danior. Gauntletted fist, two-edged sword, and devouring serpent on the north: Randir, Coman, and Caineron. Over the two western doors that opened into New Tentir were the stricken tree and the full moon of the Jaran and the Ardeth. Between them, in pride of place over the massive fireplace, hung the rathorn crest of the Knorth, highlords of the Kencyrath for thirty millennia.

One tenth of that time had been spend here on Rathillien, the last in a series of threshold worlds held and subsequently lost in the Three People's long, bitter retreat from Perimal Darkling down the Chain of Creation.

The college at Tentir dated from the ceding of the Riverland forts to the Kencyrath nearly a thousand years ago. Since that time, every cadet had added his or her stitch to the appropriate banner, building it up even as its back decayed against the dank walls. Some, such as tiny Danior, showed patches of stone wall between bare upper threads. Others, especially the Caineron, looked like ungainly, pendulous growths.

*Not unlike Caldane, Lord Caineron himself*, thought Rue, grinning.

Her horse stopped and tossed back his head, nearly jerking her off her feet. A moment later, a faint rumble came from under the earth and the hall shivered. More slates fell. Birds fled out the holes in the roof. The horse backed, eyes rolling white, jerking the reins out of the cadet's hand. Before she could recapture them, he had bolted across the hall and down the side ramp to the subterranean stables. The frightened bugling of horses already in stall welcomed him.

Rue tramped up to the cadet by the door.

"Didn't you hear my hail?" she demanded, having to raise her voice over the rumpus. She also had to look up, the other being a

good head taller than she as most Kendar her age were. "D'you
know that the outer ward is unguarded and the hall door is unlocked? I thought for sure the hill tribes had broken in and sacked
the place. Where *is* everyone?"

The Coman cadet shot her a distracted look, and winced: the
young lord of his house, looking to his standard, had set the fashion
of wearing a tiny, double-edged dagger as an earring, never mind
that with any incautious move it stabbed its wearer. "I heard you,
but this is my post. No, the guard isn't set. We aren't back to rights
yet since the last big quake, nor yet since the one before that."

"Huh," said Rue.

As far as she could see, Tentir had gotten off easy. In contrast,
sections of Mount Alban had been displaced all the way to the Southern Wastes, then north to Kithorn, before finally snapping back to
their foundation. Parts were still missing. That morning, when Rue
had left, the scrollsmen and women had been searching with increasing urgency for the upper levels' privy.

The Coman flinched as something overhead shifted. Grit rattled
down into his upturned face.

"A week we spent," he said rapidly, "sweating in the fire timber
hall below, expecting every minute for the whole keep to collapse on
our heads. They said the old buildings were the safest and no one
dared go out for fear of being swept away by the weirding, but
still...all the new cadet candidates jostled together—Ardeth, Caineron,
Knorth, the lot...No discipline. Fights. As for the Merikit, I wish
they *would* come! Tentir is a proper hornet's nest, just waiting for
some fool with a stick."

"Hall, there! *Hall!*" roared a stentorian voice outside, over the
general tumult.

The Coman threw open the door. Cadets thundered past, rank
on rank, feet booming on the boardwalk. They ran grimly in ca-
dence to the now distinguishable shouts of the drill sargent standing
in the middle of the training square:

"Run! *Run!* RUN!"

The Coman waited for a momentary break between squads,
then darted out. Rue, craning out the door, saw him reach a cadet
who had tripped, fallen, and been trampled before his mates could
scoop him up.

"*Down!*" shouted the commander of the oncoming squad.

Rescuer and victim fell flat. The ten-command hurdled over them two by two, a ripple of heads rising and falling like water over a hidden rock, lucky that none of them tripped. Then they were past. The Coman lurched to his feet, supporting the fallen cadet. They flattened themselves against the wall as the next squad thundered by, then staggered back to the door. Rue reached out to pull them in. All three collapsed in a heap on the hall's flagstones.

"Get off me!" someone in the pile said thickly.

They sorted themselves out with much cursing and some flailing of fists, one of which caught Rue on the ear. She staggered backward, shaking her head to clear it.

"What's wrong with you people?" she demanded, but instinctively she knew: the former Lord Coman had been a staunch Caineron ally, but the new one, Korey, was wavering. Caldane was said to be furious about that, and the young cadet whom they had just rescued was a Caineron. Here, writ small, were all the tensions between their houses.

The Coman shook the smaller boy until he stopped trying to fight and the teeth rattled in his head. Then he propped him against the wall.

"This...has been going on...for hours," he panted, leaning against the doorpost. "Punishment run...ha! D'they want...to kill...us all?" For the first time, he regarded Rue closely. "You're that border brat...aren't you? The one that came down...from the Min-drear High Keep. One of Brier Iron-thorn's ten-command."

"Bloody Thorn," muttered the Caineron. His nose had begun to bleed. He groped for his token scarf and snuffled wetly into it. "Damn, bloody turn-collar. S'if M'lord Caldane wasn't good enough for her..."

"He wasn't," said Rue, glaring. "Ten serves the Highlord now."

"Your ten-command was out Merikit-hunting and went missing without leave during the storm." The Coman regarded her speculatively. "We thought you'd been swept away. Better if you had been. You're in dead trouble now, brat."

Rue glowered. "We had things to do."

"Tell that to the Commandant. I reckon he's about fed up with you Knorth. We all are. Crazy, the lot of you. D'you still check under your bed every night for Gerridon, or maybe for a darkling crawler like the one your precious highlord claims to have seen here last fall?"

Rue set a pugnacious jaw.  She knew that he was baiting her, that the Coman and the Knorth were on even less easy terms than the Coman and the Caineron, but this touched on her lord's honor.

"What d'you mean, 'claims?'  D'you think it couldn't happen?  You Coman live at the southern end of the Riverland.  Here in the north, things happen.  We're closer to the Barrier than you seem to realize and what's behind that, eh?  Perimal Darkling itself!  Some days at High Keep, you can see Master Gerridon's House looming through the mist like it was about to push its way right through."

Behind the now sodden scarf, the Caineron snorted.  In that muffled sound was all the contempt with which his Lord Caldane regarded all things darkling, or anything else not of immediate use to him.

"You don't believe me?  Well then, who d'you think was behind the Waster Horde, pushing, when we fought it last winter at the Cataracts?  Darkling changers, that's who.  Our own kind, once— Kencyr, fallen with the Master, warped in the shadows of his house."

The Coman grinned.  "So the singers of Mount Alban say, especially that creepy Ashe.  If you want to label anyone 'darkling,' how about a dead woman who won't lie down, much less shut up?  As for the rest, some people will swallow any singer's Lawful Lie.  And I wouldn't brag about the Cataracts if I were you, brat:  folk may recall how the Highlord acquired a sister at the edge of the Escarpment—with a flash and a loud bang, apparently.  He's the last pure-blooded Knorth, isn't he?  So where did *she* come from?  The whole thing's another Lawful Lie, if you ask me…and what are *you* smirking about?"

"Wait and see," said Rue.

The Caineron focused blurry eyes on her.  For so young a boy, barely fifteen, he looked remarkably dissolute, like someone recovering from a vicious hangover.  He might well be:  two days ago Caldane had indulged in an epic drinking binge and passed the effects on to all the Kendar bound to him who hadn't yet learned how to defend themselves.

"Think you're so clever for getting out of this, eh, shag-head?" he said thickly, indicating the grim stream of exhausted cadets pounding past the door.  "And you got out of High Keep too, didn't you?  One more minor house dying on its feet, one more Kendar scuttling out before it falls…"

Rue's ill-cropped hair almost bristled. She had hacked it off to leave in her lord's cold hand in case she should never return—a poor substitute for her bones burnt to honorable ash on the pyre but better than nothing. If she had been glad to escape that grim place, guilt had made her chop all the more fiercely.

"I have my lord's permission to train with the Highlord's folk. Min-drear randon always do."

"Damn, bloody Mind-rear, trotting after a crazy rat-horn…"

"That's *rath*-orn, moron." Rue glanced up at the Knorth house banner, at the fierce, horned beast embroidered on it, ivory armor agleam in the darkening hall. How could anyone make fun of a thing like that, except perhaps some idiot Riverlander who had never even seen one?

The Coman glanced out the door. "Here comes your house again, lad. Up and out."

The Caineron cadet lurched to his feet. At the door, he looked back at Rue. "I'll remember you, Mind-rear. And we Caineron all remember Brier bloody Iron-thorn." For a moment Caldane seemed to leer out of the boy's heavy eyes. Rue fell back a step, making the Darkwyr sign against evil. He blinked, laughed uncertainly, and stumbled out to be swept up by his people as they thundered past.

The Coman stared after him. "Has everyone gone mad?" He looked at Rue as if tempted to make the warding sign against her. "Insanity is contagious. Ganth Gray Lord infected the entire Host in the White Hills and now Torisen Black Lord is doing it again!"

"If you want to complain to him," said Rue as the far door was forced open, screeching on bent hinges, "here's your chance."

Into the twilight of the hall came two riders, one on a tall black stallion, the other on a small, gray mare with an intricately braided white mane.

"That's Lord Ardeth," said the Coman, staring at the latter. "What in Perimal's name…" His voice trailed off and his jaw dropped.

The lord of Omiroth seemed to have brought a great light into the hall, as if at the rising of the full moon that was the emblem of his house. It shone bone-deep through his clothes, through his very flesh. *But no*, thought Rue, also staring: it *must only be that snow-white hair. And yet, and yet…*

The Ardeth were an arrogant lot, proud of their subtle lord who in his one hundred and fifty odd years had brought his house through so many disasters that even the scrollsmen of Mount Alban had lost count. The worst had been the thirty-one years of chaos after the White Hills when, without a highlord, the Kencyrath had nearly fallen apart. Only Ardeth had known that Ganth's heir lived: the boy Torisen, exile-born, who had come to him in secret and whom Ardeth had hidden among the randon of the Southern Host. There, four years ago, Torisen had come of age and at last claimed his father's seat.

The Caineron claimed that he was still Ardeth's puppet, or worse.

At the Cataracts, others suspected that the Highlord was slipping through his mentor's fingers.

Since then, his friends had begun to wonder if, after all, Torisen needed Ardeth's influence to save him from himself.

Rue knew instinctively that the old lord was now trying to reassert control over the younger man.

Perhaps that was only right, she thought, half-dazed, drawn to the old Highborn as if to the sun after bitter cold. Perhaps here was the true heart of the Kencyrath, its secret master to whom all should yield as Torisen himself once had. Her own lord was a broken man, his sons ash before him, his Kendar loosely bound to him by his faltering will. Torisen Highlord held his own people almost as lightly— through weakness, sneered the Caineron, whose own lord gripped them like cruel death; through misplaced tact, said his allies, shrugging. Rue only knew that it made her nervous. What a splendid thing it would be, she now thought, to fall at Ardeth's feet, to put her life between those thin, strong hands and hear his murmured words of welcome.

Then she shook herself, silently cursing. Everyone knew that old Adric had a taste for the exotic drugs of the Poison Courts and had resorted to them for help before now, sometimes with unnerving results. Let him glow in the dark like a rotten eel. She was a Mindrear and would hold true to her bond, if not for her lord's sake then for her mother and her mother's mother before her.

Torisen Black Lord, Highlord of the Kencyrath, rode into Tentir on his warhorse Storm like the shadow cast by the other's brilliance. Dark clothing, dark ruffled hair shot with premature gray, both horse and rider seemed to melt into the hall's shadows except for the latter's face, pale with strain floating forward wraithlike—that, and his fine-boned left hand with its tracery of white scars, gripping the reins. His right hand he carried out of sight, thrust into a dusty coat.

A large, gray wolf slunk at his side as close as he could get without being stepped on, closer than Storm liked judging by the roll of the stallion's eye. However, the Wolver Grimly only watched his old friend Torisen with unhappy concern.

If Ardeth's lunar glow seemed to promise safety, the Knorth appeared to be in obstinate self-eclipse, dark of the moon, when all things fall into doubt and danger. He neither looked at his old mentor nor seemed to listen to him. Nonetheless, he rode with all his weight on the outside stirrup, leaning away from that soft, insistent voice.

Rue got the Coman's attention by kicking him in the shin. "Go tell the Commandant we have company."

"Yes," he said, still staring, and then, belatedly, "ouch."

He stumbled out the door without looking, and brought down an entire Edirr squad.

"*Rest!*" roared a sargent.

All around the square, cadets collapsed, panting, on the boards.

Meanwhile, other riders had entered the hall at a wary distance from their lords, two columns of them, split by house. They ignored each other but their mounts, catching their mood, fidgeted and snapped.

Rue's attention leaped to the most reassuring face in the crowd, there, a respectful length behind the captain of Ardeth's guard. Teak brown from the southern sun, short cropped hair the smoldering red of mahogany, Brier Iron-thorn had come to Tentir by a long, hard road. She was older than most cadets, more experienced, and mistrusted by them for her sudden change of houses at the Cataracts. Before that, no one had believed that such a thing was possible. Not from the Caineron. Not against the will of its lord. But here she was, even more an outsider than Rue. If anyone could show these smug Riverlanders a thing or two, it was Rose Iron-thorn's hard, handsome daughter.

*Oh, please*, thought Rue, *let her start with him.*

Five-commander Vant rode glowering at Brier's back. They had all seethed with resentment when a former Caineron *yondri* had been put in charge over them, but none more so than Vant who had been forced to yield ten-command to her. If he kept in Brier's shadow now, it was because he hoped that she would draw the lightning of whatever punishment they all have earned.

Hooves rattled on the flagstones. A bay gelding danced nervously, eyes rolling, between the two lords and their retinues. Everyone looked somewhere else except Rue, who stared open-mouthed despite herself.

Like her brother, the bay's rider wore black, but her jacket had an odd cut to it, one sleeve tight and the other full. Unlike Torisen, the slim hands that nervously gripped the reins were sheathed in black gloves. What she didn't wear—and this was why no one would look at her directly—was a mask. For a Highborn lady to show her face naked to the world was indecent, much less one marked across the cheek by a thin, straight, barely healed scar. That she looked so much like a younger version of her brother was, in contrast, merely disconcerting.

So was the thin, sharp face that peered warily over her shoulder. The bay bore two riders, the second Caineron's half-cast bastard son who, somehow, had become the first's servant.

As if to compound this strangeness, a Royal Gold hunting ounce trotted after them into the hall. The cat, Jorin, was blind, which perhaps explained why he blithely plumped himself down in the path of the oncoming riders and began industriously to wash.

His tail twitched under a descending hoof. He leaped up, squalling, the bay shied, and both riders fell off.

The whole mixed retinue was suddenly in motion, horses separating by house and wheeling about to face each other, their riders' hands falling instinctively to sword hilts.

The bay, unheeded, tossed his head and trotted sedately off down the ramp.

Only the black stallion and the gray mare hadn't moved. Ardeth's voice murmured on, oblivious. Torisen stilled the commotion behind him with a raised hand—the right, its three broken fingers splinted and heavily bandaged. He looked past Rue, and his thin mouth twisted in a wry half-smile. She realized, with a start, that the Commandant had entered the hall during the confusion and was standing behind her.

She had to crane to see his face. Sheth Sharp-tongue was tall even for a Kendar, with a touch of Highborn subtlety in his features. Highborn and Kendar alike found him unnerving. Most believed, however, that he was the greatest randon of his generation. Rue remembered uneasily that Sheth was also a Caineron and that house's war-leader.

"My lords, welcome to Tentir," he said.

His gaze fell, speculatively, on the bedraggled figure in the middle of the hall, who had picked herself up and was slapping dust off her clothes. Her companion and cat both tried to hide behind her. Meeting the Commandant's eyes with a carefully blank stare, she swept up long, black hair that had tumbled down in her fall and twisted it back up under her cap.

"Who have we here?" he asked of no one in particular.

Rue couldn't help it. "'Some fool with a stick,'" she muttered.

The Commandant glanced down at her. "I daresay," he said dryly. "My lords, welcome to Tentir."

Rue ducked hastily away from him to hold Storm. The tall stallion snorted down his nose at her and stood rock still as Torisen awkwardly dismounted, favoring his injured hand.

"Honor be to your halls," he responded, preoccupied, and touched the mare's shoulder with concern. Sweat had turned it pewter gray, and she was trembling with fatigue. "My lady? Adric, for Trinity's sake...! Think of Brithany, if not of yourself."

Ardeth had also swung down and was drifting toward him like a sleep-walker, still murmuring. Sheth raised an eyebrow as both Grimly and the Highlord retreated behind Storm, the wolver keeping between the two Highborn, ignored by both. The stallion laid back his ears but subsided, grudgingly, at a sharp word from his master. Ardeth's power rippled out through the hall. The stitches on the nearest banner rustled as if trying to escape.

"You know," said the Commandant mildly, "each stitch represents a randon's bond the eternal fabric of his house. The cadet candidates here haven't yet formally earned their scarves nor set their marks, so they aren't as strongly anchored as their seniors."

"Tell him, not me!" Torisen snapped, circling behind his horse. "Adric, you should rest. Remember your heart."

"Yes, Grandfather. Please rest."

A handsome young man had slipped into the hall from the arcade. He wore a cadet's belted jacket, but of an elegant cut and material touched with embroidery as golden as his hair. Obviously, he hadn't taken part in the run. Rue's first indignant thought was

that, Highborn or not, he should have. That conviction faded, however, in the presence of a glamour more subtle than his grandfather's,
but still enough to make Rue stare. So did Torisen.

"Peri," he gasped.

"No," said the Commandant, giving him a brief, hard look.
"His son, Timmon."

As Ardeth advanced smiling on the boy, his attention diverted,
the whole room seemed to breathe for the first time since he had
entered the hall. Torisen sagged against Storm's hindquarters, and
not just with relief that the old lord was no longer focused on him.
He looked like someone who had taken a hard, unexpected blow.
The Wolver rose up on his hind legs and became a very hairy, very
worried young man, reaching out to steady his friend.

"Look at you," Ardeth was saying fondly to his grandson. "All
dressed up like a randon. Your father would be so proud."

Among the Kendar, someone turned a snort into a cough.
Timmon's father Pereden had never trained at Tentir. Nonetheless,
he had expected to lead the Southern Host and finally had gotten his
chance after Torisen put down the commander's collar to become
Highlord. On Pereden's orders, against the advice of his randon,
the Host had marched to near ruin against the vastly larger Waster
Horde. Pereden himself was believed to have died in the Wastes. A
good thing too, many thought, but no one said so in his father's
presence. Ardeth had spent the previous winter vainly searching the
Southern Wastes for the bones of his beloved, heroic son.

Now, his mind momentarily off the Highlord, the old man sagged
with exhaustion.

Timmon regarded him with growing alarm. "Please, Grandfather," he said again. "Come to my quarters and rest. Your business
with the Highlord can wait."

Ardeth patted his grandson's arm absent-mindedly. There was
a winning quality in the boy's voice that made even strangers eager to
please him, but his words had set the old lord's thoughts wandering
back to the real business at hand: convincing Torisen that his best
interests, nay, his very survival, lay in putting his shaken fortunes in
the hands of his former mentor. No one could doubt Ardeth's
thoughts, because he spoke them out loud.

"You must remember, my dear boy," he added, with devastat-
ing candor, "that many believe you as prone to madness as your late,

unlamented father." His pale blue eyes drifted to that second black-clad figure standing silent between the restless battle lines. "Indeed, once news of your latest scheme leaks out, even I may be unable to save you."

Torisen straightened with a jerk. "Young man," he said, forcing himself to look at Timmon, "if you will extend your hospitality to me and my friend Grimly, we will gladly drink the welcome cup in your quarters. Adric?"

Ardeth smiled, the drug-fired light again emerging from the cloud of his exhaustion. The hall shivered as his renewed power rippled through it. "But of course I will join you, dear boy. We have so much to discuss."

"Take care of your grand-dam," Torisen said to Storm, who snorted: *of course*. Avoiding the old man's extended hand, he slipped out of the hall into New Tentir with Grimly again on all fours trotting at his heel.

"Well done, my lord," murmured the Commandant as Torisen passed, adding blandly, "I believe I will join you." At the door, he turned.

"Conduct the Highlord's...er...guests to the Knorth quarters," he said to Rue. "As for you—" his hooded glance swooped back to the other uneasily waiting cadets "—I will have something to say to you later. In the meantime, tend to these horses. All of them."

Ardeth's guard gingerly skirted the Highlord's sister with eyes averted and thrust their reins into unwilling Knorth hands. The mutter of protest that followed them died under Iron-thorn's hard eyes. Tired and hungry, the Knorth cadets sullenly followed their Southron ten-commander down the ramp.

The Highlord's sister was left standing in the middle of the hall. She looked about her at the banners, the battle flags and, above, at the faint glimmer of randon collars hanging on the upper walls.

"So this is Tentir," said her other companion, looking down his sharp nose at the disheveled, darkening hall.

"Yes," said his mistress, in quite another tone. "This is Tentir."

Rue approached them, reminding herself that she had spoken to the Highborn before, but Jameth's face had been decently masked then. She looked quickly away as the other turned to her.

"If you'll follow me, lady."

As they climbed the stairs to the second story Knorth guest quarters, the relentless shout rose again from the training yard outside:

"All right, younglings, rest's over. Up and run, *run*, RUN!"

## Chapter II:  Wyrm Hunt

### Summer 1

### I

"WE'RE LOST," SAID Graykin, glowering about the low, dusty corridor. "Three times now, I've trod on the same loose board. Here, you!"—this, to the straw-haired cadet who led them. "Do you even know where you're going?"

The young Kendar named Rue glanced back at them, then quickly away. "Where, yes; how, no.  Most of the second and third floors are unused, except for guest quarters and the outermost rooms.  We don't like coming up here.  Besides, there are stories…"

"Oh?" said Graykin with a nasty grin, baring still raw gaps where m'lord Caldane had knocked out some of his teeth. "More 'singers' fancies'?"

Jame recognized the line that Vant—never her favorite Kendar— had taken with the young borderlander. "What stories?" she asked.

"That something lives up here in a hidden room," Rue burst out defiantly.  "That it has the paws of a bear and an axe buried in its head.  That it growls and it prowls and it eats cadets who stumble into its lair."

Graykin hooted with laughter.  Rue hunched her shoulders, the tips of her ears reddening. Jame considered. Through Jorin's senses, as they wandered, she had caught whiffs of something odd, something rank, something alive.

"The Lawful Lie notwithstanding, most songs have some element of truth in them."

"Hah!" said Graykin.  "D'you hear that, brat?  Just be careful what door you open.  Ugh!" He swatted at the cobweb that he had just walked into and spat out the husk of a fly.

"Poor Gray," said his mistress.  "Tentir isn't living up to your expectations, is it?"

"Is it to yours?"

"Oh well.  This isn't the college proper.  We'll see."

Still, thought Jame, this was not auspicious.  Neither had been falling off a horse practically at the Commandant's feet.  Then again, it was usually her departure—from anywhere—that caused the most damage. Tai-tastigon in flames, Karkinaroth in ruins, "*The Riverland reduced to rubble and you in the midst of it, looking apologetic…*"

What shape would Tentir be in when she left it?

Speaking of shapes, it was odd how every Riverland keep was so different, as if the original builders had made a point of it. Generations of Kencyr had brought their own personalities to the task but less so here, where commandants changed by rotation and no one house had power. From the outside, Old Tentir looked straightforward, even dull. Inside, it was…strange. Low halls melting into twilight, right angles that never brought one back to the same place— she was fairly sure that Graykin was wrong about it being the same squeaky board: they all squeaked—someone subtle and secretive had designed this place, disguising its nature behind a bland face.

"Jorin, stay in sight," she called to the ounce who was trotting ahead, eager to explore. Blind from birth, he only saw what she saw and remembered it, but this was all new to her.

*Lost.*

Would Tori be glad if she disappeared, gone from his life as suddenly as she had reentered it?

*Run*, she thought, *before he tells that alarming randon why he brought you here, before he proves himself as mad as they all fear—or hope—that he is.*

Graykin was grumbling again. "This is an insult!" he burst out. "You're the Highlord's sister, his only surviving blood-kin, but he pays more attention to that damned gray mare than to you!"

"Brithany is a Whinno-hir, a matriarch of the herd. She's at least as old as Ardeth, perhaps older than the Fall."

And smart. And brave. Imagine weirdwalking all the way from the Southern Wastes to rejoin her chosen master, bringing her grandcolt with her. Storm, a quarter-blood Whinno-hir, was far more intelligent than the average horse, but still a moron compared to his grand-dam.

"Damn it!" Graykin burst out, flailing at more webs. "You don't belong here!"

Jame sighed. "That's the question, isn't it? Where do I belong?"

"If you were a man," said Graykin, regarding her slyly askance, "you would be Highlord. I don't care if your brother is older than you are. You're stronger than he is…and why are you fidgeting like that?"

"I'm saddle-sore. Don't laugh." She rubbed her buttocks, wincing. When there was time to check, she would probably find them black and blue. Her knees still felt unstrung. "Highlord, huh? Your ambition is showing, Gray, but I'm not a man and I don't want power, at least not that sort. Just give me a place to stand."

"You're a Highborn lady," said the Southron stubbornly. "Stand on that."

"I tried," she said, hearing the weary exasperation in her voice, trying to curb it. "All last winter, in the Women's Halls at Gothregor, I tried."

Masked, hobbled with a tight underskirt, told over and over what a proper lady did or did not do...all to what end? She gingerly touched the scar ridge across her cheek, a parting gift from the Women's World in the person of Kallystine, Caineron's daughter and Tori's erstwhile limited term consort.

"Gray, these days Highborn women are little better than fancy breeding stock, and I'm the last pure-blooded female in the Knorth stable, just as Tori is the last legitimate male. If any house gets a half-Knorth heir out of either one of us, how long d'you think we'll last?"

For that matter, how long could Tori stand up to Ardeth pressure? Why didn't he fight back? She understood that he owed a great deal to his former mentor, without whom he would never have survived to claim his father's seat nor held it during these first, turbulent years. Moreover, he didn't want to hurt the old man. For all his drug-enhanced strength, she could sense how fragile Ardeth was, how deep into his resources he was reaching. For her brother, loyalty—yes, even love—must be at war with resentment.

And he did resent the old lord.

"When I was a boy," he had said to her in the ruins of Kothifir— had it been only the day before?—"I would have given anything to become a cadet at Tentir. But Adric forbade it."

Ardeth had protested. It had been impossible. If anyone had guessed who Tori was before he came of age...

"So you told me, Adric, when you dismissed my request as if it were a child's whim. So I lost my chance."

Such bitterness, remembered and dismissed, but never forgotten or quite forgiven.

However, if Ardeth was vulnerable now, so was Tori, and not just with exhaustion. Something about that good-looking boy Timmon had hit him hard, something to do with the boy's father, Pereden.

Worse, something deep within Torisen himself was closed off, withdrawn...dead? His Kendar felt it. So did she, and it frightened her.

Graykin hunched his thin shoulders as if against a cold wind. If he could have run away from her words, he would have. He wasn't stupid. Far from it. However, bastard and half-Kencyr that he was, his need to belong consumed him like a ravening hunger. At the Cataracts she had accidentally bound him, mind to mind, her needs at that moment matching the strength of his. Now there was no easy way to shake him off, nor should she want to. Ancestors knew, over the past winter he had earned his place in her service with scars that he would bear to his pyre, and he hadn't yet begun to regrow (assuming he had enough Kencyr blood to do so) his lost teeth. Things were going to be hard enough, though, without him clinging fiercely to her sleeve, measuring his importance by hers every step of the way.

One last try: "Gray, listen. I can't promise you anything. Not even a crust of bread every other week. Least of all protection. And you're in danger here. M'lord Caineron doesn't give up his playthings easily, much less those he considers he owns by right of blood."

"You *are* strong," he muttered, not looking at her, repeating his one article of faith as if by itself it would protect him. "I've watched. I know. Nothing stops you."

She could have shaken him.

Jorin sniffed, then dug at the lower edge of a heavy oak door. Whatever he smelled was too faint to reach Jame's senses, but she felt his interest, and his unease.

"The right door at last," said Rue with relief and tried the handle. "Damn. It's locked, and I don't have a key."

"Let me try." Jame slid between the cadet and the door, screening the latter. She extended a claw and probed the ponderous lock.

Her gloves' slit fingertips had been Marc's idea. At first she had rejected it, not wanting to use her hated nails at all, for anything, but many pairs of ruined gloves later she had had to admit that the big Kendar was right.

It still amazed her how casually he took her deformity. When her nails had first emerged, betraying her Shanir blood, her father had cast her out into the Haunted Lands, with no place to go but across the Border. Into Perimal Darkling. Into the Master's House. She had been seven years old at the time.

Then again, pure-blooded Kendar like Marc were never Shanir. Perhaps that made them more tolerant than the vulnerable Highborn.

If only Marc were with her now rather than this opportunistic half-breed—but she wasn't in a position to provide for her old, dear friend any more than for Graykin. Marc was better off with her brother. She wondered if Tori had yet offered the old warrior a place in his household. He had better, and no one deserved it more. But still...

*Lost*, she thought again, with a sudden wave of desolation. *I've lost Marc, and Tirandys, and Tai-tastigon, and now here I am where no one wants me.*

Then she gave herself a shake. Graykin was right, darkness take him. Nothing stopped her, not despair, not loss, least of all not common sense. This was a new life. She had started over before, many times, and would keep on doing so until she damn well got it right.

Tumbles ground in the lock. "There."

The portal swung slowly inward, grating on its hinges. From the darkness within came a breath of hot air—*Haaaaah...*—and streamers of cobweb floated out into the hall. With them came a sharp, acrid smell, intensified for Jame through Jorin's senses. She only realized that she had backed away when the other side of the hall stopped her. The ounce also retreated, then turned, crouched, and sprang into her arms. Her knees nearly buckled. Almost full grown, he was very heavy.

Rue and Graykin were staring at her.

"That smell..." Jame said, and sneezed violently.

"What smell?" asked Rue, too mystified for once to look away.

"The room is musty," said Graykin, impatiently. "That's all. You. Light my lady's chambers."

Rue made a face at him and disappeared inside.

"What's wrong?" hissed Graykin.

"I...don't know," said Jame, shifting the ounce's weight, and she didn't...quite.

Inside, steel rasped on flint, and candlelight danced out into the corridor. Rue gave a stifled exclamation. Without thinking, Jame dropped an indignant ounce and brushed past Graykin, into the apartment.

The cadet stood in the first room of three, holding a candle, looking about her in amazement. The low-ceilinged chamber was full of heavy furniture indistinct and sulking under filmy shrouds: a massive chair beside the fireplace, a table, a glimpse into the next room of an enormous, shadowy bed, its counterpane disordered and bulging.

"...*haaahhh*..." sighed the open vents to the fire timber hall three stories below. As the suite exhaled into the hall, its hot breath stirred walls and ceiling swathed in translucent, faintly glowing white.

"Ugh," said Graykin, peering in. "More spiders."

"I don't think so," said Jame.

She ducked, wary of the filaments that drifted down toward her as if blindly groping for her face. Not all of them were spun in single strands, she saw, but some in the round, like boneless fingers, merging higher up into flaccid sleeves. The walls and ceiling of the suite were festooned with intertwined, insubstantial shapes, afloat in the flickering light. Stirred by the hot breath of the vents and the draft from the door, they seemed languidly to grapple with each other about the room's upper margins.

"Careful," she said, touching Rue's arm to make the cadet hold the candle lower. "Let's only set fire to the keep as a last resort."

Graykin snorted.

They all felt the need to speak softly except for Jorin, who leaned in from the hall anxiously chirping at Jame to come out. When she didn't, he slunk in and crouched at her feet. A moment later Graykin nerved himself to join them in a rush that caused a momentary wake in the sea of ghosts overhead.

Jame loosened her collar, feeling sweat trickle down inside it. She didn't like heat. As for that smell... Although it had faded somewhat with the influx of fresh air, she could still almost taste it in the back of her throat, like the sting of old grief. Then she knew what it was.

"Rue, how long has a darkling crawler been loose in Tentir?"

The cadet gaped at her. "How did you...who told you..."

Another hot room, another house where monstrous shadows crawled...

*"Senethari, y-you've poisoned me."*

No wonder Tirandys had been in her mind.

"Someone once gave me wine infused with wyrm's venom. I drank it. It had that same sharp smell and taste."

The cadet sighed, almost with relief. "Most don't believe it was ever here at all. How long? Since last fall, when m'lords Caineron and Knorth stopped here on their way to the mustering of the Host at Gothregor. A darkling changer came hunting the Highlord and would have killed him, sure, if Singer Ashe hadn't pushed the changer into a fire-pit down in the fire-timber hall. His blood kindled and he more or less exploded—a proper mess all around, or so I've heard. As for the wyrm, no one saw that but the Highlord, and afterward the Caineron claimed that he'd imagined it."

"The poor, mad Knorth."

"That's it…lady," she added, remembering herself and of whose house she spoke. "They tried to say the same about the changer, but too many had seen it including my cousin, who was on duty that night outside Commandant Harn's quarters. We border brats take these things seriously."

She said this so pugnaciously that Jame laughed. "I know. I'm a border brat myself, and so is Tori, if he isn't too grand these days to have forgotten."

Her eyes kept drifting back to the ceiling. The figures that floated there were as empty as a spider's egg sack in the spring, but hot air from the vents breathed fitful definition into the flaccid forms. Here a head rose, inflating. For a moment there was the suggestion of a fine-drawn chin and an arched brow that seemed to frown. Then all features swelled grotesquely and the figure turned away with a sigh, deflating. Elsewhere limp gloves of web became elegant lace-work hands, became veined, translucent sausages, vented, and collapsed.

They were like the fitful images of a troubled dream, but whose?

Two figures emerged over and over, interacting at different points in what appeared to be a prolonged conflict. One, better defined than the other, was always turning away.

The other, more nebulous, kept changing as if trying to hold a true shape—any shape—while at the same time unraveling around the edges. Nonetheless it…no, *he* had the sharper presence of the two, a thing fiercely clung to even as errant drafts teased him apart. All over the room, his multitude of heads were turning toward her as if aware of her thoughts. Filaments floated around each like a cloud of wild, white hair.

Jame brushed a tendril of web from her neck. It left a thin, stinging line.

*…are you the one?*

"Careful," she said to the other two. "There's still a trace of venom in these threads."

There was also that ghost of words, echoing faintly with impotent rage.

*...are you the one who made bitter ash of my life?*

*No,* Jame wanted to say. *You did that to yourself and, thanks to Tori, you got what you deserved.*

She was stopped, however, by the memory of another pyre, another changer's shape melting into flame, and her eyes stung with remembered tears.

*Ah, Tirandys, Senethari. Did you deserve what happened to you? Damn Master Gerridon, honor's paradox, and all three faces of our god, for giving us impossible choices, then damning us when we choose wrong.*

"So the changer died," she said, collecting herself, "the wyrm fled, and everyone marched south to fight the Waster Horde which, incidentally, was led by other rebel changers. Meanwhile, the crawler spent the winter at Tentir, maybe in these rooms. Ancestors know, it's hot enough. Well insulated too. A proper nest."

Highborn and Kendar looked at each other.

"We should get out of here, lady."

"Good idea," said Graykin, starting for the outer door.

Jorin sat up, ears pricked. Then he jumped to his feet and trotted purposefully through the opposite door, into the bed-room. When he didn't return at Jame's call, she went after him. As they hesitated, Rue and Graykin heard an exclamation followed by a sharp summons: "Come see this, both of you."

The second room was hotter than the first, its ceiling a floating mass of loose filaments especially thick over the bed. Jame had thrown back the coverlet.

"I want witnesses to this," she said.

They stared at the bed's contents.

"A broken shell?" said Rue. She poked the pearly fragments gingerly. They dissolved with a faint hiss into a pool of viscous fluid.

"More likely a cocoon," said Jame, "or perhaps a molt. What do I know about the life cycle of a wyrm?"

The liquid had begun to eat its way through the sheets, then through the mattress.

"Ugh," said Graykin. "Whatever was in here must just have broken out—now, of all times. Why does everything always happen to me?"

Rue grinned. "Just lucky, I guess."

His indignant response turned into a stifled cry of alarm. They all stared at the clotted mass above the bed. A shape was emerging from it, as if a giant face was leaning down from the ceiling, itself a mere void but defined by the clinging web. The fading consciousness of the dead changer glared down at Jame through a silken mask already beginning to droop under its own weight.

*...are you the one who stole my Beauty?*

"What beauty?" she demanded out loud. "Whose beauty?"

"Bugger this," muttered Rue, and thrust her lit candle up into the sagging mass.

It ignited from within. In a moment, the threads had become a fiery mask distorted by rage and despair. The jaw blackened and dropped, disintegrating into a rain of ash. The rest followed, feature by feature. Fire spread in red-orange tendrils across the ceiling into the first room. Ghosts tumbled down in flames.

Driven back by the heat, they retreated into the third room. Jorin wasn't with them, but fresh tracks in the dust showed where he had gone, following a shallow groove in the floorboards worn not by use or weight but by the wyrm's corrosive passage. Both disappeared at the back wall. The stones there were slightly ajar, enough for the three to squeeze through one by one into the darkness beyond, Jame last.

Graykin's yelp of surprise receded downward.

"Stairs," said Rue succinctly.

All Jame could see at first was a fire-lit streak of the opposite stone wall, mere inches away. She put her hand on it and waited for her eyes to adjust, gratefully breathing the cool air.

"So this is how the Highlord escaped," said Rue in the dark, several steps down.

"Through a hole in the wall?" Graykin's voice came from much farther down, edged with hysteria. "I think I've broken my ankle," he added resentfully.

"Escaped?"

"Didn't you know, lady? The Caineron locked him in. He was raving." Jame could just make out the cadet's embarrassed wriggle. "Said the wyrm had bitten him."

Jame felt suddenly cold. "It *bit* him? Oh, sweet Trinity."

She could see the steps now, dimly, and went down them in a precipitous rush, past Rue, over Graykin who was sprawling where he had fallen. Their voices followed her, calling questions, but she didn't answer. What could she have said?

The wyrm bit my brother. My brother is a blood-binder, but he doesn't know it. To be a binder is to be Shanir, and Tori doesn't know that either. Our father taught us both to hate those of the Old Blood beyond reason, as he hated me, as Tori does too when he remembers what I am. If Tori finds out how alike we are, it will destroy him.

No, she couldn't say that, not to anyone.

Venom had hollowed out the lips of the treads, rendering them treacherous. Her foot shot out from under her and she bounced down the last, long stretch on her already bruised tailbone, through a wyrm hole at the bottom eaten through solid stone, into the straw bedding of an empty box stall. Horses stirred nervously all around her, the whites of their eyes flashing at her through the wooden slats of adjacent stalls. Hooves danced.

Out in the aisle, Jame paused. Which way to go? The stable was much larger than she had expected, underlying most of Old Tentir, a maze of moveable wooden partitions between the massive stone arches that supported the fortress above. The air should have been sweet with the breath of horses and ripe with their fresh droppings. Instead, a sharp tang of fear overlaid all. A tickling in her nose told her that Jorin was still on the wyrm's scent somewhere in this restless labyrinth.

Cadets were shouting back and forth: "D'you see anything?" "Not yet." "That smell...what died in here?"

Following their voices, she came to an open arena under the great hall. Secured to iron rings set in the surrounding pillars, the new arrivals fretted in their full tack. Vant was stalking back and forth behind them, impatiently slapping a brush against his leg.

"I tell you, Iron-thorn," he shouted, "the horses are spooked by that damn cat. That's all! Sweet Trinity, d'you expect me to put up this lot by myself?"

This wasn't quite fair: across the arena another cadet was struggling to hold Storm. The black stallion danced in place, jerking the cadet back and forth in his attempt to follow Brithany as the gray mare trotted from stall to stall, whickering reassurances.

The inmates quieted, but began to fret again as soon as the matriarch had passed. Their anxious calls to each other echoed off the low vault of the ceiling.

"What are you doing here, lady?"

Vant's voice next to her made Jame start. He didn't look at her directly, but his hand closed on her wrist as if to secure someone's runaway pet. On the perilous road they had all so recently trodden, he would never have dared to touch her, furious as he had been at her assumption of command. Highborn females didn't behave that way—sane ones, at least. How could he possibly have submitted to her will? How much had that weakness compromised not only his pride but also his honor? Now, however, he was in his proper place again, and all would be right.

"Listen," she said urgently to him. "There's a darkling crawler loose down here and I've got to catch it."

His grip tightened. In another moment, she thought, he would gladly slap her as a cure for hysteria, and she would try very hard not to kill him.

Then she saw Jorin. The ounce was in an empty stall directly across the arena, cautiously circling a big mound of straw. Vant saw him too. He gestured with his free hand for the nearest cadets to close in. Two of them began stealthily to climb the adjacent slat walls. Jorin daubed at the mound with a paw, and jumped back as it rustled. The wyrm's scent carried through his senses was so strong that Jame's eyes began to water.

The ounce crouched, hindquarters twitching.

"Jorin!" she shouted at him. "Don't!"

Vant glanced down at her with a kind of savage satisfaction. "Now, now," he said, grinning through clenched teeth. "No need for tears. Your pet will be returned to you…if you behave. Or maybe not."

Jorin pounced.

Something erupted from the stack in an explosion of straw. It hit the back wall and passed straight through it with Jorin in wild pursuit. The horse stabled beyond screamed and tried to jump out of its stall. Wooden slats splintered and fell. More petitions crashed down in a spreading wave of chaos. Cadets were shouting, "Stop them! Stop them!" But Brier's voice roared over theirs:

"Stop them, be damned! Get out of their way!"

Horses spilled into the arena, careening in mindless panic. Vant jumped back between the tethered mounts, dragging Jame with him, but they too had caught the madness and were plunging about in a nightmare of hooves, teeth, and eyes.

The stampede knocked Brithany off her feet, into a wall. As she struggled to rise, her forelegs tangled in the loop of her reins and she fell again. Storm screamed and reared, trying to reach her but cut off by the wild surge.

"Let me go," Jame said to Vant.

He looked at her as if she were mad and twisted her wrist. She reversed the lock on him and drove a nail into the nerve center at the crook of his arm. He swore, as much in astonishment as in pain, and she wrenched free from his suddenly nerveless grasp.

The loose horses wheeled and swerved wildly about the arena, each trying to lose itself in the safety of the herd. Jame dodged between them. Instinctively, she knew that they would trample her without a thought if she got in their way. The size, speed, and power of this living avalanche appalled her.

Here at last was the Whinno-hir, hopelessly entangled and thrashing. Jame ducked a small but lethally flailing hoof and put her hand on Brithany's shoulder. The mare instantly quieted, her large eyes bright with fear but also with that more than equine intelligence that can defy instinct. Jame drew her knife, a parting gift from the Jaran Lordan Kirien, and slashed the leather reins. She noted in passing that the Whinno-hir's bridle had no bit. Here was a creature the equal of any lord, who could only be ridden with her own consent.

Just as Brithany lurched to her feet, Storm came up roaring like his namesake, ready to kill someone. For a moment, Jame was afraid. For all she knew, this towering black stallion saw her as his master's enemy. So, for that matter, might the Whinno-hir.

Then Jorin pelted under the stallion's nose and leaped into Jame's arms, knocking her backward into Brithany and both of them nearly off their feet. Storm snorted, amused. A footstep sounded behind him, and he whirled on his hocks to find himself eye to eye with Brier Iron -thorn. Behind her Vant cradled his numb arm, looking murderous.

"Someone take that wretched cat out and drown it," he said.

The dark Southron turned to look at him. "Why?"

"Why? *Why?*" He indicated the scene behind him with a jerk of his head. "Just look!"

"I am looking."

So was Jame. The herd had slowed, their terror finally run out of them. Cadets were catching halters, soothing frightened beasts, and leading them back to whatever stalls remained intact.

"If the ounce's presence caused the panic," said Brier, "why are they calming down now? Whatever was here is gone now."

Then Jame remembered. "Sweet Trinity, the wyrm. Brier, I've got to reach Tori, to warn him."

"Not that again," said Vant, sounding thoroughly exasperated. "Haven't we had enough of this nonsense? Cadet, escort the Highborn back to her quarters."

Rue had come up, Graykin lagging warily behind her. "I can't, Five," said the cadet, with a self-conscious wriggle. "They're on fire."

"They're *what?*"

Brier looked at Jame. "Why am I not surprised."

Jame shrugged. "I didn't like the décor."

She caught a flicker of intense relief on Rue's face. Burning down the Highlord's apartment was not a good way to start anyone's life as a cadet.

"Ten, please. I've got to see my brother. This is deadly important. My word of honor on it."

The big cadet regarded her somberly. Abused by her former Caineron masters, she found it hard to trust any Highborn. They both knew that if she did as Jame asked and the mission turned out to be frivolous, it would be the end of her career.

"Very well, lady," she said. "Come with me."

# II

IN THE GREAT hall, a Coman cadet tried to stop them. Brier brushed him aside and opened the door to New Tentir, to a blur of runners and the thunder of their passage.

The Coman turned to Jame. Clearly, he didn't know what to make of her. Highborn, female, Knorth…for him, she added up to a complete nonsense.

"Lady, d'you want to get yourself killed," he pleaded, "or, worse, me expelled?"

"Relax," said Jame wearily. "You can claim that I bewildered you."

She would have liked nothing better than to sit down, right there in the midst of the quake debris. Every time she stopped moving, her saddle-sore legs threatened to fold under her. Her idea was to stick her head out the door, shout "Rest!" and hope that the running cadets obeyed.

Instead, Brier said, "*Now*," and plunged out into the storm.

Jame was scrambling to catch up before she had time to think.

They emerged on the arcade between squads, between houses too, as it turned out, and the one hard on their heels was Caineron. Caldane's cadets instantly recognized Brier and surged to catch up. Here was their former comrade, the *yondri* turn-collar, and they wanted blood.

The Danior squad ahead glanced over their shoulders. Their young lord was a Knorth ally, bone-kin to Torisen and formerly his heir. They slowed and opened their ranks to admit the newcomers. Jame stumbled. Hands caught and bore her along, her feet off the ground, her shins repeatedly kicked to a muttered chorus of "Sorry, sorry, sorry…"

Meanwhile, the back rank of the Danior was trying to fend off the Caineron without catching the sargent' attention. That, luckily, had already been captured by growing ructions between the Ardeth and the Knorth on the other side of the square.

"Keep your order! Keep your order!" came their harried shouts.

"Where to?" grunted the Danior ten-commander to Brier.

"The Highlord."

"The Ardeth, then."

The running battle pounded down the northern side of the square, turned sharp left with the arcade, and thundered on. Just when Jame thought they were going to pull off her arms, Brier grabbed her by the jacket and lunged sideways into a door. It crashed open. Jame, pitched in headlong, rolled to her feet and then off of them again as much abused muscles rebelled. Dammit, if she never rode another horse as long as she lived, she would go to her pyre smiling.

Brier faced the door, which seethed with struggling cadets. Outraged yells to the rear announced the arrival of the Ardeth, who had seen their quarters presumably under attack. Behind them, someone gave the Knorth's rathorn war-cry, shrilly and somewhat wildly, in a voice not yet broken.

"Go," Brier said to Jame. "Now."

They had gate-crashed a lower reception hall, flanked with doors, a stair at its head.

Turning, Jame found herself face-to-face with Timmon. He gaped at her, then at the boiling mass of fighters at his door. Jorin squeezed between their legs and scuttled through the inner door from which the young Ardeth had emerged and which he still held open.

"Inside," he said to Jame. "Quick."

Beyond was a communal dining room, the long tables laid out for supper but no food on them.

Timmon slammed the door. "God's claws," he said, leaning against it. "Are all your entrances this dramatic?"

He was, she supposed, about her own age, twenty or twenty-one, mid-adolescence for a Highborn whose kind matured more slowly and lived longer than most Kendar. As she had noted in Tentir's great hall, he was also startlingly handsome, if now somewhat disheveled, his elegant jacket open at the throat, his golden hair ruffled. He also held a raw, half-eaten carrot.

"Where is my brother?"

"Up there." He indicated the chamber above their heads. "With my grandfather."

They stared up at the ceiling. Footsteps sounded above, circling, circling, and the floor groaned. Whorls in the wood grain shifted with each step. They might have been looking at the surface of a disturbed pool, from underneath. Timmon's hair bristled. Jame felt her own prickle all over her body.

"What are they *doing?*" whispered the Ardeth.

"Whatever it is, it's getting worse. Oh Tori," she said to herself, "how can I help you?"

Timmon stared at her. "You don't. You stay out of the way, my girl, and so do I. Sweet Trinity, don't you think I would help Grandfather if I could?"

Jame glanced at the carrot.

"I got hungry," he said defensively, and flicked the vegetable away.

Jame stifled a sneeze. Her nose was tickling with the wyrm smell again, and Jorin was nowhere in sight. Only one door stood open in the hall, leading downward. Of course.

"*Now* what are you doing?" Timmon called after her as she hastily descended. He followed, catching up at the foot of the stair. "Trinity, you Knorth are peculiar! Your brother tears apart my quarters, and now you want to start on the cellar?"

"Nothing that bad," said Jame, casting about for the scent. "I hope. I'm hunting a darkling crawler."

"Oh. Is that all?"

The basement of New Tentir must be roughly on the same level as Old Tentir's stable, a straight shot for a creature that could pass through wood and stone at will. And they were comfortingly dark. At first, the only light came from thick candles set in wall sconces, marked with the hours of the night, newly lit. Here, the cellar was divided into many small rooms—servants' quarters, mostly, all empty.

"Where is everyone?" asked Jame. She found that she was whispering.

"Your brother told all the Kendar to leave. *Our* Kendar, you'll notice. But the Commandant seconded him and they did."

Of course Tori would try to get the Kendar safely out of the way, never mind whose they were. She would have done the same.

However, instinct told her that her brother stood in greater danger now than anyone else. There was no doubt in her mind that the wyrm would seek him out. His blood called to it, but was he its master now or was that still the dead changer? From what she had seen in the web-images festooning the guest quarters, it was one confused beastie. Of course, Tori might simply kill it, and that would be that. The last thing he needed right now, though, was such a distraction.

Here, down several steps, was the kitchen that served the Ardeth barracks, with the makings of dinner strewn about it—stew, judging by the heaps of raw vegetables and the vast cauldron on the central hearth, just coming to a boil. It all seemed very cheerful and ordinary, except that no one was there.

A loud crunch behind her made Jame jump. Timmon had found another carrot. "I'm still hungry," he said cheerfully. "What's wrong with your cat?"

Jorin stood in rigid silhouette against the flames, his back and tail arched. A singing whine came out of his throat, like a saw cutting live bone. But what did he sense? Jame edged closer, peering at the hearth, the fire, the cauldron, the water…nothing. Debris rattled down. She looked up.

"Timmon, your family crest is the full moon, isn't it? Then why is there a serpent rampant over your mantelpiece? Oh."

The wyrm lost its grip on the crumbling stones and fell. Jorin dodged behind Jame. Recoiling, she tripped over him and went down hard, cracking her head on the scoured flagstones. The crawler landed on top of her.

Knocked breathless, she barely had time to throw up an arm to protect her face. The wyrm twisted to right itself. Its sides were fringed not with legs but with fingers covered in a lacework of white scars. Her skin stung where the venom of its touch ate though her clothes; but the full sleeve of the knife-fighter's *d'hen* was reinforced to turn an attacker's blade, and so it did this creature's assault.

"*Are you the one?*"

Its features shifted inside the caul that enveloped its entire head except for a round mouth like a lamprey's. The dead changer glared at her and gnashed his ring of teeth.

"*Are you the one who stole my Beauty?*"

He thought she was Tori, Jame realized, and Beauty…Trinity, Beauty was his name for the wyrm.

The face inside the membrane whipped back and forth, changing.

"*No, no, no…*"

Tori's features emerged, haggard, desperate. "*Adric, don't…help me, help…*"

"How?" cried Jame, lowering her arm. "Oh Tori, let me help!"

His fingers slide over her face, a touch as light as gossamer but it made her skin burn. She felt her body arch under his weight. *Oh, touch me again...*

"No!"

She was with her brother, circling, circling, the old lord's glamour beating against him/her/them like the desert sun, fifteen years' experience of each other all focused on this moment, on this issue: Who would be master?

*Oh Adric, I don't want to fight. I'm tired. I hurt. And I don't want to hurt you...*

Nowhere to hide. Be a rock, a black rock in the Southern Wastes, but what shadow lies behind it?

*Adric searching for the bones of his son, which I ordered to be burned in secret on the common pyre at the Cataracts...*

(What?)

*I promised to protect him, as he once protected me. If he knew what you had done, Peri, it would kill him. I couldn't let you tell him. I keep my promises. But oh Adric, don't!*

"Don't what?" said Timmon.

He was wiping her face where Tori—no, where the wyrm had brushed it. Her skin burned as if with too much sun, but no worse. The creature's venom must almost have been spent.

"Nothing." She took a deep breath to collect herself and burst out coughing. The weakened fireplace had collapsed, overturning the cauldron onto the fire. Smoke still seeped out of the ruins, mixed with the gritty dust of stone and mortar. Jorin was sniffing at the mound of debris. Then he began to scratch around it as if trying to bury something. "What happened? Where's the wyrm?"

"Under there. It attacked you, I hit it with a shovel, and the mantel fell on it. I thought the whole wall was going to come down, maybe the whole barracks."

Both his voice and his hand shook slightly; he was not as calm as he wished to appear.

Neither was she. Just now, linked by the wyrm, she had been in that tent by the Cataracts, in her brother's mind and memory, when he had broken Pereden's neck. The feel, the *sound* of it...and here was Pereden's son who had probably just saved her life, trying to laugh off the terror that still quivered in his very bones.

*If he knew what you had done...*

What *had* Timmon's father done, to be killed in secret, his bones given to the pyre in stealth? She only knew that the sight of Pereden's son had stricken her brother in the great hall, and guilt now kept him from defending himself as he must in order to survive.

From overhead came the scuffle and thud of feet. Dust drifted down between the floorboards. Something fell with a crash.

Jame lurched to her feet, and her sight blurred. She waited for it to clear.

"How long has that been going on?"

"About as long as you were unconscious. A few minutes. Is your life usually like this?"

"More or less, and I still have to help my brother."

"Rest first. Stay with me."

She became aware of his arm around her waist, steadying her. It felt good to lean against someone.

*Oh, touch me again…*

"It's quiet here now," he said, "and safe, as long as the ceiling doesn't fall in. Stay. I've never met anyone like you before."

For a moment, she was tempted. She had never met anyone like him either, nor was she used to flattery. He certainly had a beguiling air, and he *was* very handsome.

Knorth and Ardeth, Ardeth and Knorth, circling, circling…

"No." She pulled free of his embrace. "Stay here if you want. I'm going."

"You can't help," he called after her.

She paused on the stair. "Then I'll hurt. I'm good at that."

Her first impression of the dining hall was of chaos. A mob of cadets had spilled in from the hallway, but no one seemed to be fighting now nor making much noise except for the scrape and shuffle of feet. She scrambled up on a table for a better look, catching her toe in the process and nearly falling flat among the crockery. It had been much too long a day. Knorth and Ardeth, Ardeth and Knorth were circling each other as if in a macabre dance, eyes glazed, faces twitching as if caught in a bad dream. Overhead, the ceiling roiled and groaned in a storm of wood. Jame cursed under her breath. She had seen this sort of thing before, in Restormir's main square during Caldane's epic drinking binge. When a lord let things get out of hand, it went hard on the Kendar bound to him, and these cadets were hardly more than children. She stumbled

down the length of the table, jumped to the floor, and slipped out
into the hall.

The Ardeth guards were pounding on the front door, whose
edges appeared to have grown shut. M'lord Ardeth did not want to
be disturbed.

Brier Iron-thorn was half way up the stair, hanging on to the
rail. Blood as dark red as her hair ran down her face from a split
lip, and someone had ripped the malachite stud out of her ear.
She lurched around to block Jame's way, her green eyes murky and
half-focused.

"He saved me from the Caineron. Bound me. I am his, although I trust no Highborn fool enough to trust me. I don't trust
you. You will only hurt him."

Jame blinked. "Now, listen," she began, then stopped. There
wasn't time. She ducked under Brier's arm and went up the stairs.

At the top stood Sheth Sharp-tongue, the commandant of Tentir,
waiting.

"So, girl," he said, with a faint smile, "here we are. My Lord
Caineron fears you. I begin to see why. Are you always
this…er…disruptive?"

The door was behind him and behind that, her brother fought
for his life.

"Do something!" she cried.

"Why?"

Timmon came up behind her. The Commandant ignored him.
So did Jame.

"You'd let them destroy each other?"

"Why not?"

For a moment, she saw him as a Caineron, the enemy of both
her house and the Ardeth; but something else was at work here too,
a cool assessment of power.

"Now, what kind of highlord would need my help?" the tall
randon said gently to her. "If he is weak enough to fall, better for
the Kencyrath that he should, don't you think?"

For a moment, she saw it: what chance did the Three People
have if their highlord wasn't strong enough to lead them? Tori had
weaknesses, no question about that. Suppose that in the end he
wasn't able to surmount them. So the Kencyrath would fall and so
would end their world.

No.

"Lord Caineron is strong," she said, "but strength isn't everything. There is also compassion, justice, and honor."

Behind her, Timmon turned a gasp into a cough.

The Commandant regarded her, eyes hooded and enigmatic. She glowered back. One didn't say such things to such a man as this, but she had, and damned if she would play rabbit to his hawk now.

He inclined his head and stepped aside.

"Let me," said Timmon, pushing past her. "These are my quarters, after all." But the door wouldn't open. "Locked," he said, with ill-concealed relief.

Jame put her hand on the latch. No, it wasn't locked. As below, the wood grain bound door, posts, and lintel together as if they had grown that way, with only a shallow crack between them.

Her fingertips tingled. An image began to form in her mind, intricate and verdant, deep green laced with pale gold on a bronze filigree. It was a master rune. The Book Bound in Pale Leather, that dire compendium of power, was no longer in her hands; Bane guarded it and the Ivory Knife in that pest-hole of a prison in the rock face behind Mount Alban. She had had mixed experiences with it anyway, having once accidentally set fire to a blizzard, and this rune wasn't familiar to her at all. But she could still unmake it. Already she was teasing it apart in her mind, line by line.

"What are you doing?" asked Timmon behind her.

She ignored him. It was harder to ignore the looming presence of the Commandant. Did he know what she was doing? That man had Shanir blood, although what sort she couldn't guess.

From inside came the murmur of Ardeth's voice: "...so like my dear son Pereden. Ah, what a lord he would have made. My heart breaks to think of it. You and he would have been like brothers and I a father to you both..."

Tori couldn't stand much more of this. In his place, she would long since have flared and brought down the roof, just to shut the old man up.

Jame backed away, then threw herself at the door.

It disintegrated.

She plunged into the room off balance, into a table laden with crystal, past it to the sound of shattering glass, into the folds of a curtain, through that with a mighty ripping of cloth, and onto a bed, which collapsed.

Fighting free, she saw her brother staring at her open-mouthed, as well he might. Behind him, Ardeth put his hand on his shoulder.

"My son…"

And, finally, the Highlord turned on him. "NO!"

The room shook. In all its corners, things broke, and the furniture lurched. Jame went over backward into the chasm between the bed and the wall, where she landed on top of something warm and furry that yelped.

As she struggled with whatever-it-was, both of them tangled in a winding sheet of linens, she could hear Ardeth's guard pouring into the lower hall and confused sounds from the dining room below as dazed cadets began to sort themselves out.

Closer at hand, her brother was speaking urgently. "Adric? Can you hear me? Damn, I was afraid of this. It's his heart. Commandant, does the college have a healer in residence?"

"Not at present. The Priest's College claims that we wear them out too quickly."

"Here's Grandfather's box of drugs. Which bottle?"

"The blue one, I think. Yes. Hemlock, in wine. Filthy stuff, but I've seen him drink it many times to calm himself. Damn. You pour it, boy. I'm no good one-handed. There. Is that better, Adric? That's right. Drink some more. Here's your grandson to look after you."

"Highlord, a word."

Torisen and the Commandant moved closer. Jame stopped floundering.

"Under other circumstances," panted the Wolver Grimly beneath her, "this would be fun."

"Quiet!"

She wished she could hide under the covers forever, but what would Ardeth think if he found her and Grimly there in the morning?

"Your pardon, my lord, but it would be best if you were not here when he awakes."

A deep, weary sigh answered him. "Yes. Yes, I see." Jame peeked out. Tori was rubbing his eyes. The dark circles under them looked like bruises, and the high cheekbones sharp enough to cut skin. He stood for a moment collecting his thoughts with an obvious effort. "Very well. I will ride on tonight, at least as far as Shadow Rock. As for my sister..."

Jame rose, half-sheepish, half-defiant. Grimly's furry ears pricked up beside her, just clearing the coverlet. Here it came.

"...she will be staying here as a cadet candidate and—" he paused to gulp "—as my heir, the Knorth Lordan."

From below came a crash and much shouting. The dining hall had just collapsed into the kitchen below.

# Chapter III:  Wine, Women, and Wolvers

## 2-3<sup>rd</sup> of Summer

# I

HE LAY ON the hard cot in the big, dark room, pretending to sleep.  From all around him came the deep breath of his fellow cadets, mixed with their occasional murmurs, sighs, and snores.  It should have been a time of utter peace, of deep sleep after good, hard work remembered almost luxuriously in the fading ache of muscle and mind.  He should have been intensely happy and so he was, he told himself.  He had begged to attend the college, with little hope that Father would permit it, yet here he was, against all odds, on the threshold of a new life.

Why, then, did every nerve twang with tension?

Feet shuffled on the floor overhead.  Two voices rose and fell.  Then one exploded in a shout of drunken laughter.

The Lordan was carousing late again, probably with that sly-eyed Randir who would be drinking one cup to the other's three while seeming to keep pace.

That afternoon, at the pool, he had looked up and seen them staring contemptuously down at him from atop Breakneck Rock.  Their gaze, especially the Lordan's, had made him feel not just naked, as all the swimmers were, but stripped down to his pitiful soul and left there exposed, for all to see.

He curled up shivering under the thin blanket. If only they would leave him alone…

A hand on his shoulder that made his heart leap like a startled frog.  A soft, mocking voice in his ear: "The Lordan wants you.  In his quarters.  Now."

Torisen woke with a violent start, his heart pounding.  Where was he?  Not in the Knorth dormitory at Tentir.  Tonight his sister Jame would be spending her first night there as a cadet candidate, as the Knorth Lordan.  And he…he was on the run.  From Ardeth.  From her.

"Awake?"

A shimmer of starlight through an arched window caught the glow of eyes at his feet where Grimly curled up in his complete furs, muzzle across Torisen's ankles. The long jaw altered to a mouth still full of sharp teeth but capable of human speech. "Were you dreaming?"

He sounded both worried and wary, with good cause. In the past, Torisen had sometimes stayed awake for days, even weeks, pushing himself to the edge of madness, all to avoid certain dreams.

*The Shanir dream, boy*, his father had said. *Are you a filthy Shanir?*

No, he was not, and he now knew that everyone had dreams of some sort. Still, that last really bad one had been enough to send him storming out of Kothifir and up the length of the Silver with the sword Kin-Slayer naked in his hand and his dead father's voice in his mind inciting him to murder.

*Your Shanir twin, boy, your darker half, returned to destroy you...*

Overtaken by the weirdingstrom, he and Grimly had sought refuge in the wolver's native holt on the edge of the great Weald. Then had come dark dreams. In one of them, he had found himself clutching Kin-slayer, cowering in the hall of the Haunted Lands keep where he and his sister had been born. He was hiding from her, as he had been in Kothifir all winter, but she found him. She always did. Father was there too, dead on the battlements with three arrows in his chest. No, on the stair descending, step-by-step, muttering as he came, cursing him, telling him to kill, to kill.

*The sword is in your hand, boy. You know that she is stronger than you. Save yourself. Strike!*

But Jame *was* stronger. She had cursed their father and slammed the door in his dead face. Then she had shot the bolt against his madness.

When Torisen woke, his hand was already in splints.

"You looked at Kin-Slayer and said, 'There's more than one way to break a grip,'" Grimly had told him. "Then you pried loose your fingers one by one."

Had he really meant to kill Jame? Surely not. As children they had been as close as a single soul shared by two bodies. He had played in her dreams and she in his, until Father taught him to fear both dreams and her. Still, how he had missed her after Father had driven her out, and how he had blamed himself for letting her go. Now, miraculously, she had returned to him. He loved her, if "love" was the right word for this roil of emotions.

*Father says destruction begins with love.*

"Does it hurt?" Grimly asked.

It took Torisen a moment to realize that the wolver meant his broken fingers. Grimly knew all about Torisen's horror of becoming a cripple. When they had first met, the young Knorth had been fresh from the terrors of Urakarn where Karnid torture and infection had nearly cost him both hands. He still had the lacework of white scars as a reminder of the horrible vulnerability even of Kencyr flesh.

"Pain doesn't matter," he said, "as long as they heal. And they are. Yes, I was dreaming."

He coughed, his throat parched with the memory. Grimly rose, reverting easily to full if hairy man-shape, and padded across the floor to a table where a pitcher of water stood. He poured a cup full. Propping himself up on an elbow, Torisen accepted it gratefully and drank.

He remembered now: They were at Shadow Rock, the Danior keep, snatching a few hours of desperately needed rest before riding on to Gothregor. Across the river was the Randir fortress with Rawneth, the Witch of Wilden, in residence. Dangerous. They would have to be on their way soon, but not just yet.

"I dreamed," he repeated thoughtfully, frowning, "that I was at Tentir in the dormitory, and overhead the Lordan was getting drunk."

"She didn't invite you up?"

"That was the problem. He...no, she did, and I was afraid to go. Truly terrified. And I don't know why."

"That's bad," said the Wolver, now only half-joking. He partially resumed his furs and curled up beside the Highborn, a warm presence in the predawn chill. "You don't frighten easily."

Torisen laughed, tasting his bitter fear. "Many things scare me."

Odd, how easy it was to talk to Grimly, or perhaps not. Young and friendless in that strange city, Kothifir the Cruel, one formed alliances quickly or died. He had had good reason at the time not to trust his own people. Among them, even now, only Harn, Burr and Rowan could guess his deepest thoughts. "Why do you think we're on the run now? What am I going to do without Ardeth's support and protection?"

"You really think you've lost it?"

"For now, at least. Adric has tried force. Now he will leave me to fend for myself, waiting for me to regain my senses and come crawling back."

He heard the bitterness in his voice. Up until three years ago he had been Ardeth's to command. No one but Adric had known who he was—it would have been suicide to announce himself before he came of age—but the old lord had also been both a mentor and a friend. Not to have him there now was like standing with his back to an open door, knowing his enemies were gathering in the dark beyond it.

*I opened that door when I made my sister my heir,* he thought. *I was a fool. Perhaps.*

"You're stronger than you think," said Grimly. "You must be, or the Caineron and Randir would have long since picked their teeth with your bones. Your sister is strong too."

Torisen considered this. "Yes. She's very strong. And dangerous." The word escaped him, flicking awake the terror he had felt in his dream at her summons.

*Your Shanir twin…*

By some weird quirk of fate, though, she was still only a half-grown girl while he was a man in his prime. Besides, he was Highlord, dammit, at no one's beck and call.

The Wolver grinned. "I'll tell you this: you may be my oldest friend, but it's a lot more fun wrestling with your sister."

A soft knock on the door made them both start. The Danior steward entered, shielding a candle with his hand. "M'lord," he said, "something is brewing across the river."

Torisen threw back the blanket and joined Grimly at the window.

Wilden lay across the Silver, slotted into its steep, narrow valley. A mountain stream divided at its head and hurtled, frothing, down either side into a brimming lower moat. Within its walls, the Randir fortress rose terrace on terrace, compound on compound, up to the Witch's tower glimmering white under the sliver of a crescent moon waning toward the dark. Mist was rolling out of the Witch's open door. It flowed down the empty streets, collecting at each corner, then rolling on in a slow, thickening tide, down toward the Silver's glint.

"Nice neighbors you've got," said Torisen as Grimly helped him pull on his boots. Otherwise, he had slept fully clothed. "How does she do that?"

"We have no idea. Remember, though, that the Priests' College lies literally in the shadow of her tower. Highlord, with m'lord

Danior and most of our people still at Kothifir, there aren't enough of us here to protect you."

"Time we were gone anyway." Torisen rose and stomped home the boots. The steward's worried voice followed them down the stairs:

"If the mist catches you, there will be no one to rescue you."

"We'll risk it, thank you."

"And if you leave the road, odds are that you'll get lost in the hills. After the weirdingstrom, ancestors only know where anything is. Even our balancing rock is missing."

"If it falls on us, we'll let you know."

"Cheerful fellow," muttered Grimly as he held Storm's stirrup for Torisen to mount. "No wonder your lord cousin left him behind last fall."

They rode out into an increasingly hazy night. Mist mounted silently across the Silver, then overarched it. Tendrils, drifting too low, were carried away with the current. They had to go slow on the quake-broken road or risk their horses' legs. Soon, they rode in a tunnel of fog, cut off from moon or stars, their way lit with flaring torches, the clop of hooves muffled.

Trotting at Storm's side, Grimly noted uneasily how the mist opened before them and closed behind. They were on the west bank New Road, which offered less protection than the ancient stonework of the opposite River Road. Moreover, both had been severely damaged. He didn't like the way white tendrils of mist quested blindly after Torisen like so many phantom snares cast after prey, but none of them quite managed to catch him. Even stranger, cracks seemed to close under Storm's hooves—either that, or the stallion had uncanny footing, but looking back Grimly saw that the paving had been subtly refitted. He had noticed odd, little things about his friend before of which Torisen seemed unaware and which upset him greatly when they were pointed out. The Wolver himself found them obscurely comforting.

Luckily, the Witch could only reach so far, and the sun was rising. After what seemed like hours, they emerged into a hazy dawn. Another hundred yards, and the mist burned off entirely, leaving a bright morning. It was the second of summer, and they were still some fifty miles from home.

Early afternoon found them opposite Falkirr, the Brandon keep. Brant, Lord Brandon, was also still with the Southern Host but his sister Brenwyr, the Brandon Matriarch, was said to be newly arrived home.  Torisen decided not to pay his respects.  In truth, he found Brenwyr almost as unnerving as Rawneth and preferred not to meet her without her brother on hand for protection.

They reached Gothregor, saddle-sore on tired mounts, at dusk. It, too, was held by a token garrison, but one overjoyed to see their erratic lord again.  If they could have, Torisen thought, submitting reluctantly to their fervent greetings, they would have kept him wrapped in cotton, locked away somewhere secret and safe.  Their god had played a vicious trick on the Kendar by making them only feel complete when they were bound to a Highborn.  To lose one's lord was a terrible thing.  He appreciated their concern, knowing how much they depended on him, but still…

*If only they felt free to stay or go*, he thought as he swung down from Storm and stood for a moment gripping the stallion's mane to steady himself, his legs quivering with fatigue, his splinted fingers throbbing. *If only they would leave me alone!*

Grimly snarled at the thicket of hands reaching out to support his friend, causing most of them to withdraw hastily.  But the Kendar were also giving way to a newcomer invisible until she parted their towering ranks and glided through to face Torisen.

"Highlord, the Matriarch Adiraina wishes to speak to you."

He stared down at the small Ardeth lady, his mind going blank. Nothing could be read from her masked face, but every line of her trim, tightly laced form radiated determination.

"What, now?"

"Yes, my lord.  Now."

The Wolver yelped in protest, and the lady's randon escort dropped hands to sword hilts to protect her.  By now, however, Torisen had had time to think, and his thoughts appalled him.

"Grimly, no."  He let go of Storm and stood, gathering his strength and wits.  "This might be important.  I'll see you later in the common room."

# II

TORISEN FOLLOWED THE Ardeth Highborn, with her guards striding behind him as if to prevent his escape. Something very like panic made his stomach clench. What if Adric's heart attack had proved fatal after all? Adiraina was not only an Ardeth but a Shanir. She might know if the lord of her house had suddenly died and by whose hand, for surely she would blame him for driving his old mentor to such extremes. He certainly would blame himself.

They crossed the broad inner ward, passing the original Old Keep on its hill fort foundation, incongruously small for such a mass of buildings to have grown up behind it. Foremost of these were the Women's Halls, into which he was led by the northern gate. As the scrollsmen had Mount Alban and the randon Tentir, the Council of Matriarchs had claimed the westernmost halls of Gothregor for the training of Highborn girls of every house to become proper ladies. The womenfolk there far out-numbered Gothregor's small garrison, with the Highlord as their reluctant host. Nonetheless, neither he nor any other man usually came here, where even the randon guards were female.

Only days ago, however, Torisen had virtually stormed this forbidden domain in search of his sister, only to be told that she had vanished, with two shadow assassins on her trail. His encounter then with the Ardeth Matriarch had hardly been cordial. The thought of a second interview now made him shudder, no matter what she had to tell him.

His escort led him through the Brandon, Edirr, and Danior compounds, leaving behind a flutter of ladies who clearly hadn't expected to encounter a man, much less the Highlord, at this time of night. This was the long way around, avoiding the Coman and Randir. Torisen wondered why.

But here was the Ardeth.

The tiny Highborn bowed him into a room and firmly shut the door after him. He was relieved not to find the entire Council of Matriarchs waiting for him, as it had the last time. On the other hand, this small, candle-lit room appeared to be the antechamber to Adiraina's private quarters, unnervingly intimate with its delicately scented air, claustrophobic without windows.

Torisen knew a trap when he stepped into one, but step he must.

The Matriarch sat upright in a filigree chair beside the fireplace. When they had exchanged salutes—wary on his part, gracious on hers—she indicated a chair opposite her. All too aware of the slight tremor of fatigue in his legs, he sank into it, and kept on sinking as the tapestry back slid down under his weight.

"Such an interesting design, don't you think?" Adiraina smiled sweetly. "And so comfortable, I'm told. My old bones don't allow me such luxury."

Torisen stared owlishly back at her over his jutting knees. This was her revenge for his behavior the last time they had meet, when he had nearly thrown the entire Women's World out of Gothregor on their collective ear for their treatment of his sister. In retrospect, he had probably been rude, but if he had followed his instinct, he wouldn't now be perched on his tail-bone outside a lady's bedroom.

Between them was a delicate table bearing a glass of dark, red wine and a plate of sugar cakes sprinkled with what appeared to be cinnamon.

"Eat, drink," said the Matriarch with a graceful wave of her thin, white hand. "You have had a long, hard ride. You must be famished."

Torisen was, although nerves nearly killed his appetite. This wasn't the reception he had expected. Surely, if Adric were dead and his cousin knew it, she would be far less welcoming. But if not that, then why had she requested...no, demanded...to see him the moment he set foot inside his citadel?

As he strained forward to take a cake—Trinity, how was he going to get out of this diabolical chair without falling flat on his face?—he studied his hostess. Over one hundred and twenty years old, she was a study in subtle shades of gray from the dark pewter of her gown to lace-work trim tinted the rose blush of storm clouds at sunset. Her velvet half-mask had no eye-holes: she had been blind since adolescence—the cost, some said, for her awakening Shanir powers. Although immaculate in dress and regal in bearing, wisps of white hair escaped her coiffure and the toe of a bedroom slipper lurked in the folds of her skirt. So she hadn't expected his sudden return.

Her voice flowed over him in a stream of small talk about the weather, about the coming midsummer harvest, about mutual acquaintances and friends; but hidden in the stream were rocks. She bemoaned Adric's fragile health without mentioning his recent heart attack, of which she was apparently unaware.

*So much for Shanir omniscience,* thought Torisen, a bit smugly.

"He can't help but worry, you know," the matriarch was saying. "We all do. You haven't quite found your feet yet as highlord, have you, my dear? These past three years have been…interesting, occasionally verging on the catastrophic. You really must learn to take a stronger hand and to depend more on your own kind—not that the Kendar aren't useful, when kept in their place. If you had grown up among your peers, things would be different. However, you didn't, so I suppose we must make allowances. Of course, the battle at the Cataracts was a great victory, although also a terrible tragedy for our house with the loss of Pereden. Now Adric pins his hopes on Peri's son, Timmon. To my mind, the boy is a bit frivolous and his mother over-ambitious; however, we will see how he shapes up at Tentir.

"But you aren't eating. Please do. And drink, or I will be offended."

She laughed as she spoke, making light of it, but with a silvery ring to her voice like knife-play.

Blind she might be, but her hearing was acute.

Torisen nibbled the cake and found it sweet enough to hurt his teeth, with an odd after-taste. Then again, nothing tastes right to an exhausted man. It did, however, make him very thirsty. He surreptitiously discarded the pastry and, after a struggle to reach it, seized and sipped the wine. It was stronger than he liked and made his head spin, dangerous on an empty stomach. Nonetheless, under its influence he began to relax.

"By the way, did you ever find your sister Jameth?"

He noted that she couldn't say the name without a slight shudder, and at that she still hadn't quite gotten it right. Did the Matriarchs even know that they had been trifling with a second Jamethiel, perhaps even more dangerous than the first?

"Such an…unusual girl," Adiraina was saying, with an air of sweet forbearance. "So lively. And so inquisitive. However, she will settle down with the right consort. Have you picked one yet?"

"No." The wine was making Torisen drowsy and giving his voice a faint slur. He tried not to stare cross-eyed at his knees, which was hard since they were practically under his nose. "I made her my lordan and left her at Tentir to train as a randon cadet."

"Oh!"

He could almost see the Ardeth trying to decide if he had just made a joke in very bad taste, but that would imply a lie, which was unthinkable. He had, however, rattled her. Good.

"Well, of course we would never accept her back here after all the trouble she caused."

"What, fighting off shadow assassins? I understand there was a cast of twelve apprentices under the guidance of a master, out for a blooding. How many ladies were killed?"

"One, but that isn't the point."

"It is for the eleven who survived."

Adiraina gathered her wits and temper with an effort. "Still, you really should have consulted my lord Adric. It was hardly wise to set her up as your heir, much less to expose both her and you to ridicule over her inevitable failure at Tentir. You Knorth!"

Her tinkling laugh rang with indulgence. *How we humor you*, it said. Torisen gritted his teeth.

"For the moment, however," she continued, "we must reluctantly consider Jameth out of play. That leaves you, my dear. Have you considered whom to take as your next consort? No? You should. It is your duty."

She cocked her head, as if considering a new thought. "You know, my talent lies in sensing bloodlines. Our house is very pure in that respect, almost as much so as your own. That makes you and your sister all the more puzzling. It is so important to know which lines cross, don't you think? About some matches, the less said the better. You and your sister…"

"Jame," he said helpfully, to see her squirm. Slightly befuddled as he was, he could see where this conversation was going, and he didn't like it.

"Yes…er…dear Jameth. Both of you are pure-blooded Knorth. I know that. However, all the Knorth ladies died in the massacre except for poor Tieri, who died later giving birth to a bastard of unknown lineage."

Torisen blinked. "You mean Kindrie? He's my first cousin?"

Her thin lips tightened. "A bastard is kin to no one. Really, you sound like your wretched…er…dear sister, always asking such indelicate questions. The Priests' College has a place for such people. Tieri's brat never should have left it. But we were speaking of your mother."

"We were?"

"Neither you nor your sister looks much like your father, or so I am told. Poor Ganth was always a bit unrefined—the result, no doubt, of his unfortunate childhood; even good blood can't surmount everything—but you are both pure, classic Knorth. Blind or not, I know that."

She wrapped her slim arms around herself and spoke so low that he could hardly hear.

"Sometimes, when either of you are present, my very bones shake. Did you know that, as a child, I spent hours studying the faces of your ancestors in the death banner hall? The Kendar played cruel tricks in portraying some of them but even then, such eyes, such hands; such power once flesh and blood! When your dear great grandmother Kinzi first spoke to me, I thought I would die. I hear echoes of her in your voice and in that of your sister, yet I know that both of you are closer heirs to the ancient glamour of your house even than my beloved Kinzi was. But how can that be? Tell me, boy: who was your mother?"

If Torisen had known, in his current state she might have made him answer; but he didn't, and preferred to keep any suspicions to himself.

"With all due respect, matriarch, I decline to answer."

"Will you answer this, then? I also sense that you and your sister are twins, but how can that be when she is at least ten years your junior? Where has she been all this time?"

"Again with respect, you will have to ask her."

"We did. She wouldn't tell us."

"Then neither will I."

If he could have seen her eyes, she would surely have been glaring at him. However, like her cousin Adric, she was adept at self-control.

"Please," she said, with an abrupt return to her earlier graciousness, "drink. It will do you good."

Torisen wasn't so sure about that. As a rule, he preferred cider to wine, and this was a strong, unfamiliar vintage, again with that peculiar after-taste. However, it did soothe the nerves. The matriarch's voice resumed its smooth, cool flow over his tired muscles and fretting thoughts.

"You must allow for an old woman's eccentricity. Bloodlines are rather an obsession of mine. All that really matters is that yours are pure. And they are. You really should ally yourself with our house, my dear. It would strengthen your position greatly and, if I might mention it, show cousin Adric that you truly do appreciate all that he has done for you. As it happens, the Ardeth have several young ladies currently in the Women's Halls who might suit you. May I introduce two of them?"

"I don't think..." began Torisen.

However, she had already turned to call forth the ladies in question from an inner room, where they must have been waiting for her summons.

Their entrance was preceded by a short scuffle in the dark— "You first." "No, you."—before a short, plump girl emerged suddenly as if pushed from behind. Like her matriarch, she appeared to have thrown on her best dress in a hurry, its tight bodice straining against unmatched buttons. She was followed by a taller, older young woman whose gliding step would have been more impressive if she had remembered to put on her shoes.

Torisen struggled to his feet, wincing as he jostled his injured hand. More fervently than ever, he wished that he had thrown Adiraina out of Gothregor—no, into the river—when he had had the chance.

"After your unfortunate experience with dear Kallystine," the matriarch was saying, "it is only fair that you have a chance to inspect what you are being offered. Ladies, please. Unmask."

Both girls froze, eyes widening with horror. Torisen had always considered the masks a coy embellishment, probably because Kallystine had made a game out of wearing as little as possible in bed and out of it. However, these ladies were genuinely upset—more so, perhaps, than if Adiraina had asked them to strip naked.

"That isn't necessary," he said hastily.

"Oh, but I insist. This is Pentilla." She indicated the older girl. "She has already honored two contracts, one with male issue, the other without, as specified by the terms of each agreement. Her consorts both speak highly of her amicable nature and her willingness to please. Darlie, on the other hand, is a novice, but highly trained with exceptional bloodlines. We expect great things from her. Also, of course, if the terms of your contract with her allow, you can break her to your liking."

Torisen stared at the two Highborn, who stared back at him. The older was pretty in a polished, inhuman way, as if she had made her face as much a mask as that which she usually wore. However, there was something in the depths of her eyes that made him uneasy. What kind of a life had she led, to be described as "amicable" with all that hunger locked up inside? Her child, of course, being male, had stayed in his father's house, probably with a Kendar wet nurse, while she had returned here to be used over and over again, as her house saw fit.

The younger girl wore her innocence on her face, but also some hint of her ignorance, verging on stupidity. After all, what had she been taught but how to follow orders and, in theory, to please her future consorts?

Jame's face flickered across his mind, alive with quirky humor and sharp intelligence, always asking awkward questions, dropped into this nest of females blinded and gagged with convention. The wonder was not that the Women's Halls didn't want her back but that they had survived her at all.

The Ardeth Matriarch was waiting for him to say something.

Wine unlocked his tongue. It was also beginning to make him queasy. "You sound as if you're trying to sell me a horse," he heard himself say, "or rather, a brood mare."

Adiraina stiffened with outrage, but the older girl's perfect mask of a face twitched and the younger giggled outright. The matriarch clapped sharply to restore order. They ignored her, all their attention focused on him. The older ran the tip of a pink tongue over rouged lips. The younger stared at him like a greedy child at a box of candy.

"Oh dear," murmured Adiraina. "It wasn't supposed to work this way."

"What wasn't?" Then he remembered the odd taste of the refreshments offered to him with such persistence. "Lady," he said carefully, "as you well know, Highborn are very difficult to poison, but we do react to drugs in different ways. What did you put into the wine?"

She made a gesture as if to brush away both the topic and her embarrassment at having been caught in so crude a trick. "Only a sprinkle of love's-delight. I thought you might be too tired to make an...er...appropriate decision."

"So you gave me an aphrodisiac. On an empty stomach." He seriously considered up-heaving on her pretty carpet—it seemed the least he could do—but the girls were coyly advancing on him.

"Truly, my lord, you would like me better." The sudden, naked hunger in Pentilla's eyes appalled him. "A man like you, with mature tastes..."

Darlie elbowed her aside. "I know all the best tricks...in theory, anyway. Wouldn't you like to practice them with me?"

"Ladies, please!" Adiraina cried, but no one listened.

*I'm the Highlord of the Kencyrath, dammit*, Torisen thought as he backed away. *I will not be chased around the furniture.*

Ancestors be praised. No one had thought to lock the door. Torisen slid through and closed it behind him on the uproar within—"He wants me!" "No, me!" "You hag!" "You snot-nosed baby!"—and turned to face a solid wall of women.

Most were Ardeth, these after all being their quarters, but mixed in were a few Danior, Coman, and Caineron, drawn from their own compounds in various states of dress or undress. Those farthest away could be heard demanding to know what was going on. Those closest had their eyes fixed on Torisen in a way that strongly reminded him of a mouse suddenly thrust into a calamity of cats.

Someone tugged his sleeve. He looked down into the serious face of a seven-year-old, in a nightgown, clutching a rag doll.

"Please, Highlord, will you marry me?"

He scooped her up with his good arm. "No, sweetheart. You're too young for me."

Her face lit with joy. "Then I'll wait for you!"

He tossed the child, squealing with laughter, into the arms of the nearest woman who looked strong enough to catch her.

"Put her to bed. For Trinity's sake, doesn't anyone sleep anymore? The rest of you, MOVE."

And they did, clearing a passage for him through the halls, all the way to the forecourt gate. There he was stopped by a Jaran captain.

"Highlord, my lady Trishien would like a word with you."

Torisen pulled up short, gulping. "My regards to your matri-arch—*eeerrp*—but I think I'm about to be sick."

The randon regarded him curiously. Ancestors be praised again: the Ardeth's diabolical draft didn't apparently work on Kendar.

"Pass, my lord," she said solemnly, and opened the gate. As it closed behind him, he heard her defending it against a wave of females, but was too busy heaving his guts out into a bush to care.

Across the darkening, inner ward, the common room windows cast welcoming bars of light across the grass.

*Sanctuary*, thought Torisen, and made for it as quickly as his unsteady legs allowed.

# III

THE COMMON ROOM seethed as the garrison threw together what food they could to welcome home their lord. Grimly's pack was there too, having been stranded at Gothregor some days before by the weirdingstrom, all thirty-odd of them charging back and forth in their complete furs. Pups bowled over each other. Adults paused to offer Torisen shy greetings before rejoining the wild chase under and over tables, between Kendar who grinned or cursed according to their mood, but the pack didn't care. Tomorrow they would set out for their home in the Weald with an armed escort. Torisen was taking no chances: Some Kencyr, especially the Caineron, hunted the wolver for sport. Watching Grimly gambol with a trio of pups on the hearth, he already missed his old friend.

Supper arrived—stew, fresh bread and butter and, as a treat, a plate of last season's apples. Clearly, the winter larder was nearly exhausted. The cubes of meat floating in the broth were unfamiliar.

"It tastes better than it looks," said one of the garrison, noting Torisen involuntarily make a face at the musty smell. "The weirdingstrom swept some odd game into the Riverland. Desert crawlers, dire elk, rhi-sar—Steward Rowan claims she even caught sight of a white rathorn colt."

Queasy enough as he was, Torisen forbore to ask what creature had made its way into the bowl before him. He made a show of eating, meanwhile slipping lumps of the spongy gray meat to a pup under the table, finding an odd comfort in the small, rough tongue as it avidly licked his fingertips clean.

Suddenly a fight erupted at his feet. The pups who had been playing with Grimly tumbled out, snarling and snapping at the one whom Torisen had been feeding. This was no casual game; already there was blood on fur. Luckily the young wolver with the cold, blue eyes and the enormous paws was a match for any two of her opponents.

Grimly quickly broke up the fray.

"She's a problem, that one," he said. "An orphan of the deep Weald and willing to submit to no one. We found her wandering.

Of course, we couldn't let her starve.  If we drove her back to her own pack now, though, after being with us, they would probably kill her."

Torisen regarded the orphan pup, who had withdrawn to a corner to lick her wounds.  She was certainly much more feral than Grimly's people, who in their own way were remarkably civilized, with a strong sense both of ethics and of aesthetics.  The deep Weald wolvers, on the other hand, were reputed to be savage beasts if, indeed, they were even of the same species.

A Kendar offered him a cup of mulled cider.  Although his stomach revolted at the thought, he accepted it and started to thank the man, but couldn't recall his name.  That had never happened before, not with someone bound to him.  The other's smile faltered and his ruddy face paled in blotches as he felt the bond to his lord weaken.

Soon after, Torisen slipped out of the hall into the moonless night.

*What's wrong with me?* he thought, leaning against the outer wall. *Am I finally losing my mind, or is this just exhaustion on top of Adiraina's filthy brew?*

Whichever, best to withdraw before he hurt someone else.

He crossed the inner ward to the old keep, that relic of ancient days around which the rest of Gothregor had been built.  Like the larger fortress, it was rectangular with a drum tower on each corner.  The first floor was low ceilinged, dark, and musty, its walls lined with half-seen Knorth death banners.  Someone in the common room had mentioned having to rescue the lot of them from a grove of trees, of all places, where the southern wind, the Tishooo, had swept them on Jame's last night in residence here.

He saw more evidence of that night in the second floor Council Chamber.  Here, tall stained glass windows had glowed with the crests of the major houses and, taking up the entire eastern wall, there had been a map of Rathillien glorious in jeweled light.  Now, the ruins of the latter glittered in the starlight on the inner court below—the Tishooo's work again or Jame's, he wasn't sure which and didn't care to ask.

Up again into the southwest tower and here was the small, circular room that he had claimed as his bed-chamber, dusty and dank with a winter's neglect.

*Home*, he thought, with a sudden surge of depression as bitter as bile. No, it had never been that, only a place out of the way, hard for anyone else to reach, where he could hide.

*"You haven't quite found your feet yet as highlord, have you, my dear?"*

Damn and blast Adiraina. Blind as she was, she saw far too much. Was that what he really wanted—a home? A place to belong, to love and be loved?

Nonsense. He couldn't afford such luxuries when so many lives depended on him. These quarters only missed his servant Burr's touch. He could also have used help undressing around the bandages but wasn't going to ask it of some Kendar whose name he suddenly couldn't remember. Things would be better in the morning.

Fully clothed, Torisen lay down before the ash-choked hearth and there drifted into an uneasy dream. He and Jame were children again in the Haunted Lands, chasing each other turn and turn about over the gray, swooping hills under a leaden moon. Up and down, down and up…

She pounced him and drove her elbow into his face. He yelped in pain. They rolled down the slope, scrabbling and snapping at each other in the manner of dreams like wolver pups. At the bottom, she broke free and dashed up to the next crest. He joined her there, wiping a bloody nose on his sleeve.

"Why did you do that?"

"I wanted to see how you would block the blow. You didn't. I was trying to learn something."

"Father says it's dangerous to teach you anything. Will the things you learn always hurt people?"

She considered this, idly plucking blades of grass and letting them wriggle through her ragged black hair where they tried to take root. "Maybe. As long as I learn, does it matter?"

He snuffled loudly and wiped his nose again. "It does to me. I'm always the one who gets hurt."

"Crybaby."

"Little girl."

"Daddy's boy."

"Filthy Shanir."

She sprang to her feet and looked down at him. Her eyes were silver, frosted with blue, fey, wild, and alight with mocking challenge older than her years. "I am what I am, but what are you? You don't know, and you're afraid to find out. Come, then, let's play hide-and-seek. You be Father. I'll be Mother. Catch me if you can!"

And she was off, plunging down the hillside toward the keep in a swirl of flying hair, rags, and thin, pale limbs, going, gone.

*This is wrong*, he thought. *It didn't happen this way...did it?*

If he followed, he knew where he would find her, just where he had on that terrible day over two decades ago: in their parents' bedroom, standing before a mirror whose misty depths reflected not the keep's shabby chamber but a vast, dark hall; and the face staring back at her would not be her own but that of the mother they had lost, for whom their father still desperately searched. He would try (again) to reach through the glass for her and (again) Jame would stop him. She didn't understand. Unless Mother came back, Father would turn on her, their mother's Shanir mirror-image. But she would fight him as she always did, as if his life rather than hers depended on it. And perhaps, again, she would knock him backwards into their parents' bed, where they had been conceived and born, and it would collapse on him.

That was the last he remembered. When he woke, she would be gone, from the keep, from his life, and not even in dreams would he be able to find her.

Torisen blinked. That was then. This was now. Not gray hills but heaped ash on a dead hearth lay before him, and his sister had returned.

An open west window brought him cheerful sounds from the common room, then a sudden crash followed by the cook's exasperated shout: "All right, that's it! Out, out, out!"

The parcel of wolver pups spilled yipping onto the grass of the inner ward. Torisen could hear their joyful tussle, punctuated by yelps and mock growls. Then they began to keen in unison. Their shrill voices rose and fell, first together, then in counterpoint in imitation of their elders who could shape mist with their song and bring back the ghosts of winter.

Torisen smiled. They were serenading him.

He groped in the darkness, found an old boot, and tossed it overhand out the window. The chorus broke into yipping laughter. Claws scrabbled up the stone steps of the old keep. Moments later, a half dozen pups burst into the tower room and pounced on the

Highlord as if they meant to tear him apart. He fended them off with his good hand, laughing, until they collapsed panting around him and began to snore. Lying under a blanket of small, furry bodies, he drifted off into blessedly dreamless sleep.

# IV

IN THE MORNING, the wolver pack left with its escort, the pups yipping goodbye and trotting off, eager to be home.

Grimly lingered. "Take care of yourself," he said. "This is a cold place. It doesn't love you. Your friends do, when you let them."

"And who are they?"

"You know. Harn, Burr, Rowan, maybe even your sister."

"Father always said, 'Destruction begins with love.'"

The Wolver curled a lip back over sharp teeth. "When you talk like that, I smell the dead on you. Be yourself, Tori, not someone else. Especially not him. And give my love to your sister." He grinned, suddenly all wolf. "Tell her I enjoyed our time together under the bed."

Then he dropped to all fours and sprinted after his pack.

Only when all had left did Torisen realize that the ruddy-faced Kendar hadn't gone with them as part of their escort as ordered, and that he still couldn't remember the man's name.

# Chapter IV: Testing

## Summer 1-2

## I

WHEN JAME WOKE early the next morning, on the floor under a pile of musty blankets, she didn't at first know where she was. At Tentir, of course, but beyond that...

She felt Jorin's warmth at her side and reached out to stroke his rich fur. He stretched full length, sighing, and snuggled his head into the crook of her arm. Eyes closed, she let her *dwar*-bemused memory drift over the previous evening.

The Commandant had taken Torisen's announcement that she was staying with raised eyebrows, but had only said, dryly, "I see. Very well."

Timmon, on the other hand, had gaped at her until she had snapped at him, "What are you staring at?"

"I'm not sure, but I think I like it." Then he had given her such a dazzling smile that she in turn had blinked. Dammit, what *was* it about that boy?

Tori had waited until Ardeth was resting quietly, one drug having counteracted the other, and then had called for his horse. Shadow Rock, the Danior keep, was a good twenty miles to the south. Neither he nor Storm would have much rest that night, but he was clearly anxious to be on his way before Ardeth woke.

"For Trinity's sake," he had muttered to her on his way out, "don't make fools of us both."

"No more than I can help," she had said, which was honest if hardly reassuring.

Jame considered her situation.

She hadn't known what to expect when she had rejoined her people the previous fall except to be reunited with her twin brother Tori. That he was now at least ten years her senior thanks to the slower passage of time in Perimal Darkling had come as an unpleasant surprise to them both, and would cause considerable complications if anyone found out.

Ever since her sudden appearance at the Cataracts, Tori had been under intense pressure to contract her to either the Caineron or the Ardeth, the two most powerful houses in contention for mastery of the Kencyrath after the Knorth. What she had told Graykin was true: thanks to Jamethiel Dream-weaver's role in the Fall, most lords considered the Highborn women of their houses only good for breeding and political alliances. For Jame, that was apt to mean either one of Caldane's vicious sons or the Ardeth Dari, he with the breath of a rotten eel (according to his father) whom no woman contradicted twice.

She hadn't spent most of her life trying to rejoin her people for that.

Moreover, if either she or Tori had a son by someone from another house, that boy would become the first highlord in Kencyr history not of pure Knorth blood. The balance of power would shift irreparably, perhaps disastrously.

The Kencyrath was already perilously close to losing its identity. Some, like Lord Caineron, professed not even to believe the old stories. Singers' lies, he called them, and it was true that song and history, fiction and fact, had become intertwined over time. Only Kencyr on the Barrier with Perimal Darkling—the Min-drear of High Keep, for example, or Jame and Tori's own people in exile in the Haunted Lands—had no doubt whatsoever that their ancient enemy only bided its time.

Presumably, the Merikit hillmen also understood the danger since they lived closer to the Barrier than any Riverland Kencyr except the Min-drear.

Jame's thoughts drifted back to Summer Eve in the ruins of Kithorn—had it only been the night before last?—when she had found herself thrown into a Merikit rite to placate the vast River Snake whose waking had brought on the earthquakes and the weirdingstrom. Somehow, she had emerged as the Earth Wife's Favorite. So far so good, and no stranger than a dozen other things that had happened in her short but not uneventful life. She still carried Mother Ragga's "favor," the little clay face called the *imu*, in her pocket. However, the Favorite also played the Earth Wife's lover, to ensure the coming year's fertility. To save face, the Merikit chieftain had declared Jame his son and heir until the next ritual. Then, please God, she could pass on the role to someone better equipped to fulfill the Favorite's duties.

But all of this had given the Jaran Kirien an idea.

"'Lordan' is an ancient title applied to either the male or female heir of a lord," she had told Lords Ardeth and Caineron, breaking into their interminable wrangle over which house should have the newly discovered Knorth, Jameth. "Nothing in the law forbids a female heir."

Well, she should know. Hers was a house of scholars and she herself was its lordan, no one else having wanted to leave his studies to take on the job. Torisen knew that she was female. The other lords assumed otherwise, not that Kirien had ever deliberately set out to fool them. There would be hell to pay when she came of age and claimed power.

In the meantime, "By ancient custom, the heir always has the status of a man, and 'he' doesn't form any contracts before coming of age at twenty-seven."

Jame could see her brother's mind working; that would get them both out of the fire for several years at least.

"There is this too," the haunt singer Ashe had added in her harsh, halting voice. "Traditionally…the Knorth Lordan trains…at Tentir to become…a randon."

So here she was, against all odds, against everyone's will but her brother's, and he was already beginning to have doubts.

*"For Trinity's sake, don't make fools of us both…"*

Easier said than done.

At last, Jame opened her eyes.

Over her loomed the dawn-tipped peaks of the western Snowthorns, seen through a ragged hole in the roof where the weirdingstrom had carried off both slates and rafters. Birds flitted in and out. The air was crisp enough to turn her breath into puffs of mist. She was in the attic of the Knorth barracks.

First they had tried to put her back in the Knorth guest quarters in Old Tentir, only to find them charred beyond use. Luckily, the fire hadn't spread. Unluckily, it had also consumed all evidence of the wyrm. Then there had been the third floor apartment in the Knorth barracks, where she had had such bad dreams. Finally, she had come up here, to the top of the world, it had seemed, with only the mountains and star-frosted sky wheeling through the night above her.

In a corner, Graykin stirred fitfully in a nest of moth-eaten blankets. Even his snores resounded with discontent.

Jame, however, felt a surge of excitement. She might be adept at falling on her face, but then just as often she landed on her feet. Either way, nothing had ever stopped her from jumping. She stretched luxuriously, and Jorin stretched with her down the length of her body. The old, defiant chant rose in her mind:

*If I want, I will learn.*
*If I want, I will fight.*
*If I want, I will live.*
*And I want.*
*And I will.*

This was going to be fun.

Outside, a horn blared, and birds fled out the hole in the roof. Jame scrambled to her feet, tossing the blankets over a protesting ounce. Across the dusty floor, the windows of a dormer faced eastward towards Old Tentir. As she leaned out to look, in the training square below a sargent again raised his ram's horn and sounded its raucous note.

"All right, you slug-a-beds," he roared. "It's morning. Up, *up*, UP!"

In the second story dormitories below, bare feet hit the floor in a garble of *dwar*-slurred voices. The whole college must have been out cold last night, small wonder after the previous day's events.

Turning, Jame saw that Graykin was awake. He gave her one look, then hastily averted his eyes and began to search for his clothes. He at least had slept in his underwear—a Southron custom, perhaps. She didn't know if all naked bodies upset him or only hers, but that was his problem. Ancestors knew, the rigors of the past two weeks had left hardly enough flesh on her bones to offend anyone.

Suddenly, Jame was ravenous. Nobody had eaten the night before. When had been her own last meal? She couldn't remember.

*Think of something else.*

Rubbing her sore buttocks, she twisted around as far as she could to look. Yes, those shadows were bruises. Damn all horses anyway.

But Graykin had the right idea: she needed clothes.

Her pants, boots, cap, and gloves were all right, but the jacket would never do. Why could she never arrive anywhere appropriately dressed? The last time it had been a voluminous dress "borrowed" from a Hurlen prostitute. This time, it was a Tastigon flash-blade's *d'hen*. Sweet Trinity, what if someone last night had recognized it for what it was?

That apartment below—hadn't it been strewn with neglected garments?

A central, square stairwell reached from the attic to the second floor landing. Jame ran down the steps, the chill mountain air raising goose bumps on her bare skin. The third floor was divided between a long common room overlooking the square and the lordan's private suite facing outward and west toward the mountains. Only two rooms of the latter were accessible—a dusty reception chamber and the inner room beyond. Presumably the suite continued to the north and south, but walls of chests, layers thick, blocked it off in both directions.

Jame paused in the second room beside the cold fireplace on its raised hearth, where she had tried to sleep the night before. In her dream, the floor had been covered with rich, soiled clothing, left where a careless hand had dropped them. She remembered fur and silk, velvet and golden thread, all sunk in a miasma of stale sweat, but that hadn't concerned her then. She had been sitting beside a roaring fire, drinking and laughing so hard that wine spurted out her nose like blood onto her white shirt and richly embroidered coat. That had seemed hysterically funny at the time. Sitting opposite her, her companion had also laughed but more softly. She knew he was less drunk than she and in a fuzzy way resented his self control. Damn, superior Randir. She would impress him yet.

"No, truly," she heard herself cry in a hoarse, slurred voice not her own. "Such games we used to play, my brother and I! The things I made him do!"

"Did he enjoy them?"

"Now, if he had, where would have been the fun? Once the poor little fool even tried to tell Father, who called him a liar to his face for his pains."

She was leaning forward now, supporting herself with a thick hand studded with gold rings and coarse, black hair. Her voice dropped conspiratorially. "You don't believe me? Listen. This very minute, he sleeps below in his virtuous cot. Dear little Gangrene, all grown up and come to play soldier. Shall we have him up, eh? See if he remembers our old midnight game?"

If there had been more to the dream, Jame didn't remember it. She spat into the fireplace to clear the foul taste of that voice from her mouth. What in Perimal's name had it all been about anyway? Who was "dear little Gangrene"? Surely Father had never called her brother Torisen a liar, the worst of all possible insults. As for midnight games...

Jame shrugged away the thought. It had only been a dream.

Or perhaps not.

Sprawling on the hearth like the flayed skin of a nightmare was the embroidered coat.

She picked it up. It was surprisingly heavy, its entire surface covered with thread in many colors, couched with stitches of tarnished gold. Here and there were stains as if of wine, or of blood.

It also stank.

She remembered now how she had wrapped it about her for warmth the previous night and tried to sleep in its noisome folds. Ugh. No wonder she had had bad dreams.

Jame dropped the coat and turned to the nearest wall of chests. When she dislodged and opened one, the smell was as she remembered it, with an added stale air of must and mold. Several layers down, she found a serviceable shirt and a belted jacket cut cadet style.

"Oh, very stylish," said Graykin from the doorway. "What's that stench?"

"History. Don't ask me whose."

She put on the clothes. Both shirt and coat were much too large for her, but they would do.

Below, the rumpus had subsided.

Good, thought Jame, turning up her sleeves and clinching the belt. She would slip down and keep out of sight until she knew what was expected of her.

"Try to stay out of trouble," she told Graykin as she passed him with Jorin at her heels. "Better yet, hide."

From either side of the second floor landing, stairs led down to the front and to the back halves of the ground floor, which itself was divided by the internal corridor that run all around the three sides of the square, cutting through every house barracks.

Jame bent down to peer below. To the front, nothing. That, as she vaguely remembered from the previous night, was a public area.

From the back, however, came a stifled cough and a stealthy shifting of feet. Ten long tables had been set out and ten cadets lined each of them, five to a side, standing at attention. Bowls of porridge cooled before them. At the head table, one empty seat waited. Even as she realized that it was meant for her and that no one could eat until she sat in it, the horn sounded again and everyone bolted toward the square. Descending, Jame saw the Kendar pile through doors that opened onto the common corridor, cross that, stream through their own front hall, and so out into the morning light. She snatched up a hunk of bread, stuffed it into her mouth, and followed, with a wistful backward glance at the rest of the uneaten breakfast.

Cadet candidates were forming up in tens. Jame took a position behind Brier's squad, but hands reached back to draw her forward. She found herself pushed out in front, level with the other ten-commanders, all too conscious of her reeking, oversized tunic. Timmon, also front and center before his own house, sketched her a salute in greeting. Brier stood behind her and Vant parallel, before another squad.

She chewed hastily and swallowed. "What's going on?" she hissed at Rue, a pace behind her to her right, inadvertently spraying the cadet with crumbs.

"Iron-thorn was demoted to Five. You're Ten now, lady."

"The hell I am!" But she hardly needed Vant's sidelong smirk to know that Rue spoke the truth.

"Hut!"

Everyone stiffened. Several cadets, let go by supporting hands, fell over, still lost in *dwar* sleep.

Flanked by his randon instructors, Commandant Sheth Sharptongue strolled into the yard from Old Tentir. He moved like an Arrin-ken, thought Jame, powerful, lithe, and subtly dangerous. Morning light caught the hawk lines of his face and cast his deep-set eyes into hooded shadow. He wore the white scarf of command as he did his authority, easily, as by birthright. Here were the makings of a lethal enemy. And he was a Caineron. She felt his eyes sweep over her and sensed Jorin cower at her side.

"Cadet candidates, I bid you welcome to Tentir."

His voice, light but resonant, carried easily to every corner of the square. No sound crossed it but the swish of his long coat and a breath of wind chasing last season's leaves across the tin roof of the arcade. Somewhere in a back row, a fallen cadet began to snore, grunted as a mate kicked him, and again fell silent.

"You come to us in unusual times. Last fall, almost the entire student body marched south with the Host to the Cataracts. Many died there. We honor their memory and will not forget their names. For the most part, those who survived were promoted on the battle-field and now serve with the Southern Host at Kothifir. As a result, we have very few second year cadets and no third years except for those who have returned to assist as master tens in charge of their respective house barracks.

"In addition, you may have noticed that we have several Highborn candidates, including Lord Ardeth's grandson Timmon. The Caineron Lordan is also expected momentarily."

*Is he, by God*, thought Jame. She wondered whom the prolific but fickle Caldane had picked for an heir this week, and how Sheth meant to introduce her, if at all.

At that moment, the hall door swung open and a burly, travel-stained randon stumped into the square. He stopped, blinked, and swore at the unexpected sight of the drawn up troops, who stared back at him.

"Ah," said the Commandant, smiling slightly. "My esteemed predecessor at the college and the Knorth war-leader, Harn Grip-hard, and Steward Rowan," he added as a scar-faced woman appeared in the doorway, "and Sar Burr"—this last, to a third Kendar, who had stopped at pace behind the other two. "Goodness, nearly the Highlord's entire personal staff. Have you misplaced him again?" Someone in the Caineron ranks snickered. "How may we be of service, rans and sar?"

"We're looking for Blackie," the big randon said gruffly to the yard at large. His blood-shot eyes fell on Jame and widened. "Here, boy, what in Perimal's name are you playing at?"

Jame felt a powerful urge to withdraw into her oversized tunic like a turtle into its shell.

"If I may continue," the Commandant said smoothly, "I was just about to announce the presence among us, for the first time in forty-six years, of the Knorth Lordan...ah, Jameth, is it not?"

"Lordan?" Harn blurted out. "Has Blackie gone mad?"

More snickers, louder this time.

"As to that," said the Commandant with a smile, "you would know better than I. Torisen Black Lord rode on last night. You probably passed him in the dark. A moment, please," he said, as the three turned to go. "If you will stay for a bit, Rans Harn and Rowan, you can do the college a great service. Sar Burr, no doubt you will wish to retrieve...er...rejoin your wandering lord as quickly as possible."

He turned back to the cadets. "Our three lordans, of course, will serve as the master tens of their respective houses. You will also no doubt have noticed—especially those who had to sleep last night two or three to a bed—that there are nearly twice as many candidates here as usual. One thousand three hundred and ninety, to be exact. Death has greatly thinned our ranks. However, the college is only equipped to train some eight hundred cadets at a time. I speak, of course, of those who are still here at this time next summer. Between now and then, there will be three culls rather than the usual two. Over the next three days you will undergo a series of tests to determine who stays and who goes."

*Tests.*

Jame gulped. No one had said anything about that. She was certain that her brother hadn't known. No wonder Sheth had barely blinked when Tori had presented her as his heir. Neither the Commandant nor anyone else expected her to be here long enough to matter except as proof of the Highlord's lunacy.

"We have summoned every available randon officer, sargent, and senior cadet to oversee this...ah...winnowing process. Ran Harn, if you would be so kind as to stay and assist? Thank you. I expected no less.

Good luck," said Sheth blandly, "to you all," and swept back into the shadows of Old Tentir.

A sargent stepped forward. "Tens," she cried. "Count off!"

# II

BY THE END of the first day, the randon were optimistic. There were many good candidates, judging by the first three tests, easily enough to fill the college's depleted ranks. Also, there were some promising young Shanir whose particular talents they would assess later.

As for the rest, those who couldn't wake in a timely fashion from *dwar* sleep had already been dismissed. Some of the Caineron were clearly hopeless. Caldane had over-filled his quota with every young Kendar he could lay his hands on, half of them still hung-over from their lord's excesses of the week before. Even the Caineron randon glumly agreed, more freely than they might have if the Commandant didn't habitually dine alone in his quarters. The rest, officers, sargents, and senior cadets, had gathered in the offic-ers' mess in Old Tentir to share dinner and compare notes.

There was no sign yet of the Caineron Lordan. It didn't matter. By unspoken agreement, his place was secure at the college, when-ever he deigned to arrive. After all, Sheth could hardly turn away his master's son.

"That Ardeth Timmon is shaping up surprisingly well," remarked a Danior randon, reaching for the salt. "Even if he does slide out of some things."

"Like the punishment run."

"Yes. But he clearly had good teachers at home and enjoys physical challenges. Not quite the spoiled brat we were expecting, eh? A little irresponsible and immature, though."

"I just hope he doesn't have his father's taste for the Kendar," a Coman sargent muttered to her Jaran counterpart. "That damned Pereden could charm his way into any bed, for the sheer deviltry of it."

"But this is only a boy."

"Not so young as all that, and the Ardeth start early." She raised her voice. "Did your lord get off safely, Aron?"

"Before dawn, ran," replied the Ardeth sargent. He looked exhausted. It had been a rough night, even without part of the dining hall collapsing into the cellar. "If his guard can keep him quiet with drafts of black nightshade, they hope to get him past Gothregor before he decides to tackle the Highlord again."

"Huh," said a young Coman randon. "More likely, he'll wait to see what happens here. There'll be no hiding it now. You didn't exactly help, Harn. D'you have to call your lord crazy in front of the whole college?"

Harn Grip-hard was morosely gnawing a mutton bone, his broad, stubbly face glistening with its fat. Rowan sat beside him, carefully expressionless as usual; fifteen years after the Karnides had burned the name-rune of their god into her forehead, the scar still hurt.

A Caineron laughed. "Yes. What will your precious Blackie say when he hears about that, eh?"

"Nothing," grunted the former commandant of Tentir. "The boy knows I have a big mouth, and I've known him since he was fifteen, so new to the Southern Wastes that he looked like a flayed tomato."

"What was he like then, ran?" asked a senior cadet. "Besides sun-burnt, I mean."

"Quiet. Wary. Determined. Not like his father Ganth Gray Lord at all, except in certain moods."

"It took Urakarn to unsheathe the steel in him," said Rowan. "I was there. I saw."

Harn thought for a moment, absentmindedly wiping greasy fingers on his jacket. "It's hard to explain. He isn't like most Highborn. Never has been."

"Obviously not," said a Randir, with a sidelong glance at her table-mates. Even in the close-knit world of the randon, the Randir held themselves subtly apart. There were also more female randon in that house than in any other. "To make that freak his heir and then to bring her here…"

The other randon stirred uneasily. They knew there was bad blood between the Randir and the Knorth, although not all knew why.

A senior cadet broke in, grinning broadly: "D'you see her this morning trying to wield a long sword? Trinity, I thought she was going to chop off her own toes, or maybe mine. That cadet Vant made a proper fool of her."

"Still," said an Ardeth thoughtfully, "she didn't do so badly with the short sword although I'll wager she'd never had one in her hands before. I've been watching her technique. That girl knows knife-craft, although I've never seen that particular style before. D'you see how she tried to block with her sleeve? The Commandant was watching too. 'I thought so,' he said."

"Thought what?"

"He didn't say. Still, what in Perimal's name are they teaching in the Women's Halls these days?"

"Quiet, wary, determined," repeated a Brandan thoughtfully. "What if there should be steel there too, underneath? We may be surprised yet."

This was met with general laughter and some flung hunks of bread, which the Brandan flicked away with careless, good-natured grace. "Just the same," he said, "talk to Hawthorn when she gets back from escorting M'lady Brenwyr home. I hear she had some odd experiences with the Knorth during the weirdingstrom."

"Yes, but did you see the plan she—the Knorth, that is—submitted for storming the citadel?" Like so many in his house, the Edirr cadet clearly found anything ridiculous irresistible. "I mean, a herd of goats disguised as priests?"

While he elaborated, gleefully, the older randon grumbled among themselves. It was a new idea that cadets should learn how to read and write rather than to depend, as for millennia past, solely on a well-trained memory. Things were changing. Not everyone approved.

"...ending in a rain of frogs!" crowed the Edirr cadet, "and, you know, it just might work!"

The others exchanged looks and shook their heads.

# III

BY THE END of the second day, the randon were less easy. The competition was getting ugly, and candidates were beginning to get hurt. Worse, instructors had come across possible evidence of sabotage. A notched bow had snapped at the full draw, nearly taking out a cadet's eye. Swords mysteriously lost their baited points or acquired newly sharpened edges. Horses were found to have burrs under their saddles or cinches hooked by twists of tail hair to their privates.

Practical jokes, said the Randir, shrugging.

Others feared that it was only a matter of time before someone was seriously injured or killed. In the latter case, no blood price could be demanded by the cadet's house, but such things tended to fester, sometimes for generations. Again, some glanced from Randir to Knorth.

They also spoke, with increasing unease, about the Knorth Jameth.

Most had expected that by now she would have burst into tears and retreated to her proper place, namely the Women's Halls at Gothregor. Captain Hawthorn, newly returned from escorting her own matriarch home, rather thought that the Women's World would as soon welcome back a handful of burning coals.

The Highborn girls there had barely settled down and stopped (oh, horrors) asking questions when who should arrive but Lord Caineron's young daughter Lyra Lack-wit, ostensibly to gain some polish in women's ways, actually to get her out of sister Kallystine's sight before the latter killed her. Various ladies had been heard to prophesy the end of the world, if only so that they might at last get some rest.

"However, they're apt to give the Highlord precious little of that," Hawthorn said, amused, pausing to drink from her mug of cider. "Now that his sister has slipped through their hands, I've heard that the Council of Matriarchs means to make a dead set at him for one of their own houses."

"But the Knorth Jameth. What d'you think of her?"

The Brandan captain considered for a moment. "Thoroughly unorthodox," she said, "but weirdly effective. Not unlike her brother."

The Caineron jeered at this. "What do *you* know? Your matriarch wears riding boots and a divided skirt. We've even heard that she sleeps with a death banner."

Hawthorn merely smiled. "She suits us. Perhaps we Brandan aren't all that orthodox either, anymore."

"What does Sheth intend?" one senior randon asked another quietly undercover of the above exchange. "Can he really mean to let this girl stay?"

"He accepted her into Tentir," said the other. "His honor is bound."

"Even against the will of his lord that she should fail?"

"Even so, unless he bows to that will."

"You speak of Honor's Paradox. Where does honor lie, in obedience to one's lord or in oneself?"

"Just so. The Commandant will have to decide. So will we all. But what d'you think of these sightings of the White Lady? Has the Shame of Tentir come back to haunt us?"

The other stirred uneasily. "With a Knorth Lordan here for the first time in forty-odd years…ah, I don't know. Certainly, the Lady has unfinished business with that house, if even half the stories are true."

"As to that, only the Randon Council knows. Maybe it *is* just a wandering rathorn, swept north by the weirdingstrom. Cam did swear that he saw its horns. Still, a lone rathorn. A rogue. A death's-head. That's bad enough."

The Edirr cadet could no longer contain himself.

"Did you hear about her riding test?" he burst in, claiming the room's reluctant attention. "I'm waiting at the top of the training field when she and a Jaran ten come up. When she sees what's next, she stops dead (both squads piling up behind her, mind you), and says, 'Oh no. Horses.'

"So I get everyone including her mounted and in line. As you know, the test is to ride a circuit of the fortress keeping in formation, starting at a walk, ending in a full charge, over a variety of terrain. Well, from the first the horses are all in a fret, lunging, bucking, and then the Knorth's starts backing up. She's kicking it for all she's worth but it lays its ears flat and keeps going, right into one of those quake fissures, over and down, backward. It hits the bottom and bolts and so, if you please, do both ten commands.

"The next thing I know, we're thundering down the field with the Knorth keeping pace at the bottom of a ditch.

"Then up she comes, both stirrups ripped off, hanging on for dear life, and barges into the front line. Two horses go down, three more bolt off at a tangent straight through a quarter-staff practice—sorry about that, Aron; I hope none of your cadets were trampled.

"Passing the front door, we lose half a dozen more horses when they take bit in teeth and plunge inside, hell-bent for the safety of their stables.

"Then up the southern flank of the college over hill and dale, through wood and water, between archers and their targets, apparently, because suddenly arrows are whizzing past our ears. More horses shy. More riders fall.

"By now, there are only five of us including the Knorth and that big Southron Iron-thorn who's galloping beside her and holding her in the saddle by the scruff of her neck.

"Well, finally we stop and then, if you please, the Knorth falls off."

"'Oh,' she says, looking up at me. 'Wasn't I supposed to do that? Everyone else did.'"

The Edirr burst into helpless laughter. As he beat his head on the table-top, the two senior randon exchanged glances.

"That's it," said one. "We're doomed."

# Chapter V:  A Length of Rope

## Summer 4

## I

IN HER DREAMS, Jame heard a voice:

*Kinzi-kin*, it was crying. Such a lost, plaintive sound, she thought, but fearful too, and hushed, as if afraid of being heard.

Kinzi Keen-eyed was her great-grandmother, slain some thirty-odd years ago in the massacre that had claimed all but one of the Knorth ladies at Gothregor. Who would call her by that long dead name?

She rose from her nest of blankets, went to the hole in the slanting roof, and looked down. It was early morning, barely light, with shreds of mist floating through the trees. A ghostly figure stood below, looking up. Again came that desolate cry:

*Kinzi-kin!*

Jame leaned out. "Here!" she called down.

The stranger appeared to be a woman clothed in filmy white, but the face raised to Jame was almost triangular, broad across the forehead, tapering down to a small mouth and chin. Ears pricked through the long, tangled locks that veiled half her face. Her single, visible eye was large and dark.

*Aahhh*…she breathed, in a long shuddering sigh. *Nemesis*. Then, in a pale flicker, she was gone.

The morning horn sounded and below feet hit the floor. Jame stood by the window, wondering if it had been a dream. Below, however, were hoof-marks in the rain-softened earth.

So began the third day of tests.

Hastily dressing, Jame wondered if she had been insane to believe she could ever qualify as a cadet. The Kendar against whom she was competing had prepared all their lives for this. Her own training had been at once more intense than theirs and more limited, including precious few weapons. She had only scraped through sword practice because at first her opponents couldn't bring themselves to look her in the face. Vant had broken that with a set glare, and then had thoroughly trounced her into the bargain.

She had thought she was doing well with the knife, only to be penalized for her unfamiliar style.

True, she had enjoyed plotting the overthrow of a citadel, only to realize when she turned in her closely written five pages that most cadets were still laboriously scrawling their first paragraph. That was the first time she had ever seen Brier Iron-thorn sweat.

She also thought she might eventually get the hang of the quarter-staff and bow, but not in time to help now.

As for riding, the less said, the better. Several of the horses had been found to have burrs lodged under their tails, which accounted for a great deal. Her own mount had been clean except for strange scratches along his crest that looked almost like claw marks. Jame was hardly going to explain how *those* had come about.

There were nine tests in all, three or four a day, administered at random as far as Jame could tell. For each, her ten-command was paired with a ten of a different house, and the twenty of them were sent wherever the appropriate officer waited. With so many tests all conducted more or less at the same time, Tentir and its environs swarmed with sweating cadets and shouting randon. Each time, a candidate was ranked from first place to twentieth, and the scores added as he or she went. A perfect (but unlikely) over-all score would be nine; the worst, one hundred and eighty. No one knew for certain, but the cut-off for admission to the college was believed to be around one hundred and thirty. The Randon Council, comprised of past and present commandants of Tentir, would set the final mark when all scores were in.

After seven tests, Brier was leading Vant by thirteen to his twenty-one.

Jame, on the other hand, had already nearly accumulated the fatal number. To qualify as a cadet, she would have to do very well indeed on the last two tests.

One of them was bound to be unarmed combat, the Senethar.

Jame only knew that the other took place in the great hall of Old Tentir, and that cadets often emerged from it pale and shaking. A few didn't return at all. Those who had passed refused to say exactly what had happened, on orders of the randon. Each day left a smaller, increasingly apprehensive number of the uninitiated. Finally, among the Knorth only Jame's ten had yet to face the nameless ordeal.

"I've heard some candidates choose the white knife rather than do whatever-it-is," said one of her cadets at the breakfast table.

That was Quill, thought Jame, the one whose mother had wanted him to become a scrollsman, hence the name. It had suddenly struck her that despite all they had been through together—raiding Restormir, careening down the Silver in a stolen barge in the middle of an earthquake, riding Mount Alban all the way to the Southern Wastes and back—the only two of the ten whom she knew by name were Briar and Rue. But now they were her ten, her responsibility.

"If they killed themselves, where are the pyres?"

That was Erim, clumsy, beetle-browed, and slow of speech, who looked stupid but, she suspected, wasn't.

"Idiot, they would send the bodies home for the burning."

Mint. Pretty, with green eyes and a touch of Highborn refinement in her bones. A flirt who liked to set male and sometimes female Kendar against each other, just for fun.

"Or salt them for the winter larder," said Rue. "God's claws, I'm only joking! Five, what do you think?"

Brier Iron-thorn, as usual, had drawn her bench slightly back from the table and was taking no part in the nervous chatter. "I think the missing cadets failed the test and went home, all right, too embarrassed to stay."

"Or in disgrace." Vant flung this from the neighboring table. His ten had undergone the mysterious ordeal early and all had emerged unscathed, if shaken. "What will you tell your lord, shortie, when you come crawling back to him?"

Rue flushed. "I'd rather die, or be eaten."

"Maybe they'll give you a choice. Fried, broiled, jerked…you're about the right size for a roast suckling pig, though."

"Ten," said Jame, "shut up."

Vant sketched her a salute. "As you wish, lady."

His cadets tittered nervously, unsure if they should follow his lead. He believed he would be rid of her soon, Jame thought. He might be right.

In the square, the horn blared its summons and all rushed outside to take formation.

Although they had been half-expecting it, the order that the Knorth and a Danior ten should report to Old Tentir still came as an unpleasant shock.

Entering the dim great hall, Jame looked around. It didn't appear to be any more of a torture chamber than usual—less, in fact, now that its floor was clean and its roof mended. House banners still hung portentously against the lower walls and randon collars still winked farther up in the gloom. The only difference took a moment to spot: a rope, stretched from one side of the hall to the other from the third story railings.

Behind her, a cadet gagged. Jame turned to find them all staring up at that innocent length of hemp as if they expected momentarily to be hanged with it.

Then she understood. Many Kendar suffered intense vertigo and nausea when faced with heights—a potentially fatal drawback for a professional soldier. It made sense that any cadet who couldn't overcome this weakness had no place at the college. Still, what a test to set them so early in their careers!

A cold voice spoke from the upper gallery: "Come up."

Above, a gaunt Randir officer waited for them. "So you would be randon," she said, with a thin smile at their carefully blank faces. "And what is that, eh? Would you master others? Can you master yourselves? Here, we find out."

She began to pace slowly up and down their rigid line, from the Danior ten at one end to Jame at the other and back. Her long coat swished as she moved, like the dry hiss of scales on stone. Her arms folded tight across her chest seemed to hold in and concentrate her malice. In a soft, almost caressing tone she spoke of a randon's duties, harmless stuff often heard before, but beneath the surface ran another voice like the murmur of black water under ice. Jame heard it most clearly when the woman paused before her and fixed her with dark, unblinking eyes.

*"Don't think you'll get away with it,"* came that subtle whisper inside her mind, echoing her fears and doubts.

The woman's eyes seemed to be almost all black pupil now, holes plunging into an abyss, and someone else watched through them.

*"Fail one more test, and you are gone. Pass, and how long will it be before we drive you out? Fool. Abomination. Besides, you have hurt my cousin and crossed my lady, who is far from done with you. Run. Hide. But in the end, in the dark, she will find you."*

Then she smiled. Her teeth were very white and the incisors chiseled to needle points. Then she passed on, leaving Jame as breathless as if those tightly clasped arms had crushed the air out of her.

What *was* she doing here? (*Fool.*) What could she expect to accomplish, except her brother's ruin and her own? (*Abomination.*) What place was there anywhere for such a creature as herself, bred to darkling service, in futile rebellion against her own nature?

*Wait a minute*, she thought. *I hurt her cousin? Who in Perimal's name was that...and of whom do those sharpened teeth remind me?*

Then she caught a fragment of what the randon was saying under her breath to Rue: "*Border brat. Runt. What made you think that you could fit in here, among your superiors? Give up. Go home. Die. No one cares which.*"

This randon's lady was Rawneth, the Randir Matriarch, the Witch of Wilden, who perhaps had been behind the slaughter of the Knorth women thirty-four years ago; and yes, Jame meant to cross her at every possible turn until she not only knew the truth but could prove it.

Now she recognized the power in the randon's voice. It was similar to that of Brenwyr, called the Iron Matriarch for her fierce self-control—a good thing, too, because she was a Shanir maledight who could kill with a curse.

"*Rootless and roofless...*"

*No*, Jame thought, pushing Brenwyr's words out of her mind. *I'll prove her wrong yet. I must.*

Another word floated up in her mind: tempter. That was this Randir's power, aligned with the third face of god, and that was her role: to taunt her victims to destruction, if they were weak enough to fall.

Beside her, Rue was shivering like a drenched puppy. In a moment, she would stumble forward to end this ordeal one way or another. Jame touched her arm as she moved, stopping her.

"Age before innocence."

The randon had reached the other end of the line, and so didn't see Jame step forward. A gasp from the cadets made her turn to find the Knorth already standing on the balcony rail. As they all watched, horrified, she spread her arms and stepped gracefully out onto the rope.

At last, thought Jame, something at which she was good. Not only had she no fear of heights, but a year of playing tag-you're-dead with the Cloudies across the rooftops of Tai-tastigon had given her considerable experience in such aerial sports.

She was half way across the hall when a choked exclamation from below broke both her concentration and her balance.

Jame recovered enough to part with the rope on her own terms and to catch it as she fell past. Swinging, looking down, she saw the violently foreshortened figure of Harn Grip-hard, who was staring aghast up at her.

"What in Perimal's name are you doing?" he demanded hoarsely.

"I was trying to pass a test. Sorry, ran," she added, seeing his stricken face.

"Come back." If a voice could have chipped stone, the Randir's would have.

Jame reversed and returned, hand over hand this time. She thought, as she neared the rail, that the rope gave slightly, but the stark face of the waiting randon held her attention. As she swung herself back over the rail into the gallery, she saw half the cadets bent over heaving up their breakfasts and the rest barely retaining theirs. One boy had fainted.

*Kest*, she thought. The cadet who had suffered so terribly from height-sickness on their climb up Lord Caldane's tower that even Kindrie couldn't help him.

Only Brier Iron-thorn watched her with cold detachment, as if the witness to a mountebank's failed trick.

"Now, why did you do that?" asked the Randir, very softly. Under her voice, the cold currents ran swift and deep. *"Did you think these brats would admire your courage and skill? Do you need their approval so badly? Just what were you trying to prove, and to whom?"*

Someone said, "Look!" and when they all did, there was Rue, starting across the rope hand over hand, do or die, her face white and sweating, her eyes screwed shut.

She was half way across when the rope groaned and sagged. Rue's eyes snapped open. Paralyzed with fear, she stared down at the cruel stones thirty feet below.

Her mates lined the rail, discipline forgotten.

"Come back!" some cried.

"Go on!" shouted others.

Below, Harn was roaring, "Where are the bloody mats?"

The rope sagged again. It was parting, strand by strand, some ten feet beyond the rail.

Brier started forward, but Jame stopped her. "I know you've a good head for heights, Five, but you weight half again more than I do."

As she swung a leg over the rail, the Randir grabbed her arm. "Stay here," she hissed. "Haven't you done enough harm already?"

Jame broke the randon's grip. Black rage flared in her, driving everyone back. "Never. Touch. Me. Again."

She wanted to keep her anger, to kindle it with all the misery of the past three days into a full berserker flare that would return to her all the power that others had tried to strip away. What she really needed now, however, was self-control. She regained it with a fierce effort. A moment to gauge distances, and out again over the void.

Here was the weakened section of the rope, between her hands. The outer strands had been pried apart and the inner ones notched. To all but the closest scrutiny, the rope would have appeared to be sound, and so it had proved under her slight weight. She swung past and on to where Rue helplessly dangled.

"Rue, move."

"Can't," said the cadet through clenched teeth.

"Must. Just a bit farther. Do it."

With a sob, Rue loosened the fingers of one hand, groped ahead, and clutched.

"Again. Good girl. And again."

The rope parted. Jame tightened her grip on it as it plunged away and wrapped her legs around Rue's body. They swung down with a heart-stopping rush toward the far wall and into the fibrous mass that was the Caineron banner. As Jame had hoped, it cushioned their impact nicely, if with a choking billow of dust. She let the rope slide through her gloved hands. They hit the floor harder than she would have liked, given her already sore bottom, but that was nothing compared to what it would have been like if Rue hadn't inched forward those last, vital few feet.

"Yow," said Jame, letting out her breath.

The shock-headed cadet gulped, turned, and cast herself into Jame's arms, bursting into tears. Jame held her, oddly touched. She looked up to see Sheth Sharp-tongue standing over them.

"All right, children?"

"Yes, ran," she answered for them both. "In a minute."

The other cadets came scrambling down the stair, slowing in a wary gaggle as they recognized the Commandant.

"Return to your barracks and rest," he said, addressing both squads. "You are excused this trial until later in the year, with a provisional pass for now. Your last test will take place this afternoon."

Harn reentered the hall, dragging a large, heavy floor mat. He dropped it, panting, when he saw that they were safe. "This was bundled up in a side room. And why was that rope slung three stories up instead of the usual two? What in Perimal's name is going on? Here, you!"

He stalked toward the Randir, who was descending the stair more slowly than the cadets into the hall. The Commandant sauntered over to join them.

"Take the squads back to their quarters," Jame told Brier. "I'll be along shortly."

The big Southron gave her an unreadable look, and a curt nod.

Jame was left irresolute, watching the three senior officers. Two of them were immortal in song and legend, the greatest randon of their generation. Who was she to interfere? However, she had stayed because Harn Grip-hard was her brother's oldest friend, and a berserker with reputedly failing self-control. She could easily guess what the Randir Tempter was saying to him under her soft voice, between those sharp, sharp teeth:

"*Give in to your rage. Let it devour you. Become the beast that you know you are...*"

And the Commandant merely watched, as he had when Tori had fought Ardeth for mastery of the Kencyrath's very soul.

"You say the hall was set up as you found it." Harn loomed over the smaller woman, his big fists clenched at his sides. "You say the rope appeared to be sound. But you know we don't set it that high this soon, much less without safeguards. And before that, arrows in the wood, as if anyone would conduct an archery trial there! What the hell are you Randir playing at?"

"*Let go. Give in.*"

Harn shook. Veins stood out on his neck and burst in his eyes, turning them red. Sheth drew back a step, as if to enjoy a better view. The Randir woman smiled.

This was intolerable.

Jame slipped between the Knorth Kendar and the Randir. "Ran Harn," she said, raising her voice and her hands to stop him. He caught her by the wrists in a brutal grip. Bones ground together. Both Highborn and Kendar might be called berserkers, but with the former it was a colder, more considering thing. A Kendar like Harn could rip a foe limb from limb, only later realizing what he had done.

"Harn," she repeated, louder, trying not to wince, "Blackie trusts you."

Finally he looked down at her, blinking blood-shot eyes, then thrust her aside and blundered out of the hall.

Jame watched him go, rubbing her bruised wrists.

"If he should break," said the Commandant mildly, behind her, "better it be among his peers, who can defend themselves, than among his students, who can not. You, perhaps, are an exception." She turned to find him regarding her speculatively. "I haven't quite figured you out yet, child."

"No, ran. Nor I, you."

He smiled and flicked her under the chin with a careless finger. "No doubt we will both eventually succeed." With that, he strolled away, his white scarf the last thing to melt into the shadows of Old Tentir.

Jame turned to confront the Randir. She put all the strength she had left into her voice, where it echoed hollowly. "Ropes and arrows, burrs and notched bows...whatever is going on, ran, it's between your precious Witch of Wilden and me. Leave my friends out of it."

The Randir raised an eyebrow. "You blame us? Why should we wish you to fail more than, oh, say a dozen others? You don't belong here, girl. Your mere presence tarnishes the honor of all randon, alive or dead, just as it calls into question the sanity of the brother who sent you. I, too, have reason to wish you ill, all the more so because the cause means so little to you that you can't even remember it. And who are these precious friends of yours? If they exist, which I doubt, point them out to me so that we may mark them too. Tentir has no place for fools."

Then she turned on her heel and was gone.

Alone at last, Jame sagged against the wall, feeling utterly spent. It had already been a very long morning, and quite likely it was only an hour past breakfast.

The Kendar had a phrase: to ride a rathorn. It meant to take on a task too dangerous to let go. Also, since the rathorn was a beast associated with madness, it implied that to ride one was to go insane.

Like father, like son, like daughter?

"Oh, Tori," she said, looking up at the Knorth banner with its double horned, rampant emblem. "We are truly riding the rathorn now."

# II

MOMENTS LATER, IT seems, someone was shaking her awake.

Jame surged out of *dwar* sleep to find herself in the attic of the Knorth quarters. She noted, bemused, that someone had changed her mildewed blankets for clean bedding. Brier was bending over her. Then she came fully, horrifying awake.

"How did I get here?" she cried, struggling to rise. "What time is it? Have I missed the last test?"

"You walked in," said Brier, "it's early afternoon, and the only thing you've missed so far is the noon meal. Here." She indicated a slab of buttered bread and a jug of milk on a nearby tray. "Eat quickly. The rally will sound any minute now."

Jame gulped the milk and bolted the bread, all the time scrambling to collect her wits. She remembered now walking back into the barracks to find it full of both Knorth and Danior. The sudden silence that had greeted her entrance. The stairs. The nest of smelly blankets. And escape into *dwar* sleep.

That was an unusual reaction for her, even after such a morning. She suspected that the Randir had something to do with it. However, if that woman had said anything at the end in her soft, serpent's voice, Jame couldn't remember it.

She did, vaguely, remember something else from the depths of *dwar* sleep—another voice, other words: *"What is love, Jamie? What is honor?"*

Tirandys. Senethari.

But he was dead. She had stood beside his pyre, watched him burn. A darkling changer he may have been, but whatever good there was in her she owed to him. The rest of the dream was gone.

"Brier," she said abruptly, "I'm sorry about your demotion. That was the last thing I intended, coming here. And I'm sorry I showed off on the rope. I never meant to make light of the Kendars' fear of heights."

The big Southron regarded her, no expression at all on her sundark face. "You never intend, lady. That's the problem."

# III

THE LAST TEST took place in the training square of New Tentir, under the Commandant's balcony. Cadet candidates knelt in a circle around the place of combat, ten Ardeth and ten Knorth, Timmon smiling on one side, Jame intent on the other.

She meant to be very proper and restrained this time. Remembering Tirandys had also reminded her of the dignity inherent in the Senethar, that first and most unique of the Kencyrath's unarmed fighting skills.

As with the other trials judged by single combat, two out of three contests determined victory. The winner went on to face a new challenger; the loser waited to confront whoever lost the ensuing match. After two defeats, a cadet's score was established and he or she retired to watch the superior fighters continue. Thus, at the least one fought two opponents, at the most all twenty, up to the coveted first rank.

Jame's chance came early, against a large, slow Ardeth who could hardly bear to look her in the face, much less lay hands on her. She tricked him off-balance and threw him with a crisp earth-moving maneuver that used his own size against him. The instructor, who had turned his head to speak to someone, looked back at the thud and blinked.

"Again," he said.

The second time took perhaps ten seconds longer, but with the same result.

After that, at first, things went quickly. The cautious tended to use earth-moving; the timid, water-flowing; the aggressive, fire-leaping; the ambitious, wind-blowing (usually poorly), all to the same effect or lack thereof. Their opponent had been very well trained.

"That's pure, classic Tirandys," said one senior randon quietly to another. "I haven't seen a move yet less than three thousand years old. Who in Perimal's name was her teacher?"

"Tirandys developed his form specifically for Highborn women," said the other. "Some say it was a love gift to Jamethiel Dreamweaver, although she favored the Senetha version. What if they still teach it in the Women's Halls, and their lords none the wiser?"

"Now that," said the first, "is a truly frightening thought."

Jame was aware, as the trials continued, that more and more randon were coming up to watch, but she put them out of her mind. It was a long time since she had been in regular training and she felt the lack of it acutely. Moreover, few of her adversaries in recent years had been Kencyr. She needed all her wits about her now. As she met more and more skillful opponents, she began to lose the occasional fall, but still managed two out of three wins. The instructor called increasingly frequent rest breaks.

The sun set behind the Snowthorns and shadows rolled down into the valley. Torches were kindled around the square. By now, all the other contests had ended and Kendar were returning to quarters, some to settle in as cadets, others to pack and leave. As she knelt in a space of silence during a break, amidst a growing, chattering thong, Jame tried to add up her points but couldn't. At the moment, it didn't seem important. All that mattered now was that she do her best in the last two rounds.

The instructor clapped. Timmon rose and stepped into the ring to exchange salutes with her.

Not to Jame's surprise, he favored the showy aggression of fire-leaping. She countered with water-flowing which meets and turns aside attacks, all the time studying his technique. He could be made to lose patience, and soon did, overextending in a kick that would have sent her flying if it had connected. Instead, she slid in under it and swept his foot out from under him.

"First win, Knorth," announced the instructor.

Timmon picked himself up, looking amazed. Then he grinned and came to attention, awaiting the second round.

This time he fought with more respect for his opponent, and finally caught her out with a slick, earth-moving wrist-lock.

"Second win, Ardeth."

By now, they had taken each other's measure and had found themselves well-matched. The third round moved smoothly from earth to fire to water, with a touch of wind-blowing, back and forth, give and take, though torchlight and shadow. Senethar flowed into Senetha. They no longer fought but moved together in the ancient patterns of the dance. All voices around them ceased as the glamour spread. Their movements mirrored each other. Hands moved, almost but not quite touching. Body slid by lithe body, each tracing the other's contours on the air, and the senses tingled as they passed.

Someone began softly to play a flute. It was a common exercise, by name the Sene, to alternate between fight and dance, changing instantly from the former to the latter when the music began, changing back when it stopped. The two dancers had shifted to wind blowing. They hardly touched the ground, almost weightless with balance and soaring poise. The Ardeth was good, but the Knorth...

Space seemed to open out around her. Instead of the practice square, she danced with golden-eyed shadows on a floor of cold marble shot with green. Darkness breathed around her:

"*Ahhhh*..."

The instructor shook himself and clapped twice, loudly.

The flute fell silent. Later, no one would admit to having played it, and some would claim to have heard nothing.

Jame started, suddenly awake, aware, and shaken to the core. Sweet Trinity, she had nearly reaped that boy's soul.

Timmon's hand moved past her face. She caught it, turned, and twisted. He seemed to whirl past, a sleep-dancer waking in mid-flight, too startled to break his own fall.

"Third win and match, Knorth."

"So," said the first senior randon to the second as a shaken Timmon rose, brushing himself off with unsteady hands. "Senethar and Senetha. Tirandys and the Dream-weaver both have come to Tentir, in one, small person, and with her more than a touch of their darkling glamour. What next, I wonder."

Next and last came Brier Iron-thorn.

Highborn and Southron Kendar saluted and began to circle each other. Somehow, Jame had never believed that things would go this far, nor did she know what to do now that they had. Dancing was out of the question, but she didn't want to fight Brier either. Cadets began to clap softly in unison to urge them on. This was ridiculous, she told herself. After all, it was only a contest.

She feigned a blow to draw the Kendar out. Brier slapped aside her hand, nearly snaring it in a water-flowing lock.

It occurred to Jame that she had never before seen the other fight. For such a large woman, Brier's reflexes were very fast, and she was undoubtedly much stronger than Jame. Still, this was the sort of unequal contest for which Jame had been trained.

*Right*, she thought, and settled down to it.

The first match was cautious on both sides, with a stress on defensive, water-flowing moves. The cadets clapped louder, an insistent, impatient beat. They wanted to see what these two champions could do. Jame caught Brier out and threw her.

"First win, ah...Highborn."

The second match went faster. They were striking at each other now, fire-leaping countered by wind-blowing, earth-moving against water-flowing. Brier caught Jame mid-leap and slammed her down, hard.

"Second win, Kendar."

Some cadets cheered.

Jame rose gingerly, shaken in every bone. If she had held back before, so had Brier. Now, she knew she was in trouble. Did the other's hard, green eyes see her at all, or only one of the hated Highborn? Here and now, did it matter? She tried to disable her adversary with a strike to the transverse crease of the wrist between the tendons, which should at least have numbed her hand, at best have made her knees buckle. Instead, Brier caught her wrist, pivoted and struck at Jame's ribcage with her heel. Only a quick water-flowing turn caused her to miss. Trinity, that blow could have broken Jame's ribs, even collapsed a lung. Was the Kendar trying to kill her?

"*Only a Kencyr can destroy a Tyr-ridan*," Kirien had told the haunt singer Ashe; and she, Jame, might one day become Nemesis, the personification of That-Which-Destroys, the Third Face of God.

Ironic, that an ally could kill her more easily than an enemy.

She knew she was almost spent. This kind of light-headedness only improved with rest, and the instructor just sat there stony-faced, waiting for the end. She didn't mind losing. She could simply fall down and lie there until Brier's win was called. It wasn't in her nature, however, to give up.

*Dumb, stupid pride*, she thought muzzily.

Then Brier moved—in a blur, it seemed to Jame—and she was on the ground.

"Third win and match..." began the instructor, but was cut off by a general uproar.

Jame felt hands supporting her. She spat and stared dully at the resulting spatter of blood, a tooth glimmering in the midst of in it.

Brier stood back, watching her with as white a face as her deep tan allowed.

"Careful," said Jame, thickly. "I may be a blood-binder."

*Why did you say that?* one part of her mind demanded as some Kendar recoiled. *Because they had to know*, said the other.

Meanwhile, the argument raged on:

"...a fair win..." "...an unorthodox move..." "...but effective..." "...Kothifir street fighting..." "...preserve the purity of our traditions..."

"All right, all right!" said the instructor, throwing up his hands. "Third win and match, Highborn."

"Now wait a minute," said Jame thickly, but was drowned out with cries of delight. The Kendar, cheering her? Nothing made sense.

Rue hoisted her to her feet.

"Oh no," Timmon was saying in the background. "I'm not going to fight that giantess. I'm happy with third place. Let her have second."

"I'm confused," said Jame, whistling slightly through the gap where one of her front teeth had been. "But then I usually am."

"Just take the win, lady," hissed Rue. "You need it."

While Jame tried to sort this out, someone began to clap. All other noises died. Cadets backed away. A newcomer stood at the edge of the circle, striking his hands together with slow, heavy emphasis. He was only a few years older than the cadets around him, but his rich riding coat already strained to conceal the beginnings of a pouch. And he had his father's heavy, hooded eyes.

"Well, well, well," said the Caineron Lordan. "First blood already. This is going to be more amusing than I thought."

# Chapter VI:  The Lordan's Coat

## Summer 4-5

## I

SUPPER THAT NIGHT was painful.

Throbbing head and aching muscle aside, it didn't help that cadets kept darting incredulous looks at Jame—except for Brier Iron-thorn, who wouldn't meet her eyes at all.

"What a farce!" Vant proclaimed from the next table, making no effort to lower his voice.  "For two ten-commands to rig a contest like that...well, how else d'you explain the final ranking?  I tell you, it's a shame upon us all."

Rue bristled.  "If you mean the last test, Ten, I took a fall from the lordan that taught me more than a dozen Senethari could have, and no holding back, either."

Vant laughed.  "With you, Shortie, I believe it."

"Well then, d'you think Five pulled any strikes?  Trinity, man, isn't m'lady's blood on the ground to prove it, aye, and her front tooth as well?"

Jame gave up trying to chew the hunk of bread that she had wedged into the back of her mouth.  It kept snagging on the raw gap in her teeth.  She was too tired to eat anyway.

"Oh, yes, our esteemed Five, hot from the Southern Wastes.  So that's how they fight in the back alleys of Kothifir, is it?  Rough and dirty.  I guess you showed us untaught cubs something, Iron-thorn, didn't you?"

Brier got up without a word and left the hall.  Vant laughed again, echoed by several other cadets.

"Let her go," said Jame to Rue, who had half-risen in protest. "Was that why she lost the last set?  She used Kothifir street-fighting?"

*Just as I lost for my Tastigon knife style*, she thought, as Rue nodded. *Idiots.  In a fight, what works, works.*

"Seriously, lady, who taught you?" asked another of her ten, leaning forward and dropping his voice.  "The randon are wild to know."

Jame didn't answer.  Of course they were.  Someone had broken their precious rule that highborn women should not know how to defend themselves, Tirandys be damned—as, of course, they believed him to be.

*Ah, Senethari*, she thought gingerly sipping cider, wincing at its sting. *If the randon flinch at a few unorthodox moves, what would they make of me, your last pupil, who loved you?*

"At any rate," Vant was saying, with a smug sidelong glance at her, "it doesn't matter."

And it didn't, any of it: Despite her first place in the Senethar, she had come in one hundred thirty two over all in the tests. She had failed Tentir.

Soon after, Jame went up to the attic to bed.

However, exhausted as she was, sleep wouldn't come, nor could she bear to make plans for the morrow. The moon had fallen into the dark, she noted, staring up through the hole in the roof. Wonderful. Perhaps, if she was lucky, the world would end before morning.

Jorin grumbled at her restless tossing and finally stalked off to find a more peaceful bed.

At some point Graykin slipped in. From the noise he made, clearing his throat, deliberately tripping over things or dropping them, she guessed that he wanted to rub in the news of her failure. Finally he subsided fretfully into his corner and soon began to snore.

At last Jame also fell into a fitful sleep. In her dreams, she was dancing the Senetha with Timmon. *"I know a better dance than this,"* he murmured, brushing her face with his fingertips, sliding them through her hair. *"Stay with me. Stay."*

She leaned her cheek against his warm touch. Perhaps, after all, life as a woman wouldn't be so bad. No cares, no responsibility except to please one's lord, no more knocked out front teeth...

A roughness in the texture of his hand made her pull back. She saw the white lacework of scars, and then her brother's face as he recoiled from her. They stared at each other, frozen in the figures of the dance.

Somewhere, nowhere, a tiny disgruntled voice was muttering, "...not the way it's supposed to be. This has never happened before."

But Jame was distracted by the ruddy faced Kendar tugging at her sleeve.

"I am the Highlord's man!" he cried, his face fading in patches with distress. Through the holes she glimpsed the shadowy death banner hall at Gothregor. "In the morning, he will send me away to guard his wolver friends, but if I go, what if he forgets me forever? Oh please, lady, I served your father in the White Hills and would have followed him into exile if he hadn't driven me back in the passes of the Ebonbane, as he did so many others. Forty long years and more I waited for his return, and then came his son. Now am I to be cast off again? Lady, for pity's sake, remember me!"

But without his name, how could she? As far as she knew, they had never met. He melted in her grasp, crying, crying, as if at the loss of his very soul. She could have wept herself in frustration and distress.

*Damn our blood anyway, and god-damn our god, who cursed us with it. Oh, Tori, between us what have we done?*

"What is love, Jamie? What is honor?"

"Ah, Tirandys, Senethari…"

His voice came from somewhere behind her, at least as far away as the eastern window although it might have been farther still. The predawn glimmer cast his faint, attenuated shadow on the steep inner pitch of the roof. Her own darker shadow huddled, shapeless, at its feet. Try as she might, however, she could neither rise to embrace him nor even turn her head to see once again that beloved face, now lost forever.

Then she remembered what poor use she had made of his training.

"Tentir has rejected me. I have failed you, my teacher, my mother's half-brother, you who damned himself for her love and for mine."

"Ah, not so." On the wall, the shadow bent down. Jame could almost feel the phantom touch of his hand, stroking her hair, and her eyes stung with unshed tears. "Where I failed, you need not, nor have you yet. But oh, child, you may."

"Senethari, how? Please tell me!"

He laughed, and it was a sound to break the heart. "Who am I to judge you, child—I, whom honor's paradox destroyed? There is only this: Keep faith with those who keep faith with you. And beware: our house has failed in this before now. Already, your brother is in danger of failing again, however good his intentions. How can he not, as long as he denies his true nature? And you, who have long guessed what you may become, beware as well.

Great power brings greater responsibility, and the greatest abuses. This place has unfinished business with those of our blood. I only tell you what you have already guessed. Some dreams do no more than that."

His voice faded as he spoke into a faint crackle as if of dried leaves or of fire. "Oh child, remember me."

"Senethari, wait!"

Jame struggled, hardly knowing if she wished to wake up or to sink deeper into sleep, even into death, if by doing so she could follow him, the only person who had ever accepted her knowing fully what she was.

His shadow faded as the light on the wall grew. He was returning to his pyre. Oh, not again the heat and stench and bitter taste of ashes on the wind...

Jame threw aside her blanket and jumped up, only to trip and fall over something that yelped. For a moment, struggling in folds of bedding that seemed to fight back, she was confused: *Which changer is burning? Whose beauty have I stolen? What am I becoming?*

Then her claws hooked on the cloth and ripped it away. Light blinded her. As she stood there panting, she realized that she was staring not into the flames of a pyre but directly into the newly risen sun.

"Do you mind?" said the roll of blankets at her feet. Graykin emerged from it, tousled and indignant. "The next time you have a nightmare, kindly leave me out of it."

Outside, the morning's ram's horn blared and in the dormitory two floors below, feet hit the floor.

Jame dressed quickly and went down the stair into the hall. Only when she met Vant's astonished gaze did she remember: she no longer belonged at Tentir. She sat down, feeling suddenly numb, and stared without seeing it at the bowl of porridge that a cadet thumped down before her.

*Rootless and roofless...*

So the Brandan Maledight Brenwyr had cursed her at Gothregor, within her family's own stronghold and under the eyes of its unforgiving dead.

*Blood and bone...*

She couldn't help what she was. Perhaps she couldn't live with it either.

*Cursed be and cast out...*

But where did one go from here?

Dully, she became aware of a buzz spreading through the hall. Rue nudged her. "Lady, d'you hear? The Randon Council has finally set the mark!"

"Well, what is it?" others exclaimed eagerly, craning to hear.

"One hundred and forty!"

Jame looked up sharply. Around her, a few faces had blanched, but over all a sigh of relief echoed through the room.

*I'm in,* she thought blankly. *Brenwyr's curse has failed, at least for the minute.* Then she wondered, *Why am I in?*

They could easily have stuck to one hundred thirty and been rid of her. Everyone knew that the cut-off score was fluid, and she had missed the original mark by mere points. Perhaps, after all, Tentir was going to treat her like any other cadet-candidate, which was all she had asked, and more than she had hoped for.

Suddenly ravenous, she wolfed down the congealing porridge, and thought it the best thing she had ever tasted.

In the evening, the candidates would be initiated into the randon college as cadets. Until then, they were free to prepare.

Breakfast and morning assembly done, Rue hauled Jame up to the third story lordan's quarters in search of suitable clothing for her to wear for the ceremony. While the straw-haired cadet rummaged through the chests, Jame sat in shirtsleeves on the wide, raised hearth with needle and white thread, trying to knot stitch the rathorn emblem into her black token scarf.

Graykin prowled about the apartment waiting for Rue to leave, palpably jealous that she had claimed Jame's attention first. Jorin followed him, pouncing at a ribbon snagged and trailing unnoted from his boot.

"You should clean all of this out and move in." He glared at the walls of boxes blocking either end of the room. "There have got to be apartments behind all that junk. A master bedroom. Servants' quarters. Real beds."

"I like the attic," said Jame, frowning over her stitches. "It's airy."

"Oh, it's that, all right. The wind blows in one end and out the other. You just wait until winter. Sweet Trinity, part of it doesn't even have a roof."

*Rootless and roofless...*

"I don't like being confined, and I don't like this place." She sneezed into her scarf but, at a glare from Graykin, forbore wiping her nose with it. "It smells. Besides, it gives me bad dreams. Who lived here anyway?"

"Your uncle, lady. The last Knorth Lordan."

"Ouch." Jame had stuck the needle into her thumb. "And who was that?"

Rue had turned aside to examine the shreds of a silk shirt. She didn't want to say the name, Jame realized. Interesting.

"Who?" she prompted, removing the needle.

The cadet tossed away the ruined shirt, and the name of its former owner with it. "Greshan, nicknamed Greed-heart at least among his Kendar."

*"Did you know how our father came to power?"* Tori had asked Jame in the ruins of Kithorn. *"His older brother, the Knorth Lordan, was killed in training at Tentir."*

Something very bad had happened in this airless, windowless room. Jame regarded a large stain on the wooden floor. It was barely a shadow now, sunk deep into the grain, but someone had bled here, perhaps to death. She remembered her dream that first night at Tentir and shivered.

*Dear little Gangrene.*

Ugh.

In the past her sleep had sometimes been troubled, but rarely by dire visions. Tori was the far-seer, not her. Yet that last winter at Gothregor she had dreamed truly that Graykin had fallen into Caldane's hands and that Bane was on his way to the Riverland. It was less remarkable that she and Tori had shared certain dreams; as children, they had done so constantly, thinking nothing of it. Perhaps rejoining her people was waking dormant powers in her. If so, she didn't much care for them.

Graykin turned up his nose at the pile of clothes that Rue had set aside as potentially salvageable, the plainest and most practical among all that spoiled finery.

"You should at least dress according to your rank. How about this?"

He had picked up the embroidered jacket.

Rue stared. "Why, that must be the Lordan's Coat."

"What, my uncle's?"

"Not just his, lady. Every Knorth heir for generations has worn it, and generations of Knorth Kendar have mended it."

"Here," said Jame. "Let me see that."

Graykin gave it to her, reluctantly, and she spread it out on her knees.

Although dimmed by a half century of dust, the needlework was exquisite. Tiny stitches covered every inch of the surface in shades from the autumn gold of a birch leaf to the phantom blue of a shadow on snow, from the sharp green of spring grass to the deep crimson of heart's desire. Lines swooped and curved. Fantasies of shape and color swirled, blending into each other. Half-seen images came and went with every shift of light.

"Careful!" said Graykin sharply as threads snapped at her touch.

If the coat was truly as old as Tentir, Jame thought, gingerly turning it over, probably little of its original fabric remained. The earliest needlework must long since either have been repaired or stitched over, as with the house banners in the great hall. Nearly fifty years of neglect hadn't helped. Without thinking, she tugged at a hair caught in the threads, and jumped as the coat writhed on her knees as if in pain.

"Sweet Trinity. What's this?"

Rue bent to look. "Well, they do say that every lordan since the beginning has worn this coat, and that each of them has added something…er…personal to it."

"You mean," said Graykin, with a queasy smirk, "that this is not only a heirloom but also a 'hair-loom'?"

All three regarded the strand in question. It was short, coarse, and irrepressibly curly.

Rue clapped a hand over her mouth to stifle a giggle.

Graykin blushed.

"Hmm," said Jame, with a raised eyebrow. "The Kendar really hated my dear uncle, didn't they? I wonder why."

"I wonder…" began Rue, then stopped.

"What?"

"Well, just before your uncle died, the White Lady disappeared."

"Who?"

"The Knorth Matriarch's Whinno-hir mare, Bel-tairi, sister to Lord Ardeth's Brithany. She left Valentir, where she was visiting a new great-grand-foal among the herd, but she never reached Gothregor. There are rumors that m'lord Greshan met her in the wilderness and...well, did something to her. He and Lady Kinzi weren't on very good terms at the time. Then news came that the lordan was dead, and his father the Highlord soon after him. The whole thing was a right mess, by all accounts."

"The senior randon call her 'The Shame of Tentir,'" said Graykin. "Why, I don't know. So I listen," he added crossly, seeing Rue's expression. "Is it my fault that they talk and I hear things? They also say that she has unfinished business with the Knorth and that having you here as lordan may be stirring things up."

"Unfinished business," murmured Jame, turning over the coat. So Tirandys had said: *I only tell you what you have already guessed.* It seemed, since she had rejoined her people, that she kept stepping into one ancient mess after another. Trinity, didn't her family ever clean up after itself? Then too, what was she to make of the pale lady who had called her Kinzi-kin and vanished like a ghost, leaving hoof-prints in the turf? Unfinished business indeed, and here in her hands, perhaps, was another piece of it.

The coat's peacock blue silk lining had at some point been soaked with a dark fluid. It was also ripped.

"A knife in the back?" Jame asked, only half joking. However, the tear seemed too ragged, its edges frayed, and she found no corresponding slit in the outer fabric.

Rue added the coat to her armload of saved clothing. "At least we know now why it stinks. I'll try to clean these, m'lady, and hope they dry by tonight. In the fire-timber hall, they might. Then we'll see about cutting them down to your size and repairing the coat. After all," she added, seeing Jame's expression, "it's a piece of history."

"And, in its way, a masterpiece. All right, all right. As for the rest, I *have* mended my own clothes before, you know."

Being waited on made her nervous. In the Women's Halls of Gothregor, the petty tyranny of servants had made her feel ignorant and stupid. Now it was happening again.

"Oh." She ruefully regarded the scarf. Her attempt at the rathorn crest looked like an upside-down boot with two spikes growing out of its sole; and, as usual, she had managed to sew her gloved finger-tips together.

Rue left, grinning.

"If you ever want a lock of my hair," Jame called after her, "just ask! And don't forget your own scarf."

The cadet had done her needlework the night before, and a very fine job of it too, but someone had stolen it. Jame hoped the barrack wasn't going to be plagued with a petty thief.

Graykin watched Rue's departure wistfully. "Smelly or not," he said, "there goes a royal coat."

His tone reminded Jame that, as Caldane's son, he was half Highborn. However, his illegitimacy and his mother's Southron blood barred him from even the trappings of that rank. She didn't think that he was missing much. Graykin, however, clearly felt otherwise.

"How you look and act reflects on the dignity of your house," he said stubbornly, with a discontented glance at her battered face and the purple bruises on her wrists where Harn had gripped them, all affronts to his own dignity as well. Fortunately, he had come in too late the night before to see what the rest of her looked like.

"Enough small talk," she said, gingerly biting off tangled threads, wincing as they caught on the raw gap in her front teeth. "Report."

As she had suspected, he had spent the past three days exploring the secret passages of Old Tentir, eavesdropping whenever possible.

"I would have told you last night that you'd qualified," he said with a sniff, "but you were pretending to be asleep. Anyway, the Randon Council set the mark at one hundred and forty, then waited for the Commandant to take them off the hook. But he didn't. Now they've got their breeches in a twist trying to decide how to deal with you. The Caineron claim that you've been kept on for the amusement of their lordan—his name is Gorbel, by the way."

"Gorbelly?"

"Close enough. Fun and games aside, they mean to humiliate your brother through you—and remember, the Highlord can't do anything about it short of jerking you out of here."

*The college has its own rules*, Torisen had told her at Kithorn. *If you're hurt there, I can't even demand your blood-price.*

"And that," Graykin was saying, "would be a victory for just about everyone except the Knorth. The general belief is that by admitting Gorbel without testing him, Sheth is tacitly saying that his master's son can get away with anything. The other randon aren't happy about that. They think it damages the college's integrity; but these are intensely political times."

"I have noticed," said Jame dryly.

"By the same token, although he let you in, they don't think Sheth will let you stay to the end. He's covering his ass with both lords, as it were, giving the Highlord's sister a chance but at the same time turning a blind eye to the Caineron lordan."

Sheth Sharp-tongue must be under intense pressure, Jame thought, to accept his lord's belief that honor meant nothing but obedience. Honor's Paradox had destroyed Tirandys. If Caineron could corrupt Tentir through its commander, what chance did the rest of the Kencyrath have?

"The consensus, though, is that you won't last. What Highborn girl could? The Randir called you a freak."

"Huh. They should talk. These passages in the old fortress must be giving you lots of chances to spy."

"I am your faithful sneak, mistress," he said with a mocking cringe.

"Don't call either of us that," she said sharply. "The Mistress was a different Jamethiel, and you're my...my loyal servant. Damn. That doesn't sound right either."

"Pretty titles, dirty hands."

His hands, she noticed, were remarkably dirty.

"Pick out some new clothes for yourself, while we're at it," she told him. "You look as if you've been dragged up a chimney backwards."

"Hand-me-downs," he said with disgust, kicking at a pile of moldy finery.

"I seldom wear anything else. These passages...what are they like?"

"Dark, narrow, filthy."

He wanted to keep them to himself, she thought. Knowledge was power, and the Caineron Bastard had precious little of either. Neither did she. "Once you said you would never deceive me, although there were many ways you could within the bounds of honor."

He glared at her, caught by his own pledge.

"All right, all right! From what I've seen so far, the hidden ways are much more direct than the public ones. I'll show you if you like," he added ungraciously. "I may...er...even have found the brat's hidden room. At least I thought, once, that something was keeping pace with me all down one wall, on the other side. I could hear it muttering and clawing at the stones. Then it started to pound on them. Whatever-it-is was big. And strong. The stones shook. And I'll tell you this too: The kitchen staff lays aside raw joints of meat for it. I saw them do it when I was...ah...borrowing some food. I have to eat too, you know."

"I know, I know. And so far I've been precious little good at providing for you. Well, see what else you can find out, about anything, and watch out of the Caineron. Caldane can't be happy that the Knorth have snatched both you and Brier Iron-thorn away from him."

# II

WITH RUE GONE and Graykin departed to nose out more secrets, Jame went looking for Brier.

She found the big Southron and five of her ten-command in
the third story common room opposite the lordan's apartment. They
were all bare foot, polishing a seemingly endless row of boots.

"For tonight," said Brier. "And yes, these are every pair in the
Knorth barracks except for yours and Rue's, who appears to have
run off in hers. On your orders, I take it."

"On my business, anyway. She seems to have appointed herself
my servant."

"Good," said Brier, giving her a sharp look. "You need one."
*Better yet, a keeper,* her tone said.

"But all these boots...why you?"

"Vant's orders."

"Huh. Vant's revenge, more likely. How much did you outrank
him in the trials?"

"Fifteen to thirty-six!" chorused the other cadets, grinning.

At least Vant's petty tyranny seemed to have brought the squad
squarely behind their new Five. But two faces were missing. Mint,
Dar, Quill, Erim, Killy...

"Where are Kest and...and..." Damn. She hadn't learned the
last cadet's name.

"Yel failed. And Kest left last night. The rope test broke him.
He didn't even wait to hear his score."

"Oh," said Jame, blankly. She had been so relieved at breakfast
to hear that she had qualified that she hadn't noticed who had not.

"The Knorth lost ten candidates in all," said Brier dispassion-
ately, examining a scuffed toe. "That takes us down to ninety
cadets, nearly a one-hundred command. Not bad. One of our
provisional squads will be broken up to provide replacements to
the others."

That reminded Jame that she was not only ten-commander of
this particular group but—nominally, at least—master ten of the
entire barracks.

"Wait a minute. Why is Vant giving you orders?"

"Of the ten-commanders, his score was the highest, so he stands second to you in authority. He will expect to have the day-to-day running of the barracks."

Damn. Jame would much rather have had Brier, and would have, too, if the Southron hadn't been demoted for breaking college rules on her behalf. She scowled at the formidable array of boots.

"I can countermand Vant."

"Don't," said Brier. "At least not until you've given your scarf to the Commandant and received it back from him through the hands of a Knorth senior randon. You aren't officially part of Tentir until then. None of us are, however some choose to act."

"Oh," said Jame, taken aback. She hadn't known.

"Anyway," the Southron added, following Jame's line of thought regarding her demotion, "the cadet body as a whole wouldn't have welcomed an outsider in charge over them."

"Well, they'll have to lump it, won't they? After all, they've got me."

Brier gave her another look, this one askance under the fringe of her dark red hair. Sunlight flooding in through the room's many windows gave her a fiery halo. "Sorry I knocked out your tooth," she said gruffly.

"Oh, it could as easily have been yours as mine. I think. A risk of the game. But that move you used against me...I've never seen anything like it before. Will you teach me how to fight Kothifir style?"

Brier looked up, startled. "Why?"

"It was effective, and it caught me totally off guard. I'd rather not have that happen again." She hesitated. "Just out of curiosity, were you trying to kill me?"

"Trinity, no. I'd never fought a Highborn before, much less a lady. I had no idea you were so fragile."

Jame blinked. Fragile? It had never occurred to her that she was. True, most of her adversaries in the past had been much stronger than she was, but untrained. She had usually beaten them easily. Here, that would no longer be the case.

"I've been a fool," she said, thoughtfully. "An arrogant one, at that. Thank you, Brier Iron-thorn. You've already taught me an invaluable lesson, and cheap at the price." She fingered her sore jaw.

"Just the same, I've never had a tooth knocked out before.  How long does it usually take to grow a new one?"

"About three weeks," said the Kendar.  She picked up another boot—Vant's, perhaps—spat on it, and began to polish.  "Find a twig to chew on or the teething itch will drive you crazy."

# III

IN ANOTHER PART of the barracks, Vant could be heard ordering someone else around. If she wasn't going to interfere, Jame didn't want to listen. She and Jorin slipped out the front door into the covered arcade, into the bright summer morning.

New Tentir was laid out in the same order as the house banners in the great hall: Randir, Coman, and Caineron from east to west along the north wing; Jaran, Knorth, and Ardeth along the west; Danior, Edirr and Brandan from west to east along the south. By chance or design, this arrangement grouped allies and enemies, with a scattering of neutrals between them. Jame turned southward.

For the first time, she seriously considered the physical dangers she faced at Tentir. The randon were the deadliest fighters on Rathillien, and she didn't know what rules bound them beyond the increasingly slippery concept of honor. These were her superiors, not her peers, except among the rawest recruits. Moreover, among them were bitter enemies of her house. Had she been a fool to come here? It had hardly been a considered decision, rather a spur-of-the-moment escape from an intolerable situation.

Yes, she told herself, but think of the other risks she had blithely taken in the past—the streets of Tai-tastigon, where she had stalked gods and in turn been stalked by them; the carnivorous hills of the Anarchies, where she had granted an aging rathorn mare her death wish and so gained the hatred of her death's-head foal; the Master's House itself, with its layers of corrupt history, all the fallen worlds stacked one on top of the other—all undertaken with a child's careless arrogance.

If she had known what she was doing, would she have done it? Was she growing more cautious with age, or more cowardly?

And on top of that, she had just been handed responsibility for an entire barracks, containing all her brother's precious cadets. A loner by nature, what did she know about command? Should she—*could* she leave everything to Vant?

The arcade took her by the broad facade of the Ardeth, and then turned a corner to head eastward toward Old Tentir. Jame noted that the Ardeth had appropriated not only the southwestern corner but a length of the south wing. Poor little Danior with its thirty cadets was so pinched by its larger neighbor that one half expected the building to squeak. The Edirr faired only slightly better, under pressure on the other side from the Brandan.

In front of the latter, Captain Hawthorn leaned on the arcade rail tranquilly smoking a long-stemmed, clay pipe. She raised a scar-broken eyebrow as Jame approached.

"We'd heard that you were gone, lady," she said. "Seemingly, you didn't sleep in your quarters last night, or at least not in the lordan's apartment."

Someone must have checked, thought Jame. Someone who didn't know she had shifted lodgings upward, into the attic. Vant. No wonder he had been surprised to see her at breakfast.

"Well, here I am." She sniffed her sleeve, which retained the stale reek of Greshan's jacket. "Like a bad smell, I linger."

The randon grinned. "So I perceive."

"Speaking of the lordan's suite, how is it that we can afford to leave it empty, given how full the college is? For that matter, we Knorth seem to have almost more space than we need."

"Hush, or your neighbors will hear. Actually, you can thank them, specifically your allies the Ardeth and the Jaran, that you have any quarters here at all." The randon drew on her pipe and exhaled a meditative plume of smoke. "I can remember when the Knorth barracks were nearly as full as our own. That was before your lord father fell, and nearly brought his house down with him. For more than thirty years, those rooms stood as empty as the Highlord's seat, for no one dared to seize either."

Jame gazed, frowning, back across the square at the Knorth façade. Vant could be seen intermittently as he paced the second floor, harrying a ten-command as it scrubbed the dormitory floor. Brier sat tranquilly on a third story window ledge polishing yet another boot. Heights didn't seem to bother her. Poor Kest. The Caineron barracks looming on the north side of the square were broad, five stories tall, and virtually windowless. Perhaps Lord Caldane's height-sickness ran throughout his house.

"So," said Jame, pulling her mind back to the matter at hand, "there have only been Knorth cadets at Tentir since my brother came to power? That was just three years ago."

"Aye." The randon puffed again. "Barely time for the first class to graduate, and many of those died at the Cataracts. You've much rebuilding yet to do, if your enemies give you time. Take care, lordan. Your brother can't protect you here."

Jame leaned against the rail as memory swept her back to a conversation with the Brandan Matriarch Brenwyr not long ago:

*"Kinzi and the Randir Matriarch Rawneth...they quarreled."*

*"So? Are you saying that I've inherited an undeclared blood feud, and no one saw fit to tell me?"*

*"There was no need. Anyway, it never came to blows."*

*"Let me guess. Before anything so unladylike could happen, the Shadow Assassins slaughtered every Knorth woman at Gothregor except Tieri...and no one ever knew why."*

It was still only a guess that Rawneth had been behind the Knorth massacre. Even if she was, Jame had no idea what quarrel could have led to such deadly consequences, yet she herself must still be part of it or the Shadow Assassins wouldn't have come for her that last night in Gothregor.

Huh. More unfinished business.

"Who are my enemies?" she asked Hawthorn.

The randon frowned, troubled. "I shouldn't have spoken. Not until you're a proper cadet under Tentir's protection, such as it is, and even then you should be told by a member of your own house. In a few hours, we will tell you all we know." She straightened and knocked out her pipe against the rail. "In the meantime, you'll be safe among your own people. Wait a minute while I tell my folk where I'm going and then, lady, I'll escort you back to your quarters."

When she returned, however, the Knorth was gone.

# IV

THE GREAT HALL of Old Tentir hummed with activity. Kendar scoured the flagstones while others polished the randon collars hanging against the upper walls. Beams were being dusted and retouched with gold paint by those presumably least prone to height-sickness. The rope from the trials had been removed. Delicious smells drifted up from the fire timber hall below, where whole oxen were being slowly roasted over charcoal pits for the feast that would follow the cadets' initiation into Tentir.

Jame's stomach rumbled as she and Jorin stood in the shadows, watching. With luck, by evening, she would be able to chew again, if cautiously.

She knew that Hawthorn was right. It was foolish to take chances, but damned if she was going to be delivered back to the Knorth barracks like some willful, wandering child. In a minute, she would make her own way home. Now, she had to be sure of herself. That she hadn't lost her nerve. That she would take whatever risks she must to succeed at the college, while never forgetting that this was a dangerous place, full of dangerous people.

Jorin growled.

"Good morning," said the Randir Tempter, beside her. "Or perhaps I should say 'good afternoon.'"

"We…I didn't hear you, ran."

"Ah." The other smiled. "It occurred to us that you and the ounce might be bound. You are, of course, Shanir."

"As are you." Jame listened intently. The other didn't seem to be using her under-voice, but then it had slipped past her guard before. As for physical violence, "*Never touch me again*," she had told this woman from the depths of her Shanir nature, and she suddenly knew that the Randir never would nor could. However, Jorin was still growling, which distracted her.

"Hush," she said to him.

"There are many Shanir here," said the Randir, "a few Highborn like you and the Ardeth brat, but mostly Kendar with a touch of the Old Blood. What is it, I wonder, that draws Highborn men to Kendar women? One rarely hears of the reverse. Among our own kind, we can control conception as well—or ill—as Highborn ladies. But not with Highborn lovers. They take us and use us and cast off our children as the whim takes them. They should not, for we are many and we are proud."

*What a strange conversation*, thought Jame.

She knew that the Randir was toying with her, deliberately holding her attention, but why? It was on the tip of her tongue to ask straight out what quarrel the Randir had with the Knorth, but Jorin's growl had risen to a singing whine.

As she turned to quiet him, a movement caught the corner of her eye. There was someone behind her...and a sudden blow fell on the back of her neck.

"Blood for blood, Knorth," she thought she heard the Randir Tempter say as she fell. Then darkness swallowed her.

# Chapter VII:  In the Bear's Den

## Summer 5

## I

JAME WOKE, STILL in darkness, to a savage headache.  She thought at first, dazed, that she had lost her sight, but then realized that she was only blindfolded.  And gagged.  And bound hand and foot. This, on the whole, was not good.  But where was she, besides on the floor?

Her other senses began, reluctantly, to function.

She could feel the coarse grain of wood under her cheek.  It was damp, with a curiously heady tang.  Other smells, less appealing, lurked behind it: unwashed flesh, rotting meat, human urine and feces.  Unlike the ancient miasma of the lordan's apartment, this reek was fresh, a living stink.  She had caught whiffs of it through Jorin's senses when they had been searching Old Tentir for the Knorth guest quarters.

Trinity.  Jorin.  Where was he?  If they had hurt her cat, she would kill them.

Close behind her, something large stirred and groaned.  Leather creaked.  Something muttered, then began to breathe deeply again, with the hint of a snore.

So.

At a guess, she was in the lair of the mysterious monster who ate little children for lunch and raw joints of meat for dinner.

Also, it drank strong wine.  She was lying in a spilt puddle of it. Perhaps its keepers periodically drugged it when they came to clean out its den—and they must, or the stench would be much worse.  Her captors had apparently taken advantage of this to dump her here.

"Blood for blood," the Randir had said, but not on her hands.

Perhaps they expected the beast to rip her apart.  All the more reason not to be here when it woke up.  Besides, if its head hurt half as much as hers did, it would be in a truly foul mood.

Her hands were bound behind her.  She curled into a tight ball and began to work them down her back.  Cramped muscles threatened to spasm in revolt. Halfway through, she got stuck and lay panting around the gag, trying not to panic.

This was no good. Try again.

Suddenly her hands shot up over her bent knees and hit her in the nose. She fumbled at the blindfold with fingers numb for lack of blood, then at the gag. The former, she saw, was her own token scarf. The latter was Rue's. This had been planned well in advance. The Randir must have been waiting for her to stumble into their hands, and so she had. No one would accuse poor Rue of plotting her death, but the presence of two Knorth scarves would suggest that this was a house matter, best dealt with internally by its lord. Ancestors only knew what Tori would make of such a mess.

By now, her eyes had adjusted to the dim light, most of which came from a fireplace where embers winked and tinkled in the grate. It was very hot. Opposite the hearth was a heavy door, undoubtedly locked, with a narrow, hinged panel at the bottom. There were no windows, thus no way to tell how long she had been unconscious. Damnation. If they made her miss the evening ceremony as they almost had the final test...however, that seemed to be the Randir style: traps within traps within traps.

Another deep sigh behind her. Craning painfully to look over her shoulder, she saw a low bed with a large form huddled on it. The breathing had changed. He would wake soon. And her fingers were too numb to untie her ankles, much less her hands.

The rest of the apartment was comfortably furnished, but much disordered. A chair slumped before the fireplace, its arms and back hanging in flayed strips. In the corner, a gutted bookcase spilled its contents onto the carpet. The shredded fragments of books and scrolls littered the floor.

So did little wooden figures, cunningly carved.

A monster that played with toy warriors?

One of them held a little knife as if it were a sword, firelight flickering red on the blade. She wriggled across the floor as quietly as possible, picked it up, and fumbled to lay the edge against the rope securing her legs. She had almost sawed through when the figure on the bed yawned and stretched.

Jame rolled under the bed. Her legs came free as she moved, but she lost the little knife, and her hands were still bound. The leather web of straps above her groaned and sagged. Big, bare feet hit the floor in front of her face. Overgrown toenails extended and flexed, rasping against the wood. Trinity, now what? Could she hide here until someone came to feed the brute?

Now it...no, *he* was pissing in a nearby corner. Jame edged back from the spreading puddle. Did the man have a wine vat for a bladder?

At last, the waterfall ceased.

"Hmmm?" said a deep voice, rusty from lack of use. He was sniffing the air. Surely he couldn't smell her over the room's other assorted stinks.

"*Huh!*"

The bed upended against the wall with a crash. Jame rolled to her feet and plunged for the panel at the base of the door. It flipped open at her touch, but he caught her by the hair and jerked her back. She kicked at his face. He flicked aside her foot, grabbed her by the shirt, ripping it, and threw her into the wall.

*Play dead*, she thought, sliding down the wall and lying still. Indeed, she was too shaken to do much else.

Big hands picked her up and dropped her into the chair before the dying fire. The chair sagged, exhaling a sharp breath laced with dead mice. She curled up in its hollow, knees to chin, behind the veil of her long black hair. He bent and sniffed her all over, muttering deep in his throat. Instinctively, she raised her hands to protect her face.

There was a moment's silence.

She felt his hot breath snuffling on her wrists, and then his teeth bit down on the cords that bound them.

Jame opened her eyes.

He was kneeling before her, turning her freed hands over in his own. He had claws as big as a cave bear's, three inches long at least and too large to retract. Her own ivory nails, unsheathed, were delicate in contrast. She could make out little of his face in shadow, behind its wild mask of beard. He snuffled at her fingertips, then folded them in on themselves so that the nails were hidden and cupped within his own huge claws as if in a cage of polished bone. His touch was surprisingly gentle, almost protective.

"D-d-d-d..."

"Don't? Don't what?"

"T-t-t-t..."

"Tell? Don't tell?"

The door burst open. In a blaze of torchlight, Jame saw the man's face, the savage cleft in his skull into which his wild graying hair tumbled. Something long ago had cleaved him half way down to the eyebrows. No one should survive such a blow, but this man had. He sprang back as a swung torch roared past his face, over Jame's head. His beard sparked as if infested with fireflies. The room stank of burnt hair. As he backed away, beating at his face, a big hand reached over the chair's back, grabbed Jame by the arm, and jerked her up. The room seemed to be full of giants, although there were only two of them. The one with the torch propelled her out the door into the hall and slammed the door after them. Something very big hit it on the other side. The wood shook, but held.

Harn Grip-hard backed away. The torch, unnoticed, still flared in his hand. He was shaking, his broad face white beneath its perennial stubble. From inside the locked room came strange sounds. The captive was crying. Harn dropped the torch and blundered away. Jame picked it up before it could start a fire, noting that it was wet with blood where Harn had gripped it. With a last glance at the door, she followed him.

Someone rounded a corner, fast, and almost knocked her off her feet.

"Where have you been?" demanded Graykin fiercely, grabbing her by the shoulders. She noted that he was liberally festooned with cobwebs. He also looked angry enough to kill her, presumably for still being alive. "Everyone is looking for you!"

"Tell you later. Damn. Where did he go?"

They tracked Harn by the blood drops on the floor, Graykin hissing questions to which Jame had no answers. She was touched that her peculiar servant really had been worried about her, although he hid it well behind an affronted air: How dare she upset him like that? She had no idea at first where they were, the inner halls of Old Tentir being dark enough even by day to require candles.

"What time is it?" she asked Graykin abruptly.

"Late afternoon."

"Good. What day?"

He stared at her, then looked quickly away. She became aware that her shirt was hanging in tatters over bare skin.

"The same," he said, not very clearly, but she understood.

"Very good."

Here at last was a hall slotted on one side with narrow windows. They had emerged at the northeastern corner of the third floor, near a door that opened to one of Tentir's four watchtowers. Jame recalled hearing that during his stint as commandant Harn had made his quarters in this out-of-the-place. She set the torch in a wall sconce.

"I need clothes," she told Graykin. "Go back to the barracks and tell Rue. She'll find me something. Bring it here."

When he had gone, radiating irritation that his mistress needed help from anyone but him, Jame climbed into a rush of sweet air.

On the first of two levels, windows opened to the north and south onto the sweep of the Riverland. Below, the Silver threaded through gathering shadows under as yet sun-crowned heights. It took Jame a moment, blinking against the light, to make out two large chairs drawn up before a cold fireplace. Someone slumped in the one with its back to her.

"You stink," growled the unseen occupant, "like a tavern latrine. Bathe. There." A large hand waved toward the northern window, under which Jame now saw a large tub of rapidly cooling water, undoubtedly brought here for the randon's solitary absolutions. She hesitated only briefly, then stripped off what was left of her now decidedly rank clothing.

He threw her a sharp look, as if still not entirely convinced that she wasn't Blackie in disguise.

*More like black and blue,* she thought wryly, but bruises only hurt for a while, turned interesting colors, and then went away. She was used to them.

"How did you know where I was, ran?" she asked, gratefully sinking into the tub. Harn would have over-lapped it on all sides, but it fit her slender limbs nicely.

He grunted. "I heard a rumor that you'd had the good sense to leave Tentir. I should have known better. Anyway, I went to check."

On the way, he had encountered the Randir Tempter helping a colleague back to their quarters.

"Proper shredded, his legs were. I knew your cat's work when I saw it."

Harn had found the ounce racing about the Knorth barracks, bouncing off walls, scratching anyone who tried to stop him. Vant was shouting that the cat had gone mad and calling for archers.

When no one moved (except to get out of Jorin's way), he had grabbed a bow but then inexplicably tripped, nearly impaling himself on the arrow. By then, Captain Hawthorn had arrived, looking for Jame. She and Brier had thrown a blanket over the ounce as he hurtled past and bundled him off, all teeth and claws, to a vacant room. There they had left him, from the sound of it, careening off the walls, floor, and ceiling.

Harn had put together bloody legs, a hysterical cat, and a lost Knorth. Then he had gone off to storm the Randir quarters.

Here, he fell silent.

Jame ducked to rinse soap out of her hair, then rose and slid, dripping, into the enveloping folds of Harn's gray dress coat. She picked up a shirt to dry her hair, hoping belatedly that Harn hadn't meant to wear it that night, curled into the chair opposite him, and waited.

The burly randon slumped in the oversized chair, staring blankly at the previous winter's ashes, his arms limp on the chair's rests. The knuckles of his left hand were broken and crusted with drying blood. Finally he spoke in a low, hoarse voice, as if to himself.

"So I go to the Randir. They know I'm coming, plain enough, because the door is shut. I knock. Inside, I think I hear someone snicker. Then they begin to chant, oh, so softly, 'Beast, beast, beast,' and I knock louder, to drown them out."

As he spoke, he began unconsciously to beat the wooden arm of his chair with his clenched fist, harder and harder, reopening the cuts on his battered knuckles.

Jame slipped out of her chair, knelt beside him, and wrapped her own hands around his fist as it descended. She wondered, biting her lip, if she was about to add broken bones to the day's other mementos. Harn didn't seem to notice her grip, but his blows faltered and stopped. His fingers unclenched and his big hand, relaxing, hung over the chair's arm. Blood dripped from it onto the floor. Jame cleaned the cuts with the shirt, still damp from her hair.

"I think I must have beaten down the door," he said slowly, "because the next thing I know I'm inside, surrounded by a ring of spears. No one was laughing then.

"They say, 'Leave, or we'll kill you.'

"I say, 'Bring me your bitch temptress or you'll have to.'

"So finally she comes, and I ask her where the Highlord's sister is.  She says…she says, 'Look in your future lodgings.' And smiles."

Jame considered this as she ripped strips of cloth to bandage his wounds.  That done, she wadded up the torn, bloody shirt and threw it into the back of the cold grate.  Then she resumed her seat across from him.  Sunk deep in his chair, Harn reminded her of a large, wild animal flinching away from the light, drawing back into self-imposed, self-destructive isolation.

*"Become the beast that you know you are…"*

"The man in the locked room is definitely Shanir," she said, "but I don't think he's a berserker.  That needn't happen to you.  Who is he, ran?  What happened to him?"  A sudden thought struck her.  "Don't tell me I've stumbled across the long-lost Randir Heir!"

"I won't because you haven't," snapped Harn, rousing.  "Besides, Randiroc isn't lost.  He just doesn't want to be found.  Neither would you if the Witch of Wilden and Shadow Guide assassins were after you."

In fact they were, but she wasn't hiding.  Yes, and look how *that* had worked out so far.

Harn raised a hand to rub his eyes and frowned at the bandages, clearly surprised to find them there.  "We call him Bear," he said.

"'We'?"

"Every commandant knows about him and attends to his needs.  Since we command Tentir by rotation, that means all the senior randon, not to mention the sargents and servants.  He was one of us.  The best.  Until the White Hills when a war axe did…that."

*Thirty-four years ago*, thought Jame, just after the slaughter of the Knorth women when her father's misguided revenge against the Seven Kings of the Central Lands had led to such carnage and to his own exile.  So much pain led back to that time, to those events.

"It must have been an awful wound," she said, involuntarily imagining it red and raw, white shards of skull and gray, spattered brain.  "Why wasn't he offered the White Knife?"

"His lord lay dead on the field and his heirs were already squabbling over the spoils.  No one had time for the dying."

Jame remembered Tori the previous autumn, wandering alone through the bloody shambles at the Cataracts, drawn by his Shanir power (if only he realized it) to those bound to him who lay mortally wounded, bringing them honorable release with a white-hilted suicide knife.  A true lord cared for his own—in life, in death.

"There was so much loss, and confusion, and pain."  Harn leaned forward, elbows on knees, big hands tightly clasped, fresh injuries forgotten for old.  He spoke to the ashes as if to those distant dead, as if still trying to understand.  "I was there.  I saw it all, until the Highlord's madness took me, and then—ancestors only know what I did, and to whom.  We fought our own kind, you know, Kencyr against Kencyr, the Host against our own kindred hired out as mercenaries to the Seven Kings.  It was…terrible."

"And Bear?"

"His younger brother found him on the third day, under a pile of the slain.  Oh, he was strong, was Bear, to have lived that long with blood and brains leaking onto ground already too sodden to drink in any more.  At first we thought he was dead and put him on the pyre, but then he moved in the flames and we pulled him out.  Better if we had let him burn alive.  However, his brother wouldn't let him go.  After all, our kind have recovered from worse and so did he—in body, at least.  In mind—well, you saw.  The new lord of his house didn't want him shambling around his precious keep, so the college took him in.  After all, he was…is…one of us.  For awhile, he even taught the Arrin-thar."

"The what?"

"A rare, armed combat discipline, based on clawed gauntlets.  Originally, only Shanir like Bear practiced it.  You saw his hands."

Jame folded her own into Harn's jacket.  She had completely forgotten about them while tending to his injuries.  Her gloves were with the rest of her clothes beside the tub.

"*There are many Shanir here,*" the Randir had said.

Highborn Shanir like her cousin Kindrie were often sent off to the Priest's College at Wilden—in a sense, thrown away.  It occurred to her now that Tentir would be a logical place for Kendar Shanir to gather.

"Are there other Shanir-based fighting skills, ran?"

"Many, but seldom practiced.  Most Highborn don't approve of them."

That made sense.  Given the disaster of the Fall and the Shanir role in it, Tori was hardly alone in his hatred of the Old Blood.  Most lords didn't even know that they were Shanir.  All must be, however, in order to bind Kendar to them.  The greater their power, the larger their house, except that some like Caldane added the Kendar bound to their established sons. In the old days, these new lords would have gone off to set up their own minor houses as the Min-drear had, often near the Barrier. Now, however, all nine major houses held their people close, at the most sending them out as mercenaries to support those at home here in the barren Riverland.

"But why is Bear caged, ran? To be forced to live like that, even to spread rumors of a monster to keep cadets away... It's cruel. It's intolerable."

Harn rounded on her, so fiercely that she shrank back into her chair. "Don't you think we know that? He was confined because he mauled a cadet to death. Never mind that the fool had been taunting him all winter, as we found out later."

He paused and gulped. "I...ripped the arm off someone once myself. One of Caldane's cousins. In a berserker fit. Because he taunted me. Blackie had moved north to the Highlord's seat by then. With him nearby, I can control myself. Without him... I would have used the White Knife, but Blackie forbade it and sent me instead to Tentir as commandant. That's why I set up quarters here, to protect the rest of the college."

He shook himself. "Anyway, seclusion turned Bear even more savage. Somewhere in that broken head, he knows who he is and what honor is due him. We all know it. But what can we do? He can't be allowed to roam free, to savage the next cadet stupid enough to make fun of him. We gave him a White Knife. He picked his toenails with it. Some would poison his food or rush him with spears like a cornered boar, but God curse anyone who takes the life of such a man without a fair fight."

He beat the chair's arm again in time to his words, making Jame flinch: "We don't know what to do."

Jame had no idea either, but she was going to think about it.

"Tell me why the Randir hate the Knorth."

The question jolted him from his personal nightmare and re-minded him to whom he spoke. "That's Tentir business."

"So, presumably, is Bear. That didn't stop the Randir from trying to feed me to him."

He looked hard at her. "You aren't going away, are you? You should. This making you lordan is madness. Blackie won't hold to it. He can't. One way or the other, it will destroy him."

Jame considered this. "It might. I'm not stupid, ran, nor am I some willful, spoiled brat hell-bent on playing soldier. You know that. You've watched me fight. I was blooded long before Brier Iron-thorn made me a present of my own front tooth, or M'lady Kallystine gave me this." She almost touched the scar on her cheek, but remembered in time to keep her hands hidden.

The burly randon regarded her with amusement. "How long ago, then, child?"

Jame frowned, thinking. "Honestly, I don't remember. It feels as if I was born blooded, but then so is everyone. The point is, what I don't know, I will learn, whatever it costs. The one thing I can't afford is ignorance. So, tonight I become a cadet. Tell me what I need to survive until then."

He gave an explosive snort of laughter. "I think you'll survive us all. Whether we survive you is another matter. All right. When your father Ganth was a cadet here, he was present at the death of a Randir named Roane—a cousin and favorite of the Witch of Wilden, as it turned out."

Jame remembered the stain on the floor of the Knorth apartment. "Was this in Greshan's quarters?"

"It was." Harn looked at her under craggy, lowered brows. "What have you heard?"

"Nothing." In fact, she was surprised. How did this tie into anything that had happened since?

"Mind you, your father and I were nearly the same age, but I came to Tentir the year after he left, at the same time as Sheth Sharptongue. From what I heard, though, Greshan summoned Ganth to his quarters in the middle of the night. Roane was there. He and the lordan had been drinking. Greshan was his father's darling, but...well, as a Highlord, he would have been a disaster."

"Worse than Ganth Gray Lord?"

She heard the bitterness in her voice. After all, they were discussing the man who had led his people to disaster in the White Hills and later had driven his only daughter out into the Haunted Lands to seek whatever protection she could find, even in Perimal Darkling, even in the Master's House itself.

But Harn was shaking his massive head. "It isn't that simple. Nothing ever is that really matters. Parents, children, family...and we're talking about a boy here, younger than you are now. I met

Ganth Grayling once at Gothregor, before his brief career at Tentir. His lord father Gerraint treated him like shit. Called him a liar in front of us all, although we never knew why, while that damned Greshan stood by smirking. Ganth slunk off like a whipped puppy."

Jame stared. To her, Ganth Graylord had always been a monster. She could barely conceive of him as a helpless boy younger than herself, despised by his own father.

"What happened in the lordan's quarters?"

"No one knows exactly. When the randon broke in, Roane was dead, Greshan was fouling himself in a corner, and Roane's servant was floundering around on fire. Also, for some reason, Ganth was stark naked."

Jame caught her breath, remembering her foul dream, that first night at Tentir, when the Knorth lordan had suggested calling "Dear little Gangrene" up to his apartment for some "midnight games" to impress his Randir friend. Only she had been the lordan, inside Greshan's dirty coat, inside his stinking skin. The thought made her want to crawl back into the bath and shrub herself raw to remove even the memory of that tainted touch.

"Anyway," Harn was saying, "Ganth put on some clothes and walked out of Tentir without a word to anyone. That was the end of him as a randon. A year later, Gerraint and Greshan were both dead, and Ganth was Highlord."

"Trinity. Does Tori know all this?"

"Not about Roane. That secret belongs to Tentir and Blackie doesn't. Ardeth did him no service in forbidding him to train here."

"But the randon respect him, and he loves them. He said once that the Southern Host was his true family."

"Yes. In a sense we raised him and he's done us proud. We haven't had such a decent, competent Highlord in a long time—not that those are necessarily the qualities that we need just now. These are perilous times. To survive, should we side with the just or with the powerful? Well, I made my choice when I put my hands between his in this very room and swore to follow him to the death. It's life that scares me. We totter on a knife's edge. In these treacherous times, where does honor lie?"

Jame listened, a chill running up her spine. She had thought it was only her own weakness that made her doubt, but here was one of the foremost randon of his age asking the same questions.

"You've sworn loyalty to Torisen Black Lord. Don't you trust him to recognize honor when he sees it?"

"Yes. But he still isn't one of us."

*Poor Tori*, Jame thought.

It had occurred to her before that her brother must feel nearly as rootless here in the Riverland as she did, neither of them having grown up in the heart of the Kencyrath. Still, she had envied him his link with the randon of the Southern Host. Now it seemed that that might not be as strong as she had supposed, lacking the Tentir bond, and here he was giving her this precious chance which he himself had been denied...if she lived to take advantage of it.

"Are the Randir going to keep attacking me?"

"They mean all Knorth ill. Never forget that." He scratched his stubbly chin thoughtfully, with an audible rasp. "A strange house, the Randir. Secrets within secrets. Of course, it doesn't help that the Witch has chased out their natural lord and set her son in his place, which is enough in itself to set up some fierce cross-currents."

"How did that happen, anyway?"

"I dunno for sure. The old Randir lord died, and Rawneth put a contract with the Shadow Assassins on his heir, Randiroc. Your father Ganth was to have sorted out that mess, but then came the massacre of the Knorth ladies and the White Hills. With no highlord in power to stop her, Rawneth did as she pleased."

*Another piece of the puzzle*, thought Jame, *if only I knew where to place it.*

"A strange house it was then," Harn was saying, "and stranger still it's become. Some Randir never use their true name unless among themselves. Some don't seem to have names at all outside their own house."

"Like the Randir Tempter?"

"That one." He growled, almost like Bear. If he had had claws, he would have flexed them. "Aye."

"In the hall, during the rope test, she said that I had hurt her cousin. I don't know whom she meant."

"Huh. Roane, perhaps, if she was speaking to you as a Knorth. On the other hand, the Randir tend to call all their blood-kin 'cousin.'" He shook himself. "At any rate, those here won't have so free a hand once you're an acknowledged cadet. Randon discipline tries to transcend house politics, not that it isn't getting harder and harder with lords like Caldane stirring the pot. You watch out for that Gorbel too, girl."

"That's another thing, ran. Why Gorbel? He isn't one of Caldane's established sons, is he?"

Harn gave a snort of laughter. "I'd like to see any of that lot try to fit in here. I hear Grondin is so fat that he has to be moved around his own house in a wheel-barrel, and the rest are too old. I don't know this Gorbel, but he's probably the son closest to cadet quality that Caldane could dig up and, for his pains, he gets the title 'lordan' slapped on him, not that he's apt to keep it long. He's only here because you are, as long and probably no longer. I'm not saying the boy is smart enough to cause true mischief, but he's bound to try."

"I'll be careful, ran. At least it's only for a year."

He snorted again. "One year? Try three, if you do well, and not all will be spent here under the protection of the college. You really don't know what you're getting into, do you?"

"Er...apparently not. I seldom do. And Tori didn't have time to explain much. What happens after Tentir?"

"That will depend on your final ranking, assuming you survive the autumn and spring culls. Some people have to repeat Tentir as novice cadets. That's what you'll become tonight. You get two tries. Do better, and they send you out into the field—to the Southern Host at Kothifir if you're lucky, or as an honor guard attached to the Women's Halls at Gothregor. Some third year master cadets come back here to teach and to learn advanced techniques. Some finish up with their house's randon, wherever their lord sends them. One way or another, all have to prove themselves to the Randon Council. In the end, maybe one in ten win their collars."

They hadn't noticed as they spoke that the room was falling into shadow. Then from somewhere far below came the peremptory note of a horn.

Harn sprang up, aghast as a tardy schoolboy. "It's beginning, and I'm not even dressed!"

He was, in fact, a good deal more dressed than Jame. She stripped off his coat, threw it at him in passing as if at a distraught bull, and bolted down the stairs in a glimmer of white limbs and black, whipping hair with what was left of her own clothing bundled in her arms. Around the first turn, she ran full tilt into Graykin. They tumbled down the rest of the way together. At the bottom, Jame contrived to land on top.

"I'm dead," Graykin moaned.

"No." She rolled off of him onto her feet and began rapidly sorting through her salvaged clothes, discarding most of them. "With luck, I only broke your back. You deserve it. Spy on anyone else, Gray, but not on me.

"'s not fair. You never tell me anything. Look," he said, doing anything but, struggling to sit up. "They've already started. It's too late. Give up this madness, take up your proper rank, and for God's sake put on some clothes!"

"I'm trying," said Jame, hopping on one foot to pull on a boot. "Highborn I may be, worse luck. However, I am not"—hop—"nor will I ever be"—hop—"a lady. Damn. The wrong foot, or the wrong boot. But I swear, on my honor, I'll be initiated tonight as a cadet if I have to do it wearing nothing but gloves and a surly expression."

Rue appeared, panting, with an armload of clothes. "Why'd you try to lose me?" she demanded of Gray. "Here. Hurry." She thrust the still damp but blessedly clean garments into Jame's arms. The shirt, jacket, and pants—Greshan's, no doubt—were still much too big, but at least the cuffs had been basted up. Reminded, Jame fished in the pocket of her discarded coat, drew out the two scarves, and tossed one to Rue.

Rue caught and stared at the sodden black cloth with its finely worked rathorn crest. "Where d'you find it?"

"Stuffed half way down my throat." Jame knotted her own scarf haphazardly around her neck. "I'll explain later. Damn. Where's my cap?"

Above, they could hear Harn apparently tearing apart his quarters. An anguished cry rolled down the stair: "*Where's my damned shirt?*"

Rue tugged urgently at Jame's sleeve. "God's claws, he's coming. Run!"

Too late. They shrank back as the burly randon blundered past, trying to pull himself together.

Jame started in pursuit, but Rue stopped her.

"He'll be going to join the officers by the front door. We need to come in with our house by the back." She looked about frantically. "Trinity, don't let us get lost now!"

Jame advanced on her servant. "Graykin..."

"Oh, all right."

With an ill grace, he led them through a maze of halls to an obscure, narrow stair that plunged straight down to the first floor, emerging in the short corridor between Old Tentir and the Randir barracks. Smart and stiff with a sense of occasion, answering the imperious summons of drum and horn, cadets passed the corridor's open end on the boardwalk, wheeled right, then left into the great hall, stepping proudly into their future.

"Coman," Rue breathed with relief. "Next Caineron, Jaran, and then Knorth. The other houses will be entering by the south door. We're in time."

Jame waited, fiddling discontentedly with her loose, wet hair as it tumbled well below her waist like a rain of black, blue-shot silk. It was her only vanity, but she usually kept it up out of the way, under a cap. Wearing it down now made her feel disheveled and vulnerable.

"Let me," said Graykin with irritation, beginning to comb out its heavy fall with nimble fingers. Then he twisted it up into a knot and secured it with thin-bladed knife, almost a spike, produced from somewhere on his person. "Honestly, don't you know any feminine arts?"

"Caineron...Jaran..." Rue was counting down. "Here we come."

Vant appeared, almost strutting, at the head of the Knorth cadets. He started violently as Jame slid in before him, followed by Rue. His ten wavered and fell back as Brier lead her grinning squad to the fore. If there had been room or time, there might have been a serious scuffle, but they were almost to the door and the drumbeat called them insistently on.

Inside, the massed torchlight was almost blinding. Jame stopped dead on the threshold, sure for a moment that the hall was on fire, nearly tripping up all those behind her. She had to advance before her eyes had adjusted and blundered into the rear rank of the Jaran, who fended her off with a ripple of nervous laughter. Here at last was her place, before the blazing western fireplace and under the rathorn banner, parallel to Timmon on her right and the Jaran master-ten on her left, with her house drawn up behind her. The drums in the upper gallery ended with a thunderous flourish and fell silent.

In their wake, one heard only the crackle of fire, the slough of wind through upper windows, and the breathing of nine hundred-odd younglings.

Opposite, by the front door, stood the senior randon in a dark mass. Firelight glinted off their silver collars and caught the weathered, sometimes scar-broken lines of their faces. A few were clearly Highborn, smaller and finer boned than the Kendar, but claiming no precedence over them. Here as at Mount Alban, the Scrollsmen's College, ability outranked both blood and gender: at least a third of the senior randon were women, more than Jame had yet seen at Tentir. None of the latter, however, were Highborn.

*Am I the first, ever, to come here?* she wondered, and was suddenly, profoundly, grateful that she hadn't appeared in her uncle's stinking rags.

The Commandant stepped forward, his mix of blood clearer than ever in the keen lines of his face and in his tall, rangy form. He paced down the hall, his boots clicking on the flagstones in a measured tread. Around the high neck of his austere dress coat he wore a silver collar hung thick with plaques that chimed softly as he moved. So many battles. So much honor.

"Four long days ago," he said, "I welcomed you to Tentir as candidates. Now I do so again as novice cadets. Tonight you join our ranks and receive your scarves in token of the randon collars that you may some day earn. You have passed a time of testing, the first of many. Each day from now on will bring new challenges to surmount or to fail. A year hence, only the best of you will remain."

He regarded the cadets as he passed, as if already further thinning their ranks. It was hard not to cower under that ruthless, winnowing glance.

"As you progress, consider well your goals. This is no easy path to glory. It never has been. We buy our honor with blood, and scars, and pain."

Their eyes were drawn, with his, to the upper walls where the collars of the dead hung, glimmering down on this new, raw muster of children, many of whom had never seen death, much less the horrors of battle.

"Within our ranks, all of us have lost friends, family, beloved. Some we knowingly sent to their deaths and they willingly went, because it was necessary. We remember them always and honor their names. Death can be easier to bear than life. Oh, but it is sometimes hard. Very hard. Expect no soft choices here."

Gorbel yawned. Perhaps it was only nerves on his part, but it made Jame's jaw ache to imitate him. *Ancestors, please, not now!* she thought wildly as the Commandant stopped equidistant from the three Highborn cadets. He seemed now to speak directly to them.

"We randon think of ourselves as a breed apart, an amalgam of all that is best in the Kencyrath. Our ranks transcend politics, or should. Yes, we are loyal to our houses. Fiercely so. But also to each other. Note this and note it well: While you attend this college, it is your home and all within it are your family, wherever you were born, whomever you call 'enemy' outside these walls. Here we are all blood-kin. House and college, cadet and randon, Highborn and Kendar. Honor holds us in balance, but what is honor? Consider that too, as you progress, and remember that you are bound by whatever words you swear in this sacred hall, before your banners and under the insignia of our dead so, on peril of your souls, swear honestly or not at all." He turned, his coat swinging wide. "Officers, administer the oath."

Nine senior randon stepped forth, one from each house, and advanced on their respective body of cadets.

Harn Grip-hard stumped down the hall to the Knorth. He looked as if he had thrown on his dress clothes in the dark and not adjusted them since, which was probably true. The under-shirt was the same that he had worn before, liberally spattered with grease. However, the honors suspended clanking from his massive collar out-numbered even the Commandant's. He stopped in front of Jame.

"Last chance to save yourself, girl."

"Now, ran, when have the Knorth ever showed that much sense?"

He gave a grunt of laughter. "Not in my lifetime, nor my father's before me. Give me your scarf."

She loosened the clumsy knot and handed it to him. He regarded her attempt at needlework with raised brows. "Perhaps better here than in the Women's Halls after all. Now for it. Do you swear to obey the rules of Tentir? To guard its honor as closely as you do your own? To go out and come in, to live or to die, as you are bid? To protect its secrets now and forever, from all and sundry, whatever should befall?"

As he spoke, she heard the murmur of oaths and answers, weaving the fabric of Tentir around her, each house fitting into the pattern, somber Brandan and bright Edirr, subtle Ardeth and gaudy Caineron, rough-spun Kendar and silken Highborn, the oaths like sinews binding all together.

*Now I join this pattern,* she thought, *this tapestry eternally renewed. Finally, the thread of my life will be racked into place, crossing the lives of others and crossed. Finally, I will belong.*

But then she hesitated, frowning. There was a flaw somewhere in that texture of oaths given and received. A snag. Someone was swearing falsely. How could they at such a time when it weakened the whole fabric, or was that the point? This was as bad, as treacherous, as the notched rope, waiting for the first strain to fail. She began seriously to hunt for the fatal flaw, fingering through the different textures with all her Shanir wits. If she could find the source, she knew instinctively that she could destroy it.

*But what if doing so rips an even larger gap?*

She became aware of Harn waiting for her response. Perhaps he thought she was losing her nerve. Behind her, the Knorth cadets stirred restively, waiting to take their oaths with hers. Everyone else had finished.

Jame took a deep breath and swore the strongest oath she could:

"Honor break me, darkness take me, now and forever, so I swear."

The first part she spoke alone into a startled silence. Then came a ragged echo, not just from behind her but also from all down the hall on both sides, and every massive banner shuddered where it hung:

"So I swear"…"So I swear"…"So I swear…"

Jame knew she had struck hard at someone, but whom?

Gorbel stared at her with his mouth agape, no yawn this time. Then he laughed unsteadily and said something that made his cronies snicker.

At the far end of the hall, there was a sudden stir of consternation among the Randir.

"Indeed," said Sheth softly, looking at her. "So swear we all."

Harn blinked. "That," he said, "should do nicely."

As he tied her scarf back on, correctly this time, she took the opportunity to twitch his coat closed over a particularly large grease stain. At least the bandages still wrapped around his knuckles were clean.

"Salute!" came a collective roar from the sargents.

As one, except for Jame, the cadets wheeled to face their house banners.

*Now what?* she thought, belatedly turning, and then flinched as the Randir war cry ripped through the hall, discordant and shaken; but perhaps that was how it was supposed to sound.

The deep, sure note of the Brandan answered it from across the hall. Then the Coman, small and shrill, like their house; the Edirr, in a falcon's jeering shriek; the Danior's gleeful howl; the Jaran, a shouted phrase in High Kens: "The shadows are burning!"; the Ardeth, not loud, but with a swelling under-surge of Shanir power.

*And now for us,* thought Jame.

She took a deep breath, down to the pit of her soul, and let loose with the rathorn war cry.

It began as a scream, high and wild. She could hear each cadet's voice in it, tuning to her own, ripping the air. Rathorns were called "beasts of madness" for their effect on their prey. Their cry was an assault in itself, an incitement to panic. Then it sank to a bone-shaking roar.

Yells of consternation and outrage cut it short as if with a snap of teeth. Jame turned to see that every banner in the hall but her own had fallen, half on top of their assembled companies. Heavy tapestries heaved as indignant cadets fought their way out. Angry randon crowded around the Commandant, brandishing lengths of the banners' cords and crying foul, although clearly they had snapped by themselves, without external tampering.

And all this time that wild cry went on and on, under the floor, under the flagstones. In the subterranean stable, every horse was screaming.

"Truly," said Sheth, regarding Jame over the heads of his furious officers, "we live in interesting times." He clapped his hands. "And now, we feast."

The doors to New Tentir were flung open. Beyond, the training square blazed with light, falling on long tables loaded with food and drink. Roast ox and stag, stuffed stork and crisped carp; mawmenny stew boiled in wine, garnished with almonds; baked pears and apples swimming in caramel sauce. The cadets cheered, as much with relief as joy, and rushed out to drown the taste of fear with ale. Jame and Sheth were left, looking at each other.

"I think," said the Commandant, "that you may have broken the Randir Tempter. At least, they carried her off gagged to stop her raving. A pity, that. I would have liked to hear what she had to say. Nonetheless, if you please, don't make a practice of driving your instructors mad."

"N-no, ran. I'm sorry—I think."

"At the moment, that is all I require of you: think. Now go."

But on the threshold she hesitated, stopped between past and future by the sudden memory of something she had just heard but not immediately recognized. Over the cries of cadets and horses, out in the dark, in the night, a rathorn had answered her.

# Chapter VIII:   A Forgotten Name

## Summer 5

## I

GOTHREGOR'S HERBALIST STOOD over a simmering pot, stirring it. The cream-colored paste was almost ready. From a basket at his elbow, he picked out a large, hairy leaf of comfrey and added it to the mixture, making a face as its spines stung his fingers.

Afternoon light slanted into his workroom through its southern facing windows. It also shone through the pot's stream and the glass bottles arrayed on the sill with their tinctures of iodine, decoctions of agrimony, burdock juice, and spirit of camphor, among a score of others. The Kendar's hands moved through a haze of pale green, rose, and amber light as if he were also mixing them too into his healing art, as perhaps he was.

Outside lay the broad inner ward of the Knorth fortress, with the garrison's barracks in the outer wall to the right. To the left rose the Old Keep. If one craned out the window to look east, far back beyond the Women's Halls loomed the desolation of the Ghost Walks, where the Highlord and his family had lived until assassins had slaughtered all but a handful and the rest had gone into exile with Ganth Gray Lord.

The physician sighed. He himself was a Knorth, as his family had been for generations. It grieved him that so few of his house were left. If...no, when its last two Highborn were gone, what would happen to their people?

A door opened in the wall beside the old keep. From it emerged a lady, followed by a randon guard. From their purposeful angle across the inner ward, they were headed straight for the infirmary.

"Company from the Women's Halls," remarked the herbalist, as if to himself. "I think...yes, they're Ardeth."

From behind him came a stifled exclamation from his waiting patient and a rustle of cloth. Then all was still again.

As he wrapped his apron around his hands and lifted the pot off its tripod, away from the fire beneath, the Highborn entered without knocking. He turned and saluted her respectfully.

"Lady, how may I serve you?"

The Ardeth swept into the cluttered room, black eyes darting about it behind her mask. Because of her tight under skirt, she moved in tiny steps converted by long practice into a smooth glide. However, her full outer skirt brushed against glasses, instruments, and furniture, knocking some over. As she pivoted, the belling garment toppled a chair. This, in turn, snagged the table's floor-length cover and would have pulled it off if the doctor hadn't hastily set the pot on it.

"Guard, tell this Knorth my business."

The randon sargent—a woman, as were all who protected the Women's Halls—returned the herbalist's salute. She would have been more deferential if he had been a Shanir healer or even a surgeon, but still as a soldier she had a healthy respect for anyone connected with the healing arts.

"My lady seeks the Highlord." She regarded the pot of steaming paste and raised an eyebrow, but didn't comment on it. "Matriarch Adiraina wishes to speak to him."

The herbalist bowed. "I will inform my lord when I see him. He has spent the morning searching for a missing Knorth Kendar. That, perhaps, is why you have failed as yet to…er…run him down."

"Perhaps," agreed the sargent. "Lady?"

The Ardeth had made a dart for the door leading to the infirmary. Inside, she bent down and peered under each bed in turn as if she expected to find the Highlord of the Kencyrath hiding beneath one of them. Disappointed, she returned to the workroom. There, the draped surgeon's table caught her eye. As she approached it, however, a low growl stopped her in her tracks and the guard's hand dropped to her sword. The cloth stirred. A sharp muzzle emerged, flat to the ground, followed by a pair of fierce, ice blue eyes set in creamy fur. The wolver pup glared at the two Ardeth and growled again, low in her throat, showing a dark, curled lip and the needles of her white teeth.

"Well!" said the lady. "I thought we had seen the last of these mangy creatures."

With that, she turned on her heel and glided away. The guard saluted, with an amused glance at those defiant, blue eyes, and followed.

The physician began to soak linen bandages in the cooling pot.

After a moment, the table cloth lifted and Torisen Black Lord crawled out from underneath

"The Ardeth matriarch is looking for you, my lord," the Kendar reported dutifully.

Torisen righted the chair and sat down on it. The pup slunk out and crouched warily beneath, making herself as small as possible. The Highborn looked very tired and not a little dusty, with cobwebs adding more strands of white to his dark, ruffled hair. "If Burr asks," he said, with a wry smile, "you can tell him that I've already searched under the surgeon's table."

"And for whom are you searching, my lord?"

Torisen tried to meet the other's sober gaze, and failed. That was the trouble: as in the commons room that first night, he couldn't remember the ruddy-faced Kendar's name. And now the man was missing.

"My lord?" The herbalist was regarding him with concern, probably wondering if, like his father before him, he was coming unhinged.

Was he?

Then with a sick jolt, Torisen remembered why he had come to the infirmary in the first place. Reluctantly, not looking at it, he placed his injured hand on the table.

The herbalist loosened the bandages.

"Well now, that's not so bad," he said, examining the three broken fingers, splinted together to immobilize them.

His tone was so kind, so reassuring, that Torisen looked up sharply. Yes, this man knew his dread of becoming a cripple. Perhaps everyone did. Trinity.

"The swelling has gone down considerably. And this happened...when?"

"About six days ago."

The herbalist reset the splints and began to wrap his hand with paste-soaked cloth. "Another term for comfrey is 'bone-knit,'" he said. "I've heard that some such plants of great potency grew among the white flowers in your great-grandmother Kinzi's Moon Garden, along with many other special herbs; but the way into that place was lost long ago. In another week, barring accidents, you can have your hand back. There."

Torisen blankly regarded the neat, new bandage that imprisoned all but his thumb.

The herbalist turned to straighten his work area. "My lord…" he said over his shoulder.

"Yes?"

"The missing Kendar is named Mullen.   Do you remember who I am?"

He asked it casually, without turning, but tension underlay his voice.

"I do.  Thank you, Kells."

# II

A HUNDRED OTHER Kendar names raced through Torisen's mind as he slipped out by way of the infirmary, the wolver pup following at a wary distance as if afraid he would chase her away. Harn, Burr, Rowan, Winter…no, she was long dead, cut nearly in two by his father's sword…Chen, Laurel, Rose Iron-thorn…

It was nothing, he told himself uneasily, to forget one out of so many. Yes, he was new at this, but surely such things happened all the time. Besides, this Kendar had been in his service less than a year.

The battle at the Cataracts the previous fall had opened gaping holes in the Knorth ranks which many were eager to fill. Torisen wasn't sure why, but he could only bind a certain number before he began to feel a distinct, distracting strain. At the Cataracts, he knew he had over-extended himself. Still, if he could, he would have taken in anybody who asked. One way or another, weren't they all Ganth's victims? However, as Burr had explained to him, the Knorth Kendar kept close track of status and resented any infringement of it, as many did his acceptance of that turn-collar, Brier Iron-thorn.

In their estimate, first came the Exiles, who had disappeared with Ganth into the Haunted Lands and paid for their loyalty with their lives. Of them, only Torisen, his sister and, it was rumored, a priest had survived—how, exactly, remained unclear.

Next were Those-Who-Returned, whom Ganth in his madness had driven back at the high passes of the Ebonbane.

Last came the Oath-breakers, who had chosen to stay with the Host after the White Hills when Ganth had thrown down his name and title. These Kendar had sought and for the most part had found places in other houses, whose ranks had also been thinned by battle. Torisen had heard rumors that some had gone into the Randir and remained there, implacable foes of the house that they believed had betrayed them.

At any rate, by the time Those-Who-Returned had limped back, the Kencyrath had had little room for them except as *yondri-gon*, threshold-dwellers, in whatever house would give them shelter. In token of their fervent hope that the Highlord would one day re-turn, many had branded themselves with the Knorth sigil, the same

highly stylized rathorn head used to mark the Knorth herd. It was
Torisen's goal to reclaim these first, along with their families; but
there were so many. It had been so much easier when he had been
merely the commander of the Southern Host. Then he had been
responsible for some twenty-five thousand lives, but for none of
their souls. Now, two thousand-odd Knorth Kencyr, body *and* soul,
laid claim to him, with many, many more still unredeemed. Sometimes he woke in the middle of the night, unable for a moment to
breathe under the pressure of their need. At such times, floundering
in the dark, he felt like a swimmer dragged down by a multitude of
clutching hands, desperate to cast off every last one of them. Dammit,
he couldn't save everybody.

*Ha. You can't even save yourself, boy.*

But he thought that he had at least rescued the missing Kendar—
a middle-aged Danior *yondri*, he now remembered, One-Who-Had-
Returned. When the man had knelt before him, he had seen the
three wavy scar lines of the Knorth sigil branded on the back of the
man's neck. *This is someone*, he had thought as he accepted those
broad, worn hands between his own, *who knew my father*; and he had
felt embarrassed by the glowing gratitude in that round, red face.
No one should have such power to make or break, power that he
often saw other lords abuse as his father had, power that he didn't
really want.

*Admit it, boy. You're weak and you know it, especially since your sister
returned. She's gelded you, and you never even noticed.*

Sometimes it was hard not to snap back at that voice in his
mind, behind the locked door in his soul.

*Oh yes, father?* he wanted to say. *Was it better to give up, as you did, and
let everything fall apart around you? And if my sister sometimes unnerves me, our
mother unmanned you. Destruction begins with love, you said. Remember?*

But he couldn't say that. Not yet. The image formed in his
mind of the hall of the Haunted Lands' keep where he had grown
up. He was sitting in it still, in the dust and dark, his back hunched
against the voice behind the locked door.

*Just ignore it*, he told himself doggedly. *Father is dead. Sooner or
later, he's got to shut up.*

Of course, not love but duty bound him to the forgotten Kendar.
When he found what's-his-name, he would give him a good tongue-
lashing for neglecting his duty that morning and then reinstate him.

That would show Kendar like Kells how foolish they were to have made such a fuss.

He had been headed for the garrison dormitory, meaning to search it, when a voice ahead stopped him. In the sharp diction of the Coman, a lady was demanding to know where the Highlord might be found.

Torisen turned and bolted for cover.

# III

LATE THAT AFTERNOON, a tired post horse trotted through
the north gate into Gothregor and stopped. Its rider swung stiffly
down, staggering as her feet hit the earth. One leg nearly buckled.
Steward Rowan hung on to the saddle, cursing softly, waiting for the
old injury to release her cramped muscles. She owed those damn
Karnids for more than the scars on her face.

Before her lay the broad, green inner ward, sliding into the
shadow of the western mountains as the sun set behind them. At
this hour, the Knorth garrison should have been settling down for
the night. Instead, small, determined processions crisscrossed the
darkening grass. Each was led by the gliding form of a lady followed, like a goose with her goslings, by a line of masked Highborn
girls and a random guard who brought up the rear. When two such
lines meet, they cut through each other without a word in passing.
Others were threading purposefully through the garrison's barracks,
kitchens, and other domestic offices. A few Knorth Kendar could
be seen whisking furtively in and out of sight, trying to keep out of
the way.

As Rowan stood, staring, she was spotted. A small, plump lady
turned abruptly and came at her as much at a run as her tight underskirt
allowed. Her line of girls—by far the longest and most varied in the
ward—swerved to follow her. Rowan saw as she approached that
it was Karidia, the Coman Matriarch.

She saluted, one hand twisted in her horse's mane both to keep
her balance and to prevent the animal from wandering off in search
of its dinner.

"Matriarch, how may I serve you?"

Karidia glared at her, straining within her tight bodice to regain
her breath. The garment creaked alarmingly. What could be seen
of her face below the mask was bright red. "You can tell me…where
that precious Torisen of yours…is hiding."

"Lady, I just got here. I don't know."

The Coman made a sound of disgust. "You Knorth! Always
misplacing…your Highborn. Trinity! With only two…it shouldn't
be that hard…to keep track of them."

She turned with a haughty toss of her head, but spoiled the effect by tripping over her own full hem and falling flat on her face. The girls squealed. The guard set her back on her feet and off she sailed for all the world like a righted clockwork toy, her exhausted retinue trailing after her.

Rowan sighed.

By now, the stables should have been moved from under the fortress into converted rooms set into the outer wall, opening onto the inner ward. However, given the past week's confusion, no one had had time. Rowan limped down the ramp to the winter stalls, found an empty box and, there being no one on duty to help her, put up the horse herself.

Down the row, she heard restless hooves. When she went to investigate, Storm lunged at her over the top of his open half-door, teeth snapping almost in her face. Then he recognized her and withdrew with a whickered apology.

Rowan found her lord in the neighboring tack-room, sitting on a bale of hay, trying one-handed to mend a broken stirrup leather. She sank down gratefully opposite him and stretched out her sore leg.

"I'm surprised you aren't hiding in Storm's box," she said, rubbing knotted muscles, "or under that nice big pile of manure around the corner."

"I'm keeping the latter in reserve. As for Storm, he'd hold them off all right, but he doesn't like my shadow. There," he added with a jerk of his head, seeing the question in her eyes.

In a dim far corner, now that she looked, Rowan could make out the curled shape of a pup. Blue eyes met hers defiantly over the white brush of a tail.

"Isn't that a wolver? Are Grimly's people still here?"

"No. They left this morning. We thought at first that she'd been left behind by accident, but now I think that she decided, ancestors know why, to stay. At any rate, no one can catch her and she follows me everywhere, just out of reach."

"Odd. How old d'you think she is?"

"I'm guessing about five years. Wolvers live longer than wolves and mature more slowly. Then again, she's from the deep Weald. Things may be different there."

"Yes. A lot more savage. And look at the size of those paws. If she grows into them…"

"She'll be enormous, and a shape-shifter by the time she reaches adolescence, if not before."

They regarded the pup thoughtfully. She glared back at them as is to demand, *So what?*

"Well," said Torisen, with the air of resolutely turning to business, "what news from Tentir? Burr told me about the qualifying tests."

Rowan nodded. "A nasty surprise, that. Usually, such things get sorted out before the cadet candidates arrive." She took a deep breath. "Well, when I left yesterday morning, your sister had one of the lowest scores in her class. Short of a miracle, and with a Caineron commandant in charge..."

"Trinity," said Torisen blankly. "I don't suppose I really expected her to make it through the whole year, but to have failed so quickly...Damn. I thought I would have more time to make alternate plans. This puts us back to where we were last winter."

"Worse. I'd be no friend if I didn't tell you this, Blackie, but now the pressure is really going to be on for either you or your sister to form a contract with another house. True, the hunt going on now for you is a farce. At a guess, the Council of Matriarchs summoned you and you didn't respond fast enough."

"Not the Council," Torisen murmured, still fiddling with the broken strap. Even with two hands, he didn't think it could be fixed: there were too many other weakened patches. "Just Adiraina, trying to get a jump on the game. I suspect it's every matriarch for herself now."

"Huh. Well, it doesn't help that you've picked this of all times to fight with Adric."

"Not that, exactly, but close enough. It had to come some day."

Rowan snorted. "Yes, but *now?* Anyway, in case you haven't noticed, Gothregor is up to its turrets in hunting parties, each with a bevy of prospective consorts in tow. Yes, it's ridiculous, but I know these women. When today's ruckus dies down, they'll settle in for the long chase. And I have to tell you, Blackie, we'll need help getting through next winter. If not from the Ardeth, then where?"

Torisen had been worrying about that too, but now flicked it aside. "One disaster at a time, please."

"All right." Rowan leaned forward, steeling herself. "I do see a way out of at least one mess. Take you sister not as your lordan but—" she paused, with a gulp "—as your consort."

The strap slipped from Torisen's hand. Before it hit the floor, the pup snapped it up and retreated to her corner to gnaw it.

"Well, why not?" Rowan demanded. "If you were twins, it would only be natural. As it is…well, you *are* the last two pure-blooded Knorth. How better to re-establish the line and simultaneously take you both off the…er…market. The Matriarchs might even approve. I've heard rumors that they arranged similar matches in the past, brother to sister, uncle to niece, father to daughter, trying to create the Tyr-ridan."

"Ending up with monsters, more likely."

"Well, yes. Sometimes. Usually. Nonetheless, the basic idea is sound, and some matriarchs still carry far more weight with their lords than you might guess."

"Yes, but…"

The pup's ears pricked and she growled softly. Someone was coming. Storm lunged, only to recoil at a sharp slap to the nose. A Jaran randon appeared at the tack room door.

"So here you are, my lord," she said with a smile and a salute.

They all started at a crash. Storm was trying to kick down the intervening wall. Torisen thumped on it with his good fist.

"Behave! Fair is fair. You've tracked me down, captain, and I owe you for covering my retreat that first night. How may I serve you?"

"M'lady Trishien asks if you can spare her a few minutes. She promises you safe conduct, at least where our people are concerned."

Torisen considered. He rather liked the scholarly Jaran Matriarch and, as far as he knew, none of the hunting parties above were hers. Besides, at some point he had to talk to someone on the Matriarchs' Council besides Adiraina.

"All right." He rose and stretched. "Since my work here seems to have been…er…devoured"—he glanced at the pup—"I am at your command."

Rowan watched them go, the wolver trotting a distance behind. She thought about what she had said concerning Jameth and wondered how many other Knorth Kendar had had the same idea. It might save them all, or the two Highborn in question might kill each other first.

"Just consider it," she muttered at the Highlord's receding back. "We can't go on like this much longer."

# IV

ABOVE THE STABLES lay the subterranean levels of the Women's Halls. As they threaded their way through dark corridors, Torisen thought about what Rowan had suggested. It had practically knocked the breath out of him. He still couldn't quite bring the idea into focus, any more than if someone had told him that the moon had turned backward in its course. Jame was his sister, ten years his junior, a Shanir, his twin...and she was Jame.

Images of her flickered through his mind: the half-feral child with ragged clothes and silver-gray eyes too large for her thin face; the girl on the edge of the Escarpment, crying for a dead darkling changer; the child-woman in the ruins of Kithorn, whistling up the south wind to take them home.

Then, last night, had come that strange dream that they were dancing. How she had moved, with such aching grace. Long, lovely hair had slid through his scarred fingers like black water over fissured rock, and he had hardly known if he wanted to let it glide free or to grip and wrench it out by the roots.

*Let me not see...*

Then the ruddy Kendar had interrupted them to beg that she, not he, remember his name. What business was that of hers?

*Your Shanir twin, boy, your darker half, returned to destroy you...*

No. The bolt was shot, whatever that meant.

# V

THEY REACHED THE Jaran compound without incident and climbed to the matriarch's third story chambers.

At her biding, Torisen entered and stopped short, blinded by the light streaming through the western windows. The forecourt below now lay deep in dusk, but up here the day was still dying.

"Step to the right, my lord."

When he did, the bulk of the old keep mercifully blocked the setting sun and, slowly, his sight returned. The Jaran Matriarch had risen from her writing table near the window to greet him. The lens sown into her mask flashed fire as she returned his salute, but her voice was cool and lightly amused

"Honor be to your halls, my lord. You're a hard man to find. My sister matriarchs have been complaining about it most bitterly."

She resumed her seat, sweeping her full skirt around the chair legs, and picked up her pen. Torisen noted that it had worn a permanent groove in her index finger and that her hands were ingrained with ink spots. He carefully moved a stack of manuscripts to the floor and perched on the window ledge.

"What do you write, my lady?" he asked as she dipped the quill and resumed her flowing, rounded script on the page before her.

"That you look tired, but far better than the last time we meet."

It was hard to remember that that had only been six days ago. So much had happened. "My thanks again, matriarch, for telling me where to find my sister. Without you, I probably still wouldn't know."

She smiled slightly. "Oh, I think Lady Jameth will always, eventually, make herself known. One might more easily conceal an earthquake. I also write that you seem to have acquired a new…er…pet? Dear me. One never quite knows how to refer to a wolver."

She regarded the pup thoughtfully, then extended a hand to her. Torisen held his breath. The pup crept forward, touched the matriarch's fingertips with a cold nose, and immediately retreated.

"Well," said Trishien. "That will do for a start. My greetings to you too, little one. Still, how very odd. Have you bound her to you, my lord?"

"No!"

"Would you know if you had?"

"I'm...not sure. I think so."

"Ah." Torisen wished that he could see the Jaran's eyes more clearly. Glassed over as they were and reflecting the sunset sky, it was impossible to guess her thoughts. "You came into your power late, my lord. We scrollsmen have wondered before now how well you understand it."

"Do you write that too?" Torisen asked, watching the quill move. He spoke more sharply than he had intended.

She might have read his mind; assuredly she did his tone. "My lord, when you assumed your father's seat, you took responsibility for your people and consequently opened wide tracts of your life to them. I speak here of the entire Kencyrath. Of course we discuss you. I am sorry if you find that offensive—and I can see that you do—but you must learn to accept it." Her lips twitched. "I also write that your hair is laced with cobwebs and straw, from which I deduce that you have recently been in a stable...and perhaps under various articles of furniture?"

Torisen relaxed with a wry laugh. "Your sister matriarchs press me hard although not," he added, thinking of the manure pile, "to the last extreme. Yet."

"I think you will find only the Ardeth, the Danior, and the Coman in hot pursuit. Yolindra of the Edirr may also try her hand, if only to tease Karidia. Luckily, the Caineron, Randir, and Brandan matriarchs are not currently in residence at Gothregor, although you may well hear from them."

"I've already heard from the Brandan, but not about my sister. Brant wants to conclude negotiations for my cousin Aerulan, but I don't understand. Aerulan died a long time ago."

Trishien put down her quill. "Thirty-four years ago, my lord, with all the other ladies of your house except for poor Tieri. It's Aerulan's death banner Lord Brandan wants. Before the massacre, he negotiated a contract with your father for her in perpetuity."

"Yes, for a huge sum of money not yet paid, but now he's dead and so is she." He grimaced and rubbed his temple.

"Are you unwell, my lord?"

"Not exactly." Dealing with the Women's World made his head ache. There were always things left unsaid that he was supposed to understand. "I told Brant last winter that he could keep the banner with my blessings. Sweet Trinity, how can I profit from so much grief?"

"I...see." She picked up the pen and resumed writing. "Your generosity does you credit, especially when you need funds so badly. Yes, yes, we all know about that. But here your tact may be misplaced."

There it is again: the unspoken message, this time unmistakably a warning, but he knew from experience that she would tell him nothing more.

Trishien sighed. "This would be so much easier if your house had a matriarch. Have you considered your sister..."

"No!"

"Very well. I will only say that it would be better if you let Lord Brandan pay the dowry in full, but I can see that telling you will do no good. You don't mean to profit from anything your father did if you can help it, beyond claiming his power."

This hit too close for comfort. Veer away.

"You mentioned four houses in pursuit," he said, attempting levity. "What, have the Jaran no taste for the hunt? I seem to remember that you also wanted to see me when I first arrived."

"That was only to tell you that Lord Ardeth has recovered from his illness and is on his way home, although in a fragile state of health. As to the other matter..." Trishien sighed in vexation and rubbed the side of her nose, leaving an ink smudge. "I admit that I am tempted. After all, we have one lady who would suit you very well whom you already like; but she would hardly thank me for interrupting her scholarship."

"You mean Kirien."

He considered the Jaran Lordan with her intelligence, good nature, and dry wit. Yes, if forced to it he could do worse; but no, she would never leave her studies. He wondered how she would find time for them when she came of age and assumed control of her house, if as Highlord he still permitted it. She might prefer that he did not. As Kirien had explained it to him, the entire Jaran had flipped a coin for lordship and she had lost.

"However," said the matriarch, resuming her usual brisk manner, "I did ask you to come in part because of her. Earlier today, Kirien sent this message."

She handed him a paper containing a half dozen lines of Kirien's distinctive, spiky script.

He read quickly. "Jame has passed the tests after all, but since then she has disappeared. Harn is searching for her."

His hands felt cold, his mind an echoing vault. *I endangered my sister when I sent her here last winter without protection. I didn't know. I didn't know. But this time I've done it well aware of the risk she faces. Do I want to see her dead?*

"Your pardon, lady," he said, rising quickly. "I must leave for Tentir at once."

He was half way to the door when she called after him: "Wait!"

Her hand was writing again, but the letters that emerged jagged across the page, interrupting her normal, smooth flow. Kirien was sending another message.

*The Matriarch is a Shanir,* Torisen realized, and despite himself drew back a step. *Perhaps Kirien is one too.* At the same time, another, cooler part of his mind observed, *So that's why Trishien's news is so much more recent than Rowan's, although my steward half killed herself bringing it to me.*

Trishien read what she had written, and smiled. "Ah. The lost is found. Your war-leader Harn has rescued your sister from the bear's den—now what could that be? A metaphor perhaps?—and even now she is accepting her scarf as a cadet from his hands."

The sun set. Cool mountain shadow swept into the room with the first breath of night. Torisen shivered, then wondered why.

*She is slipping out of your control, boy. I said she was too strong for you.*

But Jame was safe…for the minute at least. Surely Harn could keep her out of future trouble.

*And since when, boy, has anyone ever managed to do that?*

A rap on the door made them both start. Outside, Karidia's voice rose over the captain's protests like the shrill yap of a lap dog out for blood: "Trishien, you open this door this minute! I know you're hiding him in there!"

"Oh dear," said Trishien as Torisen looked frantically for another way to out. "I'm afraid there's just the door. And the windows. I *am* sorry."

Plump little fists pounded on the door. "You selfish, glass-eyed, book-loving snob, let me in!"

"The window it is, then," said Torisen, and swung his legs over the sill.

The wall below was thick with ivy, but he was still three stories up, and he only had one good hand. His feet scrabbled for purchase in the tangle of tough vines. Stiff leaves poked him in the eyes. The trick was to step down, secure a foot, then let go and grab a lower handhold, quickly, before gravity pulled him off the wall. Above, the pup leaned out the window yipping with distress. Torisen was about half way down when she launched herself after him. Instinctively, he let go to catch her and they both fell, straight into Burr's arms. The burly Kendar set Torisen on his feet and the pup leaped to the ground.

Trishien laughed down at them. "I do believe that you and Lady Jameth are related after all. Now please excuse me, my lord. Someone is at the door."

"Run," said Torisen to Burr, and followed his own advice.

# VI

THEY STOPPED IN the forecourt, hard against the stone flank of the old keep.

"Trinity," said Torisen, laughing, holding a stitch in his side. "I'll never regard a stag hunt the same way again." Then he saw Burr's expression. "What's the matter?"

"My lord, Steward Rowan has found the Kendar Mullen."

His formality set Torisen back. "Found who? Oh. Of course. Where?"

"In the death banner hall."

They were almost at its door. Torisen hesitated a moment, his hand on the latch, then entered, followed by Burr. They left the pup, forgotten and rigid, on the threshold.

The hall took up the old keep's first floor, a low-ceilinged, unfurnished, windowless chamber. A torch set in a bracket by the door brought flickers of false life to the gallery of faces crowding the walls. There hung the Knorth dead. Most were Highborn with the family's sharp, proud features, not a few of them betraying the mad twist that ran also through the Knorth blood. These were portrait banners, but also sometimes caricatures; in death if not in life, all Highborn faced the judgment of those over whom they had had power. Also among their serried ranks were a few Kendar, mostly noted randon, scrollsmen, or artisans. Every banner was woven out of threads unraveled from the clothes in which each, man, woman, or child, had died. The air stank of cold stone and old, moldering cloth, laced with the unexpected reek of fresh blood.

Rowan sat in the middle of the floor, cradling the head of a missing Kendar. When she looked up, her scarred face, never expressive, seemed less animate than the dead that surrounded her.

"I looked here first, my lord, and found him."

Torisen knelt beside her. It took a moment to realize what he was seeing.

The Kendar's broad face was relatively unmarked, but whatever ruddy color it still possessed now came from torchlight alone. Below that, the broad chest and gnarled arms seemed to hang in dark, clotted tatters, as if he had started cutting the wavy lines of the rathorn sigil into his clothes and gone on to the skin beneath, slicing deeper and deeper except where old battle scars had turned aside the blade. Much of the blood had long since dried. Some still welled in sluggish surges from his throat, where the white hilted knife had at last cut too deep. The blood in which Torisen knelt was still warm. He could feel it seeping through his clothes.

The man was still breathing, but just barely. His eyes half opened like those of a tired child reluctant to wake. Then he saw who bent over him and smiled.

"My lord."

Torisen gripped the Kendar's worn hand. "Mullen. Welcome home."

The smile remained, but the eyes lost their focus and no breath returned.

Torisen sat back on his heels, feeling dazed. He stared at the pattern of blood, fresh and dried, spread out around him in a pool, then running dark into the flagstone's cracks. "This took time."

"Probably most of the day," Rowan agreed. She regarded her lord steadily. He could also feel Burr's eyes on him, and a weight as if all his dead ancestors lining the walls also watched in judgment.

"You want me to understand," he said to them all, "but I don't. Why here? Why like this?"

"D'you mean why'd he turn himself into the raw material of a death banner?" Burr asked gruffly. "To be remembered, of course, and what better place for it than this?"

"My lord…Blackie…" Rowan spoke gently, as if to a slow-witted child. "Did you have any sense that this was happening?"

"Of course not!"

"You would have if he had been one of your people dying at the Cataracts."

Torisen started to answer, then stopped. He remembered that restless and, to him, inexplicable urge that had driven him out after the battle to search through the carnage for the mortally wounded of his house, to bring them honorable death and release from pain by the white-hilted knife.

"Are you saying that he did this, and took so long about it, hoping that I would come to find him?" He looked from one impassive face to the other, appalled. "Trinity! You know I didn't cast him off on purpose!"

"We know," said Rowan. "You just forgot his name, and the bond broke. But you did remember him in the end." She paused, then asked carefully, "Will it happen again?"

Torisen rose, greatly perturbed. He started to run a hand through his hair, then stopped, seeing that it was still wet with Mullen's blood. "I don't know. I don't know why it happened this time, unless I took too many new Kendar into my service at the Cataracts and just couldn't hold on to them all."

But there was more to it than that. They all sensed it, without knowing what it was, much less what to do about it.

*Ha, boy. I told you: you're weak.*

Torisen looked from Burr to Rowan and back again. After everything the three of them had been through together, over nearly two decades, they trusted each other with their lives, their souls, and their honor. But then so did every Kendar sworn to him. Where was the flaw that had let this man slip away?

*Didn't you abandon me, your father and lord, to my death? For that I died cursing you. Lack-faith, oath-breaker, do you wonder that your title rings false and your people fall away?*

Words echoed in the hollow shell of his soul, and he still couldn't turn to answer them. The dead watched, their judgment hanging over him like the blade Kin-Slayer, bane of the unworthy.

*I must find my own way*, he thought, steeling himself. *For my people's sake if not for my own. The old times have passed, but not honor.*

"I swear to you," he said, swinging around to address all the watching faces, alive and dead, "I will find out why this happened and I will never let it happen again. My word on it."

A shiver went through the hall, as if all in it had been holding their breath.

"What of this man?" Rowan asked, Mullen still limp in her arms.

"He deserves to be remembered, as he wished. Let his body be given to the pyre and his clothes to the artisans, that his banner may hang here forever with his peers."

*Noble words*, Torisen thought as he watched Burr and Rowan gather up the corpse. With his broken hand, he couldn't help even if they had let him, nor would it have been his place to do so. Mullen had passed into the care of his own people. Noble words indeed, but with a muffled echo in this place of the dead that chilled his

heart.  If he couldn't make them good, the Third Face of God,
Regonereth, would have precious little mercy on his soul.

*Nor you either*, he thought. *My sister. My nemesis.*

On the threshold, the wolver pup threw back her head and
howled against the coming of the night.

# Chapter IX:  School Days

## Summer 6-32

## I

AND SO RANDON training began at Tentir.

After the first testing, roughly a thousand cadets were left at the college—still too many, but more were expected to fail prey to the autumn cull.  As expected, the Caineron had lost the most candidates in the first few days, but with Lord Caldane's eight established sons adding their numbers of sworn Kendar to his, they were still the largest contingent at the college.  Following them in numbers were the Ardeth, the Randir, and the Brandan, all houses with Kendar bound to more than one Highborn.  Lord Hollen's little Danior could only muster three ten-commands.  The Knorth mustered nine, just shy of a one-hundred command.

For the most part, school days followed the pattern established in the testing.  The horn usually sounded at dawn, although sometimes earlier to surprise those who still depended too much on *dwar* sleep.  Following breakfast and assembly, there were four two-hour lessons—half before lunch, half after—then a free period, then supper.  Evenings were spent studying, mending gear, or attending to other house business.

Sometimes, after a particularly dismal lesson or because an instructor had had an especially bad day, a ten-command was obliged to repeat a class far into the night.

Often, depending on the season, cadets were called on to perform one of the thousand or so chores that the college needed done to function properly.

Every seventh day they were free to do whatever they pleased.

While each house ate and slept in its own hall, cadets continued to train together, two different ten-commands at a time under whatever randon or sargent was best suited to teach them.  In this way, the college hoped to forge bonds between houses that even their lords could not easily break.  Whether this stratagem would work or, indeed, ever had, was a subject of perennial debate in the officers' mess.

To Jame's relief, most of the classes began with reviews of the basics—to correct bad habits, the randon said, and they found much to criticize. However, she had no habits whatsoever in many disciplines and so was glad for the chance to learn whatever she could, as well as to regain the physical edge that a winter in the Women's Halls had badly dulled. It was hard, muscle-aching work, but she enjoyed it.

The situation in the Knorth barracks was less to her taste.

From the start, Vant barely consulted her in the running of her own house. He assumed she knew nothing about such matters, which was true, and proceeded to arrange things to suit himself. For the most part, Jame couldn't fault his competence. For example, it would never have occurred to her to detail cadets to guard the doors to the inner, common corridor when they stood open. Like any other house the Knorth could always gain access to either half of their first story by going up the stairs to the second floor landing (which straddled the corridor) and descending on the other side, but it was considered rude to seal off the barracks during the day and positively hostile to obstruct the corridor itself, as any house could by closing the great gates at either end of their section.

Other house duties included cooking, cleaning, and serving at table, done by rotation. Unlike the Caineron or the Ardeth, the Knorth had no Kendar servants, its lord having none to spare. Whatever needed to be done, the cadets had to do.

And then there was house discipline.

Vant could assign individuals or whole ten-commands such necessary but unpleasant chores as mucking out the Knorth stables, de-worming the hunting pack, and unclogging the kitchen well after a seething of eels set up residence in it.

The boot-polishing incident turned out to be the first of many for Jame's ten. Vant was always finding fault with one or another of them, for example when Erim tripped over his own feet and more or less threw a bowl of soup in Vant's face (Jame wondered about that: Erim might be clumsy, but he had very good aim), or when Niall, Kest's replacement, woke the whole barracks by screaming in his sleep.

Her own ten didn't want Jame involved in the punishments earned by these mishaps.

"Don't you come with us, lady," Rue insisted as the ten-com-mand geared up during what should have been their free time to tackle a trog-infested latrine. "He's got it in for Five, sure, but he's also trying to get at you. He thinks if he makes things nasty enough, you'll give up and leave." She laughed. "Doesn't know you yet, does he?"

He knew her well enough to have put her in a fix, thought Jame glumly, watching her ten go. Whether she went with them or not, should she submit without comment to Vant's unfair punishments and look weak, or complain and look petulant, or pull rank and tell him to lay off them altogether? Being a master ten was awkward to begin with, not (presumably) like being a one-hundred commander with clear-cut lines of authority. If she hadn't come to Tentir as a lordan, Brier would be master now and Vant her second in command. Brier would know how to run the barracks. Jame didn't. If this was another test, to see how each master ten handled his or her house, she was failing miserably.

As it happened, that afternoon she couldn't have gone with them anyway. At breakfast, a sargent had arrived and called out a dozen names including Jame's with orders to report to various randon after classes. A bit nonplused (after all what had she ever had to do with birds?), Jame went off in search of the Falconer.

The mews occupied a long second story room in Old Tentir, overlooking the inner square. Half the windows were screened with oiled cloth to keep out drafts. Rank after rank of goshawks, peregrines, gyrfalcons and eagle owls rustled on their perches in the subdued light, the bells tied to their legs ringing softly. Their hooded heads jerking toward the door as Jame paused on the threshold, waiting for her eyes to adjust.

"Well, come in, come in!" a shrill voice called from the other end of the room. "D'you think we have all day?"

The far window was uncurtained. A misshapen figure stood black against it in a shaft of light smoky with dust. This half of the room seemed as messy as the other half was obsessively neat. As Jame made her way forward, stumbling over debris and colliding with work tables, she saw that a dozen cadets from various houses had arrived before her and were perched precariously on stools around the cold fireplace, watching her progress. She found an empty stool off to one side. It rocked under her on uneven, rickety legs.

The Falconer had spoken to her as sharply as to any tardy cadet. He must not know who she was. Good.

"Right," he said as she gingerly settled. "We were discussing how bonds form between Kencyr and animal."

Jame felt her tension ease. She had worried how Tentir would regard someone so clearly aligned with the Third Face of God, That-Which-Destroys, especially given the chaos her house had already caused along those lines. However, of all her Shanir traits, this surely was the one least apt to get her into trouble.

Seen momentarily in profile, the Falconer's hooked nose looked like a beak, and there was something strange about his eyes. His apparent hunchback consisted of a small, alert merlin and the padded shoulder that served as its perch. As the bird's head jerked to and fro, so did its master's.

"A select few," he was saying, "have always had this ability. Perhaps we all did, in the beginning, but lost it with the thinning of the Old Blood. You, sirrah!"

A Danior cadet straightened abruptly on his stool, nearly falling off of it.

"How did you and that beast come to be bound?"

Squinting against the light, Jame saw that the great, sprawling mass at the cadet's feet was alive. It raised a massive head, yawned with cavernous, nearly toothless jaws, and went back to sleep.

"W-we were born on the same day," the boy stammered, "and b-both our mothers died. The old lord valued his Molocar as much as his Kendar. Torvo and I were suckled by the same wet nurse."

That meant the hound was fifteen or sixteen years old, a great age for his breed. He began to snore in great, gusty sighs, with an unnerving catch between breaths.

"We've been together forever," said the boy, bending to stroke the gray muzzle.

"Well, now," said the Falconer, not unkindly. "You have the talent. There will be others."

"It won't be the same!"

"No. Alas, that we should outlive so many of those whom we love."

He ruffled the breast feathers of his pretty little merlin. The bird raised its tail and squirted a white stream of excrement out the window. Someone below cursed.

"And you, boy?"

The cadet addressed didn't answer, didn't seem to have heard. His dreamy face was turned toward the window, eyes unfocussed. The Falconer stalked over and slapped him. He came back to life slowly, like a sleeper waking, and sat there stupidly rubbing his cheek.

"Cast your mind after your companion, yes, but, never, ever, lose yourself! All of you, take note: some of us never come back.

"And you, girl?"

The Randir cadet whom he had addressed scowled sullenly at the floor. Like many of her house with some Highborn blood, she had thin, sharp features and hooded eyes. "I don't know what you mean, ran. I don't even know why I'm here wasting my time…and yours."

"The answer is up your sleeve." He whistled, a sweet, wavering sound that made the hound twitch in his sleep. "Ah. Here it comes."

The Randir's jacket bulged and rippled as if with new, strangely placed muscles. Something golden flowed out of her sleeve onto her lap. There it collected itself in thick, molten coils and raised a triangular head with glittering orange eyes. At its soft hiss, the others drew back and the merlin bated, screaming.

"It's a gilded swamp adder!" someone exclaimed.

Jame liked snakes, and this one fascinated her, being at once so beautiful and so grotesque. She leaned forward for a better look.

"Is it blood-bound to you?" she asked, genuinely curious.

Randir and serpent both hissed. The wicked little head wove back and forth, black tongue flickering.

Jame withdrew hastily.

"You Randir have odd tastes," the Falconer said dryly.

"It was a gift from my mistress."

"Dear Lady Rawneth. That explains everything. And you, girl? Where's that ounce of yours?"

He *did* know who she was. "Back in the Knorth quarters, ran."

"Sure of that, are you, or only guessing?"

Jame reached out to Jorin's senses. As a rule, he used hers much more easily than she did his.

"Well?" the Falconer demanded. "What d'you see?"

"Nothing, ran."

Or rather, only memory: she was on a ropewalk between Tai-tastigon's inner and outer walls. Below her, a man carried a wriggling sack. He threw it into the water.

...close, wet, and all those other weighted, pathetic sacks bobbing lifeless in the current...

She gulped, swallowing the sense of something so precious, so nearly lost forever.

"He's a Royal Gold," she heard herself say. "Extremely valuable, if sound, but Jorin has been blind since birth. His breeder ordered him to be destroyed. He was drowning when we bonded and I rescued him. Now I am his eyes and, sometimes, he is my nose."

"Ah," said the Falconer. "A spontaneous bond, and not one by blood. Interesting. Those in distress must be particularly vulnerable to you. Be careful whom you touch, and when."

*Too late for Graykin,* thought Jame, not that he seemed to mind except when she failed to live up to his grand expectations.

"And you, boy?"

He spoke to the shadows behind Jame. She had been aware for some time of the buzz of flies but had assumed that they were attracted to some bit of food left out too long in the general mess. Now, turning, she saw a Coman cadet hunched in the corner, surrounded by a blur of wings.

"It isn't always flies, ran," he said, with a lop-sided smile. "Sometimes it's wasps or moths or jewel-jaws. They don't bother me—much—because they never land, but they don't tell me anything either."

Jame reflected that insects seldom bothered her either, which was fortunate. The last thing she needed was a swarm of bloodbound mosquitoes.

"Hmm," said the Falconer, tapping his yellow teeth with a dirty fingernail. "You should talk to Randiroc, the next time he swings by. Then again, he doesn't talk much to anyone."

The name stirred Jame's memory. She sat up straight. "The missing Randir Heir?"

A stool crashed over. The Randir cadet had sprung to her feet. "There is no 'missing heir,' only a hunted renegade and traitor to his house!"

Jame recoiled, not so much at the finger thrust almost in her face as at the sinuous, golden form gliding down the other's arm toward her. Her stool broke. She turned a backward fall into a roll, fetching up on her feet in the corner with the Coman cadet. For a moment, she was surrounded by a sizzle of tiny wings.

Then the swarm launched itself at the Randir.

The latter backed away, flailing, tripped over the supine hound, and crashed into the Falconer.

Snake and merlin went up, the former inadvertently flung into the air, the latter launching itself after it. The bird caught the serpent behind its wicked little head and shot out the window clutching it.

Half the hooded hawks screamed and leaped to follow, but their jesses stopped them short in midair, leaving them to swing upside down from their perches, wings bating and beaks angrily panting.

The Randir lurched to her feet and fled the mews, pursued by a furious cloud of flies.

"Well!" said the Falconer as some cadets hauled him to his feet while the others rushed to help the frantic birds before they injured themselves. "At least we've discovered one thing your talent is good for, boy. Myself, I wouldn't care to be your enemy."

In the process of brushing him off, Jame saw his eyes clearly for the first time, or rather didn't: the sockets were sunken and the lids were sealed shut over them with tiny, neat stitches.

He groped for a chair and sat down. "Well, well, well. That's quite enough excitement for today. Come back next week and we will continue."

# II

IT HAD BEEN a short session.

When Jame emerged from Old Tentir, a Jaran and an Edirr ten-command were still practicing swordplay on horse back in the training square. Timmon leaned on the rail before his compound, watching as if the display were being staged purely for his amusement.

He greeted Jame with a smile and a jerk of his chin toward second story window of the mews.

"Did you have fun up there? First a hawk with a snake in its beak and then a Randir with a ball of flies for a head. She half-drowned herself in the water trough getting rid of them."

"I think," said Jame ruefully, "that I've made another enemy. Why aren't you in class?"

"Oh, I didn't feel like hammering nails."

From behind them within the Ardeth quarters came the ruckus of reconstruction, where Timmon's ten-command (minus Timmon) was apparently being kept busy.

"I wish they'd finish," he said. "We haven't had a hot meal since you dropped the dining room into the kitchen."

"Sorry about that, but it wasn't entirely my fault. I mean, buildings don't necessarily fall down or burn up whenever I walk into them."

"Only on special occasions, I suppose. Speaking of which, have you ordered that gaping hole in your barracks' roof to be repaired yet?"

Jame grimaced. There it was again: the question of command, when she didn't even like telling Rue to clean her boots. Of course, Rue did it anyway, with the air of helping the helpless.

"I like to sleep under the open sky."

Timmon shot her a grin. "I was teasing. As the senior Knorth randon, Harn Grip-hard should tend to any structural repairs, now that he's decided to stay on for the term as an instructor."

"Is Harn also the Knorth one-hundred commander?" she asked hopefully.

"No, silly. In the barracks you are, in all but name, as I am in mine—although," he added with a note of complacence, "the Ardeth have twice as many cadets as you do. No, Harn Grip-hard will only intervene there if you make a real mess of things."

So it *was* a test of sorts. Damn, blast, and hell.

"Seriously, Timmon, how do you handle being a master ten?"

"Oh, I leave it all to my second ten-commander, of course. So does Gorbel, from what I hear. Why should we lordan be bothered with such mundane trifles?"

"Because we're training to become randon officers and the heads of our respective houses?"

Timmon laughed. "D'you really think the three of us will ever assume lordship? Gorbel is only at Tentir because you are. Why you're here, ancestors only know. I came because I enjoy sports and, frankly, to please my mother, who has ambitions for me. I may have older half-brothers, you see, but my parents were half-siblings, which counts for a lot in our house." He grinned. "Are you shocked? In the Knorth, don't twins often mate?"

"Not since Gerridon and Jamethiel Dream-weaver."

*And if the High Council knew that Tori and I are twins*, she thought uneasily, *what then? Would they throw us together or make sure that we never met again? Between them, the Master and the Dream-weaver bred the Fall. Between us, what might Tori and I produce?*

"Don't you have any ambitions of your own?" she asked Timmon.

"To enjoy myself, mainly. I wouldn't mind commanding the Southern Host as my father did, provided my staff did all the work. He was a great man, my father. But lordship sounds too much like hard work. Let cousin Dari have it if he wants it. Grandfather will probably live forever anyway, so why fret."

Before them, two horses collided and their riders tumbled, laughing, onto the ground. Jame flinched, then wondered why. The fall was nothing, given their training. What was it about horses in general that set her teeth on edge? Granted, her encounter last fall with the rathorn mare and her death's-head colt hadn't helped, but this—call it what it was: fear—predated that. Forgotten events still lurked like assassins in the shadowy pockets of her childhood. The ghost of one now rose—something about a dark gray stallion stained black with sweat and flecked with white foam...

She remembered. It had been her father's warhorse Iron-jaw, the one that had turned into a haunt. The changer Keral had threatened to feed her to it.

Timmon was looking at her sideways.

"I have to ask: why *are* you at Tentir? What do you want?"

"A place to belong, I suppose. You wouldn't understand. Half of the time, I don't either."

"What a strange way to live. Don't you miss the Women's Halls?"

"No!"

He laughed. "I've heard something about your adventures there. No doubt they don't miss you either. My mother says Highborn girls often go through a hoyden stage. Obviously, you reached it later than most. You ran wild too long, she says, like a filly that's never been broken to ride. Someday, though, you'll settle down and realize what you really want."

"And what, pray, is that?"

"Why, what any woman wants: a good man, of course, or maybe several of them, preferably one at a time."

Jame grinned, showing the half-filled gap in her front teeth. Brier had been right both about the timing of regrowth and about the teething itch. "Like you? Like your grandfather, who worships tradition? Like Caineron, whose only god is power? Like Tori, who can't face who or what he is? The best man I know is a seven foot tall, ninety-five year old Kendar named Marcarn whom, ancestors know, I miss with all my heart."

"You," said Timmon, "are adorable. And more than a bit peculiar. I'd like to see you properly dressed or, better yet, undressed. We could have pleasant times together, you and I."

He wound a loose strand of her hair around his finger, using the excuse to trace the curve of her neck. Jame shivered and drew away.

"You'd only be disappointed," she said over her shoulder, turning to leave. "I've often been mistaken for a boy."

His voice, gay with laughter, followed her: "Now, where's the fun in that?"

# III

THE DAYS PASSED, edging toward midsummer.  Up and down the Riverland, the bad-tempered black cattle had been driven up into the mountain pastures to graze and the long horned sheep with them, shorn of their thick fleece.  Flax was sown, cherries and strawberries picked.  The apple crop was thinned to make the remaining fruit grow larger and swine feasted on the discards under drooping boughs.  Grass grew thick toward hay-time; called the Minor Harvest, while oats, rye, and wheat ripened in the riverside flood-plains and water meadows for the Major Harvest at summer's end.

So far, so good, reported the Kendar harvest-master.  Despite the previous year's neglect, when the Kencyr Host had marched south to fight the Horde rather than stay home to mind the fields, the Riverland might yet squeak through the next winter without famine.

Meanwhile, last year's stores were beginning to run out.  Oatmeal, moldy cheese, and black bread hard enough to drive nails were supplemented by whatever forest, field, or sky could provide by way of fruit or game.  Hart season would begin soon.  Streams were eagerly fished or set with traps.  The Silver itself, however, was left alone:  anything hooked there was likely to snap the line or pull the fisherman in, never to be seen again.  Anyway, as Rue said, why risk offending the River Snake?  Vant might laugh at that, but he didn't meddle with the Silver either.

The weirdingstrom had swept other, stranger game into the valley, both from the north and the south:  black swans and fierce little hawks with pearly feathers shading to pale blue; dire elk whose eight foot antler-spans kept tangling in the undergrowth; lumpy desert creatures that caught cold in the crisp, mountain air and rent the night with their hacking coughs; flying frogs and things like black, leather kites that killed by wrapping themselves around the heads of their prey.

And there was something else.

One morning Jame and her ten went with the bowlegged horse-master to bring in fresh mounts from the upper field where the Knorth horses pastured.

It proved a frustrating task.  The herd was on edge, easily spooked but unwilling to stray far from the paddock's lower fence.

"There's a predator somewhere about," said the master, peering up the slope from under his shaggy eye-brows and mopping his bald, perspiring head. He sniffed as if for a scent, but it would be a wonder, thought Jame, if he could smell anything, given that at some point long ago his nose had been smashed almost flat to his face.

At its top was a jumble of enormous boulders, many newly tumbled down from the mountains above.

Jame glimpsed a flicker of white among them and immediately thought of the phantom Whinno-hir Bel-tairi. As she shifted for a better look, however, the horses suddenly surged around her, all wild eyes and great, swinging flanks.

"Don't crowd the mares!" the horse-master was shouting. "They'll kick you if you get between them!"

Jame ducked under a gelding's belly and jumped for the fence. What she hit, though, was the gate, which swung open, taking her with it. It stopped with a jar that sent her tumbling over its top rail, down between the gate and the fence. The herd plunged through the opening and thundered off down the slope, pursued by sweating, shouting cadets. Brier gave Jame an unfathomable look and then, more sedately, followed them as the whole mob, equine and Kencyr, made for the underground stables at a dead run.

"Perhaps in future, lady," said the master in his nasal voice, eyeing her askance, "you should leave horse-wrangling to others."

Jame glanced again at the upper slope. Nothing white showed now, but it had been there, and it hadn't been a Whinno-hir.

# IV

A LUNCH OF bread, hard cheese, and milk followed, with much subdued laughter and glances at the top table. By then, everyone had heard about the stampede through the great hall and the chaos it had caused below.

Afterward, Jame and her ten tried to stay awake during an interminable lecture on strategy, delivered by a randon so battered that he appeared to have made every mistake against which he was now warning them. When he got excited, he pounded the desk with a wooden fist or sometimes detached and threw it at a dozing cadet.

Their next class was held in the great hall of Old Tentir. They entered to find Senethar practice mats spread out on the flagstones and half a ten-command lounging on them. Jame slowed, recognizing Gorbel's heavy-lidded face, so like his father Caldane's that it set her teeth on edge. His four Highborn toadies eyed her askance as she approached and snickered among themselves. Behind them stood five young Caineron Kendar, their personal servants and cadets in their own right, watching Brier Iron-thorn with hard, set faces older than their years.

Gorbel rose casually to acknowledge the arrival of their instructor, a small, red-faced Coman sargent. His friends followed suit, waiting just long enough to make clear their opinion of a teacher so far beneath them in social rank and blood.

The lesson began with a demonstration of a simple water-flowing throw. One pulled an opponent off balance, pivoted back to belly, and threw him over one's hip. It didn't call for great strength, only good balance and proper leverage. As for falling, the mats were an unexpected luxury.

"Form a circle!" ordered the sargent and they did, one house taking the inner ring, the other the outer, face-to-face. "Salute and begin."

Jame's first opponent was a grinning Caineron Highborn who used the excuse to let his hands wander.

"I know a better game than this," he breathed in her ear.

"Perhaps, but can you play it without balls?"

She reached behind her, low, and squeezed. He gasped. As his grip involuntarily loosened, she threw him, hard.

The sargent frowned, knowing that something had happened but not what. He clapped. "Change!"

The pace quickened. Throw, fall, change; throw, fall, change, over and over. The cadets grimly settled down to the rhythmic thud of bodies hitting the mats. It seemed to go on forever, until breath burned in the lungs and sweat stung the eyes. Thirty minutes, sixty…sweet Trinity, did he mean to keep them at it the full two hours? However, if someone fell off onto the stone floor, he or she was permitted to quit. Jame saw first one, then another and another of Gorbel's cronies roll free and settle back to watch the fun. She was tempted to join them. This was the most sustained practice yet, worse than when she had tested in the Senethar because this time there were no rest breaks, or rather only one.

As he fell, a cadet grabbed both her cap and a handful of the hair coiled beneath.

The sargent glared as she interrupted the lesson's flow to disengage the other's grip. "You should cut that short, lady. Anyone who can grab it in a fight is going to have you at a disadvantage."

Grinning, the cadet tugged. Hard. Jame bent his wrist until he yelped with pain and let go. Then she twisted the black skein of hair back on top of her head and defiantly tugged the cap down over it. Other randon including Harn had said the same thing, admittedly with reason, but be damned if she was going to lose the only attractive feature she had left.

The lesson continued.

Throw, fall, change…and here was Gorbel.

This was the first time that the rotation of classes had brought them up against each other. He was younger than she had thought. Breathing hard, hair plastered with sweat to his bulging forehead, the Caineron lordan stared at her.

"You," he said heavily.

"Me," Jame agreed. She expected a sneer, but he looked merely exhausted and dogged. "Ready?"

In answer, he grabbed her jacket and threw her awkwardly. For a moment, she thought his legs were going to buckle under them both. On impulse, when her turn came, she threw him near the edge of the mat. His friends pulled him off, laughing at his half-hearted attempt to resist.

That left only a half dozen cadets in the game, Brier Iron-thorn among them. The Southron flowed through the moves, the only sign of effort a sheen of sweat that made her dark face gleam like polished wood. Her expression was calm and remote, as if her thoughts dwelt on the far side of the moon. It didn't change when one of the Caineron Kendar first threw, then kicked her viciously in the ribs.

Jame had heard that muffled thud before over the course of the practice without realizing what it was. Four times? Five? More? She should have recognized the hatred in the Kendars' eyes for one of their own who had escaped their lord's cruel grip. Their masters snickered. Her own ten stirred and muttered; they had seen what was happening long before she had. So must the instructor, but he had done nothing. Perhaps he felt that a turn-collar deserved no better. Brier picked herself up more slowly than before. That last kick had hurt.

Jame felt rage stir in her. *Careful*, she thought, as her current partner backed hastily away. *Don't overreact*. Then, *the hell I won't*.

She stalked across the mat toward the Kendar, who shrank back and looked quickly away. Here was one who either could not or would not met her eyes. They hadn't been matched before; he had been avoiding her. She clapped, and he jumped like a spooked horse.

He was taller than she was by at least a head. She had to reach up to touch his face and turn it, nails out only enough to prick although they still drew tiny drops of blood.

"Look at me." Her voice roughened with the undernote of a purr. "There. That's better. One should always meet one's enemies face-to-face, don't you think?"

He was a handsome, almost pretty boy, or would have been without terror distorting his face. A sudden stench announced that he had lost control of his bowels. She tapped him lightly on the cheek and let her hands slide down to grip his sleeves.

"Now, let's play. Throw me, or try."

Stiffly, he assumed the proper stance, took a deep breath, and turned to lift her over his hip. She leaned back and shifted her weight so that his buttocks shot past her. Nervous laughter rippled through the cadets. They had often played this trick on each other, but the Caineron was too rattled to counter it.

"Again."

White face beginning to blotch with red, he tried, and was caught off-balance, bent backward with her knee in the small of his back.

"Again."

This time she moved even as he did, rolling over his arm, landing on her feet in a crouch before him. Her grip shifted to a lock on his wrist. She twisted. He somersaulted over this fulcrum of pain and slammed down on the stone floor.

"There," said Jame, straightening up. "Isn't that better?"

The instructor clapped twice. "That's enough," he said. His voice shook and so did he. "Never, ever humiliate a fellow cadet that way."

"If not respect for one, then why for any?"

He gaped at her, mouth opening and closing. At another time, it would have been funny.

"Let it go," said Brier behind her.

Jame glanced at her. "If you wish. For now."

Dismissed, the rest of the command except Rue scattered to practice on their own until dinner.

Brier gave Jame an unreadable look. "What you did back there during the lesson, lady...it didn't help."

With that, she turned and walked away.

Jame stared after her. Dammit, the Southron was right. Terrorizing Kendar only made them more stubborn unless it broke them altogether, and what right had she to do either? Blood right, some would say. She was Highborn, and had just demonstrated everything that she hated about her own kind's casual abuse of power, to someone who had already suffered far too much from it.

"Has she had to put up with much more of this harassment?" Jame asked Rue.

The cadet squirmed. "A lot," she admitted, "usually not so obvious. She says she can deal with it. I wasn't supposed to tell you."

It seemed that either she scared people shitless or they thought she was too weak to protect her own. What a choice. Jame sighed. In every way, the road ahead was longer than she had realized.

# Chapter X: Battles Old and New

## Summer 41-2

## I

SOMEONE SCREAMED.

For a blurry moment, half asleep and half awake, Jame thought it might have been herself.

She had dreamed again that she sat on the hearth of the over-heated Lordan's chambers, drinking and laughing drunkenly with that sly Randir, Roane. A servant had gone to fetch "dear little Gangrene" from the dormitory below. Anticipation stirred in her gut, and lower down. It was a long time since she had indulged in the old, sweet midnight games with her darling little brother. The poor fool probably thought he was safe here at the college.

*Ha. You are my meat, boy, and Father has given you to me to devour, just as he will all the Kencyrath with his death. May it be soon. I am empty, and I hunger.*

A hesitant footstep on the threshold and there he stood, flanked by two guards, the boy Ganth Grayling with sick terror on his face. Out of his eyes, however, stared someone else, as she did out of Greshan's. Sweet Trinity. Torisen.

Then had come the scream that had woken her, but not from either of them.

From below, Jame heard Vant's voice raised in a shout of exasperation. She grabbed the first clothing that came to hand, a long-tailed shirt, and pulled it on as she went quickly down the central stair to the second floor with Jorin dashing on ahead.

The dormitory was divided into two sections. To the left, as one faced the square, were the ten-commanders' individual rooms. To the right, each squad slept in a canvas cubicle rather like camping out inside, except that during the day the partitions were folded back against the walls. On a hot summer night like this, Jame would have expected them to be left open to catch any stray gasp of cool air. However, the Kendar apparently suffered less from extremes of temperature than the Highborn, for which she envied them. If only it would rain!

As she threaded through the canvas maze, pulling her long, black hair free of the shirt and letting it spill loose over her shoulders, Jame heard sleepy voices within raised in protest:

"Not again." "Let us sleep, can't you?" "Somebody, please, gag him with a dirty sock."

A scowling, tousled head popped out between canvas flaps. "Do you mind...oh!"

"Go back to sleep," Jame told him, and went on toward a murmur of voices. It came from the quarters closest to the southern fireplace, a position of honor held by her own ten.

"If you can't keep your filthy nightmares to yourself," Vant was saying with a kind of throttled fury, "go home. We don't need your sort here."

He spoke to the new cadet, Niall, who was sitting up in bed, knees clasped tightly under his chin. Thin and quiet by day, he looked gaunt and haunted by candlelight, and he was shivering. The rest of Jame's ten had gathered around him. Brier, as usual, held aloof but watchful in the background.

"You leave him alone, Ten," snapped Mint, to a mutter of agreement from the others. She sat on the edge of the cot and put an arm around the boy's hunched shoulders. "If you'd seen what he saw, you'd probably wet your bed every night."

Before Vant could answer, they all became aware of Jame.

"What's the matter?" she asked.

"Nothing that need concern you, Lady." Vant gave her a smile that was mostly bared teeth. "Sorry you were disturbed." He turned back to Niall. "As for you..."

"This is my ten-command, you know." Jame slipped around him and perched on the chest at the foot of Niall's cot while Jorin dove under it and began happily to play with whatever he found there. "Now, what was it you saw?"

When the cadet only gawked at her, Mint answered.

"Lady, last winter while the rest of us stayed snug with the garrison at Gothregor (including you, Ten), Niall stowed away in a supply wagon and went south with the Host. He served as a messenger in the battle at the Cataracts. We don't know exactly what he saw there—he won't tell us—but it must have been awful. Now he's afraid that he'll fail Tentir because he can't stop the nightmares. He thinks only cowards have bad dreams."

Vant started to jeer, but Jame stopped him.

*Not another Kest*, she thought, *lost for lack of the right word.*

"I was at the Cataracts," she said. "It *was* terrible. The noise, the smell...the very ground shook. Then the Waster Horde came, wave on wave, breaking against the shield wall, until the grass was slimy with blood and all the horses screamed. The whole thing was a nightmare. Brier, you were there too, weren't you?"

In the shadows, the big Kendar stirred. "I was, but after the battle."

"So you missed the fun." Vant made it a sneer, as if glad at last to score a point against his rival.

"Fun?" Brier considered the word. "Not exactly. I was with the Southern Host when m'lord Pereden marched it out into the Wastes to meet the advancing Horde. Three million of them, some fifty thousand of us. Our center column clashed head on and was ripped apart. The sand drank our blood and the Wasters ate our flesh. I saw Commander Larch flayed and dismembered. It took her a long, long time to die. I was there when Pereden—" she paused, hunting for the right word, saying it at last with a curious twist—"fell. We didn't know that the left and right columns had survived. Those few of us who escaped joined one or the other of them and harried the Horde all the way to the Cataracts."

"Which is why," added Jame, "the Northern Host was able to reach the bottleneck at the Escarpment first. Otherwise, that would have been the end of us all."

There was silence for a moment as the three unlikely veterans remembered and the rest tried to imagine what horrors they had seen. For once, not even Vant could think of anything to say. Jame heard a murmur on the other side of the canvas wall and soft voices saying, "Hush!" The other ten-commands were listening.

Distant thunder grumbled and the air shifted restlessly. The walls stirred. Under the bed, Jorin engaged in mortal combat with a stray sock.

"Did you kill anyone in battle, lady?" asked Erim.

"Probably." Jame grimaced. "I had Kin-Slayer, y'see, and was trying to hack through the thick of things to give it to my brother. If ever a sword thirsted for blood, it's that one."

"And you actually managed to hang on to it?"

Vant, rallying, caused a ripple of nervous laughter. In practice, one way or another, Jame almost always managed to lose her weapon.

"This one I could barely get rid of," she answered grimly. "I tell you, that damn blade *likes* to kill, and it can cut through anything…if you know the trick."

The "trick" was to wear Father's emerald signet ring on one's sword-hand, as she had discovered by accident. She had tried to tell her brother, but didn't know if he had taken her seriously.

"Do you ever dream about it, lady?" asked Niall, looking at her askance. "The battle, I mean."

Jame considered. "Occasionally as a bloody muddle, which most of it was. Sometimes, though, it's all too clear. I have to get Kin-Slayer to my brother or he will die, but I don't know where he is and there are so many people in the way. Some of them are changers. They wear Tori's face and beg me to throw them the sword. When I don't, they change into my father and curse me: 'Child of darkness, filthy Shanir, die and be damned…'"

They were all staring at her.

"And then," she finished, somewhat lamely, "I wake up."

Quill's face had twisted with concentration. "Isn't there a song about a randon who shrieked all night long in his sleep before a battle, until his Kendar had to stuff tufts of wool in their ears? The next day he fought like a demon, but in silence because he was too hoarse to make a sound."

"I remember that one," said Killy eagerly. "He got behind the enemy and cut down a score of them before they even knew he was there. With everyone else roaring battle-cries, y'see, they didn't hear him until it was too late."

"Another Lawful Lie," said Vant scornfully.

"Maybe." Jame considered the story. "To me, though, it has the ring of truth."

"Then you don't think I'm a coward, lady?"

"Because you have nightmares? Of course not. Everyone has them. The more you see, the less these particular ones should bother you; but if you start running away from them, you may never stop."

Like Tori, in a way. He wasn't running now, but somehow he had been stopped dead in his tracks, and that wasn't good either.

She roused herself. "Enough. Go to sleep, all of you, and dream sweetly if you can. If you can't, well, it isn't the end of the world. And if you give Niall punishment duty for this," she added softly to Vant in passing, "you're a bigger fool than I thought…if that's possible."

A breath of fresh air met her on the stairs. As she reached the attic, the hole in the roof briefly flooded with light, followed at a slight interval by the thunder's growl. Jorin retreated to a corner; he disliked storms and hated getting wet. Jame crossed to the hole and leaned out of it.

The storm was approaching from the north, rumbling down the throat of the valley. Snake-tongues of lightning flickered across the sky, throwing the mountain sides into sharp relief and making the river gleam like its name.

Watching it come, Jame considered nightmares, specifically the one from which Niall's scream had woken her. No one now alive knew what had happened in that close, hot room, the night that Greshan had summoned his younger brother up to it; yet, somehow, the memory lingered, like the stink of the gorgeous coat that her uncle had worn, now resigned to a chest in his former apartment. Each dream brought her closer to some terrible truth. For herself, whatever it was, she felt she could endure it, but could Tori? It hadn't occurred to her until that night, when she had seen his eyes set in their father's terrified face, that it might also be dragging her brother along, one nightmare at a time, toward an ultimate horror.

Damn and blast. Tori was stronger than her in so many ways, but not in this.

The air fidgeted this way and that, now hot, now deliciously cool, lifting tendrils of Jame's loose hair. Leaves began to fret. Now came the wind, roaring in the tree tops, making boughs toss until the whole forest heaved like an ocean gone mad. A blinding flash, a boom like the end of time, and rain fell in a shower of icy arrows mixed with stinging hailstones.

Well, they would cope. Whatever haunted Tentir wasn't stronger than both of them, as long as they supported each other.

She stayed, drinking in the tumult, until at last the storm rumbled off down the Riverland, and one by one the stars crept out of hiding.

# II

AT BREAKFAST, NIALL still looked haggard but more in control of himself, answering her raised eyebrow with a slight, shy duck of his head. Talk and laughter moved freely back and forth across the hall, as if the previous night's storm had broken more than the oppressive heat. Only Vant looked sour, as if he had swallowed something nasty. Jame sat at the head of her table and Brier at the foot. They both tended to be quiet in company, but for the first time Jame felt included in the group even while it respected her reserve. She wondered if Brier Iron-thorn felt the same way.

Then she remembered: the Southron had said that she had been there when Pereden...fell. What an odd, ambiguous word. Did Timmon know? Should she tell him? Better not.

The day's first class—archery with a Jaran ten—passed without incident, except for Erim hitting the mark every time. His aim was indeed very good, almost uncanny, for someone who looked as if he shot at random from a truly awful pose.

Next came sword practice with the Danior, which again provided no surprises. As always, Jame was quickly disarmed.

"Next time maybe we should bind the hilt to your hand," said the randon in charge, not altogether joking.

After lunch came a work detail with an Edirr ten.

The largest of the quake fissures in the outer training field had been spanned halfway down with a wooden bridge. Normally, the steep ditch was dry, but the previous night's storm had sent a flash flood down it to the Silver, piling debris against the bridge's footing. Until the mess was cleared away, it was impossible to know if the structure had been damaged. Consequently, the two tens were set to removing the tangle of broken branches under the guidance of a red-faced sargent.

It was hard, dirty work. Mud cemented the makeshift dam together and mud backed up against it, under a foot of murky water. Moreover, the sides of the fissure were slick with more of the same, where they weren't jagged with exposed boulders. Cadets kept slipping and falling while the sargent got redder and redder with shouting at them to watch what they were doing and to stop playing silly buggers, dammit.

Then he was called up-field to help the horse-master. A stallion had gotten loose among the mares and must be captured before they, not being in season, kicked their eager suitor to pieces.

Dar started to climb out of the ditch, but an Edirr cadet pushed him back in. When he had scrambled up the opposite side, outraged, the Knorth all found themselves on one side and the Edirr on the other. There was a moment's speculative silence, then a grin that seemed to spread from face-to-face.

"Red clover, red clover, send Rue over!"

Rue plunged down the slope, plowed through the muddy water, and scrambled up the opposite side. At the top, the Edirr girl who had called caught and flung her back down to land with a great splash at the fissure's bottom. She rejoined her own side, muddy from head to foot.

"Red clover, red clover, send Honey over!" she called back to her opponent in a kind of throttled shout, as none of them wanted to attract attention.

Honey, in turn, was sent flying to a chorus of muted Knorth jeers.

Then Erim bulled his way up and through the enemy line. "I capture you," he said to Honey, and bore her back to the Knorth side.

Jame, Brier, and the Edirr ten-commander watched from the bridge, or rather the Edirr kept watch against the sargent's return. If he had any hesitation about his role, it was only that he couldn't join in the fun.

Jame didn't know what to do. The cadets were clearly having a wonderful time, but they weren't doing the work assigned to them and would be in trouble if the sargent caught them at it. "I should stop this," she said, "or shouldn't I?"

Brier gave her an impassive look. "You are master ten of your house," she said—that, and no more.

It hadn't been fair to ask her, and Jame knew it. She had to start making her own command decisions.

Swearing under her breath, she approached her cadets from behind and touched Dar on the shoulder. Before she could speak, he reached back and seized her, apparently thinking that she was the captured Honey bent on escape. The next moment, she was in midair. Sky and earth wheeled past, dotted with startled faces, and then the brown water at the ditch's bottom leaped up to meet her.

Jame emerged sputtering, mud in her eyes, her hair, her mouth. A rock in the river bed shifted under her hand as she tried to rise and she lurched forward again into the mire, face first. The cadets on both banks were staring down at her, appalled. She sat in the filthy water, feeling it seep through her clothes, considering her situation,

*For Trinity's sake,* Tori had said, *don't make fools of us both.*

Had she come to Tentir for this? What hope was there that she would do any better in future? Maybe she should give up, go back to Gothregor, stop trying to accomplish the impossible.

But was this really that much worse than the Women's Halls? Jame thought about that for a moment, then burst into laughter.

"Knot stitches," she said.

The sargent returned, horrified to find his lord's sister sitting at the bottom of a muddy ditch, laughing like a lunatic. He didn't understand why she found a needlework phrase so funny. Neither did the cadets, but it was infectious. As they resumed work, one only had to catch another's eye and murmur "knot stitch" for them both to burst out in giggles.

It was in this high good humor and in wet, filthy clothes that the Knorth reported for the last lesson of the day. And that was where things began to go seriously wrong.

# III

THEY SHOULD HAVE been bound for a reading lesson—hard work for most but a welcome rest for Jame. Instead, they were told to clean up as best they could and then to report to a third story room in Old Tentir where none of them had ever been before.

Their destination overlooked the inner square, high enough to make some of the cadets turn pale. Gorbel's ten-command waited for them. The Caineron were jeering at the Knorths' muddy clothes when the Commandant entered, followed by a richly dressed, unfamiliar Highborn.

A surprised murmur ran through the Caineron ranks: "Corrudin." "It's Corrudin, Lord Caldane's uncle and chief advisor." "What's he doing here?"

If Gorbel knew, he didn't say. Jame thought she saw a flicker of alarm in his eyes, but he instantly hooded them, his face becoming as expressionless and dull as a toad's.

"Sit down, all of you. I see that some of you recognize our guest."

The Commandant's manner was as suave as ever, his half-smile as elusive and ironic, but he was wary too, and watchful. He reminded Jame of Jorin, feigning nonchalance before the pounce.

"M'lord Corrudin has gifted us with his presence today in response a certain…er…incident that took place during a recent lesson."

It *was* about the Senethar class, thought Jame as she and the other cadets settled crossed-legged on the floor, furtively tugging at wet clothes to ease their cling. Could this elegant, elderly Highborn be here to lecture the Caineron about their harassment of Brier Ironthorn? Then she caught a fleeting smirk on the face of the Kendar whom she in turn had humiliated. No. Justice for the Southron wasn't on anyone's mind.

"Normally," the Commandant was saying, "this subject arises later in your training. However, since there are no fewer than three lordan currently at Tentir and some of you have already experienced their…er…effect, it was thought wise to bring up the topic early. This is for the benefit of you, the Kendar who serve with them. M'lord, if you will…?"

He invited the Highborn forward with a sweeping salute and withdrew to the shadows at the back of the room where he stood, a motionless, alert presence.

The Highborn advanced at his leisure, his dark purple robe, crusted with gold embroidery, swishing across the floor in the silence. His face was finer cut and more austere than most Caineron, his silvery hair slicked back from a sharp widow's peak. He looked far more like the leader of a house than his overweight, overbearing nephew. Jame wondered why Caldane was Lord Caineron and not his uncle, and whether Corrudin resented it. He didn't look like a man to suffer fools, gladly or otherwise.

"I thank Commandant Sharp-tongue for this opportunity," he said, "and for his faithful service to our house." His voice, smooth and melodious, made Jame twitch, as if at something just beyond her range of hearing. Out of the corner of her eye, she saw Gorbel's stubby hands tighten on his knees.

"As you Kendar know," he said, ignoring the two lordan, "you are bound by our god to obey the Highborn. Normally, you are given no choice in the matter just as, normally, you are given no choice in what house you serve. You stay where you are born." His gaze flickered over Brier, who returned it wooden-faced. "Now, it would follow, would it not, that you are bound to obey every command given to you—even if some are...ill-advised?"

Jame leaned forward, listening intently. Was Caldane's chief advisor about to warn them about Honor's Paradox, which Caldane himself was doing everything he could to circumvent?

"I do not speak of those orders issued by our liege lords, of course," Corrudin continued smoothly. "Who is the judge of honor, if not they? No, I refer to lesser Highborn, not so old or wise as their masters, whom they too must obey."

Cadets were nodding. Born to servitude, they liked to hear that all Highborn but a few also had limited power. Jame tried not to fidget. She suspected that this was all about her, but didn't yet see how.

"That said, it follows that as future randon, and as valuable assets to your respective houses, you must learn how to resist the folly, even the malice, of such minor Highborn as would misuse their power over you, as has recently occurred."

Ah, that was it. No wonder the Caineron boy had smirked.

"I believe a demonstration is in order." The Highborn turned suddenly to Gorbel. "Lordan, if you would oblige, give one of your comrades a foolish command."

Gorbel blinked and stirred, taken as much by surprise as Jame and the others, but hiding it better. For a moment he returned his great-uncle's sleek smile with a stony glower, and then he twisted around where he sat to regard his ten. His hooded eyes swept over them, and all but one failed to meet his stare. That one, a Highborn, grinned back at him, but his amusement quickly faltered.

"No," he said, with a laugh shaken by disbelief.

"Yes. Kibben, stand on your head."

The cadet gaped at him, then lurched to his feet, his face twisting between astonishment and horror. Jame recognized him as the master of the Kendar boy whom she had made pay for Brier's harassment. Neither master nor servant was smiling now.

"Resist," murmured Corrudin. It was more than encouragement.

"You heard me," said Gorbel. Sweat trickled down his face, channeled slantwise by the heavy lines of his scowl. "Do it."

The cadet staggered between the Cainerons' opposing wills. Both ten-commands had scrambled to their feet and were backing away from the conflict.

Also instinctively in retreat, Jame shot a glance at the silent figure at the back of the room. Why didn't the Commandant stop this? All three were Highborn of his house, and two were cadets presumably under his protection as the current master of the college.

Then she remember Sheth standing outside the door that first night while within her brother fought with Lord Ardeth for his very soul, and again, in the hall when the Randir had tempted Harn Griphard to become the beast that he feared he was. Here again was that cool assessment of power, Lord Caineron's chief advisor against the Caineron's future lord. If either should break, better here, better now, than later when so many others might fall with them. Such had been the bitter lesson of the White Hills, when her own father's ruin had nearly brought down the entire Kencyrath.

Kibben made an odd, choking noise. He bent, put his hands and the top of his head on the floor, and swung up his legs. For a moment he tottered upside-down, the long tails of his foppish jacket falling into his face. Then he crashed over like a tree falling, all of a piece. The wooden floor shook.

Gorbel smiled. "Good boy," he said softly.

Suddenly Jame realized something that perhaps she should have guessed before: these Highborn cadets weren't Gorbel's friends. They were his father's spies. No wonder Caldane had received news so quickly of the training incident and sent his uncle to assess the situation.

Corrudin stood unmoved. He might never have exerted himself if not for the flicker of thwarted rage in his eyes, quickly masked. However, Jame had seen it. He hadn't expected to lose against his lumpish, despised grandnephew. Now he knew, as did she, in whose blood the true power ran; and for all his smooth veneer, that knowledge infuriated him.

"Well," he said lightly, as Kibben's servant helped the shaken Highborn to his feet and tried to prevent him from again attempting a head-stand. "There you see a perfect example of misused authority. My thanks, lordan, for your assistance. However, we have yet to see how such abuse affects a Kendar. So, another demonstration. My lady, if you please."

He turned to Jame and drew her forward with languid wave of his hand. Then he did the same to Brier Iron-thorn.

"I think this time I will propose the order," he said, slowly circling them, beginning again to enjoy himself.

Jame's skin crawled. This was going to be bad. She met Brier's eyes, as green and cool as pond moss, and as lacking in expression. Only weeks of observation told her that the Southron was braced to show no emotion, whatever happened.

"My," said the Highborn, still circling, looking them up and down. "How dirty you both are, but especially you, my lady." A ripple of nervous laughter went through the cadets. Under it, Corrudin's voice sank to a murmur. "Been playing in the mud, have we? How appropriate, given all that your house has dragged us through. I was in the White Hills. I saw. Blood, and mud, and more blood, pooling in the hollows where the wounded drown in it. There also the honor of your house died, as we see yet again in your presence here. And you, Iron-thorn, were once one of us. Your mother died in our service. You disgrace her memory."

The Kendar stirred, but silver-gray eyes locked and held jade green: *Look at me, not at him. Don't listen. Don't react. Don't give the bastard the satisfaction.*

Corrudin made a slight sound of annoyance.

"So you are theirs now, body and soul. Very well. It is only fitting, then, that you kiss their filthy boots. Girl, give this turn-collar the order."

Jame lurched as his will crushed down on her. Such power...! How had Gorbel contested it? But then he hadn't been its primary target. As if from a great distance, she could hear the cadet Kibben struggling to obey Gorbel's last command, over and over again. Between them, grandnephew and granduncle had broken him, perhaps beyond repair.

"You heard me," Corrudin whispered in her ear, a smile lurking in his voice. "Do it, you stupid little bitch."

She turned on him. "Back. Off."

The Highborn stiffened. His look of astonishment changed to utter horror as, step-by-step, he found himself retreating backward towards the window. The low sill caught him behind the knees. He flailed for a moment, trying to regain his balance, then fell. They heard him hit the tin roof of the arcade two flights below, then the ground.

Gorbel gave Jame a slow, sleepy smile. "Good girl," he said.

# IV

CONSIDERABLE CONFUSION ENSUED.

Cadets rushed to the window and those hardy enough to brave the height leaned out to gape down. Alarmed cries and questions rose from the square below. The cadets answered in a babble of shouts that enlightened no one and, in future days, gave rise to some truly startling rumors.

Meanwhile, freed from restraint, Kibben stood on his head in the corner.

Jame hadn't moved. She felt as if she had blown out her brains with one searing act of will power. Trinity, where had that come from...and was it apt to happen again? What she had done to the Randir Tempter was nothing compared to this. It had been like a berserker flare, but much more focused and ruthless. If she had ordered the very stones of Tentir to collapse on them all, perhaps they would have.

Brier held her elbow, steadying her.

"Lady, sometimes you worry me."

Jame gave a shaky laugh. "Not half as much as I worry myself."

The Commandant winnowed through the swarm of cadets, separating Caineron from Knorth—not that either stunned house had thought yet to turn on the other.

"This...er...lesson is concluded, and with it the class day. Dismissed. Someone, please escort Cadet Kibben to the infirmary, if you can get him upright. You," he said to Jame, "wait for me in my office."

Only then did the consequences of her act strike her. Sweet Trinity, he was going to expel her immediately. No, the entire Randon Council would set her up as the butt for archery practice and then award prizes for the best shots. Erim was a cinch to win that one, if they let him compete.

"All right?" asked Brier. It took Jame a moment to realize what she meant: *If I let go, will you fall over?*

"I think so," she said, somewhat confusedly, and the Southron withdrew her support.

The cadets filed out, shooting her stunned looks in passing. They took Kibben with them, horizontal, one cadet at his head, another at his feet, while he continued to grope desperately for the floor. Only when everyone had gone did Jame realize that she had no idea where the Commandant's office was.

Well, that wasn't quite true: he sometimes reviewed the cadets from a second story balcony. That might be attached either to his living quarters or to his office, or perhaps to both. In fact, leaning out the window, she could see it below, to the left. Until she meant to cap her day's exploits with a demonstration of wall-scaling, she needed a stair. That should be easy enough to find. After all, her ten had used one to reach the third floor.

However, she hadn't taken into account Old Tentir's confusing innards, or her own rattled wits. Once away from the windows and daylight, she quickly became lost in the maze of dusty corridors. *This is ridiculous*, she thought. After all, as the Talisman she had mastered the layout of an entire city. However, complex though it was, Tai-tastigon hadn't been deliberately built to bewilder. Here, even straight hallways seemed to take a perverse pleasure in wandering. Where was Graykin when she needed him? Dammit, she was going to be late for her own expulsion.

A dingy, long-tailed rat made her jump as it broke cover and scurried down the passage away from her.

Suddenly, a great paw of a hand, all claws, shot out of a swinging panel down by the floor, seized the rat, and snatched it back inside. Jame hadn't realized where she was, much less that the feeding flap to Bear's prison was double-hinged. She knelt and cautiously pushed it open a crack. A gust of hot, foul air breathed through it into her face. She could see Bear's massive form hunched against the glow of the fireplace. He bent his shaggy head to what he held in his hands. The rat screamed once, and then was silent. Jame eased the panel shut on the sound of strong teeth ripping wetly at the small, furry carcass and crunching its bones.

Around the next corner came a glimmer of daylight. Jame followed it to a window which again overlooked the inner square. For all her wandering, she had ended up in the room next to the one where she had started out. On the other hand, the Commandant's balcony was now directly below her, one story down. She surveyed the square. In this, the free period before dinner, it was nearly empty.

The Coman cadet from the Falconer's class whom she now knew as Gari crossed the arena, surrounded to the waist by a swarm of bouncing grasshoppers. He didn't seem to have any control over what kind of insect he attracted, although they did seem in some way to reflect his current mood. A cry of dismay greeted him as he entered his barracks. *They shouldn't complain,* thought Jame. The last time, after a particularly miserable work-detail cleaning latrines, it had been a swarm of stink-beetles.

Swinging her legs over the window ledge, she dropped lightly onto the balcony.

"Most people use the door," said the Commandant's voice from inside.

"Sorry, ran." Jame brushed aside a filmy curtain and entered, wet boots squelching, leaving a trail of muddy prints. "I got lost."

It was a large room, indirectly lit by windows on either side of the balcony. These were shaded with taut, peach-colored cloth, probably old tent canvas, vertically slashed to allow the breeze to edge through. The filtered light cast a mellow glow over walls covered with exquisitely detailed murals.

The Commandant lounged in a chair slightly back from one of the windows, his long, elegantly booted legs stretched out before him and crossed at the ankles. Silver flashed: he was whittling a bit of wood with a small knife. Although it was hard to tell with his face in shadow, Jame thought that he sounded tired.

"This is the Map Room," he said, with a languid wave of his hand. "Here you see accurate depictions of all our major battles on Rathillien, and in the cabinets below are accounts of the participants. Yes, that one is the Cataracts."

The mural in question occupied a large portion of the northern wall. Jame recognized Hurlen, that town of wooden towers built on many islets at the convergence of the Silver and the Tardy. There was the Upper Meadow where the Host had camped; there, the Lower Huddles, along which she had been riding when the Caineron charge had come over the crest on top of her; there, off to the left, the mysterious, lethal Heart of the Woods where her brother and Pereden had fought.

Looking closer, she saw tiny figures including one in black, repeated at different places in the field. By their growing size, she could trace her brother's progress through the conflict, except that several times he appeared to be two places at once.

"That is one of the mysteries of the Cataracts," said the Commandant, watching her. "Who was the rider in black on a white horse who suddenly appeared in the midst of the battle? My lord Caldane claims that the High Lord sent a decoy into the field to lessen his own chances of being killed. Why, then, a white horse, when everyone knows Torisen's mount is black?"

"That was by accident," said Jame, still looking at the map. "So was my presence in the Caineron charge. I was just trying to get across the field. Also, I'm the one who...er...borrowed your warhorse later. Sorry, but it really was an emergency."

"I will take your word for it and not press to know why you, of all people, tried to ride Cloud bareback. Interesting. That answers quite a few questions, if not why you arrived there and again here wearing a Tastigon knife-fighter's jacket."

"It's called a *d'hen* and with due respect, ran, that's all I will tell you about it."

"I see." He leaned back, hands dropping with their work into his lap. "Now, did I or did I not request that you not break any more instructors?"

Jame swallowed. "You did, ran. Sorry. Is he badly hurt?"

"A cracked collarbone and many bruises. Worse, only by concentrating can he prevent himself from backing up, regardless of what lies behind him. I would say that Kibben is avenged, and then some. Out of curiosity, may I ask what happened?"

So he hadn't been close enough to hear. Jame told him what Corrudin had tried to make her do. "It would have destroyed Brier," she concluded, "and she's already been hurt far too much by my kind. It might also have destroyed me. I suddenly thought, maybe that's what he wants, and be damned if I'm going to be forced into it."

"A good instinct," murmured the randon. "It was his desire, no, his demand, that he be allowed to try. A powerful Shanir, that, and dangerous. After all, he brings out the worst in everyone. Truth for truth, Knorth. You would have done my house a service if you had broken his neck, but then we would probably have had civil war. There will be trouble enough as it is, but that needn't concern you. He may have also influenced the worst in me when I allowed the test; however, I had just heard that you were sitting in a mud puddle, having hysterics."

"And, as lordan, if I should break, better here than later."

He gave her a shadowy, fleeting smile. "I see you understand."

"But ran, what I did to Corrudin, whether he deserved it or not, wasn't that also a gross abuse of power? I can't seem to get it right. First I can't exert control over an arrogant twit like Vant; then I force a Shanir Highborn to commit defenestration. Maybe I don't belong here after all."

"With that power, where would you go?" He spoke softly, a voice out the gathering shadows, giving shape to her own fears. "Untrained as you are, who is safe against you? Not enemies, not friends, perhaps not even own your brother."

He shifted to prop his chin on his fist. She felt the pressure of his assessing eyes and the keen mind behind them at work on the problem. On her. "It seems to me," he said, "that you hate your own blood and its inherent power. Perhaps that mistrust is warranted. Dark things stir in you, girl. I sense them. But part of what you are is also the blessing, or the curse, of our god. Your position in the Kencyrath is unique. You are a Shanir, a Highborn, the Knorth Lordan, and a female. If you don't learn how to control your innate abilities, either they will destroy you or you will fall back into the trap that you came here to escape. Do you see another course?"

"N-no, ran." And she didn't, short of leaving her people behind forever. But if she returned to Tai-tastigon as the Talisman, she would still be herself. *If you start running away*, she had told Niall, speaking of nightmare, *you may never stop*. The same held true here, even more so.

He leaned back again, into shadow. "Tentir is a testing ground. If it eases your mind, I promise that by the time you leave, you will know beyond a doubt if you have succeeded or failed."

Jame's heart gave a leap.

"Then I'm not expelled, ran?"

"No. You are riding the rathorn now, to what fate I have no idea, but it would be unwise of me to interfere. I believe, however, that I should assign you extra duty for damaging the arcade roof, say, by repairing it. Please leave the normal way, through the door. The college has had enough excitement for the time being."

Her foot was on the threshold when he spoke again, out of the gathering darkness:

"By the way, you also should know that the Randir Tempter has returned to her duties at Tentir—prematurely, I would have thought, but here she is. Take care, Knorth. She has no love for your house or for you."

"Yes, ran. Thank you." She saluted him and left.

Only on the way out did she recognize what the Commandant had been carving. It was a little, wooden soldier.

This time, she found the stair easily and was descending to the main hall when a mound of dirty clothes on a pair of muddy legs entered from New Tentir. Jame wasn't sure about the legs, but she recognized the mud.

"Rue?"

The clothes dropped and there was the border cadet waist deep in them, gaping at her.

"Lady! You're still here!"

"Of course I am. Oh, you mean I haven't been kicked out yet. No, but we have to repair the roof."

"That's all?" A huge grin split the girl's face. "My, won't Vant be surprised."

"What's all this about?" Jame asked, indicating the sprawling heap.

Rue shrugged. "Vant gave our ten punishment duty for the mud fight. It's laundry day down in the fire timber hall, and we have to wash the entire barracks' dirty underwear."

At that moment, Vant himself entered the hall. "You, shortie, what're these clothes doing on the floor? Can't stay out of the dirt, eh?" Then he saw Jame, and turned his start into a sideways salute with eyes averted. "You're possessions are packed, lady. We can have you on the road to Gothregor before dinner."

"Oh, can you." Jame finished her descent at a leisurely stroll. She had no impulse whatsoever to lose her temper: after Corrudin, this seemed like a minor affair and Vant, for all his six feet of arrogant bluster, a bug not worth squashing. "Such unseemly haste, but then every time you turn around, you apparently expect to find me gone. Well, now you can relax. At least this side of the autumn cull, I'm not going anywhere."

Others of her ten had entered as she spoke, each with arms full of laundry. Vant was staring at her now, open-mouthed.

"You throw Lord Caineron's chief advisor out a third story window, and the Commandant doesn't expel you? Is he insane?"

"You may ask him that, with my blessing. In the meantime, I rescind your punishment order. Each ten will do its own washing, as usual. And in future you will clear any such order with me before you issue it. I'll be making a list"—*as soon as I can find a reliable master ten to consult*, she thought—"specifying what duties are yours and what are mine."

Vant stood rigid, staring straight ahead. "Lady, I can't read."

Jame remembered that he had indeed lost most of his points in the entry trials on that score.

"Learn," she said, and walked out.

Rue followed her, trailing clothes as she sorted out the muddiest of them. "What about yours, lady?"

Jame plucked at her shirt, feeling it unglue from her skin and bits of half-dry mud rattle down between her breasts. Head to foot, she was a mess.

"I need a bath," she said, "or better yet, a swim."

# Chapter XI:  The White Lady

## Summer 42

## I

NO ONE SWAM in the Silver by choice: those who did tended not
to come out, nor were their bodies ever found.  The Merikit blamed
the River Snake.  Jame believed them, having been dropped halfway
down the Snake's gullet at Kithorn.  However, the river's tributaries
were generally considered to be safe.

South of Tentir, one such stream tumbled down through a series of falls, basins, and rapids.  Jame heard the water's roar as she
approached on a path hacked through rampant cloud-of-thorn
bushes, also the laughter of cadets who had had the same idea and a
head start on her.  She stripped off her filthy clothing as she went,
mindful of those reaching three-inch thorns.

Here a rock thrust up into the afternoon sun.  Dropping her
bundle of clothes at its base, she climbed toward the sound of
water, untangling her mud-clotted hair as she went.  At the top she
was met by the delicious tingle of cold spray on her bare, hot skin
and a cool breath that lifted sweaty tendrils from her face.  Across
the gorge, the stream plunged over boulders, half rapids, half falls,
into a wide, oblong cauldron.  The swiftest water flowed past on
the far side of some large, flat-topped rocks into a stony bottleneck,
then down into the next pool.  The rest of the basin swirled slowly
in an ever-renewing backwater.  Heads bobbed in it, turned up open-
mouthed to stare at her.  Well, let them look.  She poised defiantly on
the brink for a moment, then dove.

It occurred to Jame in midair that jumping headfirst into unfamiliar water was not very smart and, sure enough, she barely missed
a submerged ledge.

Fed by mountain snows, the water was cold enough to jolt the
heart.  It was also surprisingly deep once away from its treacherous
margin.  A chasm opened in its bed, gaping down below the reach
of light—the work, surely, of the River Snake's writhing rather than
of mere erosion.  Fish hung over its terraces, motionless except for

the shimmer of their scales in the mottled light. Then, in the flick of an eye, they were gone. Through the cloud of dirt drifting off of her skin, Jame thought she saw something below in the abyss, something that stirred and began slowly to rise.

A hand touched her shoulder. Jame lost her breath in a flurry of bubbles and surfaced, gasping. Timmon's golden head bobbed up beside her.

"You scared me," he said. "People don't usually dive off Break-neck Rock head first." He looked at her closely. "Your teeth are chattering and your lips are turning blue with the cold. Come on."

He swam to one of the flat midstream rocks and climbed up onto it. Turning, he offered her his hand. Mindful that her gloves were with the rest of her clothes, on shore, Jame scrambled up without his help and stretched out face down on the rock, hands tucked under her elbows. The stone was blessedly warm. Slowly, the memory faded of what she thought she had seen in the depths. A leviathan in a puddle indeed—not that it would have been the first time she had seen such a thing.

The other swimmers were slipping out of the pool and departing, either through tact or out of sheer embarrassment. At that moment, Jame didn't care which.

"Ah," she said with a contented sigh, relaxing. "This is nice."

Timmon cradled his head on folded arms, regarding her askance. She thought he was going to ask her about the defenestration of Corrudin, but word of that mishap apparently hadn't yet reached him.

Instead, he said, "No one would mistake you for a boy, but I can count every one of your ribs. You really should eat more."

"So everyone tells me, but I think my sense of taste was permanently damaged in the Haunted Lands. How would you like to dine day after day on whimpering vegetables?"

"Not much. Did they really?"

"When they weren't groaning or screaming, and the potatoes' eyes followed you reproachfully around the room. We won't even discuss the cabbage heads or what was in them."

"Thank you. I think I've already lost my taste for supper."

He, at least, needn't worry about starving, any more than about growing fat. Through streamers of wet, black hair, she regarded the slim, nicely muscled body stretched out beside her, alabaster white except for his tanned face where the sun had brought out an unexpected garnish of freckles. He grinned at her and she looked quickly away, surprised to discover by the heat in her own face that she was blushing.

They were lying close enough together to feel each other's warmth. Timmon ran a fingertip lightly over her skin. With an effort, Jame held still, although the hairs on her arm quivered and rose.

He smiled. "You aren't used to being touched, are you?"

Hit, pushed, kicked, occasionally thrown off high buildings, yes...but no, mere touching wasn't a common experience for Jame. Neither was being hit by rocks.

"Hey!" said Timmon, rousing, as a pebble bounced off his bare back.

Two figures stood on Breakneck Rock. For a moment, Jame had the strangest feeling that all of this had happened before, only that man in a bright coat had been someone else, and so had she. A scrap of dream, a bitter rind of helplessness and shame...or had it been she on the rock, looking down scornfully at a thin, naked boy trying futilely to cover himself?

But the newcomers proved to be only Gorbel, his scarlet coat aglow like a banked fire in the gathering twilight, and one of his friends. The latter leered down at them.

"Fast work, Ardeth!" he shouted over the waterfall's clamor. "At least save us a bit of Knorth thigh!"

As Timmon swore back good-naturedly, Jame regarded the Caineron Lordan, who stared back at her without expression. Clearly, he had been pleased by her handling of his granduncle, as had been the Commandant. Corrudin must normally keep well in the background for his name never to have come up before outside his own house. Was he the brains behind Caldane's otherwise mindless drive for power? Caineron politics obviously were far more complex than she had realized.

Someone was shouting. The words were broken by distance, water, and tree, but they were coming closer. Again came the cry, clearer now:

"...rathorn! There's a rathorn in the woods!"

The second Caineron plunged out of sight—from the sound of it, into a thorn bush—but Gorbel had turned and now stood as if rooted to the spot. Then he began, slowly, to retreat backward toward the rock's slippery edge.

Jame and Timmon jumped to their feet.

"Watch out!" Timmon shouted, but too late: Gorbel's foot came down on vacant air. He tottered for a moment, arms windmilling wildly, then fell. He landed with a great splash and immediately sank. The water turned red. Trinity, if he had hit the ledge...

Timmon dove in after him. On the verge of following, Jame froze.

Something white had emerged on top of the rock; something like a horse, but clad underneath in bands of ivory armor from throat to loins. Ivory also masked its face like a battle helm, and out of it grew two horns, the smaller between flared nasal pits, the larger, wickedly curved, between deep-set ruby eyes. It stared down at Jame, and bared its fangs with a long, soft hiss of satisfaction.

Jame felt her jaw drop. The last time she had seen the rathorn colt, it had only been a foal. Time passes: it had grown.

Timmon surfaced with a thrashing, sputtering Gorbel. The backflop had apparently saved the latter's neck, but not taught him how to swim.

"Help!" Timmon shouted, and flinched as Gorbel's flailing fist caught him in the nose. Then the weight of sodden clothing dragged them both down again.

Rathorn be damned. Jame dove in.

Again, the shock of cold water, again the glimmering depths, with two figures sinking into them. Their struggle had taken them out beyond the ledge. Timmon was trying to strip off the deadly coat, which seemed to have developed a dozen extra arms, while Gorbel clutched at him with a drowning man's panic. Jame swam after them. Her ears throbbed in time to her heartbeat and her lungs ached by the time she caught up. The Caineron, mercifully, finally went limp. She hooked her nails in the coat and ripped, releasing a fresh cloud of red dye. They wrestled the remains off a now unconscious Gorbel and struck out for the surface, taking him with them.

Far below in the rock shadows, eyes as large and unblinking as dinner plates thoughtfully watched them go.

Gasping, Knorth and Ardeth dragged the Caineron ashore. Gorbel made a gurgling sound. Timmon turned him on his side as he began to vomit water and what was left of his lunch.

They were on a spit of rock between the upper basin and the first of a series below, with water thundering down through the narrow throat of a chasm at one end. The noise covered the sound of approaching hooves. Jame had no doubt, however, what had just breathed down the back of her neck. She turned and found herself eye to eye with the rathorn colt. His nasal tusk came up almost gently under her chin, lifting it, obliging her to rise or be impaled.

Something red flew out of the water with a wet sound—*p-toot!*—as if it had been spat. Gorbel's coat whacked the colt in the head and flung its dismembered arms around his neck. He squealed and reared, fore-hooves flailing, rear slipping on the wet rock. Over he went, backward, to a shout of alarm from Timmon and a squawk from Gorbel.

Jame ran.

Below Breakneck Rock, a wall of thorns kept her beside the river as it snaked down the mountain side from wide pool to narrow rapids, from outthrust rock spit to cleft gorge. The roar of water deepened as more streams joined it, covering any sound of pursuit, and she must watch where she placed her bare feet rather than look back. There was no turning to fight such a thing anyway, no chance at all except either to lose it or to reach safety before it caught her.

Jame paused on top of a boulder the size of a small house. Rubble spilled precipitously down its far side to a narrow rock ledge. Beyond that gaped the mouth of Perimal's Cauldron with the river thundering down into it and mist billowing out. From here, she could see no way out below. She was turning to backtrack when a stone shifted under her foot and suddenly she was falling.

There are probably worse things than tumbling, naked, down a steep, rocky slope, but at the moment Jame couldn't think of any, unless it was the abrupt stop at the end. Bruised and breathless, she found herself sprawling on the stone ledge at the cauldron's smoking rim, amazed that she hadn't broken anything or gone over the edge.

But she wasn't alone.

*Kinzi-kin.*

On the far landward end of the ledge stood a figure wreathed in mist, haloed with thorns. Long white hair—or was it a mane?—

stirred in the updraft. Ears pricked through it. Jame wondered if in her fall she had cracked her skull without noticing it. As the mist shifted, at one moment the other's form appeared to be that of a thin, pale woman; the next, that of a spectral horse, and yet not quite.

Trinity. Was it a Whinno-hir? A name came back to her: Beltairi. The missing White Lady.

One dark, liquid eye regarded her warily.

*My lady Kinzi bade me find you.*

Jame sat up, wincing.

"Your lady...my great-grandmother Kinzi...is dead. Sorry. It was a long time ago."

The dark eye showed a white rim.

*How long?*

Jame thought fast, doing sums. "Er...thirty-four years."

The other flinched. Jame saw her clearly for a moment as a small, painfully thin mare who pawed the ground in denial and tossed her head as if to dislodge those words that threatened to shatter her already tottering world. The hidden half of her face emerged briefly from the veil of silvery hair. Something about it was terribly wrong.

Then she was a woman again, with trembling hands clasped over her ears as if to hear nothing more.

*No, no, no. Dead? And for so long? Oh, Kinzi, for me it was one endless night full of terrible dreams. Kinzi-kin, my lady bids me warn you...but my lady is dead, yet she summoned me, spoke to me. In a grove. Under the eyes of so many silent watchers.*

That must have been the stand of trees where the Tishooo had left the Knorth death banners hung as if in some aerial hall, Jame thought.

"Kinzi's banner called to you, lady?" she asked, to make sure.

*Yes, yes. Oh, her blood must have trapped her soul in the weave of her death.*

Damn. Jame had suspected as much with Aerulan. The wider implications appalled her, but there was no time to consider them now.

"You said my great-grandmother sent you to warn me. About what?"

Rocks rattled down, followed a moment later by the rathorn like a bolt of white lightning, all horns, hooves, and fangs. The

Whinno-hir screamed and vanished. Where she had stood was a gap in the cloud-of-thorn bushes. Jame bolted through it, the rathorn roaring on her heels. The path ended in a wall of thorns. Beneath them was a dark hole, a burrow leading to some animal's lair. Jame dove down it. Wet skin and damp soil turned it into a slick, muddy chute, with a quick glimpse at the bottom of furry hindquarters scuttling for dear life out the back door.

The rathorn crashed down on the bush. Thorn and dry branch snapped against his armor and between the twin scythes of his horns. Jame started up, but her loose hair caught on the brambles. Trapped, through a fretwork of thorns she saw something white eclipse the darkening sky like a falling moon. Then the rathorn smashed down again, and she scrambled free.

Her wild flight ended abruptly against a pair of legs. There was a crescent of them, and a spiked ring of spears leveled over her head at the bush. In its ruin, the rathorn reared and screamed his defiance. His sides and flanks were bloody from the bite of thorns and his red, red eyes glared into hers.

*Come away from them*, said his voice in her mind. *Come away with me and let us be done.*

A hand on her shoulder stopped her.

The colt snorted. *If not today, then tomorrow, or next week, or next year. Wait.* Then he turned and plunged away.

Captain Hawthorn grounded her spear with a sigh. "One thing about having you around, lady," she said to Jame. "Life is never dull."

# II

THEY ALL ENDED up in the Commandant's office, which turned out to be adjacent to the Map Room.

Timmon had found his pants. Jame was shivering naked inside a borrowed jacket. Gorbel, in his pink-stained shirt, was throwing a tantrum.

"You *have* to let me hunt it!" he raged, leaning over the Commandant's desk and fairly shouting in his face. "No one has ever bagged a rathorn before! When am I ever likely to get another chance like this?"

Gorbel, obviously, was an avid hunter. Jame had never seen him so animated or less like the miniature version of his father that he always tried to be—not that Caldane didn't hunt too, she thought, remembering the Merikit skins, scalps still attached, strewn about his bedroom at Restormir.

No one had mentioned the pale Whinno-hir. Jame began to wonder if she had imagined their strange conversation. Great-grandmother Kinzi's soul trapped in the web of her death? A warning never quite delivered?

"You've *got* to let me hunt him!" Gorbel cried, adding in a rising note of triumphant, "Father would insist!"

The Commandant regarded him thoughtfully.

"Something does have to be done about that beast, sir," said Hawthorn, regretfully. "I've never seen its like, all white and red eyed—magnificent, in terrible a way—but it's clearly a rogue. A death's-head. No rage will let it join, and they're social creatures, rathorns, for all their filthy tempers. On its own, it will go mad, if it hasn't already. It's dangerous."

The other randon murmured agreement.

"At least we know now why the herd has been acting up," said the horse-master. "Of course it would, with something like that on the prowl."

"Yes, but why here? True, some of them are man-eaters, but to attack so close to a keep and with such determination…"

Everyone looked at Jame.

She glared back through a tangle of wet, muddy hair with enough broken thorns in it to build a respectable bird's nest and wished she could stop shivering. It wasn't just that she was cold and wet, or that under the coat her body was laced with stinging scratches. The colt had been inside her mind. She could still taste his fury, but beneath that the grief and aching loneliness. She had taken away the only thing he had ever loved. Now she was all he had left, and he wanted her dead only a shade more fiercely than he wished for his own death.

"Indeed," said the Commandant, "something must be done. But not by cadets."

Gorbel looked stunned, then furious. The Commandant ignored him.

"Organize a hunt. Take randon and sargents, war-hounds and hawks. The Falconer will be our eyes, as usual. See to it. Dismissed."

And they all found themselves trooping outside, including a stunned, stammering Gorbel. "B-b-b-but the Commandant is a Caineron!" he said with genuine, almost hurt bewilderment.

Timmon shrugged. "Perhaps Daddy's reach isn't as long as you supposed. Perhaps Sheth will let you kill something later. Something small."

"Ah!" Gorbel snarled and stalked off, squelching loudly in his wet boots.

"I'll see you back to your quarters," said Timmon to Jame, sounding a shade too pleased with the situation.

"No, you won't," she snapped, shrugging off his solicitous arm.

"Don't you at least want this?" he called after her, holding up the borrowed coat which had come off in his hand.

"No!"

Cadets stared, aghast, or dove for cover as she stormed down the arcade. One, his arms full of armor to be cleaned, fell with a great clatter head first over the rail into the training square.

Rue met Jame at the Knorth door. The cadet's jaw fell. "Lady, you...you're..."

"Wet, cold, muddy, and in a foul temper. Just get me some hot water before I kill somebody. And stop staring at my ribs!"

# Chapter XII: Unsheathed

## Summer 43-44

## I

JAME WOKE WITH a start, heart pounding, tangled in sweat soaked bedding. Trinity, when would these nightmares stop? But this one had been different. No hot, close room, no drunken laughter or unholy hunger. They had been chasing...someone. Her, she thought. In pain. In despair. How her face had throbbed.

*Was* that me? Jame wondered, touching her cheek, surprised to find the scar so slight.

In her dream, it had sprawled across half her face, and she had been running very fast on all fours.

There had also been terror.

They would finish what he (who?) had started or, worse, they would give her back to him.

*Oh, Kinzi, is this all that honor has come to mean?*

And he hunted with them in his gilded armor, as avid for blood as the hounds that bayed on her trail.

"Ho! So ho! Hark, hark, hark!"

There *were* voices below in the training square, in the predawn glimmer.

Jame scrambled out of her disordered bed and crossed to the inner window, snatching up clothes as she went. The square seethed with subdued, purposeful activity. Horses, dogs, randon and sargents...of course. This morning they would set out to kill the rathorn colt.

Downstairs, she found most of the college's cadets lining the rail, watching and chattering excitedly.

"I reckon they've called up every hound in the college except Gorbel's private pack and Tarn's old Molocar," Dar was saying as Jame slipped between Brier and Vant to a place at the rail.

"Tarn is as mad as fire about that," remarked someone from Vant's ten. "He won't admit that old Torvo isn't up to it. Anyway, the lymers are already out casting for the scent."

"They'll start at the pool," said Quill wisely. "I hear it crashed through the thorns, so there'll be a blood trail, at least at first. Once the direhounds catch sight of it, well, that will be that."

Not far away, the Commandant was checking the tack on his tall, gray stallion Cloud. The horse wore a coat of iron rings interlaced with strips of *rhi-sar* leather, protecting his chest, sides, and flanks with skirts long enough, hopefully, to foil a rathorn's upward thrust. His rider wore corresponding light armor, designed for the hunt. Man and horse had the same sheen of misted steel, the same chill of purpose.

Two direhounds, impatient for the chase, turned on each other snapping and snarling. They moved almost too fast for the eye to follow, a blur of lean, white bodies, black legs, and square, black heads. Huntsmen grabbed them by their spiked collars and wrenched them apart, but not before one had caught the other's foreleg in its powerful jaws and snapped the bone with an audible crunch. The hunt-master knelt to assess the damage. The hound whined and was licking his face as he slipped a blade between its ribs.

"First blood of the hunt," said Erim uneasily as the randon cradled the dead hound, "and it's ours."

*There will be more,* thought Jame, eyeing the array of swords, boar-spears, and bows.

"I wish," she said to no one in particular, "that they would just leave him alone."

Vant gave her a sidelong glance. "Now, lady, we can't have a brute like that on the loose, can we? Or were you thinking you'd like to ride him?"

That caused a ripple of laughter; Jame's poor horsemanship was fast becoming the stuff of legend. The horse-master swore that she had found every way to fall off known to man or beast, and then invented a few more.

"Look," said someone.

They all leaned over the rail, craning to the left to watch as Gorbel entered the square. He was dressed in hunting leathers and carried a boar-spear as if he knew how to use it. The hunt-master stroked the hound's head one last time, lowered it to the ground, and rose to meet the Caineron Lordan.

What they said was inaudible to the onlookers, but Gorbel's growing anger spoke for itself. He turned, blustering, to the Commandant.

Sheth shot a sidelong smile at Harn Grip-hard, who stood stone-faced by the rail, watching, clad in his everyday, rumpled clothes. "Since the Highlord's commander does not deign to hunt down and kill the…er…emblem of his house," the Commandant announced in his clear, light voice to the college at large, "he stays here, in charge during my absence. Ask him."

Even as Gorbel turned, speechless and baffled, Harn was shaking his massive head. No.

Vant laughed as Caineron lordan stalked back to his barracks. "Better luck next time, Gorbelly!"

"Be quiet," said Brier.

Vant turned to her from his haughty height although, indeed, he was slightly shorter than she. "*What* was that, five?"

Jame spoke without looking at either of them. "She meant, 'Shut up, ten.' It's tacky to gloat."

As Gorbel stalked past the Randir, they called out sympathetically to him. One named Simmel put his arm around the Caineron's shoulders and shook him playfully.

*Mmm*, thought Jame, remembering her uncle's ill-fated Randir crony, Roane. Whenever there was trouble, there seemed to be a Randir somewhere behind it, pushing.

In the crowd by the rail, she saw a thick coil of gold wrapped around a cadet's neck. The Randir seemed to feel Jame's eyes and glared back, one hand rising to caress the triangular head that rose from her collar to meet it. So. The Shanir had gotten her snake back, apparently uninjured. Good.

Was it really possible for an entire house to go rotten? Some Randir randon seemed all right. Others…she remembered the Tempter and the calculating, alien darkness that had seemed for a moment to peer out through her eyes. The Commandant had said that she was back, but Jame hadn't yet encountered her, nor did she wish to.

The Falconer's merlin swooped over the square with a scream, then wheeled toward the upper window of the mews where his master awaited him. Simultaneously came the belling of distant horns.

"They have the scent!" cried several voices. "Hurrah!"

Riders swung into the saddle and took the boar spears handed up to them. Archers strung their bows. Hounds yelped and pressed eagerly against the hall doors, black tails whipping in excitement. The doors opened. They surged through, down Old Tentir's hall, and out into the growing dawn. Swift feet and hooves followed.

Cadets leaned over the rail to watch them go, cheering, but then fell silent as the tumult of the hunt faded into the distance. Gorbel threw down his spear.

After that, it seemed quite prosaic to go in to breakfast with another round of lessons ahead.

# II

HOWEVER, IT TURNED out to be a day of distractions.

Whatever the class, the cadets' attention kept turning to the hunt.  For a long time, snatches of it could be heard in the distance—the bell of hounds, the sound of horns—borne on a shifting wind.  The rathorn colt, it seemed, was keeping close to Tentir, playing hide-and-seek with its pursuers.  In this, it was no doubt helped not only by the Riverland's odd topography but also by the disruptions caused by the recent weirdingstrom and quakes, which between them had displaced large chunks of the landscape, some as far south as the Cataracts.

Perhaps, some whispered, it could even use the folds of the land as the Merikit did.

Others laughed at this, but uneasily: no one knew for sure how the northern tribesmen could pop up wherever in the Riverland they chose.  Some, like Lord Caineron, welcomed the odd native hunter as good sport, to be hunted in turn.  Others remembered the fate of Kithorn and kept watch especially against the autumn cattle raids, but it did little good.

*We are strangers here*, Jame thought, not for the first time, *and the land doesn't welcome us.*

She and her ten were on their way, finally, to the day's last lesson.

The previous three had been exercises in confusion, with whole files of lancers tripping over each other's weapons, arrows loosed at random (except for Erim's, who couldn't seem to miss if he tried), and an irate strategy instructor dismissing half his class mildly concussed for inattention.

Harn had finally emerged and bellowed that the whole college had better settle down or, by Trinity, he would work off their fidgets with a punishment run the likes of which they had never seen and probably wouldn't survive.

Gorbel, bound for the same lesson as Jame, was still seething: "God's claws, I can track down that brute if anyone can.  I'm the best hunter at Restormir except," he added hastily, "for Father."

While his cronies assured him that this was true and Jame's ten bit their tongues under Brier's stony gaze, Jame unhappily considered the rathorn. The Riverland wouldn't be safe for her, or at least as safe as it had ever been, until he was dead, but what a terrible waste!

Here was their classroom, a large chamber on the ground floor of Old Tentir, where they would practice with some of the more obscure weapons in the Kencyrath's armory. Jame stopped short on the threshold, her ten piling up behind her. Hanging on a rack were suits of protective leather armor, face-guards, and beside them, in pairs, heavy gauntlets tipped with steel claws.

Their instructor was a dark Brandan who looked as if he had had entirely too much experience with the wicked blades behind him. Indeed, one puckered eyelid drooped over an empty socket while three seamed scars ran parallel to it slantwise across his face.

"The Arrin-thar," he announced, gesturing to dangling weapons. "You see the intended connection with the lethal claws of the Arrin-ken, also with occasional rare Shanir. Find the pair that suits you best."

Alone among the excited chatter of her classmates, Jame fumbled through the swinging scythes, hoping desperately that none of them would fit.

"Here, lady," said the instructor, and thrust a pair at her. "These were made for a Kendar child—as playthings, no less—but you have hands almost as small." He pulled on his own and flexed their articulated fingers. Clink, clink, clink. "Well, Jameth?"

Jame stood holding the gauntlets in her own gloved hands, feeling numb, then nauseous.

"My name is Jame, ran, not Jameth." She gulped. "And I think that I'm going to be sick."

"Not good enough." He flipped down his face guard. "Defend yourself."

And he sprang at her.

She dropped the gauntlets.

The next moment passed in a blur of action, two figures at the heart of it leaping, striking, withdrawing.

The instructor looked down at his shirt—he hadn't bothered to don body armor against a novice—and watched it fall apart in five long gashes. The hairy chest beneath was similarly slashed, and the cuts just beginning to bleed.

Jame backed into a corner, hands gripped tightly behind her.

"…sorry, sorry, sorry…"

The randon stalked after her, cadets scattering before him. "Show me."

White faced and miserable, she held out her hands. He stripped off the gloves and examined her fingertips. Then he pressed her palms to make the ivory claws extend.

Gorbel's moon of a face appeared at the randon's elbow, wide-eyed and goggling.

"Oh, how splendid!" he breathed, and then, as his friends pushed up behind him. "I mean, how grotesque. Father always said you were a freak."

For this, he got the randon's elbow casually jabbed into his eye and retreated, swearing.

"You'll need special training to use these properly," said the instructor in a matter-of-fact tone, releasing Jame's hands. "Gloves aren't a bad idea, though. Take note, all of you: always keep a weapon in reserve, the more unexpected, the better. D'you have clawed toes as well…er…Jame? Too bad. They can be useful. Now, on to practice."

The rest of the session passed in a daze for Jame. Wearing armor against the others' inexperience, encumbered by her own, she countered their flailing attacks automatically, initiating none of her own. Nor did it help that the instructor kept watching her, although he said nothing. At last the class was over and the cadets dismissed.

Outside the room, Jame almost ran head first into the Randir Tempter. All the more startling, the woman wore a heavy veil across the lower half of her face. She stepped aside without speaking, but the lines around her dark eyes shifted as if she smiled, unpleasantly: *Why should I interfere? You will destroy yourself soon enough.*

Jame had meant to slink back to her attic, but word of what had happened preceded her.

Timmon was waiting on the boardwalk. "From all the ruckus," he said, "I thought you must at least have sprouted fur and fangs." When he craned to see her hands, she presented them to him with a defiant glare, nails out. "Now these," he said, examining them, "are quite elegant. Just the same, you'll have to be careful how you use them in bed."

Jame realized that her ten had bunched up behind her, watching and listening, Vant with distaste, Brier without expression, the others obviously fascinated.

"Do you mind?" she snapped at them. As they reluctantly departed, she rounded on the Ardeth. "As for you…"

Timmon also retreated, throwing up his hands in mock surrender. "Keep 'em sheathed! I'm off too. And sleep well tonight, Lordan of Ivory," he called after her as she stalked away. "I'll see you in your dreams."

At the door of the Knorth barracks, Jame paused, hearing a babble of voices within: "Did you hear…" "Did you see…" "Oh no." "Oh yes!"

Sudden silence fell as she stepped over the threshold. Nearly everyone was there, back from the last lesson, and all had turned to stare at her. Instinctively, she thrust her hands behind her back. Her movement broke the spell. At least half the room rushed at her, shouting questions:

"Oh, lady, can we see? Rue says they're five inches long" ("I did not!" Rue protested from the back of crowd) "and as sharp as knives!" "Did you really make cat's meat of the instructor?" "We knew you were a true Knorth!" "Oh please, lady, show us!"

And, hesitantly, Jame did, flexing her long, black gloved fingers, the ivory nails, honed to lethal points, sliding out of their sheaths.

"Ooooh!"

"So *that's* why the king post in the attic is all scratched up!" Rue exclaimed, suddenly enlightened.

Jame bolted up the stairs.

In her own quarters above, she leaned out the hole in the roof to gulp down cool mountain air, to wonder if, after all, she was going to be sick.

But here came Jorin, trotting across the floor, greeting her as if she had been gone a year. She sank down against the wall, gathered up as much of the ounce as would fit into her lap, and pressed her face into his rich fur. His purr shook them both, or perhaps not his purr alone.

*"Shanir, god-spawn, unclean, unclean!"*

Words shouted at a frightened child with bloody fingertips and nails. No: claws. Hide them. Chop them off. But too late: Father had seen. So much hate, such loathing for who and what she was.

Worse, Tori felt the same way, on a gut level perhaps inaccessible to reason. Father had trained him well, even as he had rebelled against that legacy of hate.

She, too, had rebelled, over and over again…but she had never quite lost the sense that it was all her fault. The claws. The rejection. Everything. That lesson, too, had sunk in deeper than reason.

Now Kendar who previously couldn't look her in the face had been avid to see what she had kept hidden in shame all her life. True, some had expressed horror. But not all. Not even most.

She remembered Marc's easy acceptance of her…deformity. Perhaps he was more typical of the Kendar attitude than she had thought. "*We are many,*" the Randir Tempter had said, speaking of the Kendar Shanir, "*and we are proud.*"

Jorin stretched backward over her arm, bracing himself with a paw against her cheek. She took it, feeling the warm, thick pad, the hidden menace. Press here, and out they came, hooked and sharp. Jorin took back his paw and began to groom it, pausing to crunch on the tip of a nail.

The most natural thing in the world.

No. It wasn't the same…or was it?

She cupped his sleek, golden head with her ivory nails. He leaned back into them. *There. Scratch there.*

All her life, she had mistrusted her own judgment, depending instead on that of Kendar like Marc, like these cadets, like Brier.

But her brother's feelings still mattered. Dreadfully.

And there was far more to her Shanir nature than ten embellished fingers. As yet, Tentir had no exact knowledge what it had on its hands.

Below, the dinner horn sounded.

Had so much time passed? Apparently. Her stomach rebelled at the thought of food, but she couldn't hide here forever. Jame pushed Jorin off her lap and soberly went down to a meal for which she had no appetite.

# III

*I MUST BE dreaming,* thought Jame.

She had expected to fall asleep with difficulty that night—after all, one's life didn't turn upside down every day—but now she barely remembered falling into bed.

Not this bed, though. The attic offered nothing so soft nor such silken sheets, deliciously cool on bare, bruised skin. Eyes still closed, she stretched luxuriously, like a cat, and found that her hands were bound above her head.

*...be careful how you use those claws in bed...*

Her eyes snapped open. Surely, this was a dream. Curtains of red ribbons surrounded her, rippling, whispering together. More ribbons bound her wrists, but loosely as if to say, *Relax. Blame us if you must, but enjoy what you can't prevent. Truly, is it so bad to be a woman?*

There was a flaw in that logic—probably several—but Jame found it hard to think clearly over the seductive suspiration of silk on silk. Anyway, did it matter what happened in a dream? And this felt so very, very good...

The ribbons parted. Timmon stood over her, naked and smiling. "I promised you some fun," he said.

Abruptly his expression changed. "Oh, no. Not again."

He seemed to go flat, and then his image separated into long strips...no, into more ribbons, fluttering in futile protest.

Through them stumbled someone else. A spare body wired with muscle and laced with scars, black hair shot with white, silver-gray eyes...

Brother and sister stared at each other. "Oh *no!*" they said simultaneously, and Jame woke with a start in her attic loft on rough blankets, alone.

*What a strange dream,* she thought as her pounding heart slowed. *Even for me. Especially for me. Oh well.*

She curled up again in her scratchy nest, but this time sleep eluded her for a long, long time.

# IV

DAWN CAME AT last, but no word from the hunt. The distant sounds had faded under a leaden, overcast sky. Not even the keen eyes of the Falconer's merlin, circling above, could pierce the clouds that mantled the lower slopes of the Snowthorns.

After assembly, Gorbel again demanded that he be allowed to lead out his private pack of hounds, and again he was denied. Simmel led him off, whispering in his ear with a twisted smile that the Caineron did not see.

The Danior Tarn also begged for permission to join the hunt with his Molocar Torvo and also was denied, but more gently. The old hound gave a cavernous, nearly toothless yawn and fell asleep at his master's feet.

When Jame's ten set out to do their stint in rebuilding the quake-broken outer walls, she was told to stay behind. It occurred to her, watching them go, that she hadn't been outside Tentir since the rathorn attack at the river, that the class schedule had deliberately been changed to keep her in. The college was a large place. Nonetheless, she suddenly felt cramped and restless.

Having nothing else to do, she took Jorin and went in search of Harn Grip-hard.

On the way, she ran into Timmon, arm in arm with a Kendar girl of his house.

"Have any good dreams last night?" asked Timmon. "Because I didn't. At first. Then I remembered Narsa here, and the rest of the evening was quite jolly."

He toyed with a lock of the girl's dark hair as he spoke, glancing sidelong at Jame. It occurred to her that he was trying to make her jealous.

"Play your games, then," she said, lightly. "I wish you joy of him, cadet."

Timmon blinked at her and the girl glared, clutching his arm even more tightly.

Jame went her way, annoyed to find that she *was* vaguely, fleetingly jealous. But, after all, he hadn't been all that impressive naked, even in a dream.

…anyway, not compared to that other lean, neatly muscled body tempered by hardship and battle, those beautiful hands that wore their scars like elegant lace-work gloves, those silver-shadowed eyes…

*Stop it*, Jame told herself crossly. *Things are complicated enough already*

At length she found Harn in the subterranean stable.

A commotion drew her to the southernmost row of stalls, hard against Old Tentir's foundation. Over shouts of warning rose the eerie shriek of a terrified horse, followed by a series of crashes. Edging closer, Jame saw a large, piebald horse in its stall, on its back, with all four hooves in the air. She burst out laughing. Harn turned around and boxed her on the ear, hard.

"It isn't funny," he said.

The blow sent her reeling. Rage surged over shock and she came back at him, claws out; but his expression, impatient and pre-occupied, stopped her like a dash of ice water in the face:

*Not now.*

The horse began to thrash again. A flying hoof smashed through wood, caught, was wrenched free. The animal kept rolling back against the wall and pausing to pant, its pale belly heaving. Then it lashed out again.

The bowlegged horse-master jerked a cadet out of the way. "D'you want your face flattened like mine, youngling? You and you. Pin him down."

A sargent and a third year cadet threw themselves on the horse's head and neck.

"Steady, steady…"

The master shook out a coil of rope and expertly snaked it around the far hind leg near the hock. "Now, let go!"

They sprang back.

The master pulled, aided a moment later by Harn, and the horse crashed over in a cloud of dust. It rested for moment, looking dazed, and then lurched to its feet. Harn grunted approval when he saw that it was uninjured and turned to walk away. Jame followed him, rubbing her ear.

"Listen," he said, rounding on her. "When a horse gets cast in a stall like that, it can't get up by itself. It will struggle until it dies."

"Ran, I'm sorry I laughed. It wasn't funny at all. And yes, I did nearly flare at you."

"Huh." He gave her a brooding look. "But you didn't."

"Ran," she said as he turned again to leave, "tell me about the White Lady."

He swung back, so suddenly that she shrank from him. "Why?"

"Because I've seen her, first outside my quarters, calling to me, and then beside Perimal's Cauldron."

To her surprise, behind its garnish of grizzled stubble his broad face paled. "I said your being here was madness, and now this."

"Now what, ran?" she asked, bewildered by his agitation. Did he mean to hit her again, burst into tears, or faint? "Has it something to do with her being called 'The Shame of Tentir,' and why that, anyway?"

He loomed over her like a cliff face, as if poised to crush her questions with his sheer bulk, and perhaps her as well.

"Just leave!" he roared down at her, causing heads to turn across the stable and Jorin to bolt. "D'you hear me? Get out!"

She stared after him as he stumped off.

The horse-master came trotting up to see what all the shouting was about. "Now, now, remember what the Commandant said about not driving your instructors mad, lady," he said, adding, "not that it looks like with Harn Grip-hard you'd have far to go. What in Trinity's name d'you say to him?"

"Just that I'd seen the White Lady. Was that so awful?"

The master's shaggy eyebrows rose, as if attempting to scale the mottled heights of his bald head. "Well, it's a surprise, given that the poor thing's been dead these forty years. And no, I'll not tell you how or why if the senior randon of your own house won't. I've heard tell, though, that if a Knorth sees her, it means they're going to die."

"Oh," said Jame, digesting this. "Ran, did Harn just expel me from Tentir?"

"No, no." He clapped her bracingly on the shoulder as he might have to reassure an nervous filly. "You've still got a mort of tests to fail and horses to fall off. All things in good time."

# V

THE HUNT RETURNED at dusk the next day in shocking disarray.

Everyone in it was muddy and bruised, with ripped clothes and shattered weapons. The dogs limped, heads down, and most of the horses had gone lame. The Commandant led his own mount with a sargent swaying on its back, his head wrapped in bloody rags. Other injured randon entered supported by friends or on makeshift litters.

"Trinity," said Harn, staring, as were most of the cadets who had gathered as the morning before at the practice ground rail, this time in stunned silence. "That damned colt did all of this?"

"Hardly any of it," answered Sheth, helping down the sargent. Members of the man's house rushed to help him. "I've sent for a healer," the Commandant told them. "There are some broken limbs. Otherwise, this is the worst of it.

"No, not the rathorn," he repeated to Harn, preoccupied, as he turned to help the other wounded. "We ran into a tree, or rather a tree ran over us."

The rest of the story had to wait until dinner in the officers' mess. Nearly everyone attended, bandages, splints, and all. A healer, borrowed from the Scrollsmen's College at Mount Alban, was with the injured sargent. Otherwise, even the Commandant was present for once, although this was a mixed blessing: no one dared to speak of the hunt before he did and there he sat, calmly sipping the wine that he had ordered served instead of the customary cider, clad in a coat of rich, purple velvet trimmed with royal blue. Unlike most of his fellow huntsmen, he had found time to bathe.

Harn, too, drank, more deeply than usual. He had been rattled by Jameth's sighting of the White Lady and, no doubt, had made a fool of himself, luckily during the Commandant's absence. Since then, he had had time to think. Whatever his feelings about Bel-tairi and the terrible events following her death, or disappearance, or whatever-it-had-been, he felt now that he had underestimated the Knorth Lordan. It was hard not to see her as a frighteningly vulnerable version of her brother or as a fragile child when compared to her fellow Kendar cadets, but Bran's news heartened him.

On the other hand, as usual, he found Sheth's reticence maddening. At last he slammed down his glass, ignoring it when it shattered. His neighbors flinched at the flying shards.

"Well?" he growled. "D'you mean to sit there all night smirking like a cat in cream? What *happened*, man?"

Sheth picked a splinter of glass out of his venison stew and laid it beside his plate. "Patience never was one of your virtues, was it, Ran Harn? All right."

He folded his hands and spoke as if to them, a thin smile wryly twisting his saturnine face. "As you may have guessed, we saw precious little of the rathorn. His trail kept ending up in a hopeless muddle, crossed, recrossed, and crossed yet again. Clearly, he was playing with us and no doubt enjoying himself enormously. Then too, we kept stumbling on stray patches of weirding and the occasional case of arboreal drift."

Someone laughed, like Harn a bit drunk. "S'true. I got caught in a creeping grove of sumac and was nearly carried off, Trinity knows where."

"You were lucky," said another morosely, his hands such a welter of bandages that he could only glare at his untouched meal. "The cloud-of-thorns were on the move too. So were the wild roses. And the raspberry canes."

"Ah, the thorns of life," murmured Sheth. "So sweet. So sharp. Things didn't get really…er…interesting, though, until last night. We were bedding down when we first heard it. From the approaching lash of branches, I thought we were in for a storm, but there was no wind. Then it burst into our camp. I think," he added judiciously, "that we were simply in its way."

"In whose way?" demanded Harn, just short of an explosion.

"Why, didn't I say? It was a golden willow. Rampant."

"God's claws, Commandant! Don't y'know how to tell a story?" The bandaged randon leaned forward, elbows planted firmly in his dinner.

"Listen. First, as Sheth Sharp-tongue says, we hear this mighty thrashing in the forest. Myself, I wondered if the Dark Judge and judgment itself were about to fall on us. Then the earth begins to writhe. Roots are surging out of it and rocks are sinking in. See, the ground has turned as soft as quicksand and I'm fighting in its grip, all tangled up in runners like so many ropes of steel. Then comes the tree.

"God's truth, we all thought we were dead. Some were sinking, others picked up and flung aside. It had no more regard for us than...than for so much straw flung in its way. Less, if possible. Myself, I don't believe that the Riverland is alive and conscious, much less that it doesn't like us crawling over its wrinkled hide like...like..."

"Fleas?" suggested an Edirr, helpfully. "Lice? Wood ticks?"

"Argh. Brute nature. Brute Rathillien. That's all it is. Like a hundred other worlds before it."

"Ah, but we don't know about them, do we?" said the Commandant gently. "Only that none of them have put us to the test the way this world has."

"It needs to know its master," a Caineron muttered into his glass. "That's all."

"And if it refuses?" asked a Randir, with a sidelong smile at the others of her house.

"Then, I say, break it all to bits."

"Leaving us to stand on what?" Harn snorted. "This is ridiculous. Look at you, bandaged up to the eyebrows. Who broke whom? You Caineron and you Randir, who cut down all the trees around Wilden to stop them from drifting away. What has that gotten you? Mud-slides in season and a rain of frogs out of it. Is all the Chain of Creation to be bent to your will?"

"Yes!" shouted the Caineron, and banged their glasses on the table, more shattering in the process.

"If this keeps up," murmured one senior randon to another, "we'll have to start drinking from tin cups, or from cupped hands."

"So we are to rule the whole of creation," said Sheth, with a wry smile, regarding their battered ranks. "Never mind the Master or Perimal Darkling or a trail of lost, fallen worlds. Never mind betrayal, heartbreak, and thirty millennia of failure. And for whom, after all, do we accomplish this great feat—our hated god, our...er...beloved lords, ourselves?"

He had spoken this last softly so that most of his fellow Caineron hadn't heard. But Harn did.

"Which do you serve, randon?"

"Ah, my dear brother-in-arms. Grant me the space to decide."

Harn looked hard at him. "Choice, yes, so that it be done with honor."

The other inclined his head, acknowledging ruefully the Kencyrath's fundamental dilemma.

"I dunno about Rathillien," said one of the hunters with satisfaction, "but we spent all day chasing down and settling for that damn tree. It's chained to a boulder now, waiting for the axe. Prime bows, its wood will make, among other things."

"It's a prize all right," another agreed, "for whichever house reaches it first."

This sparked a widespread, increasingly loud argument: to whom did the willow belong? It turned out that the randon of the two nearest major houses—Caineron and Randir—had sent urgent messages to their lords requesting foresters. The Brandan claimed that they had put their mark on it first, the previous fall. Others pointed out, however, that they had subsequently lost it: when the sap began to run that spring, not surprisingly so had the tree, right across the river south of the Danior's Shadow Rock. Other houses, smaller, farther away, or more altruistic, insisted that it belonged to Tentir, hard won with blood, bruises and sundry broken bones.

Before the randon could become too heated, Harn loudly broke in: "We stay-at-homes have some news too. Bran, show 'em."

The dark, scarred randon obligingly opened his shirt to reveal five scabbed-over gashes across his hairy torso. Then he explained how he had gotten them.

"So," said someone, after a blank moment. "Our kitten has claws."

"And why," murmured the Commandant, "am I not surprised?"

"We already know that she's a reasonably controlled berserker," Harn growled. "I'll swear to that."

"We won't," snapped a Randir. "When our tempter first chewed through her gag, she induced the Kendar in charge of her to jump down a well. Something at the bottom ate him."

"Trogs, probably," muttered someone. "And poor sanitation. Never trust a rock with teeth, or a midden that burps."

Hawthorn glanced around to make sure that the randon in question was absent. "Yet Lady Rawneth has since sent her pet tempter back to...er...grace our halls."

Since her return, she had, in fact, kept mostly to the Randir barracks, to no one's disappointment except (perhaps) the Randir.

"Odd," remarked a Danior. "We've been watching the Highlord for any of his father's destructive traits, and here they pop up in his sister. True, it's not as if she could read runes or reap souls…"

He paused, perhaps remembering when Knorth and Ardeth had danced and darkness had gaped. But nothing, after all, had come of that.

"Just the same," said another randon, maybe following the other's thought, maybe not, "d'you think Torisen knows?"

"He might," said Bran, securing his shirt. "We all know how the Highlord feels about the Shanir, and his attitude toward our Jameth has been…puzzling. Does he want her to succeed at Tentir or not? Does he really mean to keep her as his heir, perhaps to become the first highlady in our history? Does he even know his own mind in the matter?"

"Or perhaps," murmured a Randir, "he's lost said mind altogether. It's been known to happen in his family. Ask the Knorth: how secure do they feel in his power since the battle at the Cataracts, much less since he fled Kothifir for the Riverland as if the Shadows themselves were snapping at his heels?"

Harn started to rise, but Sheth's fingertips on his arm stopped him. "Time will tell," the Commandant said gently. "Shouting won't."

"No offense, rans," said a Coman, his eyes flickering nervously from face to face, "but the rest aside, we all know there's only one person at Tentir qualified to train a natural Arrin-thari."

He jumped as Harn's fist crashed down on the table.

"No! We agreed that that was far too dangerous. Remember the mauled cadet. And look what he did to your face, Bran."

"Oh, I don't blame him for that. After all, at the time we were forcing him at spear-point into a cage."

"Just the same…"

"Enough," said the Commandant quietly, and the room lapsed momentarily into a strange, almost embarrassed silence.

Behind the wall, in the gloom of Old Tentir's secret ways, Graykin listened with interest.

"Speaking of the Highborn," said Hawthorn, "I'd watch out, if I were you, for the Ardeth Timmon."

"Why?" demanded a member of that house.

"Because you also produce strong Shanir, as we know to our grief from Pereden. Because his son may also be a dream-stalker, as well as a charmer. Because he's already snared a Kendar girl with his glamour and bedded her. We all know what damage that can cause, and how many Kendar Pereden ruined."

"Nonetheless, it's a house matter," said the Ardeth flatly. "Don't interfere."

"Still, he's bound to try for the Knorth Lordan."

"I pity him if he does," Harn said with a sudden bark of laughter. "God's teeth and toenails, didn't you hear? Our kitten has claws."

# Chapter XIII:  Blood and Ivory

## Summer 45

## I

JAME WOKE WITH a start, dew beading her eyelashes.  She had taken to sleeping directly under the hole in the as yet unmended roof, to Jorin's dismay, but in the past few days it had made her feel less like a prisoner.  During the night it had rained, hard, driving her back to shelter.  As soon as the storm had passed, however, she had returned to watch the hazy stars emerge one by one.

Although she thought that she had dreamed again, after that, she remembered little except a voice calling:

*...come, come, come...*

Perhaps that was what had woken her.

She rose, taking care not to disturb the ounce, and looked out. The heavy cloud cover of the past few days had condensed into slow rivers of fog rolling silently down the mountain slopes to the river.  Above, a crisp night sky sparkled with stars, the sliver of a waxing moon having long since set.  It was either very late or very early, and deathly still.

In a corner, Graykin stirred, grumbled, and went back to sleep. He had told her the previous night of the conversation that he had overheard in the officers' mess.  That had given her several things to think about.

*...come, come...*

This would be the third day of the hunt, and the seventh in the college's weekly rotation, meaning no classes.  One might even sleep in and skip breakfast.  If she could slip out unseen, no one would know she was gone until evening.

*...come...*

She dressed quietly, choosing her black, knife-fighter's *d'hen* over a cadet's jacket.  It felt good to have the Talisman's old tools back in hand for a night's prowl, if through a different maze than that of Tai-tastigon.  Solitary by nature, how she missed the freedom to come and go as she chose.  As she extracted grapnel segments from the *d'hen*'s full sleeve and snapped them together, she wondered if she would ever become accustomed to acting with or through others. A long talk with the earnest Brandan master ten had given her a list of her responsibilities as head of her own barracks, which she had memorized and then passed on to Vant, to his ill-disguised disgust. Well, if she had to lump it, so could he.

Attach the line, anchor the hook, and swing out into the night. Hopefully, the Kendar with their dislike of heights would never think of such an escape route. On the ground, she freed the grapnel with a flick of her wrist and caught it as it fell.

The fading summons drew her northward across the foggy training fields, over the bridge under which the mud battle had been fought, to the outer wall. Despite ongoing repairs, parts of it were still down, tumbled by the quake, and the whole length unguarded. Of all the Riverland keeps, ironically, Tentir possessed the fewest fortifications. When Jame had asked Vant about this, he had snorted:

"The other houses defend themselves mostly against each other. Who would attack a school where all young randon train?"

The Merikit, Jame had said. The Seven Kings. The Shadow Guild. A rising of *rhi-sar*. Caldane, Lord Caineron, on a bad day.

Vant had only laughed, as if humoring a moron.

Beyond the wall was the orchard that each year supplied the college with its apple cider. The boughs were heavy with fruit ripening toward the autumn harvest, the ground beneath fragrant with windfalls that squelched and slipped underfoot. Beyond again were sloping pastures dappled with sleeping cows and sheep and other indistinct shapes that could have been anything. Although the eastern sky now showed the black silhouette of peaks, it was still very dark here in the valley below, and rather foggy.

Jame tripped over a stump hidden in deep grass, then over another. A hare, breaking cover almost under her feet, made her heart leap. Ahead loomed the forest, in this light a solid black mass poised like an avalanche to topple over the land stolen from it. Under its eaves, seedlings had already begun to reclaim what was theirs.

Jame stopped just short of those reaching shadows. For the first time, she wondered what she was doing here.

Two by two, in perfect silence, points of light sprang up in the trees, some low, some high, more and more and more.

*The forest is watching me*, she thought, and fished the imu medallion out of her pocket.

"I have the Earth Wife's favor," she said, holding it up, wondering even as she spoke if that was still true in all senses of the word.

She had promised to carry the little, clay face with its big ears into places where Mother Ragga otherwise was deaf, but she hadn't done anything yet about the duties foisted on her by the Merikit chief Chingetai. Damn the man anyway for making her his heir and, by implication, male, just to get out of a tight spot.

Still, wasn't that exactly what Tori had done too, following the Merikit's lead and Kirien's advice?

So here she stood at the boundary between two worlds, assigned much the same role in each, in danger of failing in both.

The forest's eyes blinked. Then out of its shadows burst a flight of luminous moths. They swirled around Jame with the flash and flutter of a thousand wings, dusting her with their glow. One landed on her wrist and flexed pale gray-green wings overlaid with a tracery of silver. Its furry antennae twiddled furiously.

"Have you a message for me?" Jame asked it, only half in jest.

If so, there was no time for it. The next moment the moths spiraled up into the sky as rushing bodies parted the thick grass. Jame found herself surrounded by a milling pack of hounds. They were muzzled lymers, she saw, scent trackers with fringed dewlaps and busy, intrusive noses.

One gave a muffled yelp and their black ranks parted to let through the direhounds. Jame stood very still among the glimmer of white backs. Teeth and eyes gleamed up at her. While not up to a Molocar's weight or strength, these hounds were killers. She had seen them practice on the weaker of their own kind: their mothers first taught them to eat meat by ripping apart the runt of each litter and feeding the bloody scraps to its stronger siblings.

Then horsemen rode among the roiling pack, whipping them off. But there were too few of them to be the college hunt—a bare dozen or less.

Someone laughed. "I don't believe it. First that Danior brat slinks out of Tentir with his mangy mutt and now here's the Knorth freak. Ho, my lord! Shall we loose the dogs again and see how fast a Knorth can run?"

Jame recognized the voice: it was one of Gorbel's Highborn cronies. The Caineron Lordan himself rode apart, leaning down from the saddle to let the lymers sniff a white cloth with dark stains—

at a guess, rathorn blood wiped from thorns. The dogs milled excitedly around him, although some shrank away, whimpering. A Kendar cadet lashed them back into line. Then they were off, black on black under the trees, casting back and forth for the scent.

"My lord!" called the Highborn again.

Gorbel straightened. "What?" he said, preoccupied, intent on the dogs.

One gave a muffled yip and plunged into the forest, the rest a black tide flowing on his heels.

Gorbel shouted: "Ha!" and spurred after them.

Direhounds and horsemen followed. Jame dodged among them, sure they meant to ride her down. Instead, someone grabbed her by the collar and jerked her up across a horse's withers. A saddle horn punched her in the stomach with every stride. Branches whipped her buttocks and tore at her streaming hair. She started to slip. The horse shied violently as her nails bit into it and the rider cursed.

Trinity, anything to stop this nightmare ride.

Occasionally, prayers are answered.

Something hard clipped Jame on the back of the head and she tumbled into merciful darkness.

# II

SOMEONE WAS GROANING.

Jame swallowed, dry-mouthed, and the sound stopped.

Incautiously, she opened her eyes and winced as sunlight stabbed into them. Time had passed. The day must be well advanced. Before her lay a dappled glen carpeted with ferns, lined with slender, gleaming birch trees. She frowned, trying to remember something, anything. Shouts, dogs yelping, pain.

That last was still with her. Her head throbbed with each heartbeat and her shoulders ached. She tried to straighten to ease the strain and discovered that her hands were bound tightly behind her, around a tree trunk.

Footsteps.

Someone sank onto his heels before her, bringing their eyes level.

"So. Awake at last."

She fumbled for a name to fit that narrow face with its mocking eyes. Simmel. A Randir.

"Where…"

"North of Tentir, lost in the folds of the hills. More than that, I can't tell you. The cursed land keeps shifting. Worse, that damn colt has crisscrossed it so often over the last few days that the lymers have run off in all directions and all but three of the Caineron after them." He laughed. "That house. So easily led."

"You mean…misled."

"That too. M'lord Gorbel insists, however, that we are on the true scent. Why? Because that Danior brat and his mangy mutt are still ahead of us. But it really isn't necessary to track the rathorn any farther." He brushed loose hair back from her face and let it slide through his fingers. "You see, now we have something he wants. You."

Jame tried to answer, but the words stuck in her dry throat.

"You'd like some water, I suppose," said the Randir, making no effort to get her any.

Behind her back, she extended her claws. Her hands were so numb that she didn't know if she was breaking the rope that bound them, strand by strand, or merely shredding her own wrists. She hawked and spat froth, wishing a moment later that she hadn't turned her head to do so. The Randir's hand had dropped to finger her *d'hen*.

"What a strange jacket," he murmured, spreading it open at the throat, regarding with detached interest the slight swell of breasts beneath her white shirt, the quick, secret pulse.

When he raised his eyes, his pupils had expanded until only a rim of white remained. From the abyss within, whatever lived in the Randir Tempter's eyes regarded Jame with amused, indolent contempt.

"So here you are, the last of Kinzi's female bloodline, the last Knorth lady."

As he spoke, his voice shifted timber to a drowsy half-purr that made Jame's skin crawl.

"And what do you think your great-grandmother, dear Kinzi, would make of you? Why, you're no lady at all, just a scrawny, maskless hoyden playing soldier. Scarred, too. Damaged goods." His fingertips brushed her cheek, with a touch more of long, sharp nails than of his own short cut ones. He made a slight moue of disappointment. "I thought Kallystine had cut deeper, but never mind; even now she is paying for that mistake, and for many others."

"Who *are* you?"

"Even now you don't know. But then my name is legion, as are my forms and the eyes through which I see. Do you recognize these?"

He opened his jacket at the throat. Around his neck was a string of human teeth, the incisors chipped to sharp points. "The roots never stop bleeding," he said, more in his own voice than before, and bared his own sharpened teeth in a feral grin. "Ah, my family have been good servants to my lady, and my mother was one of the best. After you were done with her, my lady returned these to me, lest I forget. I will never forget, and neither should you."

Then Jame remembered, with a shiver. Rawneth had used the soul of one of her randon captains, a former instructor at Tentir and guard at Gothregor, a woman whose name Jame had never been able to learn, to create a demon to hunt Kindrie. There under the shadow of the Witch's tower at Wilden, Bane had literally ripped open its seams with the Ivory Knife and the demon essence had spilled out onto the pavement as a sort of black sludge with a set of teeth—these teeth—afloat in it before they too sank.

So that had been Simmel's mother and the Tempter's "cousin," caught in a situation not unlike Bane's own after the priest Ishtier had used his soul to create the Lower Town Monster—except that the Knife had presumably destroyed the randon's soul, but not necessarily her body. With Bane, the reverse might be true. Or not. Jame's head hurt enough as it was without trying to untangle such a riddle.

The Randir put a finger to his lips. "Shhhh. You mustn't frighten her away."

"Who?" Jame demanded, thoroughly confused as his voice changed again.

"Why, Kinzi's pretty little Whinno-hir, although not so pretty now. I thought she was dead. No matter. Today we finish what my sweet Greshan began."

A Caineron Highborn appeared behind him. "What, trifling with our bait? No fair, Simmel. We've earned that dubious pleasure, not you."

The Randir flinched. His face, sallow before, went white with shock as his pupils suddenly contracted back to normal. He lurched to his feet and stumbled behind a bush, where they could hear him violently retching.

"Odd people, the Randir," commented the Highborn.

Jame recognized him from her first class with the Caineron, the one who had wanted to play games. Now he watched her with bright-eyed intensity, and licked his lips.

"No," said Gorbel, behind him.

"But, my lord, think how proud your father will be of you! Besides, afterward who could tell?"

"I said, no." As the other withdrew, grumbling, Gorbel knelt and raised a leather water-bag to her lips.

Jame drank, feeling as if she could drain a lake.

"Enough," he said, and withdrew the bag.

"Why?"

"Once you helped the Ardeth Timmon save me from water," he said gruffly. "Now I save you with it. We're even."

That wasn't what she had meant. The Caineron was right: after what she had done to him and to his pet advisor, Caldane would love anyone who brought her to grief; and even as his current lordan, Gorbel's position in that snake-pit of a house was none too secure.

A shiver passed through the forest. Leaves rustled, trunks groaned, stirred by no breath of wind. Jame stiffened and tried to draw up her cramped legs.

"I think," she said, as casually as possible, "that I may be sitting on a snake."

"More likely a root. The rain last night loosened the soil. Arboreal drift, you know. Some trees prefer to spend the summer upslope where it's cooler. Also, that damn willow is stirring things up."

"It's here?"

"Close enough, and on the move, dragging a chunk of mountain after it."

He had risen and spoke in a preoccupied voice, listening. The woods quivered again.

"Take cover. As for you," he looked down at Jame, expressionless, "wait."

Left alone, unable to do otherwise, she waited.

# III

SOMETHING WAS COMING, something that glimmered between the white birch. The forest seemed to shift around it. Late spring flowers bloomed in the shadow of new leaves, stirred by a fresher breath than that of near midsummer. The Whinno-hir seemed to drift into the clearing like smoke, like mist. There at its edge she paused, shy as a doe with one delicate hoof poised in midair. Her coat was the color of fresh cream, her mane, tail, and stockings white, as were the dapples on her back and flanks. Large, dark eyes darted here and there, warily. Ears flicked. Then she snorted, tossed her head, and stomped.

Jame caught a trace of what she had scented: the infinitely personal reek that clung to the Heir's Coat. But she had long since laid that aside.

The hills fold space. Sometimes perhaps they also fold time. This wasn't the ragged creature that Jame had seen before, but what she had been. For a moment, it was forty-three years ago, and Greshan lurked behind her in ambush.

"Lady!" Her voice came out as hollow as an echo in an empty room, straining to cross decades. "It's a trap. Run!"

*Twangggg...*

The note of the bow seemed by itself to flick a crimson line across that cream colored shoulder, so fast did the arrow fly.

The Whinno-hir screamed, wheeled, and fled.

Simmel leaped from the bushes to follow, already fitting another arrow to his bow, but Gorbel caught him by the jacket and swung him around, hard.

"Never." Slap. "Hurt." Slap. "A Whinno-hir." Slap.

He let go and the Randir fell.

"I challenge you for this, lordling," he snarled through blood spilling from a split lip.

"Do. Then you can explain to the Commandant why. Oh, Perimal."

Half a dozen direhounds erupted from the undergrowth. They might not be scent trackers, but blood shed almost under their noses whipped them to frenzy. Most charged after the wounded

Whinno-hir. One made for the Randir. Gorbel caught the hound on his dagger as it leaped and flung it aside.

"Damn waste of a good dog. Horses!" he roared, turning. "After them, you fools, before they catch her!"

The three Caineron plunged away, two of them riding high in their stirrups, whooping, the third grim-faced with spurs clapped to his mount's sides.

Simmel lurched to his feet and smeared blood across his white face with a shaking hand. His trembling fingers caught the necklace of teeth and broke it. He looked beyond sick, like an apple half-devoured from within by worms. His skin grew taut over bone and his eyes sank.

"My lady honored me," he said, in a drying thread of a voice. "Then she left me. She left, with her will unfulfilled."

He was Randir. His lady was Rawneth, the Witch of Wilden. Of course. That was who had spoken to her through him.

"Your mistress has hag-ridden you," Jame said, to distract him, to gain time as she strained against her bonds. "I've seen this before, with a…a creature named Bane. Where is your shadow, Randir? What's happened to your soul?"

His lips peeled back, teeth already falling from oozing gums, and went for Jame in a shamble. At last she wrenched her hands free. One came up with a rock in it. She smashed him on the side of the head and his skull crumpled like paper, empty. He fell, and in falling crumbled to dust and to a rain of bloody teeth within his cadet's uniform.

# IV

JAME SCRABBLED OFF the remains of rope, noting that her claws had indeed picked apart one length, but they had also badly lacerated the opposite wrists. Her own blood, still flowing freely, had loosened the knots.

A moment to tear strips of cloth from her shirt, another to bind up the bleeding wounds, and she was off, stumbling after the hunt. No tracker, she quickly went astray in the restless landscape. Somewhere hounds were baying and men shouting but, it seemed, in different directions. Perhaps Gorbel, that mighty hunter, had also gotten lost.

The ground rippled with roots to trip her. Aspens quivered, reaching for the cool heights. Valley oaks dug in their gnarled toes. A grove of sumac scattered wildly in all directions. The whole Riverland felt unstable, shifting—from the crack on her head or blood loss or arboreal drift, Jame couldn't tell. Dense undergrowth, swaying trees, a sky rapidly clouding over—which way was north, which south? Lost. And under it all was the nightmare sense of needing to get somewhere, fearing that it was already too late.

Shouts, crashes, a high, terrified whinny.

Jame floundered through bushes and stopped, staring. She had caught up with the wrong hunt. Again.

The Whinno-hir Bel-tairi plunged against the ropes that held her, jerking her captors back and forth. She was small and delicately made, but terror gave her strength. A violent lunge yanked a Kendar off his feet. She stood poised to trample him, but restrained herself, snorting, and he scrambled out of her way.

"Hold her, damn you!"

The man who spoke bent over a fire, stirring it with a metal rod. There was something of Torisen in his features, something of Ganth in his voice, but both on the turn. Though still young and handsome, he looked like a man with a secret taste for spoiled meat, his own flesh just beginning to ripen on the bone.

Jame stood rooted, staring at him. This, without doubt, was her long-dead uncle Greshan.

"Having been on your travels," he said to the Whinno-hir in a conversational tone, "you may not know this, but your mistress Kinzi, my dear grandmother, has seen fit to stand between me and my chosen consort. She has even talked Father into sending my brother to seek the contract that should be mine. Dear little Gangoid. Sweet little Gangrene. As if he were man enough for Rawneth, or for anything else. I will have her, you know. I always get what I want. But your lady must be taught not to meddle, and you will bear that message to her."

He drew out the iron, which by now was glowing red hot, and spat on it. Fixed to its end were the three curved lines of the rathorn sigil, incandescent with heat.

With an effort, the mare controlled herself, although her wide, dark eyes still rolled white. The men gasped and fell back a step. Their ropes now hung loosely around a slender woman with long, white hair and a triangular face.

*Please*, she said. *Please.*

"Well, well, well." Greshan thrust the iron back into the heart of the fire and rose. "I've heard that your kind can shape-change, but never believed it. Now, is this form true, or an illusion? Shall we find out?"

He sauntered around her, stepping over the slackened ropes. "You aren't bad looking...for an animal. I've had worse. Perhaps we can handle this another way, if you please me."

As he came up behind her, his hand dropped to loosen his belt. In a flash, she was again equine, lashing out with small, sharp hooves. He fell over backwards with a yelp and scuttled away. Once clear, he rose, his face going from white to blotchy red with anger.

"You mangy, flea-bitten nag, look what you did!"

She might have cracked open his skull. Instead, she had ripped his coat and knocked him into a mud puddle.

He grabbed the hot iron and stalked toward her.

"Bring her down!"

Ropes tightened around her legs. She crashed over on her side.

"You. Hold her head.

A wooden-faced Kendar forced it to the ground and knelt on her neck, one hand brutally twisted in her mane. Greshan stepped forward and thrust the glowing iron into the Whinno-hir's face.

Her scream and the stench of burning hair shocked Jame from her trance. She sprang at Greshan, the rathorn battle-shriek tearing from her throat and her claws out. He saw her. His eyes widened and his jaw dropped.  So did the brand.  But at the end of her lunge, he wasn't there.  Face down in deep mould, she heard the fading echoes of shouts as the mare freed herself and then the receding beat of hooves.  She was alone, the glen undisturbed by fire or struggle.

*Did I dream it?* She wondered, but then she felt a hard shape under her hand, under the loom of decades and drew it out.  It was a rusted metal rod, its end bent into the sigil of a Knorth branding iron.

You can visit the past, Tirandys had once told her, speaking of the Master's House, but you can't change it.

"Damn, damn, *damn*!" said Jame.

However, this terrible story wasn't over yet.

*Today, we finish what my sweet Greshan began.*

The hounds were still on the trail of their prey and she was still lost. Jame pulled herself together and rose.

Water flows downhill.  Find water.

# V

SOME TIME LATER, how long she hardly knew, Jame found herself stumbling up a slope. Something beyond the ridge above her was moving, something big.

Overhead, golden leaves undulated against a leaden sky. Supple withes swayed back until the trunk invisible beneath them groaned, then surged forward with a great *swooshhhh*.

From the crest, she looked down on the errant golden willow. It had just passed by, a shimmering hillock of narrow leaves on long, wand-like stems, fighting its way up the bed of a mountain stream. Beneath, its roots writhed in a serpentine node, cracking out like whips to anchor and pull, digging into the stream bed to push. Its trunk swayed back, then surged forward. As it did so, the chain fettering it rose dripping from the stream and the huge boulder to which it was attached ground forward another inch. Back and forth, back and forth.

This was the tree that, not so long ago, had carried Jame and her cousin Kindrie across the Silver, away from the Randir's ravening pack, not that it had probably been aware of them clinging like a pair of aphids to its boughs. Now here it was, all but trapped, wood for the axe.

A moment's dizziness, and suddenly she was slithering down the steep slope, into the stream. Half obstructed as it was below by the boulder, it had risen far above its natural bed. Moreover, the willow's roots had churned it to the consistency of thick oatmeal lumpy with stones and apparently bottomless.

Flailing about, she managed to grab the overhanging branch of a tree that had survived the willow's passing. Whether she clawed her way out or the tree pulled her up, Jame had no idea. As she lay panting on the bank among its hunched roots (why did she have the impression that they had pulled themselves out of the willow's way?), a hoarse, hollow voice spoke above her, sounding not altogether pleased:

"You again, girl. I might have known."

Jame looked up.

The tree's trunk was a knobby, thick affair, easily twice as wide around as her arms could have reached. Shaggy bark clung to its bulges like an ill-fitting dress. Some eight feet up was a broad burl that suggested a contorted face, with a large hole where a major branch had long since broken off. The whole looked not unlike a natural *imu*.

"Earth Wife? Mother Ragga?"

"G'ah," said the voice, as if clearing its throat, and the hole spat out a shower of leave mold mixed with old bird bones, twigs, and one very angry squirrel. "Step-mother to you, if that. Get off my feet. Your blood is poison."

Jame let her head droop. The rag around her wrist was dripping red. "…could have told you that," she muttered, trying to tighten it with teeth and her free hand. "…'s hardly a secret anymore."

"Get up," said the hollow voice as the squirrel furiously scolded them both from a nearby branch. "G'aaah up! They have her."

Then Jame heard the Whinno-hir's despairing cry. Over it soared the rathorn's scream, mingling with the mad howl of the direhounds.

# VI

JAME CLAWED HER way to her feet, bark shredding under her nails. The sounds were surprisingly close. Trinity, had they all been running in circles? She fought her way down stream through brambles, past the boulder, up the far slope. The ridge above was crowned with throttle-berries and under them ran the narrow paths of wild things. Clothed this time, but otherwise as wet and slippery with mud as she had been at the falls, Jame slithered between the roots until she could see into the hollow beyond.

On the far side, the Whinno-hir huddled, a pale blur, against the trunk of a giant fir. Bare, lower branches thrust out around her like so many brittle arms seeking to protect a ghost.

The rathorn colt also stood between her and the hounds. Three lay dead and mangled at his feet. A fourth dragged itself in circles, snapping furiously at its own useless hindquarters. The last two, one on each side, darted back and forth, trying to draw their quarry off balance.

The colt reared up, presenting his horned mask, greaves, and ivory sheathed belly. Head on, only his hind legs were vulnerable. Hackles rattled and rose, lifting the lower half of his mane, a spiky wave down his spine, and his tail. As the hounds lunged, he pivoted on his hocks and struck at them, fangs snapping, with the whip-crack speed of a snake. One came too close, and was impaled on the twin horns. As the colt flung him off, his mate lunged for the rathorn's throat, broke his teeth on the ivory armor, and went down with a shriek under sharp hooves.

The hound with the broken back had stopped circling. It snarled as the rathorn loomed over it. The hooves drove down again in a precise blow to the skull that shattered it.

Sudden silence.

There in the midst of carnage stood the rathorn like some fabulous cross between a dragon and a warhorse, all white except for his own blood and that of the hounds. The latter ran down the curved horns into grooves in the ivory mask, between the glittering red eyes, down to the mouth where it was caught by the flick of a pink tongue between white fangs.

Then he gave himself a very equine shake that set his mane flying and uttered a loud snort of satisfaction.

Jame could feel his eyes fix on her. He snorted again: "*Huuh!*"

She crawled out from under the bushes and stood, swaying slightly. "All right. You can see me and I can see you. What next?"

Below, undergrowth crackled and parted for Gorbel, closely followed by his two men. He gave a grunt of satisfaction, not unlike the rathorn's, and swung down from his mount, a wickedly sharp boar spear in hand. His companions kept to their saddles, but with difficulty: all three horses had caught the rathorn's disturbing scent. The colt lowered his bloody horns at them and snarled. They backed, wild-eyed, barely under control.

The Caineron took up a stance, perhaps by accident, between Jame and the ivory-clad beast. One of his own hounds lay disemboweled at his feet. Jame didn't like the odds for either man or beast. She slid down through the bracken to Gorbel's side and touched his sleeve. "Please. Don't."

He shot her a look askance, taking in her filthy condition. "Been playing in the mud again, have you? Father would love to see you now."

"Well, I've seen him turning handle over spout in midair, filling his pants. Who d'you think is ahead so far?"

The sound he made might almost have been a laugh.

Then both horns and spear swung around to cover the opposite side of the hollow. Someone or thing was approaching. A snuffle, a sneeze, and the Molocar Torvo shambled panting into the clearing, followed by his master Tarn.

Both were utterly disheveled and matted with burrs. One of the Caineron snickered. Gorbel looked exasperated. When Tarn saw the rathorn, however, his face lit up with delight.

"See?" he demanded of them all. "*See?* I don't know what trail you lot followed to get here, but we came by the true one, every step of the way." He dropped to his kneels and threw his arms the enormous, shaggy hound. "Good boy, Torvie, good boy!"

Torvo licked his master's face and slowly collapsed in the boy's embrace.

Tarn shook him. "Torvie, you idiot, this is no time for a nap. There's the rathorn. There! We still have to take it." The hound breathed in long, rasping sighs, with a rattle at the end of each, his half open eye-lids fluttered. "Torvie!"

Everyone was watching now, transfixed.

"Torvie, wake up! You're not going to die. No, no..."

The rathorn colt began to quiver. His hackles had fallen and he seemed somehow smaller than he had been, more vulnerable. His own grief had scabbed over, Jame realized, but never healed, like an abscess on the soul. What he saw now was not a boy and a dying hound but himself in the last moments of his dam's life, frantic that she not leave him, knowing that she must, but not yet, please, not yet.

The hound's breath rattled and stopped.

For a moment, no one breathed.

Then the rathorn screamed.

His grief and despair blasted the clearing, withering every leaf, killing every blade of grass. Jame fell to her knees, hands over her ears, but the sound was in her heart, in her soul, ripping open old scars.

She was with her first teacher and nurse, Winter, as Kin-Slayer in her father's hands sheared the Kendar woman nearly in two.

She was on the edge of the Escarpment, watching her mother plummet into the abyss.

She was crouching beside the body of the man who had taught her honor and given her love under the eaves of darkness.

*Good-bye, Tirandys, Senethari. Good-bye.*

A hand on her shoulder...Torisen? No. Gorbel.

"B-but I never cry," she told him, feeling tears track down her muddy face.

"Neither do I," he said, and perfunctorily wiped a streaming nose on his sleeve.

Somewhere beyond her own grief, she had glimpsed a fat man beating a woman over and over, despite her screams, until she lay still on the floor in a pool of blood that inched toward a child's bed.

Tarn bent over Torvo, sobbing. "It's my fault! It's all my fault!"

Otherwise, the clearing was empty.

Jame glanced toward where the Caineron had been.

"They ran away," said Gorbel flatly. "I might have too, if I'd been on horseback."

"The rathorn?"

Then they heard him shriek, not far away. He sounded terrified. Gorbel grabbed his spear and plunged off in the direction of the sound, with Jame hard on his heels.

# VII

THEY CAME TO the churning stream, the boulder, and the willow. The latter two had progressed perhaps a foot since Jame had last seen it, but where was the rathorn?

The willow swung back and surged ahead, its leaves flowing molten gold. The chain rose dripping, and there was the colt, brought up with it. In his head long flight, he had plunged into the quagmire and somehow gotten his lesser horn wedged into a link of the chain.

"Oh, shit," said Jame.

The colt snorted out mud, wheezed, and began feebly to struggle. The willow swung back and the chain sank again, dragging him down with it.

"Damn," said Gorbel. "There goes my trophy."

"Quit on me now and I'll hand you something you'll be even sorrier to lose. Come on."

Seen close up, the boulder really did look like a dislodged chunk of mountain. A very big chunk. With muddy water boiling around it. Jame took a running jump and for a moment hung from its slick rock-face by her nails. The roar of the water echoed in her head. Then she forced the world back into focus and clawed her way up. Luckily, the boulder was full of cracks and niches. When she reached the top, she looked back down to see Gorbel trying to follow her, still stubbornly clutching his boar spear. She grabbed its shaft below the head and braced herself. He climbed up hand over hand and collapsed gasping beside her.

"This…is…insane."

"But interesting. Look."

The willow was shedding wands. As they floated down, they grew thread-like roots and clustered around the rock's base, busily prying into its fractures. The cap of each rootlet excreted an acid that allowed both the saplings and their parent tree to anchor themselves with startling speed, years of erosion accomplished in minutes. Still, that might not be fast enough.

"Can you use that pig-sticker to pry this open?" she asked, shouting to make herself heard.

He examined the link that hooked the chain's ends together. "I might. Why?"

"Just do it, once I reach the colt."

He caught her arm. "Again, why?"

"Because I killed his dam."

Rathorn ivory is the second hardest substance on Rathillien, and it never stops growing. If they live long enough—and some scrollsmen argue that, like the Whinno-hir, they are potentially immortal—their armor eventually encases them in a living tomb.

The mare had been staggering under its weight, breathing in hissing gasps through bared fangs because the nasal pits of her mask had grown shut, as had one eye hole. He had walked beside her, crying, now a yearling foal, now a slender, white-haired boy with red, red eyes: *No, you're not going to die! No, no...*

"You bagged a rathorn?" Gorbel's goggle eyes were suddenly those of a child, wide with wonder. "How?" he demanded eagerly. "With what weapon?"

"There isn't time..."

"Tell me, and I'll help."

"With a knife."

*If you kill me, my child will kill you.*

"Through the eye."

*Kill me.*

"At extremely close quarters."

The chain was rising again, and the rathorn with it. Gorbel still held Jame's arm, for a moment supporting her as she sagged. He peered at her face, white under its muddy mask, but if the cloth around her wrist was more red than brown, he didn't notice.

"Are you all right?"

*I'm bleeding to death,* Jame thought with odd detachment. *Well, either I have enough blood left in me to do this or I don't.*

"Besides," she said out-loud, "I owe the tree too."

He was surprised into letting her go, and she stepped out onto the taut chain. The colt's weakening struggles barely caused a tremor, but at least he was still alive. The links were slick and knobby underfoot (who brings a chain on a hunt? They must have sent to Restormir or Wilden for it), but it was at least as thick as the rope that had stretched across the great hall.

When she reached the colt, she slid into the roiling water, onto his back. His red eyes snapped open and he began feebly to thrash, but already they were sinking again. Jame took a deep breath. Opaque water, almost liquid mud, closed over her head. Eyes squeezed shut, she slid her hands up the rathorn's neck and down his mask to the trapped horn. There. She began to work the link back and forth, inch by inch, up the length of ivory. The air in her lungs was turning to fire when the slack went out of the chain and they rose again.

Above water, she clung gasping to the colt's neck. He hung limp. She drove her nails into his crest.

"Wake up, dammit! You can't kill me if you die first!"

# VIII

GORBEL WONDERED IF the Knorth madness was indeed contagious and if so, whether he had caught it.

After all, here he was on top of a bloody big rock *(don't think how far off the ground you are; don't think)*, trying to break a Trinity-bedamned chain with an ancestors cursed boar spear, while trying to fend off a swarm of willow saplings. The boulder's face seethed with them as if with so many leafy snakes *(ugh)*, all industriously rooting themselves in stone. Debris rattled down on all sides, along with occasional larger chunks.

Father had told him clearly enough what to do with the Knorth bitch: humiliate her; make her suffer; show the entire Kencyrath how insane both she and her brother were for thinking that a Highborn girl could ever become a randon.

But it wasn't so easy. She kept throwing him off guard.

This...this was insane.

She had killed a rathorn mare. There, he envied her. She felt she owed a debt to the rathorn's foal. All right. He could see that, vaguely. But to a *tree*?

Madness.

And what about that sudden flash of...memory?...back in the clearing when the rathorn had let off that god-awful cry? Father beating Mother, smashing her skull, spattering blood and brains...no. His mother had died when he was still only a squalling brat. He didn't remember her at all, and he cried for no one. But his nose did run. It was running now.

Sudden pain lanced through his foot. A sapling had crawled onto it unnoticed and had sunken its roots through the boot into flesh. He yanked out the leafy wand as if it were a weed, but only the top part came. His foot continued to throb as if splinters had been driven deeply into it.

The willow swayed back and forward again with a rush. The chain around the boulder tightened. Its length rose, bringing with it a muddy mass that resolved itself into two figures, one clinging to the other. The rathorn hung by his horn like a slaughtered hog on a hook. Then he snorted mud out of his nostrils and again began struggling weakly to free himself. He had guts, that one. So (*face it*) did the Knorth.

But Trinity, what a way to ride a rathorn!

Stone shifted under foot. Gorbel wobbled, terror clutching his heart. One side of the rock sheared away, trailing saplings, and hit the water with a great, drenching splash. The rest of the boulder was breaking apart, the chain paying out link by link, faster and faster, as the willow pulled and its anchor gave way.

Jump. *Jump*!

Gorbel did, and nearly fainted on impact from the stabbing pain in his foot. He limped to high ground and clung to a tree, watching, as the boulder disintegrated. Set loose, the dammed stream crested in a muddy flash flood. Two figures tumbled with it, around a curve in the river bed, out of sight.

# Chapter XIV: To Ride a Rathorn

## Summer 45 - 53

## I

…DROWNING, TUMBLING OVER and over, battered, coughing on water, choking on air, arms and legs wrapped around the colt, her face pressed against his neck, white mane and black hair streaming together in her eyes…

…hang on, hang on, hang on…

Thick with debris, the river swept them on in the flash flood of its sudden release until, finally, the crest left them behind. The colt righted himself with a snort and struck out for the shore, but the water was still too deep and the current too swift.

Jame clung to him, her head spinning. No, she and the colt both were, around and around in a wide eddy. Here, sharp rocks like teeth rimmed the shore, gnashing the water to foam. The clear center of the vortex revealed stony terraces below, gaping like a vast, ribbed gullet. At the bottom, eyes as big as dinner plates reflected the moon, waiting.

*It wasn't the River Snake,* Jame thought, with intense if momentary relief. They hadn't yet reached that monster's abode beneath the Silver. However, Rathillien came in layers of reality. Either she had hit her head once too often or this was some new dimension of the Merikits' sacred space, from which the Four—water, air, earth, and fire: Eaten One, Falling Man, Earth Wife, and Burnt Man—ruled Rathillien in their singularly haphazard fashion.

"Great fish! Eaten One!" she cried to the maw beneath, sputtering through a face-full of spray. "What have we done to you? Spit us out!"

*Bloop.*

Monstrous bubbles set the water boiling around them and burst with the stink of fish breath.

*Ah, why should I bother with you, who are no spawn of mine? Go your way. Go.*

The whirlpool disgorged itself into a waterfall. They fell from what surely was an impossible height. Stranger still, an old man fell with them, his dingy-white beard whipping up over his shoulder. He was almost but not quite seated on a throne that fell just beneath him.

"Falling Man, South Wind, Tishooo!" Jame cried to him. "You helped me once at Gothregor. Will you again?"

"Pshaw." Needles clattered in gnarled hands. A knobby scarf laddered with dropped stitches flew upward and tried to wrap itself around his neck. He fended it off impatiently. "Knit one, purl two…I already did my part in blowing away the weirdingstrom. Leave me alone. I have a kingdom to rule."

"Tishooo, you're knitting your beard into your scarf."

"Well, how do *you* catch a dragon? Go away, girl. I'm busy."

They crashed into the pool at the base of the falls, into water throbbing with the pulse of its own descent, and were sweep on. Jame could no longer feel her chilled hands or feet. *Much more of this*, she thought, not very clearly, *and I'm off.*

One last try.

"Earth Wife…"

WHAP.

They had tumbled into a tree's drooping limbs and one had slapped her smartly across the face. The colt snagged the bough with his curved horns. Half-dazed, still clinging to his back, she felt him swing around in the current, then clamber out of the water and up the bank. Wet, tangled roots that should have snared his hooves instead shifted, groaning, to provide footholds. At the top he stood for a moment with his head down, sides a heave and quivering legs astraddle. Then he gave himself a mighty shake.

Jame was lying on the ground before she realized that she had fallen off. Cracks of bright sky showed through a dark canopy of leaves overhead. She stared up at them, too tired to move or think. Between one blink and the next, or so it seemed, the light shifted and darkened toward a night fretted with stars. Time had passed. How much?

The air was very still, yet nearby leaves stirred.

"Talk, talk, talk." The words rustled and creaked as stiff leaves rubbed together. "Earth Wife this. Earth Wife that. Always wanting something. Always meddling. *Errr-eeek*…Wear down a mountain, you would, girl, or tear up a forest by the roots. And now this."

Jame rolled her head toward the voice. She lay not far from a large holly bush. Broad, glossy leaves edged with faintly luminous gold stirred fretfully. Some drew back, others bowed forward or curled into rolling lines. Light, shadow, and movement defined a crude, constantly changing face as large as the bush itself. It glowered down at Jame, spiked leaves rippling into a scowl.

"Said your blood was poison, girl, didn't I? What shall we do with you now, eh?"

*Something has happened.* Jame thought, fumbling through shards of memory. *What?*

She raised an unsteady hand to her head. The makeshift bandages had long since unraveled and been swept away by the current; the scratches, if one could call them that, oozed. She could see white tendons laid bare and veins narrowly missed. Trinity, had she cut that deep and never even felt it? A diagonal swathe of mingled fresh blood and dried was smeared across her fore-arm. Vaguely, she remembered hot breath on her wrist and a sense of bitter triumph not her own. A pause. Then had come the first, almost tentative rasp of a tongue against her bleeding flesh.

Sweet Trinity. He had tasted her blood.

Somewhere, someone was crying. It was a terrible sound, compounded of grief, rage, and a helpless, hopeless despair that shook her very soul.

"D'you want to see what you've done, you wretched, wicked girl?" hissed the leaves, rasping against each other in such agitation that spines snapped and flew in a stinging shower. "Then look."

Foliage peeled back layer by layer, opening not into the heart of the bush but into the dim, earth-floored lodge of Mother Ragga, the Earth Wife. Two figures huddled on the cold hearth, both white-haired but one a naked, shivering boy and the other a woman who held him in her arms. It was he who sobbed in deep wrenching gasps through pale lips stained with blood.

*My blood*, thought Jame.

The woman bent her head to draw the curtain of her hair over him and across the ruined half of her face. One dark, liquid eye regarded Jame askance.

*Oh Kinzi-kin, child of darkness. How much worse than your uncle you have proved.*

Then she froze, ears pricking through her tangled mane.

Jame heard it too.

Something was moving in the gathering dark. With it came a crackling and the stench of burnt fur.

"Now look what you've called up," hissed the Earth Wife, closing her branches like so many leafy arms. "As if we needed him!" Then she turned her face inward and disappeared.

Undergrowth and small trees snapped beneath a heavy tread, though the footfalls themselves were felt rather than heard as slow, deep shudders in the earth. Something huge prowled and growled through the darkening wood, circling, circling. Too weak to rise, Jame turned her head to catch glimpses as it passed, now a black shape defined by a hole in the star light, now by glowing cracks that opened and closed as it moved as if some terrible conflagration still smoldered deep within its flesh.

*In the Ebonbane, by the chasm*, it was muttering over and over. *On the hearth, in the Master's hall…*

Its words crackled and growled in Jame's mind, impatient, hungry. If fire had a voice, so it would have sounded. There was something else in it, though, something terrifyingly familiar, but her dazed brain refused to track down the memory.

An enormous head suddenly blotted out the sky above her, blunt, feline, and very, very close. The ears were charred stubs, the eyes caverns lit by deep, internal flames, the whole face a contorted mask of scar tissue.

*Huh.* It breathed waves of heat and greasy smoke in her face, then snuffled in her scent. *You.*

Jame had been expecting the Burnt Man who, Ancestors knew, was bad enough. But this was something else, or perhaps something more.

"Who…what *are* you?" she gasped, trying to cringe away.

The great head swung above her, scarred lips rippling back from white fangs bared half in grin, half in snarl. Flecks of bitter ash stung her face and clung to her lips, rank with the taste of ancient holocaust.

*On the hearth, in the Master's hall, the changer Keral burned out my eyes. So many of my kin lay dead around me. So many. And all the while the Dream-weaver smiled and smiled as she danced out the souls of the fallen. But I did not fall. Dancer's daughter, in the Ebonbane, by the chasm, you escaped my judgment. But* these *mountains are mine.*

Trinity, of course: it was the blind Arrin-ken whose presence she had sensed in her flight from Gothregor and up the Riverland, when the entire Snowthorn range had seemed like a crouching cat that held her under its paw.

Then, he had let her go. Now...

*You have called on water, air, and earth. Now call on me. Do you seek judgment, Nemesis? Ask, and I will give it, blind justice for blind destruction. Ask!*

The pressure to confess welled up like vomit. She had done so many bad things, or at least things for which she blamed herself. The great cat's will bore down on her, his hot breath scorching her face.

*Confess. You know your guilt.*

The Arrin-ken were the third of the three people who made up the Kencyrath. The Highborn ruled, the Kendar served, and the Arrin-ken kept the balance between them and their god—or had until millennia ago the great felines had withdrawn into the wilds of Rathillien for reasons still not entirely clear. However, they still sometimes used the so-called God-Voice to speak through unwilling Kencyr lips.

Oh. That was where she had last heard that terrible voice. In the subterranean Priests' College. Though the mouth of the renegade priest Ishtier.

Grief, pain, and rage had driven the great cat insane, but did that matter?

*For us*, the Arrin-ken Immalai had said, *good is no less terrible than evil*, nor were the two easily told apart. Who was to judge between them, if not those whom their ruthless god had chosen for that role? Least of all, who was she to question such a judgment?

In a moment, she would give this dark avenger what he wanted, and with it permission to burn her alive. Or would she become one of the Burnt Man's pack of the damned, the Burning Ones, with whom he hunted down those with the stench of guilt on them? An Arrin-ken's justice or the Burnt Man's? Kencyrath or Rathillien or both? It was all very confusing.

Yet again came the demand, singeing her eyelashes, rattling her to the depths of her being: *All things end, light, hope, and life. This you know full well, darkling-born, none better. Why delay? Come to judgment. Come!*

...get away, get away, get away...

She was still too weak to move, but her will to survive leaped out and seized that other mind now blood-bound to her own.

With a shriek, she/he/they burst out of the undergrowth. Before them, a monstrous darkness crouched, gloating, over its prey.

*That puny thing is me?* thought Jame.

Then the Arrin-ken raised its blind, smoldering face to them, and the stench of it rolled out in waves of heat that made the air quiver. The colt stopped short, appalled. Jame felt his hindquarters gather as if they were her own. The next moment, they had leaped over the great cat and were in wild flight down the riverbank.

...run, run, run...

# II

THE COLT'S TERROR at this sudden invasion of his soul fed on Jame's of that which even now might pursue her. Their flight was madness and mindless, an eternity in growing darkness of crashing into, through, and between things that raked their sides and snatched at their feet.

After what felt like a millennium, Jame began to gather her wits. So did the colt. She could feel his revulsion at her presence in his mind and his attempts to throw her off. If she had indeed been on his back, he would have been rid of her long ago, and she of him. As it was, she felt his hatred and rage trying to pry her loose even as she struggled to free herself from him, but they were bound, body and soul. How could one throw off oneself?

To ride a rathorn...

Trinity, who would have thought it would be like this?

*Hush*, she found herself crooning to the colt. *Gently, gently. What good will it do to run yourself to death?*

*Good enough to kill you*, came the fierce answer.

And so he would, if he could. She felt the air burning in his lungs and his heart pounding. So did her own, back where her body lay.

*So this is blood-binding,* she thought, sickened to the bottom of her solitary soul. *No one should have such power over another being, and I don't even like being touched. Graykin was bad enough, but this...this is obscene. Am I too, for letting it happen?*

Gorbel's moon-like face hung over her, his lower lip pendulous with dismay.

"What's wrong?" he said, as if from a great distance.

She clutched his arm, and he flinched at the bite of her nails. "Gorbel, for Trinity's sake, kill me and set us both free!"

"What?"

"Just do it! Daddy will love you for it."

"Huh. I may not be clever like some, but I'm not stupid. Caldane, Lord Caineron, loves no one but himself. We don't play for love in my house, only for power. And survival. You've made a fine mess of your wrists. Hold still while I bind them. I said, hold still!"

She barely saw his hand before it caught her in the face with a jolting slap.

"Damn," she heard him mutter as the world dimmed.

# III

IT FELT AS if they had been running forever, on and on and on.

Sounds came and went.

Jame was vaguely aware of hounds baying and someone (Gorbel?) shouting to attract the hunt's attention.

Time passed.

A thin, cool hand touched her brow, then held something to her lips, forcing her to drink. "I don't know what's wrong," said a voice which, surely, she should know. "These injuries are bad, but nothing that *dwar* sleep won't heal...if she lets it. This constant agitation is killing her."

*You try to calm down*, she wanted to say, *with a bloody great cat breathing hot ash down your neck!*

Yes, there had been a cat. A blind Arrin-ken. Hunting them. Somehow mixed up with the Merikits' Burning Man.

And there had been a Whinno-hir mare—Bel-tairi, the Shame of Tentir, whatever that meant. She had tried to stop their mad flight crying, *Kinzi-kin! Nemesis! Do you want to kill him?*

Herself, perhaps; the rathorn colt, no.

Then the blind Arrin-ken had erupted from the undergrowth, roaring, and the branches around him burst into flame. The colt jumped out of his skin, literally. One moment he was bucking like a lunatic, as if that could unseat a disembodied rider, the next he and Jame were looking down at his collapsed form. With its fierce animation gone, it had looked almost as pathetic as Jame had under the Arrin-ken's paw. And then the blind brute had come at them again, not to be fooled by mere flesh and blood.

The rathorn bolted.

...run, run, run...

But where were the mountains, and what were these hills that rose and fell, swooping on wings of withered grass under the leaden eye of the moon? In a hollow, a patch of bloated flowers burst with a carrion stench under the colt's hooves. He slowed, snorting with alarm.

*Oh no*, thought Jame.

There probably were ways to step straight from the banks of the Silver into the Haunted Lands, several hundred leagues to the east on the other side of the Ebonbane.

With luck, though, this was only a nightmare, or the onset of terminal delirium.

However, given past experience, it was just as likely that she had somehow stumbled into her brother's soulscape. Again.

From the crest of the next rise, they looked down on the desolate ruins of a keep, just as Jame knew they would. Every line of it was familiar to her, from the squat tower to the broken walls, from the dry moat to the cracked, moon-like solar aglow over the lord's hall. She and Tori had grown up here, and here their father had died.

Memories: helping Cook dig poached eyes out of boiled potatoes, carefully, because if they burst they poisoned the food; the randon Tigon so hungry for meat that he cut off and roasted his own toes; Winter refusing to teach her how to fight because she was not a girl but—that awful thing—a lady. Ha. She had pounced her brother after that, hoping to learn something from his reaction. Instead, she had only given him a bloody nose.

*"Father says it's dangerous to teach you anything."* Tori had said, snuffling into his sleeve. *"Will the things you learn always hurt people?"*

Jame had considered this, as she did again now, wondering if the answer had changed. *"Maybe. As long as I learn, does it matter?"*

*"It does to me. I'm the one who usually gets hurt. Father says you're dangerous. He says you'll destroy me."*

*"That's silly. I love you."*

*"Father says destruction begins with love."*

Love had destroyed their father, or rather the loss of it had with the gradual fading of their mother out of their lives and his increasingly desperate search for her.

Another memory, as sharp as a splinter of glass and as hard to forget: That day, she had played hide and seek with her brother (*"You be Father, I'll be Mother).* There. Below. In the keep. And ended up dancing to entertain a warty faced death banner in the great hall.

At first, she had hadn't seen Father watching her. Then his husky voice had stopped her in mid-step.

*"You've come back to me."* He had looked half dazed with a relief so intense that it wiped twenty years off his face. *"Oh, I knew you would. I*

*knew…*" But as he stepped hastily forward and saw her more clearly, the softness had run out of his expression like melting wax. *"You."*

*I don't want to remember this,* Jame thought, gripping the colt's tuft of a mane.

Simultaneously, she realized that she was not only in the rathorn's mind but on his back. Also, her hands had gone small and childish, without nails. The colt likewise had dwindled to a frightened foal, with mere bumps between his eyes and on his nose instead of those lethal horns.

Maybe this was a nightmare after all, and she was trapped in it. Perhaps this was a taste of the same terror that sometimes kept her brother awake for days on end rather than risk never being able to wake up again.

But fear only sharpened memory.

There in the hall, Father had stuck her hard across the face and slammed her back against the wall.

*"You changeling, you impostor, how dare you be so much like her? How dare you! And yet, and yet, you are…so like."* His hands rose as if by themselves to cup her bruised face. *"So like…"* he breathed, and kissed her, hard, on the mouth.

"My lord!" Winter stood in the hall doorway.

He had drawn back with a gasp. *"No. No! I am* not *my brother!"* And he smashed his fist into the stone wall next to Jame's head, speckling her face with his blood. Then he had raged out, shouting for his horse, hell-bent on storming the Master's House itself to reclaim his lost love.

Winter had knelt beside her. *"All right, child?"*

Jame remembered nodding, and not being able to stop until the randon touched her shoulder. Then Winter had risen but paused, briefly, looking down at her. *"It isn't entirely his fault."* she had said, and gone out to ready her lord's gaunt, gray stallion before someone got killed.

*If not his fault,* Jame had wondered as a child, *then whose?*

Now, the half-grown part of her mind caught the glimmer of an answer, and felt an unexpected stab of pity. From the miseries of his own childhood, her father had risen to the pinnacle of power, only to fall with the loss of the one thing he had ever wanted. Love.

And for all his flaws, he was *not* like his brother, although Greshan had shaped him in ways that she was only beginning to understand.

*So, who is the monster in the maze?*

The question sprang into her mind as if asked by someone else. She recognized the test it posed, and the importance of the answer. Who was her true enemy?

Trinity. There were too many possibilities. Master Gerridon, the Witch of Wilden, Ishtier, Caldane, Torisen...

No, she told herself fiercely. Not him. Never.

Here and now, or rather down there in the keep that had become her brother's soul-image, the enemy was a mad, muttering voice behind a locked door.

"Tori!" she cried. Both she and the foal flinched as her shrill, child's voice cracked the leaden silence. Every nerve in her body cried, *Shut up, you fool! Run! Hide!* But she tried again, louder. "Daddy's boy! Come out; come out, wherever you are!"

The rathorn shook as the sky rumbled, or perhaps it was the earth. The sour wind shifted, this way and that, and the grass rustled like so many ribbons of dry snake skin.

Someone stood in the keep door, a thin, dark-haired boy her own age, give or take a minute either way. A white wolver pup crouched at his heels, just out of reach. The twins stared at each other. It was then. It was now. All they had had together lay between them, close enough to touch and yet years out of reach. The wind blew hard and the grass cringed, beginning to whine.

"Tori, get out!" she cried down at him, into the teeth of the rising gale, across the abyss of time. Could he hear her at all? "Go somewhere, anywhere, as far from here as you can!"

The wind veered again, now pushing at her back. It brought with it an all too familiar smell of must and dust and ancient sickness. She knew what was there before she turned to face it, but heart and stomach still lurched at the sight.

The Master's House loomed over them. Mist obscured its lower stories but the upper leaned as if poised to topple. Ashes of the dead blew in veils off its many roofs and gables, clouding the moon, thickening the air. Darkness stared out of a thousand broken windows and the reek of dull hunger exhaled—*HHAAAaaaa...*— through a hundred gaping doors. From the shadows within came the grinding of stone on stone as at a glacial pace the whole massive pile edged forward, for this was only the blind head of the House. The rest of it stretched back into Perimal Darkling and beyond, from fallen world to world, down the Chain of Creation. All those rooms of darkness drove it forward with a vast, inhuman momentum while its shadow rolled before it over the hills, and the grass wailed under it.

Jame gulped down nausea. If Tori's soul-image was bad, hers was worse. In the House was a hall with a green-shot floor. There, the woven eyes of the dead and the damned stared down from the walls at a sleeper huddled on the cold hearth, on a pile of Arrin-ken pelts.

*And when the Master, finally, enters his hall, what then, Dancer's daughter? Will you rise and fight, or open your arms to him as you so nearly did once before? For what else, after all, were you bred?*

Ah, but that time had not yet come.

"Hush," Jame breathed to the foal, her hand on his quivering neck. An ear flickered back to listen, then forward again, then back. "Hush. The Master is still in his house, the monster in its maze. In the end, either he will come out to meet us or we will go in after him. There. Aren't you glad now that you tried a taste of my blood?"

Perhaps she had spoken too soon.

A clot of darkness detached itself from the shadow of the House and rushed toward them over the swelling hills, glimpsed and gone and glimpsed again. Part of the rumble separated into pounding hooves.

"Oh no," said Jame.

The Master's gray stallion burst over the next rise and roared down on them. Its gaping jaws spewed foam and its steel-shod hooves threw up divots of turf that turned to dust in midair. The foal shrieked for his mother and bolted.

They dodged away among the rolling hills, the foal running in blind panic, Jame trying to keep him in the hollows, out of sight. This was hide and seek with a vengeance. It was also that buried childhood nightmare only recently unearthed by her abysmal attempts at horsemanship.

*If you fail the Master, we'll just have to feed you to Iron-jaw, won't we?*

She remembered the gray stallion charging her, ears back and teeth bared, when he had been only a horse and she only a child who had strayed into what might laughingly be called his pasture, given the noisome herbage of the Haunted Lands. Another time, Tori had dared her to ride him and, of course, she had been thrown, hard.  There.  That was the origin of the sick fear that curdled her stomach to this day every time she put foot to stirrup and herself at the mercy of such a strong, unpredictable creature.  Then her father had ridden the stallion to death and the changer Keral had claimed the haunt that it had become for his master.

The foal skidded around a mound, his hind legs nearly flying out from under him, and they swept down on a lone, white-haired figure on foot.

"Stop, or you'll kill yourselves!" he shouted, then jumped out of the way as they hurtled past.

"If we stop," Jame yelled back over her shoulder, "we'll die!"

Around another curve and there he was again, directly in their path with his thin hands up, terrified but determined.  "I'm not joking!"

"Neither are we!"

The foal ran into him, stumbled, and fell head over heels.  Thrown clear, Jame scrambled to her feet and spat out a mouthful of wriggling grass before it could take root.

The cause of their fall sat holding his head and groaning.  Belatedly, Jame recognized her cousin Kindrie Soul-walker.  Of course.  That was the other voice she had heard in her sleep or delirium or whatever this was, and those were the thin, sensitive hands that had held a cup to her lips.  Now he had entered the soulscape as a healer to help her, and been trampled for his pains.

"Sorry," she said to him, then "Run!"

The ground was thrumming like a vast drum.  Over the crest came Iron-jaw and hurtled down on them, roaring.  Kindrie stared, aghast, then abruptly vanished.  The foal shied, squealing, directly into the stallion's path and went down under his hooves.  The haunt wheeled and went for him, teeth bared.  If he caught the young rathorn, he would shake him to death or snap his neck.

Jame leaped at the haunt's head.  She meant to go for his eyes with her claws; however, her fingertips were still without nails.  Instead, she found herself clinging to the stallion's neck, his hot breath reeking in her ear.  One dead, white eye rolled toward her.  He reared and tossed his head, trying to throw her off.  If she fell, he would surely kill her.

*So*, she thought with an odd detachment, *do I die a helpless child or, finally, accept what I am and grow up?*

Her body seemed to decide for her.  Skin split and bloody claws erupted from the tips of her fingers, just as they had when she had turned seven and faced her father over the dying Kendar Winter.  She wrapped her legs around the haunt's neck.  When he reared again, swinging her upward into his face, she drove her claws into that white marble of an eye.  It burst, spraying an arc of black blood that clotted as it hit the air.  Up he went and over, crashing down on his back.  Jame sprang clear and ran.  She heard him thrashing behind her, trying to roll away from such agony.

*So some haunts can still feel pain*, observed part of her mind. *Interesting.*

Another part, the one that wanted to live, thought only...*run, run, run*...and so she did, on and on and on, too scared to realize that she ran alone.

## Chapter XV:  Back to the Soulscape

### Summer 53

# I

SOMEONE WAS CALLING her.

"Jame."  And again, "Jame."

She knew that voice, although it seemed a lifetime since she had last heard it.

"Jame.  Come on now, lass.  Wake up."

Part of her was still running, lost among hills that rolled on forever, but the rest of her would rather die than not answer that call.  Her eyes fluttered open.  The moon glowed through tall windows, throwing tranquil bars of light on the floor, onto facing rows of cots empty except for the one in which she lay, but not alone.  A strong arm held her.  She knew that touch, that very smell, clean and honest as the man himself.

"Oh, Marc," she said.  "I had such an awful dream."

But then, when she raised her hand to touch him, to be sure he was really there, she saw that her arm was heavily bandaged from wrist to elbow.  No, it hadn't all been a dream.  The worst part was true.

"Marc, I've done a terrible thing."

"Have you now."  His big, rough hand gently stroked her hair.  "You'd better tell me about it, then."

For a long while, however, neither of them spoke.  They hadn't seen each other in nearly a year, not since the battle at the Cataracts.  It seemed more like a lifetime ago, Jame thought, settling against the Kendar's broad chest, feeling him breathe and listening to his heart beat, steady and strong.

She remembered how they had first met.  Dashing around a corner in Tai-tastigon with the stolen Peacock Gloves tucked into her wallet and the city guards on her heels, she had run head-on into what she at first had thought was a wall.  Then it had put out big hands to catch her on the rebound.

He had walked all the way from East Kenshold—a big Kendar in late middle-age, turned out by the new lord of a minor house for defending the old lord's Whinno-hir mare from being ridden against

her will.  Before that, he had been a Caineron yondri with the Southern Host; before that, the last survivor of another minor house that
had held Kithorn until the Merikit slaughtered everyone except Marc,
who had been out hunting at the time and had come home to red
ruin.  By the time he had reached Tai-tastigon, seventy-odd years
later, he had been tired unto death and ready to die, sure that at his
age no Kencyr house would ever accept him again.

He had, however, woken in time to save her from a brigands'
attack in the alley below—this, by climbing down two stories from
the inn's loft "and then, to save time, falling the rest of the way," as
he had put it later.

He was the most solidly decent person Jame had ever known,
and she trusted his moral sense far more than she did her own.

However, he had assumed that she was Kendar with only enough
Highborn blood to account for her various strange attributes.  After
all, Kencyr ladies were a breed apart, seldom seen outside their own
halls and then only heavily masked.  That one of them should be the
infamous Talisman, apprentice to the greatest thief in Tai-tastigon,
had never crossed his mind.  At the time, Jame hadn't been sure
herself what she was, and certainly hadn't guessed that the Highlord
of the Kencyrath was her long-lost twin brother Tori.

Then she had found out, and so had Marc.

Would there ever be that easy friendship and equality between
them again?  Could there be between a Highborn and a Kendar?
They hadn't yet crossed that bridge, yet here he was.  Hang on to that.

Just then, Jorin trotted into the room and jumped up onto the
cot.  Jame yelped as his weight landed on her bandaged arm.  Marc
scooped up the ounce and rolled him over between them, upside-
down.

"Hello, kitten," he said, rubbing the exposed, furry stomach.
Jorin stretched, back arching, paws in the air, and began to purr.

"Where did you spring from?" Jame asked the Kendar over the
cat's rumble.

"Oh, Gothregor.  Everyone is back, except for those still attached to the Southern Host or elsewhere.  Your lord brother will
need every hand he can get for the haying, come midsummer."

Jame tried to imagine the seven foot tall Kendar wielding a
scythe instead of his usual two-edged war axe.  "He's got you out
cutting the grass?"

"Nothing wrong with working the land, lass. I'll take that any day over a battlefield, where naught grows but bones from the earth after the first frost. Mind you, they say blood is a good fertilizer, but not one I'd use by choice."

Marc had never cared much for fighting, come to that. In battle, he usually feigned a berserker fit and scared the enemy into headlong flight. She had seen him once empty a hostile tavern the same way, with brigands flying through the doors, out the windows, and even up the chimney.

"Mostly, though," he said, "I've been seeing what can be done to put that big stained glass window back together. You know, the one facing east in the old keep, the map of Rathillien. A gorgeous thing. Somehow, though, it got smashed to pieces."

"Er...I'm afraid that was me. At the time, I had a pack of shadow assassins after me and used a rune to blow away their souls. Unfortunately, the window blew out too. So did a lot of death banners from the lower hall. Sorry."

There was a short pause, followed by a resigned sigh. "Ah well. I should have guessed as much. That's all right then, as long as it was in a good cause."

She started to turn to look at him, but stopped herself, in case he wasn't there after all. If this was a dream, she didn't want to wake.

"Are you teasing me?"

"Not at all. The window can be replaced. I hope. You can't. Besides, I enjoy the work."

*He would,* thought Jame, a bit envious given her own lack of talent. Marc had always had an artistic bent but precious little chance to develop it.

"Here."

He dropped something smooth and cool into her hand.

"We were melting down some salvaged shards of red glass— did you know the color comes in part from real gold?—when your lord brother nicked a finger and a drop of his blood fell into the mix. The result was...interesting."

Jame held the fragment up to the moon. Even such faint, silvery light woke a ruby glow in the heart of the glass. It seemed to her that she held something alive, but with a sort of life beyond her experience or comprehension.

"I'd like to experiment with other colors," said the big Kendar wistfully. "It's awkward, though, asking the Highlord of the Kencyrath to bleed on request."

Jame braced herself. She had to know. "I suppose," she said carefully, "that Tori has offered you a place in his—that is, in our house."

He shifted, to muffled protests both from cot and cat. "He did, yes. I declined the honor."

"But...why? Ancestors know, you've earned it."

"Oh," he said, trying to sound casual, "I thought I'd wait a bit, just to see what else might come along."

Jame nearly sat up, but the effort made her head spin.

"Marc," she said urgently, clutching his jacket, "you can't count on me ever having an establishment of my own, much less being allowed officially to bind Kendar to me. Think! Is Tori likely to give me that much power?"

"He made you his lordan, lass."

"Yes, but that was only to buy time. He can pitch me back into the Women's Halls whenever he wants, assuming the matriarchs don't toss me out again. Why, he hasn't even come to see if I've managed to get myself killed yet."

"Oh, he came." Marc chuckled. "You called him 'Daddy's boy' and told him to go away."

"Oh," said Jame blankly. "Oh dear. Wait a moment. How long have I been unconscious?"

"More than a week. Your cousin Kindrie went into the soulscape to see what was keeping you, and came back with two black eyes. He said something about being trampled by a rage of rathorns."

For the first time since waking, Jame remembered the rathorn colt. Trinity, where was he? It struck her now that she hadn't felt his presence since they had ran in different directions to escape the haunt stallion. Surely she would know if he was dead...wouldn't she? What if she had left him trapped in the soulscape?

"I have to go back," she said, struggling to free herself from Marc's arms. "He won't know how to get out. He'll wander there, lost, until he dies."

"Gently, gently. Who will?"

"The colt. Marc, I said I'd done something awful, and I have. I've blood-bound a young rathorn."

He didn't push her away, but she felt his breath catch. "I didn't know you were a binder," he said, with a careful lack of emphasis. "Still, I suppose it's nothing you can help. Why bind a rathorn, though, of all creatures?"

"It wasn't intentional. He bit me."

"Ah. Well, there's no accounting for taste."

Jame felt a surge of relief. "Now you're laughing at me." If he could accept this, the worst thing she knew about herself, perhaps their friendship would survive after all.

But that didn't help the colt.

"I brought someone to meet you," said Marc, deliberately changing the subject.

She felt him move, then heard a flint rasp. The sudden flare of light momentarily blinded her. When her eyes cleared, she saw a child's wisp of a shadow cast on the far wall. Marc had set a lit candle down behind a lumpy saddle-bag on the table.

"This is my sister, Willow. Willow, meet my Lady Jamethiel. If you're good, she may let you call her Jame."

"I would be honored," said Jame, a little shaken, as the shadow sketched a wary salute.

She knew, of course, that her brother had found the child's bones at Kithorn the previous autumn and for some reason had carried them all the way south to the battle at the Cataracts. A little girl, trapped in death for decades under the ruins of her house...there she had hidden while her family was slaughtered above her, and there she had starved to death. But blood and bone trap the soul until fire sets it free, so here she still was.

Jorin's head popped up. He wriggled free, hopped down, and bounced at the shadow, which recoiled from him.

"He's frightening her," said Jame sharply.

"Give them a moment. Ah, that's my girl."

Cat and shadow had begun to chase each other back and forth, up and down the wall, while Marc moved the candle to give the game more scope.

"I keep meaning to give her to the pyre." He sighed. "After losing her once, though, it's hard to let go again."

In his tone, Jame heard the boy that he had been, who had lost everything he had ever loved. The old ache had never really healed, nor the loneliness gone away except, perhaps, for a time when two unlikely friends had shared a loft in Tai-tastigon.

"D'you suppose," he asked, "that it hurts her to stay like this?"

"I don't think so," said Jame, watching ounce and shadow child play, "but what do I know?  You should ask Ashe."

He took a deep breath. "So I will.  Until then, I'll hold on to her a bit longer, just to see what else might come along."

Neither spoke after that.  Jame settled back against his shoulder and closed her eyes.

## II

SOME TIME LATER she woke, or thought that she did.

The room had tarnished to a kind of thick, half light that belonged neither to day nor to night and cast no shadows but two. One was her own. The other sat cross-legged on a blanket, watching her, or so she assumed. It had a child's shape and some hint of shadowy features, but she could see through it to the wall beyond, to shelves thick with dust, lined with broken jars.

"This is a dream, isn't it?" she asked the silent watcher. "You're Willow, and this is where my brother found you, in the still room at Kithorn, under the charred hall."

No answer. Jame gathered herself to rise, but hesitated as the other drew back. "You're afraid of me. Why?"

Then she saw that her hands were tipped with six inch long ivory claws that rasped on the floor and would not retract. Her clothes had also changed to the close-fitting costume of a Senetha dancer with its oddly placed slashes. There were more of them than she remembered. *Reaper of souls*. Who had called her that? *Dancer's daughter*. She felt her Shanir nature stir, dark, dangerous, and seductive.

"Is this what you see in me? Is this what you fear...for yourself? No. For your brother."

She settled carefully back against the wall.

"I'm sorry. I didn't mean to take your place in his life. When Marc and I first met, I'd lost my family too. I was...almost feral. You know," she added, reminding herself that, after all, this was only a child, "like a kitten that's grown up wild and never learned how to purr."

She frowned at her overgrown claws and clicked them together irritably. "Even for a dream, this is ridiculous. Maybe I should take up knitting. Knit one, purl two...but I'd only end up making cats' cradles and tying my hands together. I can't even pick my nose with these things without picking my brain, and there's little enough of that to begin with."

The shadow child uttered no sound, but something about her suggested a suppressed giggle.

*Good*, thought Jame, relaxing slightly, and continued, as much now to herself as to the child.

"It's hard to be Kencyr, much less a Highborn Shanir. Honor as we practice it is a cold, hard thing. It breaks some people. It turns others into monsters. I could easily be as bad as you fear I am…no, much worse…if I hadn't been shown kindness. First there were the Kendar at my home keep, then Tirandys, then Marc, and I love them all for it. I especially love your brother for reminding me what decency is, simply by being himself. I would rather die than hurt him. My word on it."

More tension left the small, shadowy figure, but a question lingered.

"Why can't I give him what he needs most, a home?  Because I don't have one myself and perhaps never will."  Jame thrust fingers into her loose hair in an exasperation which grew when her claws became entangled.  She tugged, nearly poked herself in the eye, and swore in a language hopefully unknown to a child from remote Kithorn.

"So far, by accident, I've bound a half-bred Southron and a rathorn colt out for my blood (which he got, ancestors help him).  Oh, and let's not forget my dear half-brother Bane, who flays little boys alive for sport, or used to.  Maybe I don't deserve anyone better.  The point is, though, not what they owe me but what I owe them, and so far as a bounden Highborn I've done a rotten job all around.  I'm not going to promise Marc anything I can't give him.  He deserves better than that."

*Now,* Jame thought, *comes the hard part.*  She leaned forward, looking as serious as she could with both hands still tangled in her hair as if she was trying to tear it out by the roots.

"Willow, I need your help.  This is a dream, part of the dreamscape.  I need to go deeper, into the soulscape.  I've gotten there before accidentally (and by now you probably think that 'Accident' is my middle name), but I don't know how to do it deliberately.  You helped Kindrie to enter my brother's soul-image last winter on the march south, when he fell asleep and couldn't wake up.  Will you help me now?  Please.  The colt is still trapped there.  He's bound to me, however reluctantly, so I have to rescue him if I can, at the very least.  Tirandys and the Kendar taught me that."

She didn't know how Willow would respond, or even if she understood.  After all, this was a child, and one long dead at that.

Time stretched on and on in silence, until it lost all meaning. Dust drifted down. Flesh began to melt. The dancing costume now hung on wasted limbs and her hands had fallen to her lap, each still loosely gripping a mass of black hair with bits of dried scalp attached to it. Jame felt, dimly, that this should concern her, and there was a niggling sense of something else important, forgotten; but it was too much trouble to remember. All she wanted was to lie down and to sleep forever, but she was cold, so cold. Crawl across the floor through thick dust, lift the edge of the blanket...but someone was already under it, waiting, with eye sockets full of lonely shadow.

Those who receive kindness owe kindness in return.

Jame crept under the blanket and took the small bones in arms hardly less clothed in flesh. Dust fell. And silence. And the long night of the dead without a dawn.

# III

THEN SOMEONE SPOKE her name, or rather that hated corruption of it: "Jameth." And again, "Jameth."

The voice was muffled, but it was also clearly angry.

Jame stirred uneasily. She would rather sleep on and on, with no worries except perhaps that her teeth would eventually fall out, like her hair.

Wait a minute. That had been a dream, hadn't it? Trinity, she hoped so. Yes, she still had a full if rather tangled head of hair, and no clothes.

That last was changing, though. She felt her name draw her on, into a web of unseen thread. Coarse strands touched her, lightly at first, then with more persistence, snaring, entangling, thickening. And they stank. It was like being pressed face-first into dank, moldy cloth. Just as she was about to panic, she found herself on the other side, in a circular room. Like the death banner hall at Gothregor, it was dark and windowless, with an oppressively low ceiling. Torches flared at intervals around the stone walls. Between them hung dark tapestries full of lurking shadows that seemed furtively to shift as if aware of her presence. Opposite, however, firelight flickered on a familiar, gentle face.

Jame had never actually met her cousin Aerulan. After all, it was more than forty years since the massacre that had claimed all the Knorth ladies but one, the child Tieri, whom Aerulan had died protecting. However, over the past, dismal winter confined in the Women's Halls at Gothregor, wearing her dead cousin's clothes because Tori hadn't thought to provide her with anything more suitable, she had often visited Aerulan's banner where it had hung among the ranks of her family's dead—that is, until that last night when the Tishooo had blown them all out the window.

Now here they both were again, except...except it appeared to be Aerulan herself standing there, smiling back at her.

Blink. Look again.

While the other's face had the shape and fullness of life, it was marked by the fine weave of death, and its smile was a mere tug of stitches. Nonetheless, Aerulan's soul gazed out through warp and woof, clear-eyed and wryly amused.

*So here we are again, cousin.*

Was this another dream, or had she indeed reached the soulscape? If the latter, whose voice had drawn her and where was she now?

The answer came in the click of boot-heels and the jangle of heavy spurs, both muffled by the stone and thick cloth of the walls.

Brenwyr stalked past in a swirl of her divided riding skirt, arms folded tightly across her chest as if holding herself together. No longer smiling, Aerulan watched her pass. As the dead girl turned her head, Jame saw that it had no back except the concave reverse of her face, rough with tied off threads.

The Brandan Matriarch seemed oblivious to them both. What comfort could she take in that which she could not see, and who could see anything through an eyeless seeker's mask? In the Women's Halls, Jame had sometimes been forced to wear one herself as punishment for her restless wanderings. More commonly, though, the mask was used in a child's game. The girl wearing it lost not only her sight but her identity until she managed to catch another player. Then she passed on the mask and assumed the new seeker's name. In the end, everyone was someone else except for the girl left wearing the mask, who became no one, nameless and lost. Sometimes, she wore it for days until an older girl took pity on her and removed it.

But who could free a matriarch blinded by her own despair?

"What can I do? What can I do?" Brenwyr was muttering to herself in a rant as circular and obsessive as her pacing. "We had a contract, dammit! You were to have been mine forever. But then you died and the Gray Lord went into exile, and now his son tells my brother to forget the price. Adiraina says that he's only a man, that he doesn't understand, that he means to be kind. Ha! How can I keep you, and yet how can I bear to lose you again? This will destroy me. Worse, what if it drives me to destroy others?"

The shadows stirred in the tapestries as she passed, creeping forward, gaining definition. Her demons. Her memories.

Here stood a child grotesque in her brother's oversized clothes, a knife in one hand, a hacked off hank of long, black hair dangling from the other. Every line of her unhappy face said, *It didn't work. I still hate myself.*

In the next tapestry, the same girl knelt beside the body of a woman who, arms full of boy's clothing, had tumbled down a flight of stairs and broken her neck.

Brenwyr beat her blind face with clenched fists. "Oh, mother, I didn't mean to curse you. I didn't. I didn't. But I am a Shanir maledight, a monster. What can I do but harm? Adiraina, grand-mother-kin, you tell me to be strong and so I have been. The Iron Matriarch they call me, but they don't know. They don't know. Aerulan, sister-kin, you gave me strength, and love, and then you died. Oh, I cursed your murderer and doom fell on him, but you are still dead. And now must I lose your banner too? He tossed you to me, ancestors damn him, like a bone to a dog! The insult, the shame. I should curse him. No, no, I have already cursed his sister. 'Rootless and roofless'...damn you, Jameth!"

Jame flinched. That was the same harsh, heartbroken cry that had drawn her here.

Then she fought to keep her balance. Only now did she realize that she was again wearing Aerulan's clothes, including the tight underskirt that practically bound her legs together. To fall over at the Brandon's feet would be awkward, to say the least. She won-dered in passing if "damn you" counted as a maledight curse.

Brenwyr said it again, with a breaking voice. "You stole her, seduced her with that accursed Knorth charm. Ah, how well I remember it. How I have felt it, even with you. On the road. In the cold. Did you sleep with her?"

That, thought Jame, still tottering precariously, was one way to put it. She had retrieved Aerulan's banner from the tree where the Tishooo had left it and taken it north with her. Yes, the nights had been cold. Yes, she had used the banner as a blanket for warmth and sometimes woke to feel her cousin's comforting arms around her. Willow wasn't the first of the dead with whom she had shared comfort. It probably wouldn't help, though, to say that she had slept not only with Brenwyr's beloved but under her.

As the matriarch paced on and on, the shadows kept pace with her from tapestry to tapestry, mirroring her thoughts, mocking them.

*You are ugly, dangerous, a killer,* they said. *Who could love you but one of the mad Knorth, and now she is dead. Maledight, monster. Curse yourself and die.*

Jame watched the roil of dark stitches and wondered. Doubt-less, the Brandan Matriarch had a terrible opinion of herself, and the possible loss of Aerulan had stirred up all the destructive self-loath-ing at the bottom of her soul, but this seemed extreme. Moreover, she sensed another presence in the room, slyly lurking. If she, Jame, was here, why not someone else? As if in answer, the stitches of the nearest tapestry seethed like so many maggots into the semblance of a masked face that turned to look at Jame askance. It smiled.

*I told you. My name is legion, as are my forms and the eyes through which I see. Miserable orphan of a ruined house, do you know me now?*

"Oh, yes," breathed Jame, her fists clenching, nails biting palms. "We met in the eyes of your tempter and again when you spoke through that wretched boy whom you hag-rode to his death. Worm in the weave, I name you, and witch in the tower. Rawneth, the great bitch of Wilden."

The other began to laugh, and Jame went for her, claws first. The face distorted in a soundless scream as her nails hooked in it and tore downward. The fabric disintegrated into striped, twitching threads and slimy clots that slopped to the floor, stinking like the contents of an unplugged drain.

"Ugh," said Jame, regarding her befouled nails, wondering if she would ever get them clean again.

Brenwyr had spun around. "Who's there?" she demanded harshly. "Name yourself, so that I may know whom to curse."

Jame floundered to her feet, fighting not only the tight under-garment but the full outer skirt. Trinity, neither had been this bad in the real world. In them, she might hop or roll, but little else. The Brandan Matriarch was advancing on her, arms blindly groping. Her sleeves, her very hands, trailed threads as her entire soul-image began to unravel. Over her shoulder, Jame saw Aerulan.

*Go,* mouthed her cousin, so urgently that the stitches sealing her woven lips snapped and bled.

Jame ducked away, lost her balance again and, in a sharp ripping of undergarments, toppled through the hole left by the disintegrat-ing tapestry. As she fell away into the outer darkness of the soulscape, she saw the receding image of Brenwyr. The matriarch had stopped, her shoulders slumped. Then she drew herself up and began slowly, grimly, to pull back together the frayed threads of her being.

# IV

THE SOULSCAPE SEEMED to connect all individual soul-images, but it wasn't clear to Jame exactly how. One could get lost in here forever, or stumble into something really nasty, as she just had.

Trinity, could Rawneth wander here as she pleased, or did she only infest Brenwyr's soul-image? There, she had clearly found a chink in the Iron Matriarch's armor, and Brenwyr was too blinded by grief and rage to defend herself. Jame sensed that she had expelled the Witch at least temporarily. But there were other banners in Brenwyr's soul-image, other "eyes" through which that malignant creature might peer. Somehow, the matriarch must shed that accursed seeker's mask. Aerulan, or rather her banner, was the key, but one problem at a time.

It was hard, though, not to think what power it would give one to have free range of the soulscape. Trinity, what a way to find things out, if not to destroy one's enemies outright. She pictured herself armored and deadly, cutting a swathe through the rotten patches of the soulscape, up to the Master's very door. But why stop there? Why not pursue the monster into his maze and there destroy him once and for all? Why have such power if not to use it?

*Nemesis.*

The word emerged out of the darkness as a harsh cough, as if it were trying to dislodge clinkers in the throat. With it came the stench of burnt fur.

*What have you done now?*

The name drew her, but not as strongly as "Jameth" had done. After all, while she was clearly a nemesis, aligned with That-Which-Destroys, she wasn't yet *the* Nemesis, Third Face of God. Dammit, what had she done now except defend herself…and rip the guts out of a putrid banner in someone else's soul-image…and blood-bind a rathorn.

Where was the colt? What if she had really killed him…but wouldn't she know if she had? She reached deep into her own soul, to a part that ached like an overtaxed muscle. Weakness sent quivers through all her limbs. He hadn't the stamina for this. She felt his exhaustion threatening to undo them both.

*No*, she told herself. *Be strong. Be angry.*

That blasted cat, Arrin-ken be damned. If he must prowl the soulscape, why didn't he go after the Witch for tormenting Brenwyr? So much was rotten in the Kencyrath, both openly and in secret. Honor had been twisted until for some Highborn it was nothing but a Lawful Lie, and the breaking of it of little more importance. Where were the judges that should call such oath-breakers to justice? What worms ever now were undermining from within the fabric of the Three People so that all in the end might fall to ruin?

Her throat hurt. She had shouted her questions into the darkness. Now she waited for a reply.

Nothing.

Then, faintly, she heard someone calling her:

*Kinzi-kin. Come. Please.*

When she turned toward the voice, another tapestry hung before her. This one depicted a garden in full bloom, and all the blooms were white. Pushing it aside, she stepped into the Moon Garden.

# V

FOR A MOMENT, Jame thought that she was in the real garden at Gothregor, which she had discovered the previous winter during her ceaseless wanderings through the empty eastern halls. It occupied a secret courtyard abutting the Ghost Walks, where the women of her house had lived before the massacre and, when she had last seen it, it had been a riot of snowy blossoms in the early spring.

So it still was, although the year had passed well into summer. Moreover, the lofty comfrey, lacy yarrow, heart's ease and self-heal all glowed softly in the dusk while pollen floated, glimmering, on the still air. At the north end grew a flowering apple tree where none had been before. Under it sat a pale lady, with the head of the rathorn cradled in her lap.

*Lully lully lullaby*, she sang in a low murmur, stroking his white neck and mane. *Dream of meadows, free of flies...*

"Isn't this Kindrie's soul-image?" Jame asked, perplexed. "How did you get here?"

The lady paused and raised her head, the right side turned away. *Who is Kindrie?*

Her lips didn't move. They never had, Jame realized, when she spoke, and that was only when she wore the aspect of a woman.

"Kinzi's great-grandson. He was born in this garden—the real one, I mean. His mother Tieri, Kinzi's granddaughter, died here."

She glanced at the southern wall where Tieri's death banner should have hung. Moss and shadow suggested that gentle, sad face against the stones, but nothing more. For that matter, she supposed that while all soul-images were unique, people must model them after something familiar to them. She would have liked the garden for her own soul's haven, although for her it probably would sprout carnivorous daisies and flights of bright-winged carrion jewel-jaws.

The White Lady was shaking her head. *Names, names, names. Never born, never lived, never died.* Her hand stole up to her hidden cheek, touched it, jerked away. *Someone hurt me. Who? And my lady dead? No, no, no. This is all a bad dream, and so are you. Go away.*

She bent again over the colt, crooning,

*Dream of friends who never lie,*
*And of love that never dies...*

The whole garden had a strange texture, best seen out of the corner of the eye, a sort of cross-hatching.

At Perimal's Cauldron, the Whinno-hir had said that she had spoken to Kinzi, that the matriarch's blood had trapped her soul in the weave of her death.

Jame touched a nearby lily. Its white petals looked like cool, living velvet, but they felt like coarse, damp cloth. "I think," she said, "that we are in the background of Lady Kinzi's death banner."

If, however, this was the remnant of her great-grandmother's soul-image, might some element of her still inhabit it?

*But all life must end in sighs,*
*So lully lully lullaby.*

A square of candlelight glimmered on the garden, silvering grass and flower, changing their shadows to pewter. It fell from an open window set high in the northern, outer wall, where the Ghost Walks began. During her visits here in the flesh, Jame had noticed the bricked up aperture, but had not known to whom that lovely view down into the garden had belonged, much less why it had been obstructed. Now a figure stood at the open window in dark silhouette against the flickering light. She had heard that Kinzi was a small, trim woman, and so was this silent watcher, although nothing could be seen of her face. What a long shadow that tiny figure had cast, until assassins cut it short.

Jame felt suddenly, acutely, self-conscious. She still wore the remnants of Aerulan's clothes, little better than tatters, and no mask. Moreover, the rags stank with the residual effluvium of the shredded tapestry. This time, not only had she arrived inappropriately clothed but reeking like an open sewer. She saluted the figure in the window with as much dignity as she could muster. Perhaps the other nodded slightly in reply, perhaps not. Life, death, and the abyss of time lay between them.

*Lully lully lullaby...*

The sad little song began again, lamenting all that had been lost. Lives, hope, honor, all gone, and only the victims were left to pay, and pay, and pay. A house in ruins. Her house. A family put to the knife, and that too hers. Vengeance be damned. Where was justice?

*Be strong. Be angry.*

Jame was pacing now, impatiently plucking off sodden rags. She felt dangerous. She felt deadly. All that she had shouted into the darkness echoed in her mind, the challenge unanswered. Her god was no help—long ago, those three faces had turned away—and his judges went their own inscrutable way, far from the walks of those whom they were to have served.

The garden fell gradually into shadow, the inner light of its blooms flickering out one by one.

"You leave us in the dark, and damn us when we stumble."

Her angry voice came back flat and muffled, off stone walls that were in fact cloth, threadbare leavings of the dead.

"You let honor perish and those who flaunt it prosper."

*Remember that all men do lie,*

*If not in words, then deeds belie...*

"You demand that we fight your battles, yet the weapons that you give us shatter in our hands."

To whom was she speaking? Did it matter? She flung out the words like knives, not caring whom they hit.

"Yet through this all, we are bound to keep faith?"

"Watch where you tread."

The voice grumbled down, huge, like thunder in the mountains. This time, there was an echo. Jame stopped short. During her rant, space had changed around her. She could still see the lit window, but it seemed lower than before, the fire in it dying in a wrought iron grate. Of Kinzi, if indeed it had been she, there was no sign. Instead, Whinno-hir and rathorn colt huddled together in the embers' ruddy glow. Walls still surrounded them and the drum tower of the Ghost Walks still loomed over head, but then the latter shifted on its foundations. Stone ground on stone. Grit rattled down. Was it going to fall? No. Slowly, ponderously, it began to rock. Back and forth. Back and forth. And it had gone all lumpy, more toward the bottom than the top, against which a faint, full moon seemed to be rising.

...click, click, click...

Needles, knitting—what, Jame couldn't see, but as for who... She gulped.

"Mother Ragga, how did I...that is, how did we get into your lodge?"

A grunt of disgust made the air shake, as if something massive had fallen. What Jame had thought to be the moon leaned over her, glowering. Mother Ragga had a face not unlike a monstrous dumpling gone bad, soft here, bulging there, alight with mottled indignation.

"This is what the Merikit call sacred space—Rathillien's soulscape, as it were. You always did creep inside, girl, whenever you found a chink. Since those idiots invited you through the front door as my Favorite, though, there seems to be no keeping you out, short of killing you. I'm considering that."

"What? But why?"

"Look where you have trodden."

The upper reaches of the room might be the lodge, grown large enough to swallow an army whole, but the dirt floor where Ragga kept her earth map was still the Moon Garden, or what was left of it. Jame saw with dismay that in raging back and forth she had destroyed a wide swathe of it. Comfrey, yarrow, and heart's-ease lay not just broken under her feet but rotting, with the threads of Kinzi's banner showing through like tendons laid bare. She flexed her hands, staring at the ivory gauntlets that gloved them. She wore armor from throat to loins but, like the rathorn, only on the front. The draft from behind was disconcerting.

She had dreamed of slashing through the soulscape, a warrior clad in gleaming ivory, destroying all that was rotten in it. What if, however, like the Ivory Knife, everything that she touched died, the fair with the foul? Was that what it meant to be the Third Face of God?

"You asked why," grumbled that enormous voice. "You ask much. But what will your answers cost? It isn't the Favorite's role to ask but to act, yet that might be worse. What about the summer solstice, eh?"

Jame had nearly forgotten, and it wasn't far off.

"Didn't we take care of my part in that on Summer's Eve?" she asked nervously. "After all, I've already fought last year's Favorite— sort of. It wasn't my idea to combine that rite with establishing the boundaries, nor to get dragged into either one of them, for that matter."

"Huh. Well I know it, and little it matters. There are rules. Remember, not only does the Favorite mate with the Earth Wife for the fertility of the land, but then she passes off her lover to her consort the Burnt Man as their son. It's called 'fooling death.'"

"Who makes up these games anyway?" Jame asked.

The rocking stopped for a moment. "Don't know. Doesn't matter. They just are. I might blink at some of 'em, but the Burnt Man won't. Not now, anyway. Since you became involved, he's somehow gotten mixed up with that blind judge of yours. Bad breath, a worse attitude, and he's out of his tiny, little cinder of a mind. Then there's you, another disaster waiting to happen. Oh, you may regret it afterward and try to make amends, but some things once broken can never be mended."

*And they will hunt you till you die*, sang the Whinno-hir Bel-tairi on the Earth Wife's hearth, rocking the white-haired boy that was the rathorn colt.

*And then your mouth will fill with flies,*
*So lully lully lullaby.*

The Earth Wife's face filled half the sky, and her anger pressed down as one feels the weight of a mountain from within a cave or that of a boulder poised to fall. "Did you hear that, you wretched girl? What did you people do to this poor creature? She came to me wounded in body and soul. I sheltered her in my lodge—days, years, what does time matter? Then her lady called her forth. Is her torment to begin all over again? I tell you straight, I'd rather destroy the lot of you than go through that again. Don't think that I can't! And what's the matter with that colt?"

As Jame fumbled for the answer least likely to get her killed, the Whinno-hir spoke again:

*My lady bade me find you.*

They might have been back at Perimal's Cauldron, but the shock of that first meeting had passed into a dreamlike acceptance.

*My lady bids me warn you. Of the Knorth Highborn, only three of you are left.*

Jame blinked. Three? "Lady, who…?"

*One is still too wounded to know himself, and the other's mind is poisoned against his own nature. You are the closest of the three to realizing who and what you are, but you also have the darkling glamour bred into your very bones. The haunt singer Ashe has warned my lady, and my lady has warned me.*

"Wait a minute. How does Kinzi know—I mean, about the third? This side of the shadows, except for Tori and me, there's only our cousin Kindrie, and he was born long after the massacre."

*The dead know what concerns the dead. My unfortunate granddaughter Tieri is dead, and so am I. While our blood traps us, we walk the Gray Land together, two of a silent host.*

The Whinno-hir's voice changed. Her fire-cast shadow lengthened and thinned, as if cast by someone else, small and trim.

Jame gulped. The Gray Land? One by one, all the things she thought she knew about death were proving false, but she must keep to the point. "Lady, Kindrie is a bastard, or doesn't legitimacy count after all?"

*It does. Blood of my blood, some things that matter very much are unfair, but true. It is also true that I told your father to draw strength from his anger, but he did not have the discipline to control what he called up. How could he, while he denied what he was?*

Be strong, Jame had told herself. Be angry.

"Great-grandmother, I know who I am and what I may become."

*Ah, but what if you are truly alone, with neither That-Which-Creates nor That-Which-Preserves to balance you? Have you the strength, alone, to balance yourself?*

"Huh." The Earth Wife leaned back, her face a pocked moon rising, and the tower groaned as she resumed her slow rocking. "That's the kernel of the nut. Balance. We four have it—most of the time; you three don't. By stone and stock, you don't even seem to know who you are. As I understand it, you people have ruined world after world. Should Rathillien topple as well for your faults?"

"I think," said Jame carefully, "that without us this world is doomed. Mother Ragga, have you looked into the face of the shadows that loom over you? I have. As everyone keeps reminding me, I was raised among them. If I remembered more of those lost years, perhaps there would be less of me left to recover."

She paused, surprised by her own words. Of course, her lost childhood still bothered her. (Confess.) What had she done under shadows' eaves and what had been done to her? (You know your faults.) Perhaps, after all, she had deserved the latter, and much more beside.

Huh. I know who I am, she had just said, and of this much she was sure:

"Thanks to my Senethari Tirandys...and to Bender, his brother...my honor has survived."

"So far," grumbled the Earth Wife.

"Well, yes, but who can say more than that?"

*Enough. I am sorry, child, but desperate times, desperate measures. Ashe is right: Tentir will test you as it has all Knorth lordan. Succeed or fail. Live or die. Now give back this poor boy's armor until you earn the right to wear it. Besides, he is cold.*

So was Jame, all up her bare back. Half clothed was far worse than stark naked, but must she face the outer darkness in nothing but her skin? What if the blind Arrin-ken was waiting for her? On the other hand, did she really want to back out of the Earth Wife's presence or, worse, turn bare buttocks on her great-grandmother? Oh well.

At the thought, she felt suddenly lighter, with good reason: the armor was gone, or rather back where it belonged.

"I cared for the mare," grumbled that huge voice, thunder receding. "I will keep what watch I can over her fosterling until (if ever) you assume your responsibilities. Here."

Something scratchy dropped around her bare shoulders—a kind of blanket, knit of moss and lichen.

"Now sleep."

And, despite herself, she did.

# Chapter XVI: Midsummer's Eve

### Summer 53 - 60

## I

JAME WOKE IN Tentir's infirmary and, to her great annoyance, was forced to spend another seven days there. She had never been flat on her back for so long before, nor was this usual for the fast-healing Kencyr.

"You should be glad you aren't dead," said Kindrie, who had been summoned to treat the wounded of the rathorn hunt and had stayed to keep an eye on her. "Soul-walking is dangerous, even when you aren't bled nearly dry."

Her slashed wrists had all but healed, settling into a random pattern of thin, white lines which, hopefully, would soon also disappear. She had to admit that Tori's scars were much more esthetically pleasing, but then his had been the work of Karnid fanatics, to whom everything formed a pattern.

More to the point, she was missing vital training. All too soon after midsummer would come the autumn cull both of unworthy cadets and of beasts unlikely to survive the coming winter. For herself, Jame would rather be salted for the larder than sent back to the Women's Halls at Gothregor. The sound of cadets at practice outside in the square made her fidget under the Earth Wife's thick, mossy blanket. So did the blanket itself, which tickled. Besides scratchy lichen, she suspected that it harbored a hidden population of woodlice, if not spiders and centipedes, but so far none had been fool enough to bite her. Then too, the moss was cool and comforting on this hot summer day.

"It would help if you ate something." Rue presented her latest offering. "Look, here's a nice bowl of gruel."

"Yum, yum," muttered Graykin from the far corner where he was pretending to be invisible.

"I wish," said Jame, exasperated, "that all of you would stop treating me like a moron."

"Then stop acting like one." Kindrie took the bowl and offered her a spoonful.

*The Scrollsmen's College must agree with him,* Jame thought, unconsciously drawing back from the dripping, gray gunk.

(*Toad eggs, dog vomit...*)

When she had first met her cousin that spring, he had seemed to have all the backbone of an angle-worm and a beaten air that had made her long to hit him. Of course, at the time, he had just escaped from what must have been a nightmare winter in the Priests' College at Wilden, in Lady Rawneth's shadow and under her thumb.

"You won't regain your strength if you don't eat," he said patiently.

"I'm not hungry."

(*Maggot larvae, cow drool...*)

Food had seldom been more than a necessary evil in her life, given her early acquaintance with the shrieking carrots and oozing onions of the Haunted Lands. Now the very thought of it nauseated her. Marc might have coaxed her into eating. However, after assuring himself that she was out of danger, or at least as much so as she ever was, he had gone back to tend an unpredictable glass furnace at Gothregor.

"If it decides to blow up," he had said, not too comfortingly, "I should be there."

Harn Grip-hard had gone with him, to prepare for the Minor Harvest. Tomorrow, Midsummer's Day, all cadets would go home to help with the haying.

Kindrie put down the bowl. "Very well. You can serve a rathorn rabbit, but you can't make him eat it. Before I forget, my lady Kirien sends her congratulations."

"For what?"

"Not being dead yet, I suppose. Also, Index says he's going up into the hills with you for the summer solstice."

"Damn that man. How often do I have to tell him that I'm not going at all?"

"Every day from now until then, I suppose. The solstice comes, what, six days after our Midsummer? You'd think our ancestors would have paid more attention to Rathillien's calendar, but we always have tried to impose our own systems on any threshold world where we happen to land. Anyway, you can hardly blame Index. Herbs are only his practical job. The Merikit were his field of study before your friend Marc wiped out a score of them, avenging Kithorn."

"For what it's worth, that winter killed Marc's taste for bloodshed for the rest of his life, which for a professional warrior is awkward."

"It also closed the hills to all Kencyr except, apparently, you."

"That wasn't my idea."

"No. A lot of things aren't, but they still happen."

"Oh, bugger this." Jame threw off the Earth Wife's gift, tripped over Jorin, and fell flat on her face. Rue returned her to bed while Graykin modestly averted his eyes.

"What *is* this thing?" asked the cadet, regarding the fibrous mat suspiciously.

"A reminder." Not that she was likely to forget, Index notwithstanding. What would the Merikit do on the solstice without the legitimate Favorite? Oh well. That was their problem.

"Even if you wanted to go up into the hills," said Kindrie, "I doubt if you would have the strength, especially if you carry on like this."

Jame growled at him, echoed by Jorin under the bed, nursing the paw on which she had trodden.

"You're enjoying this, aren't you?"

The ghost of a smile flickered across his thin face. "A bit," he admitted.

"Huh." She glowered at him for a moment. "Rue, Graykin, I want to talk to my cousin alone."

Rue sketched a salute and turned to leave. Graykin tried to sidle into the shadows behind the open door, but the cadet fished him out and pushed him before her, protesting, into the hall. The door closed behind them. Kindrie sat down on the opposite cot, looking nervous.

"Have you been mucking around with my soul-image again?" Jame asked him bluntly.

That, after all, was how a healer worked. Each person, consciously or not, visualized his or her soul in a particular way. The Knorth favored architectural models. A healer might spend what felt like a year inside an injured person's soulscape, rebuilding a fallen wall, and emerge an hour later to find his patient's broken ribs well on the mend. What repairs she might need now, Jame couldn't imagine.

But Kindrie was shaking his head, the window behind him making a halo of his white hair.

"No. The last time, remember, you threw me out so hard that I cracked my skull on an inconveniently placed anvil. This time, all you needed was a solid stint of *dwar* sleep. That, and food. Still, battered, half-drowned, and nearly exsanguinated—a busy day, even for you. But why did you ask about your soul-image?"

"I'm not sure." She frowned, trying to recapture impressions that had hardly registered at the time. "Something about it this time was…different. First, I was on the edge of Tori's soulscape—no, I didn't meddle with it, although I did shout a bit. Then there was the Master's House, but I was outside of it. In fact, it came after me. What in Perimal's name was that all about?"

"I'd forgotten," said Kindrie slowly. "We haven't had a chance to talk since Summer's Eve when I tried to heal your face."

Jame touched her scarred cheek. "And I never got a chance to thank you for your work on this. I know, I know: you could have done more if I hadn't thrown you out. That wasn't deliberate. Sorry about the anvil."

She still had to fight her revulsion at his priestling background. What the Shanir were to her brother, priests were to her, with better reason. Still, she kept reminding herself, Kindrie hadn't chosen to grow up at Wilden in the Priest's College. Born after the Knorth had nearly been wiped out by Shadow Assassins, Shanir, and (worse) illegitimate, he had been dropped into the priests' laps, so to speak, as an alternative to drowning him like an unwanted pup.

She wondered what those who had thrown him away so casually would think if they could see him now. Besides having become a powerful healer, he was beginning to show the fine-drawn Knorth features that one could trace on death banners back to the Fall. There was much of his mother Tieri's gentle melancholy in his eyes, but also much of his great-grandmother Kinzi's deceptive strength in the elegant bones of his face and hands. In fact, physically, he was starting to look like a cross between Tori and herself, except for the white hair and pale blue eyes. Were they a legacy from his unknown father? Who in Perimal's name could that have been, anyway?

*Of the Knorth Highborn, only three of you are left.*

And those three were the Kencyrath's last chance to produce the long-awaited Tyr-ridan, through whom their god was supposed to manifest himself and do battle with that ancient enemy, Perimal Darkling.

*One is still too wounded to know himself, and the other's mind is poisoned against his own nature.*

If she was becoming That-Which-Destroys, Tori presumably was destined to become That-Which-Creates, if he could overcome the poison instilled by his father, if he ever got the chance to make something new out of their increasingly compromised society.

As a potential third, That-Which-Preserves, who else was there and who better than the healer Kindrie, wounded by his past but slowly recovering from it?

Except that he was a bastard, and blood still mattered.

"About your soul-image," he was saying, "I know you believe that it's the Master's Hall. I thought so at first too. When I went into the soulscape to work on your injury, all of the hall's death banners had been slashed across the face, like you, then stitched up again with coarse thread to form raised welts. I wasted a lot of time unpicking stitches before I realized that they were only a diversion."

"I'm confused. Aren't disfigured faces what you would expect to find?"

"Yes, but there were too many of them, and they were laughing at me. Then I saw something white on the hearth. It was you, the real you, asleep, wearing partial rathorn armor, with a bleeding crack across the cheek. That's what I was trying to close when you woke up and threw me out."

"Oh."

Jame considered this, rather blankly. Perhaps she had worn the ivory armor in the soulscape before borrowing it this last time, as it were, off the colt's back. On that level, just as different versions of the Moon Garden might shelter more than one soul, so armor might shield whoever needed it, and she already had close links both personal and familial with those horned beasts of madness.

"I think," said Kindrie, "that it means you've begun to protect yourself against your past, like growing a callus, only in you it takes the form of an outbreak of ivory. Sleep could be another defense, if a passive one. There, they couldn't get at you. But now you're awake and out. Of the hall. Of the Master's House."

Jame snorted. "Into the Haunted Lands. Back among the dead. Not quite like my brother, though."

"No. For some reason he's still confined to that awful keep where you both grew up. You, though, seem to be free in the soulscape, though travel there is perilous and I'll thank you to re-member that it just nearly killed you."

"At least Tori has the keep, and you have the Moon Garden. Will I ever have a true home or must I always wander, armored and perhaps armed, but roofless and rootless?"

The question burst from her with a force that surprised them both.

"That's what you really want? A home?"

"More than anything." Until she said it, she didn't realize how painfully true it was. What had her life been so far but a desperate search for a place where she belonged? Brenwyr hadn't needed to curse her, although it probably hadn't helped; she was the eternal out-sider, the arch-iconoclast. Given her nature, what else could she be?

"I'm sorry," said Kindrie, seeing that she was upset. "Still, soul-images do change as we grow. You're only—what, nineteen years old? Twenty? More?"

There was no answer to this: thanks to the slower, erratic passage of time in Perimal Darkling, Jame didn't know. She felt ancient.

"I should tell you," said the Shanir, this time not meeting her eyes. "In the soulscape, your servant Graykin was guarding you in the shape of a half-starved mongrel dog, chained to the hearth. He's intensely jealous of anyone who gets close to you. That's his soul-image, and it's a pretty miserable one. It's not my business, but you should consider more carefully how you treat him."

Jame brushed this aside. Graykin was the least of her worries.

"Has Tori accepted you as a Knorth?" she asked abruptly.

"No." Again Kindrie looked away, biting his lip. "He tried, but...do you know how psychic bonding works? Most of the lords don't really understand, but when they bind a follower they give that person a small piece of their soul image, or maybe they give him, or her, a niche in their own soulscape, or maybe both. It's hard to explain, but there's definitely an element of give, whereas with blood binding it's all take, like...like..."

"Rape versus love?" Jame suggested, deliberately probing her own sense of guilt over the colt.

"In a way. When the Highlord offered me a place in his house, I was overjoyed." He looked at her askance through a fringe of white hair. "I'm looking for a place to belong too, you know, and I am Knorth, if only by bastard blood. That wouldn't matter to Torisen, but you know how he feels about the Shanir."

"He hates and fears us," said Jame flatly. "Father taught him that."

"Just the same, he tried. You know what his soulscape is like. Well, he gave me his hand, and there I was in that desolate keep. At the back of the hall was a door. Something was on the other side. Something that muttered and cursed and shook the handle."

Jame remembered being in her brother's soul-image and slamming that door against their father's madness, to save Tori's sanity, to give him peace.

*The bolt is shot.*

"Well," said Kindrie, taking a deep breath, "what he offered me was the lock on that door. I couldn't accept it. He isn't ready."

"Little man," said Jame, impressed, "you've grown."

His pale face flushed. It took Jame a moment to realize that he was angry. "I couldn't hurt him. You know that. But since then I've wondered: is it good for him to have part of his soul-image locked off? That was your doing, wasn't it? I nearly caught you at it. Perhaps it seemed like a good idea at the time, but somehow it's weakened him. I've heard rumors. He's having trouble remembering his people's names."

This struck cold. "But if he can't remember…"

"The bond breaks. One Kendar has already killed himself because of it."

"Oh. Poor man. And poor Tori. Kindrie, this is awful. Can't we do something about it?"

He shook his head, frustrated. "I've thought and thought. He has to come to terms with what's behind that door, and he has to do it by himself. I think. At any rate, the way things stand right now, neither of us can get close enough to him to help."

Silence fell between them. The room was falling into shadow, the sounds outside of the day's last class fading as cadets dispersed for their free period before the Midsummer Eve's feast.

"So," said Jame at last, "that's why you're at Mount Alban instead of at Gothregor."

"Yes. The Scrollsmen's College has taken me in and the Jaran Lordan, Kirien, has been very kind. Of course," he added with a twist to his smile, "she's pleased to have a healer on hand. For a community mostly of aging scholars, the scrollsmen and the singers get into as many squabbles with each other as a bunch of children. Academia seems to have that effect on some people. I'm also helping Index put his herb shed back in order after the weirdingstrom."

Index, who knew where every bit of information could be found, be it in some ancient scroll or in a colleague's capacious memory. Besides supplying medicines, in its organization the herb shed was a mnemonic device—Index's index, as it were. Jame wondered if Kindrie had discovered that yet. She herself had only found out by accident.

"Well, he's not going to talk me into going up-river for some blasted fertility rite, and so you may tell him. I just want to go back to being a normal cadet."

"That," said a rough voice, "you'll never be."

Gorbel limped into the infirmary and dropped heavily into a chair. "Still here, are you?" he said to Kindrie. "Good. Do something about this damned foot of mine. Now."

"You'll have to excuse him," said Jame. "The Caineron consider good manners a weakness. Gorbel, this is Kindrie Soul-walker, my cousin and blood-kin to the Highlord."

"The Knorth Bastard, eh? Well, don't just stand there, man. This hurts!"

The Shanir gave Jame an unreadable look, then knelt to pull off the Caineron's boot. This took some effort: the foot within was badly swollen, with green lines radiating out from a central, raw puncture.

Kindrie sat back on his heels, staring. "I thought I'd dealt with this. All right. Let's see what's going on." He cupped Gorbel's broad, dirty foot in his long, delicate hands and bent over it.

"One of your blasted willow saplings sank a root into me," Gorbel explained to Jame, then flinched. "Trinity damn it, man, be careful! Anyway, the surgeon dug it out like a splinter, which hurt like Perimal. Now this."

"Gently, gently…" said the healer, and Gorbel's stubby toes slowly unclenched. He sagged in the chair, small eyes losing their focus and toad face relaxing.

"It's a forest in here," Kindrie murmured, deep in the other's soul-image. "Strange. He doesn't know what he is yet, hunter or prey. At the moment, he's trying to be a tree."

"Perhaps because trees don't feel pain, although I'm not so sure about that anymore. What about the willow?"

"That's the problem. I couldn't help while he had a physical object jammed through his foot—how would you like to be healed with an arrow still sticking out of you?—but the sapling's rootlets are loose now in his soulscape and, I suppose, in his blood. Damn. Have you ever tried to uproot a particularly persistent weed? Just when you think you've gotten it all, it springs up again on the other side of the garden. This is going to take awhile."

"Am I interrupting anything?" asked a voice at the door, and there stood Timmon with an armful of daises, beaming over them like a particularly self-satisfied sun. "You're awake at last. Good!"

"What are those for?" Jame asked as he appropriated a water jug for his bouquet.

"Why, hasn't anyone ever given you flowers before?"

"No. Once picked, they just die. What's the point?"

"You're supposed to admire them," murmured Kindrie, "and be grateful to the donor."

"So this is about you, Timmon, not about me or an armload of wilting greenery, however pretty. Does your girlfriend admire flowers too?"

"Everything is always about me," said the Ardeth cheerfully. "What girlfriend? Oh. The Kendar. Narsa. It's a nuisance how possessive some females get, especially when the fun is over. You'll be more sensible, of course. Actually, that Coman cadet Gari picked these flowers, but he asked me to bring them because he's come down with an infestation of termites."

"How uncomfortable for him."

"Oh, he's all right, as long as he keeps moving. Otherwise, the floor collapses under him. The master-ten of his house has him sleeping outside. Hello, what have we here?" He wandered over to regard Gorbel, who blinked slowly at him.

"A ssslight case," said the Caineron, slurring his words, "of in-grown tree." He made a sound like a small explosion that turned out to be a laugh. "That tickles," he informed Kindrie.

"My. I had no idea the infirmary was so entertaining."

"Nodd from where I'm sittin'. Want to change places?"

Jame propped herself up on an elbow, then surprised herself by modestly pulling up the moss. A spider scrambled down between her small breasts, diving for cover. "Timmon, you can't treat people that way, especially not Kendar. They're too vulnerable to the Highborn as it is."

Kindrie shot her a look: *remember Graykin.*

"Ah, you sound like Grandfather," said Timmon, pouting. "Now, my father Pereden amused himself however he pleased and he..."

"...was a great man. So you've said. Repeatedly."

"There." Kindrie sat back on his heels with a sigh. "I hope I got it all. The swelling should go down soon. If it doesn't, or comes back, we'll try again."

"Come on," said Timmon, pulling Gorbel to his feet and scooping up the boot. "Let's get you back to your quarters. Good evening, my lady. Sweet dreams."

As they lurched out, one supporting the other, Kindrie turned to a rank of bottles on an infirmary shelf and took down a blue-tinted vial.

"Lord Ardeth's favorite," he said, uncorking it and pouring a small amount into a glass of water. "Tincture of hemlock. This will help you sleep."

Jame took the glass and sniffed it. "Ugh. Distillation of dead mouse, more likely."

"Now, now. If you're a good girl, maybe we'll let you go back to the Knorth barracks tomorrow."

She glowered at him, and drank. "You're enjoying all of this far, far too much."

Kindrie smiled, lit a thick candle with the hours of the night marked on it by bars, and left her alone.

# II

BY NOW, IT was early evening. The day's last light flooded through the infirmary windows and shadows crept after it up the walls. Below, cheerful, muted chatter spilled into the square from the barracks' dining halls.

Jame floated on the light, then sank into shadow. The hemlock began to take effect almost immediately on her empty stomach. It was a little like being drunk, as far as she could remember from her one experience, but with an unpleasant tingling of her limbs as if they were falling asleep. She drifted in and out of consciousness fitfully, not quite trusting herself to the drug. That was too much like losing control. The candle flame seemed to expand and contract as it flickered in the breeze through the open window. Light and dark, dark and light...

Fleetingly, someone touched her, leaving a slight, supple weight on her chest that had not been there before.

Jame blinked. The candle had burned down two rings. The college would be settling for the night and soon she would be only one sleeper out of hundreds, as was proper. She sighed and let go.

A low growl roused her, followed by a soft hiss.

"Can't you let the dead rest in peace?" she muttered, and with difficulty pried open her eyes.

Jorin had his forepaws on the edge of the cot and was leaning forward over it, every hair a bristle. Moonlight reflected in his wide, blind eyes. He growled again like distant thunder.

A hiss answered him, and the weight on her chest stirred. Whatever it was, it was so close that she had to stare cross-eyed at it to focus. A coil of molten gold had settled into the mossy blanket. Above it, weaving to and fro, rose a triangular head with glittering eyes. The gilded swamp adder hissed again, showing wicked white fangs and a flickering black tongue.

"For this you woke me up?" said Jame, hearing the hemlock slur in her voice. "Settle down, both of you. Jorin, here." The ounce slunk onto the bed and settled by her feet, still glaring. Bit by bit, his eyes closed.

Serpent and girl regarded each other.

Candlelight gleamed off the zigzag pattern running down the adder's back, ochre at the top, shading to rich gold with a ridge of gilt at the bottom. Scales rustled softly as it breathed. Its throat and belly were the color of pale honey, its eyes a fiery orange.

"Oh, you beauty," Jame murmured and stroked its gleaming throat with a fingertip. It flowed over her hand and up her arm in a ripple of muscles to settle in a band of gold around her throat. Its tongue tickled her ear.

"Your mistress is going to be furious with you," she told it, "but never mind. Hushhhh."

And again the room was quiet.

# III

WHEN JAME WOKE again, someone tall stood over her. She blinked at the candle. It must still be an hour shy of midnight. What a long, confusing day.

"I thought," said the Commandant, "that I would check on you during last rounds. The healer makes a good report of you, except he says that you won't eat. Now why is that, I wonder?"

The answer was there, waiting, as if she had known it all along. "Ran, I've blood-bound a rathorn colt. He's very upset. I think he's trying to starve himself to death and take me with him."

"I...see. You Knorth do get yourselves into interesting scrapes. How will you handle this one?"

Jame frowned. "I'm not sure. Go up into the hills and find him, I suppose, when Kindrie lets me out of this bed. Between us, Bel and I should be able to do something."

"Ah." The Commandant drew up a chair and settled back in it, hawk-features receding into shadows over the glimmer of his white scarf of office. He folded his hands under his chin, stretched out his long legs, and crossed them at the ankles. "You refer to the Whinno-hir Bel-tairi. The White Lady. Recent sightings of her have been reported to me, but I dismissed them. To the best of my knowledge, she has been dead these forty years and more."

"My great-grandmother Kinzi sent her to find me."

"Ah. That explains everything, and nothing. I had believed that the last Knorth Matriarch was also dead. Have I perhaps been misinformed on that point as well?"

Jame didn't feel up to explaining, assuming that she could. Instead, she asked a question that had bothered her for a long time:

"Ran, why is Bel-tairi called 'The Shame of Tentir'? What could she have done, to deserve that?"

"It wasn't what she did but what was done to her."

"Do you mean my uncle Greshan branding her?"

A sigh answered her from the shadows. "That was only the start of it, or not quite the start."

Jame remembered her glimpse of the brutal past in that clearing on the hunt. "Greshan was courting Rawneth, but Kinzi forbade it.

He took out his revenge on her Whinno-hir mare. Was that before or after my father stormed out of Tentir in the middle of the night?"

"After, by about a year. Now, where did you hear that? Have you spoken to your brother or to Harn Grip-hard?"

"Not to Tori. I don't think he knows anything about it. And when I asked Harn about the White Lady, he just roared that I should leave Tentir before it was too late. Then he stormed off."

"Did he now?" The dry voice sounded amused. "My dear brother-in-arms. Always so excitable. But then we are speaking here of a very painful topic, both for your house and for Tentir. I will tell you this much: yes, your uncle the Knorth lordan put a branding iron to a Whinno-hir's face, and then he bragged about it to the whole college. That was bad. Worse followed. The Highlord, your grandfather, ordered that the entire affair be hushed up, as if that were possible. But his darling son mustn't be seen for the worthless bastard he was. Oh no. Even if it meant hunting down and killing an injured Whinno-hir. He hadn't finished the job, you see. He simply let her go, maimed as she was and weeping blood."

Silence fell for a moment. The Commandant seemed to taste again that bitter memory, holding it on his tongue like a drop of poison that must be swallowed. His voice, when he resumed, had flattened, all emotion suppressed.

"The entire Randon Council went on that grim hunt—nine in all, one from each major house and all former commandants of Tentir except for the Knorth, Hallik Hard-hand, whose turn it was to wear the white scarf. Greshan went too, all gay in his gilded leathers, but he came back slung across his saddle. A hunting accident, Hallik said. He also said that the mare must be dead. They had pursued her up a steep mountain trail and she must have fallen off into river below. The way ended in a sheer rock face, you see, with no sign of her."

He paused again, remembering. "I scaled that path as a cadet. Many of us did, afterward. It's a hard, rocky climb, even at a walk, and she was injured, running for her life. On one side, stone. On the other, far, far down, the black, roaring throat of the river. At the top...a curious thing. I thought at first that I saw the outline of a door in the rock wall, and the suggestion of carving around it. But the crack was barely fingernail deep and behind it, only more stone."

For the Whinno-hir, Jame thought, that door would have stood open into the Earth Wife's lodge, which could be found wherever it was needed. So that was how the White Lady had come to shelter, and yet left those behind sure of her death.

Her mind began to drift again. That damn hemlock. The next time Kindrie wanted her to sleep, he would have to do it another way, say, by hitting her over the head with a rock.

"I see that I am tiring you." The Commandant rose, his tall form seeming to stretch up to the ceiling. "Anyway, there is little more to tell. Hallik killed himself with the White Knife, your grandfather Gerraint died of grief, and your father Ganth Grayling, unprepared and unworthy, became highlord, to the near destruction of us all. If you want to know more, ask Harn when he returns. After all, Hallik was his father."

"Wait," she said, as the Commandant turned to leave. Hallik Hard-hand was Harn's father? And he had killed himself over a mere hunting accident? There had to be more to the story than that, but the questions she wanted to ask roiled in her drug-numbed mind like a handful of worms, impossible to sort head from tail. "Please," she heard herself say, "return this to the Randir. She must be worried about it."

Jame didn't realize how still the Commandant had become until he moved again, bending over her and carefully pinning the swamp adder behind its wicked little head. It gave a sleepy hiss as he lifted it from her neck and by reflex coiled itself around the warmth of his arm.

"You favor strange bedfellows," he said, in an odd voice. "How did this come to be here?"

She could only shake her head, which set everything spinning. "Someone brought it. Dunno who."

"I...see. Be careful what you say about this, and to whom. The lords can collect no blood-price for anything that happens here, but the college has its own forms of justice. Good night."

"G'night, Senethari."

He paused in the doorway, gave her an enigmatic look, and went out, carefully holding his lethal charge.

# IV

SEVERAL MORE TIMES Jame half-woke during the night, thinking she had heard some disturbance. More likely, though, it was the
echo of a dream.

Shouts, battle-cries, and then sargents bellowing, "Run, run, run!"
to the thunder of feet on the boards of the arcade...obviously her
drug-befuddled brain had drifted back to that first day at Tentir and
the punishment run.

Oddly, each time she surfaced a different member of her ten-
command was in the room, on guard. This puzzled her, but not
enough to ask why they were there. When she at last fully woke in
the early morning, Brier Iron-thorn sat on the window-ledge.

Jame regarded that hard, strong profile, that distant, proud expression. How little she truly knew about this woman. She remembered a bloody Brier on the Ardeth stair, blocking her way to the
room above where Tori fought for his soul if not for his life:

"He saved me from the Caineron. Bound me. I am his, although I trust no Highborn fool enough to trust me. I don't trust
you. You will only hurt him."

Such a bitter insight, and so tangled even in the Southron's
own mind.

"You haven't yet taught me how they fight in the streets of
Kothifir," she said.

Brier glanced at her. "There hasn't been time, lady. Do you still
want to learn?" She turned back to contemplate the empty square,
across which dawn was edging. She looked tired, and her clothes
were dull with dust. "The randon would hardly thank me for cor-
rupting your classic style."

"It's only classic because it's all I know—that, and some
knife tricks."

When she pushed back the blanket of woven moss, it slid to the
floor and crumbled to dust. Spiders scurried off in all directions.
She stood up and swayed, suddenly light-headed. When her sight
cleared, she found that Brier had moved swiftly to support her.

"Thank you. Now, where did Kindrie hide my clothes?"

Jame was nearly dressed when the healer arrived.

"I'm not sure about this," he said, watching her wobble on one foot as she tried to pull on a boot, then sit down abruptly on the bed. "I hear you didn't have a restful night, which is hardly surprising under the circumstances."

"Damn. Who else knows?"

"Everyone," said Brier briefly. "The Commandant sent me word late last night about your uninvited bed-mate, and Vant overheard. He's already tackled the Randir about it."

"Trinity. Have there been fights?"

"A few. Then the sargents stepped in and ran us all ragged. They're still keeping a thumb on the pot, hoping it won't come to a boil before the general exodus later this morning."

A sudden commotion erupted outside the infirmary door.

"No!" Rue was saying loudly. "Stay away from my lady, you...you..."

A scuffle, a yelp, and the door burst open. Rue tumbled into the room and rolled to her feet between Jame and the intruder. Brier instantly joined her. Peering between them, Jame saw a Randir cadet framed in the doorway.

"I did *not* put Addy in your bed," the Randir said.

By now, Jame had recognized her as the Shanir cadet from the Falconer's class, and had noted the rising bruise under one eye. Vant's work, probably.

"Who is Addy? Oh, I see."

Around the other's neck hung a thick, living, golden loop, which she half-steadied and half-caressed with one hand.

Slipping between the two Knorth, Jame offered her hand to the Randir's snake. Behind her, Rue yelped in alarm, but she had already welcomed the serpent as it slid, glittering, over her fingers.

"No," she said, having by now had time to think. "I don't believe you would risk Addy that way. It...that is, she...might have been killed, and you would certainly have been blamed. Besides, Highborn are almost impossible to poison, so as an assassination attempt it wasn't very bright." She didn't add that a shot of venom to the throat, in someone already weakened, might not have been all that easily shrugged off, but the Commandant wanted this incident played down, and so did she. "When did you miss her?"

"Around dinner time." The Randir regarded her with sharp mistrust. "You believe me?"

"I know what it means to be bound to a creature—human, animal, or reptile. Someone has tried to play a nasty trick on both our houses, and to take advantage of our differences. That offends me. If you find out who it is, will you let me know?"

"Agreed, if you will do the same for me."

Below in the square, the rally sounded and the barracks woke with a surly roar.

The Randir turned to leave, but Jame stopped her.

"If you'll wait a minute, I'll go down with you."

"Why?"

On her second attempt, with Rue's help, Jame managed to pull on her boot. She rose and stomped to settle the heel. "Brier tells me that there were clashes overnight. If we're seen together, that's one step toward calming things down, at least over this business. Another time, it may be different."

The Randir considered this, then gave a curt nod. "My name is Shade," she said, as if to seal this temporary truce.

"And mine is Jame."

When they entered the square, all nine houses had assembled. A ripple went through the waiting ranks and a murmur that the sargent on duty instantly quelled. Shade joined the Randir. Jame, walking on to the Knorth, felt eyes follow her and saw marks on a dozen faces of the previous night's unrest. The Commandant stood on his balcony watching. When Jame met his hooded gaze, he gave her a slight nod: Well done.

After breakfast, Jame ran down Vant.

"It wasn't the Randir," she told him bluntly, "or at least not the snake's owner."

"She told you that, I suppose," he said, baring his teeth. Two of them had been knocked out. "Did she also happen to mention that she's the Witch's granddaughter?"

*Whoa.*

"Lord Randir is her father? I didn't know that he had any children."

"Only one, begat by way of experiment before his tastes settled. Anyway, did you think that the Caineron are the only house whose Highborn make sport with their Kendar?"

He spoke with such unusual, throttled rage that Jame blinked. She hadn't realized that he felt so strongly on the subject. It also occurred to her that she knew nothing of Vant's background, except that he was presumably descended from Those-Who-Returned, Knorth Kendar driven back by her father as he had stormed into exile and forced to serve as *yondri* in other houses until her brother had reclaimed both power and as many of his scattered people as he could hold, perhaps overreaching in the process.

But Vant's past was a puzzle for another day.

"Shade may be half darkling changer for all I know or care. On this, I believe her. So lay off."

As Vant departed, sour-faced, to organize the cadets' departure, Jame found Rue at her elbow.

"I assume that we're all under house rather than college discipline once we leave Tentir. True? Good. Saddle me a horse, a nice, quiet one, and wait for me with it outside the north gate. No, I'm not going with you. If my brother asks, tell him that I have unfinished business in the hills."

Brier had come up to hear this last. "Is it wise to go off on your own, lady? The land is treacherous. Besides, someone has just tried to kill you.

"I suspect that he...or she...will be marching out with the others. I'll take my chances with Rathillien." She paused and gave a snort of laughter. "Besides, I'll probably have company soon enough."

# Chapter XVII:  Into the Wilds

## Summer 60-65

## I

JAME STARED.  "YOU have got to be joking."

Rue gave a self-conscious wriggle.  "All the others are going home for the harvest, but Chumley here pulled up lame.  Myself, I think he faked it for the inspection.  He's perfectly sound now.  Anyway, you asked for a quiet horse."

"I should hope so.  If he gets frisky, the earth is going to shake."

They regarded the animal in question, a placid chestnut gelding with blonde mane and tail, built along the lines of an equine mountain range.  He dropped his huge head to scratch a heavily feathered fetlock.  Somewhere under all that hair must be a hoof the size of a buckler.

"Oh well," said Jame.  "As long as you can find me a ladder."

Some time later, horse and rider ambled out of Tentir by a lesser gate—*the fewer spectators the better,* thought Jame, not to mention what people would make of her departure in the wrong direction.

Chumley might have grown bored pulling a cart, but he didn't object to a rider if, indeed, he even noticed her most of the time. He seemed quite happy to shamble along, head down, eyes half-closed under a heavy thatch of mane, finding the easiest way as if by accident.

Jame could have made faster time on foot.

However, then she would have had to carry the bulging saddle-bags that Rue had stuffed with as much food as she could lay her hands on in a hurry.  Left to herself, Jame would have forgotten about provisions altogether.  As Tirandys had once remarked, she never could remember to pack a lunch.  Only by resolutely thinking about something else had she managed to choke down some breakfast.

On top of bags was strapped a bed-roll; and on top of that, Jame's knapsack, containing several things that would have made Rue stare if she had known about them.

They were following roughly the same route as the rathorn hunt, northward, across the toes of the Snowthorns.  Sometimes

the Silver glinted below as it wound down the valley floor. Sometimes voices floated up from the New Road as Jaran and Caineron
cadets rode north to their home keeps of Valantir and Restormir,
outpacing the slower travelers on the upper slopes. Mount Alban
also lay in that direction, as did the ruins of Tagmeth and Kithorn, all
three on the opposite bank. Beyond that were the hills claimed by
the Merikit, then the Barrier that separated Rathillien from Perimal
Darkling. However, Jame had no intention of going that far.

Actually, she didn't know where she was going or particularly
care. The rathorn colt was out here somewhere, probably more
aware of her than she was of him. She sensed that she could draw
him to her by force if necessary, but that might break him and would
surely defeat her purpose in seeking him out. They had to come to
some understanding before he starved himself to death and either
took her with him or left her unable to face a meal without nausea
for the rest of her life. Besides, she felt responsible for him.

*My stupid, stupid blood.*

Meanwhile, it was a beautiful midsummer's day, warm in the
sun, cool in the shade, with the tang of the evergreen ironwood in
the breeze blowing off the heights. Clouds sailed southward down
the valley against a sky as blue as a kitten's eye, their shadows drifting
after them as if leisurely grazing on the upland meadows. Lavender
true-love and pink shooting stars spangled grass that dipped and
swayed in the wind. Among the trees, wood rose and bluebell lit the
dappled shadows. Then the land plunged down into fern-laced
ravines and up into stands of fluttering aspen which had at last
achieved their summer arborage. Here a creek gurgled in its bed.
There a jumble of boulders loomed as if tossed by some petulant
giant at play. Above loomed the gray, misty heights of the
Snowthorns, capped with white. Below, birds stilled at the clop of
the travelers' approach, then burst into song when they had passed.

Jorin trotted ahead, occasionally dashing after butterflies when
they caught Jame's eye. Mostly, however, she dozed, swaying on her
mount's broad back, lulled by his placid, steady gait.

*Take me where you will,* she thought, just this side of sleep, hardly
knowing whom she meant. *Dreamscape, soulscape, sacred space, over the
hills or under them...wherever he waits for me.*

Once or twice she thought she glimpsed a keep sprawling
below, but surely that was a waking dream. Valantir was some

twenty-five miles north of Tentir and Restormir, the Caineron strong-hold, that much farther again. At this pace, given the rough terrain, she would be surprised if they had made ten miles by the time the sun dipped below the peaks.

At dusk they halted beside a stream. Above, it coiled out of sight around pine and tamarack with a muted roar beyond that suggested a waterfall. Below, it slowed to meander down through a rich, sloping meadow fringed at the bottom with trees. This would do nicely.

Jame slid down from Chumley, and fell over. Her feet were numb. Also, it was a long, long way to the ground. Recovering, she unloaded the gelding and set him loose to graze in the meadow. Then she pitched camp under the boughs of a mountain ash with the chuckling stream nearby. As she gathered kindling, Jorin slipped off to hunt his dinner. Night fell.

A huge shape loomed out of the darkness, making her start, but it was only Chumley come looking for company. The gelding sank ponderously to his knees, then eased over onto his side with a groan of pleasure, his back to her small fire. Presently he began to snore. Leaning against him, Jame watched glow-bugs trundle about over the grass with their tiny lights like so many lost search parties while crickets sang derisively up at them.

At length she settled down under her blanket, devoutly hoping that the horse didn't roll over on her in the night. Only at the edge of sleep did she remember that she had forgotten to eat any supper. Jorin returned some time later and curled up beside her with a contented belch of raw muskrat.

In the morning, the rathorn came.

# II

JAME WAS KNEELING on the pebbly margin of the stream, splashing cold water in her face, when a flash of white caught the corner of her eye. She rose, absently wiping her hands on her pants, and watched the rathorn colt canter toward her through the tall grass, the Whinno-hir Bel-tairi a pale shadow at his side.

Chumley was grazing by the river. His head jerked up as he caught their scents and he whickered uneasily. Bel swerved aside to reassure him, but the colt came straight on, gaining speed.

Hackles rose down his back, lifting his mane and the streaming flag of his tail. His head dropped to level the tips of his twin, curved horns. Jame watched his rapid approach, half terrified, half transfixed. He seemed to flow in a ripple of muscle and shifting ivory. If death were poetry, it would have scanned to the beat of those lethal hooves. And he wasn't slowing down.

*I should climb a tree*, thought Jame, just as Jorin did so behind her with a wild scrabble of claws and a shower of bark.

However, something told her to hold her ground and so she did, even as the rathorn hurtled down on her like an avalanche, filling the world with white thunder.

At the last moment he swerved aside in a stinging spray of gravel. Jame felt the wind of his passing and a sharp tug on her jacket where his nasal horn had plucked it open, drawing a bead of blood in the hollow of her throat. He skidded to a stop and wheeled on his hocks.

Here he came again.

This time just short of her the colt again slammed to a halt and reared, ivory hooves slashing the air on either side of her head. She noted almost with detachment that the light feathering concealed sharp dewclaw spurs, growing from the back of each fetlock joint. As his wild, musky smell filled her senses, she knew that he was trying to panic her into moving. Just a flinch either way and he would smash her skull, but he couldn't kill her outright.

Both realized this simultaneously. The rathorn dropped back to all fours and glared at her, nose to nose. Then he snorted, pivoted, and trotted away, tail arched, farting loudly.

"Hello to you too," said Jame, and abruptly sat down in the stream as her legs gave way under her.

The Whinno-hir had paused beside the gelding to snatch a few bites of grass. Against his looming bulk, she seemed no bigger than a foal, slender limbed, insubstantial. When Jame rose and wobbled toward her, she jerked up her head and froze in wide-eyed terror.

Suddenly the colt was between them. This time Jame couldn't help recoiling as his fangs snapped in her face, even though she was reasonably sure he didn't mean to bite it off. Before she could recover, both equines had galloped away.

Jame watched them out of sight, then went to coax Jorin down from his tree.

She spent the rest of the morning sorting out the supplies sent by Rue into what would keep, what wouldn't, and what was for her by definition inedible short of starvation, notably a wad of over-cooked sprouts mashed together in a bag like so many soggy, de-formed little heads. Among the second group, snatched from an-cestors knew what larder, was a whole roast chicken. After some thought, Jame shoved it and the other perishables back into a saddle bag, waded out into the stream, and wedged the lot in among stones so cold with mountain run-off that they numbed her hands.

Then she and Jorin went exploring.

To the west, hidden by trees, there was indeed a very respect-able waterfall, tumbling into a deep pool, from there spilling into the swift stream that ran past her camp. Host trees overhung the water, their pale foliage fluttering upward in the misty draft. In the fall, the leaves would take flight for other hosts farther south. Some already seemed on the fret to go, as if sensing that the season was about to turn and the days to shorten.

This sheltered place would have been a much better campsite than the one she had chosen, Jame thought, and then saw that some-one had had the same idea. Several yards from the waterfall, a shallow cave opened into the escarpment. Tucked under the cliff's overhang was a stone-lined fire-pit, with embers still smoldering in a deep bed of white ash. More rocks formed a semicircle outside. As Jame cautiously stepped between them toward the pit, her al-tered perspective suddenly changed them from random heaps to the crude semblance of human forms. One looked vaguely like a figure half-reclining, small boulders for the extended body, a pile of flat rocks for the torso, a round rock for a head, by nature even given the hint of a face. Imagination turned three more piles into seated men.

As Jame backed away from the cave, something made her look up. On top of the escarpment, on the lip of the falls, stood a man, looking down at her. She only saw him for a moment, long enough to note the hood that concealed most of his face and his hunting leathers, worn to a mottled green almost invisible against the undergrowth. She had barely drawn breath to hail him when he melted back into a clump of shrubs.

Jame scrambled up a spill of rocks to the top of the falls. By the time she got there, however, the stranger was gone leaving not a footprint, not a broken leaf, only a flight of azure-winged jewel-jaws spiraling up through the trees. If she hadn't stumbled across his campsite below, she would have thought that she had imagined him. Even so...

Turning, Jame looked back the way that she had come. From this height, she had a view over the host trees and pine spinney, down to the meadow where the chestnut gelding was rolling on his back, feathered hooves kicking the sky. For him, this must be paradise. Neither the rathorn nor the Whinno-hir was in sight, although a twinge in the bond that they now shared told her that the colt at least had not gone far. Beyond the trees at the meadow's foot there seemed to be a gap, and beyond that a high bluff crowned with more trees. She could hear the distant, hollow roar of water running between rocky walls. Could that be the Silver? Sunlight glinted on it farther upstream where it converged with another, smaller torrent. Between their fork rose the lower reaches of the northern Snowthorns, dismissed in the local parlance as "hills." Higher, more jagged mountains loomed beyond, including one at some distance whose heights were wreathed with smoke.

*Wonderful*, thought Jame. *Earthquakes, weirdingstroms, floods, and now maybe a volcano.*

She was about to descend when something across the river on top of the opposite cliff caught her attention. Although nearly masked with leaves, it looked like the remains of a curtain wall, enclosing a shattered tower. She had never seen it from this angle before, but it looked alarmingly like the ruins of Kithorn—which made no sense whatsoever. The nearest keep on the east bank to the north of Tentir was Mount Alban, home to the Scrollsmen's' College, but that would place her within spitting distance of the west bank Jaran fortress, Valantir, of which there was no sign.

Then she remembered that the Riverland fortifications had originally come in pairs, built by the ancient kingdoms of Bashti and Hathir to glare at each other across the Silver. Since then, a number had disappeared altogether, their stones dismantled to rebuild the nearest Kencyr keep. There must once have been at least a tower opposite Tentir. Perhaps this was its ruin, although that would place her much closer to the college than she had thought. Still, better that than opposite Kithorn, on Merikit land, only days from the summer solstice.

"Either way," she said to Jorin as they started back toward their camp, "there's not much we can do about it short of running like hell, and I can't go anywhere until I've settled matters with that blasted rathorn."

Jorin ignored her in favor of a glittering, golden beetle that whirred past his nose. With a snap he ate it, and then was noisily sick. It had tasted awful. That night neither he nor Jame had any desire for food.

Perhaps it was the rumble of her empty stomach that roused Jame sometime later. *It can't be very late, though*, she thought, only half awake, looking up at a swollen gibbous moon that would soon be full. Just in time for the solstice. Odd. On Rathillien, was there some correlation between a full moon and the longest day? *Will have to ask Kirien or Index*, she thought drowsily.

Before she could sink back into sleep, however, some slight change in the stream's chuckle made her blink.

A man was bathing in it. Jame thought at first that it was Kindrie, but only because of the long white hair—too long, surely, unbound, waist-length, clinging to the stranger's shoulders and back. Moonlight turned his whole body into gleaming alabaster except where blue shadows traced wiry muscles and the threads of old scars. He scooped up water and dashed it in his face. It ran down, gleaming, over the hard lines of his chest, stomach, and loins.

*Since when do I dream of naked men?* Jame thought. *All right. Since Timmon. And Tori. But who is this? Trinity, I'm not dreaming...am I?*

The stranger waded ashore. He made hardly a sound on the pebbly bank, nor as he dried himself with wisps of grass, nor as he slipped back into his well-worn hunting leathers.

Glow-bugs traced his movements. He played with them, sculpting their flight with his white hands, expanding his gestures into wide, glowing sweeps. They danced with him, and he with them, wind-blowing kantirs in a moon-silvered field. At times, in flight, his feet barely touched the bending grass. So her mother the Dream-weaver had danced, free of earth, free of pain or regret, free as the wind blows. Jame longed to join him, to shed all that weighed her down—her past, her responsibilities, herself—but dull flesh bound her, helpless. Instead, she watched until the moon set and sleep took her into dreams of aching grace.

# III

IN THE MORNING, a strange mare grazed beside Chumley in the field. Jame didn't see her at first, so perfectly did she blend with the play of sun and shadow on the grass. Even then, Jame didn't at first believe her eyes. Of the many strange things she had encountered in her life, a green horse ranked near the top. The mare greeted her with a friendly whicker, long, moss green tail swishing at flies. On closer inspection, Jame saw that although her eyes were the color of new leaves, her coat was actually pearl gray, subtly stained in all the shades of leaf and lichen, wood and stone. In fact, thought Jame, tracing the swoop of a line down her shoulder—tawny gold tinged with a rosy haze the color of ripening wheat—she was beautiful, a true work of art, and also excellently camouflaged.

Around her neck was a leather band. Curious, Jame slid a finger under it. Immediately, blood began to trickle down the mare's neck from a small, neat hole in her throat. It stopped as soon as Jame hastily released the band, which she now saw had a small plug on its inner surface. The mare had raised her head with a look of mild inquiry, but dropped it again to graze when she saw that nothing more was required of her.

How very odd. A campsite with stone figures for company, a naked man bathing, and now this. It seemed that she had encroached on someone's territory, but whose?

She was gnawing a wedge of rock-hard bread, hoping she wasn't about to break another tooth, when the rathorn returned, again accompanied by Bel. He swerved to inspect the newcomer, who squealed and kicked him in the face when he got too close. Jame winced, feeling his head ring inside its ivory mask. He retreated, then began to prance back and forth, slashing at weeds, deliberately ignoring both Jame and the strange mare.

Now that he wasn't trying to kill her, she had a chance to observe him more closely. For all his fluid stride and proudly cocked head, his white coat was dull and staring, his mane and tail tangled into elf-locks. As for his ribs, she could count them as easily as she could her own.

Despite that, he was no fool. She sensed that he understood as well as she did that they were now bound together, and had as little idea how to handle the situation. Of course, he was furious and resentful. If the situation had been reversed, she would have been tearing out her hair—or better yet, his. To be in the power of one's worst enemy...how did one live with that? How had she, during all those lost years in Perimal Darkling? But then at some fundamental level she had still been free, still been herself, thanks to Tirandys' subtle distortion of his master's orders. That would have ended in Gerridon's beribboned bed, where she would have taken her mother's place in more ways than one. Instead, someone (Bender?) had handed her a knife and she had reclaimed her life with its sharp edge.

This bond would be much harder to sever than the Master's wrist. If the old songs were right, it bound her and the rathorn together to death and perhaps beyond. Even more surely, she knew that if she pushed the colt too hard against his will, he would lash back as best he could, even to his own destruction. This had to be subtle. A courtship. Even a seduction.

Still, things weren't as bad as they had been. Their experiences together in the soulscape, while terrifying, had taken some of the edge off his anger at her. After all, they had arguably saved each other from the haunt stallion Iron-jaw and she had gone back for him, even if the Earth Wife's protection had turned out to make that unnecessary.

More important, he now had the company of the Whinno-hir Bel-tairi. As different as they were in many respects—not least in that she was prey and he a predator—both were herd animals. Much of his previous despair and incipient madness had been rooted in his isolation after his mother's death at Jame's hand. Captain Hawthorn had called the colt a rogue, a death's-head, adding that no rage would let him join it. Jame wondered if he had tried and been repulsed. That long, half-healed scar down his side above the protective armor suggested the work of another rathorn stallion's nasal tusk. For that matter, maybe he had been lurking around the Knorth horses not in search of meat but of companionship. After all, he hadn't attacked any of them. Poor boy.

Boy. When they had first met, she had judged him to be either a weanling or a yearling, but what did she know? Her only real experience with horses before that had been with her father's warhorse Iron Jaw and the monster that he had become.

How old was the rathorn colt now? Less than two years, at a guess, and, for all his inches, not yet full grown. She wondered at what age it would be safe to ride him, assuming they got that far without killing each other. Working in the stable, she had overheard the horse-master speak of a two-year-old filly whose knees had finally closed, whatever that meant beyond that she was now old enough to work. It made sense after all that a foal couldn't bear the weight of a rider before it was strong enough.

Then again, this was a rathorn, not a horse. As far as Jame knew, no one had ever ridden one before, at any age, or at least not lived to brag of it. "To ride a rathorn" was madness—wasn't it? Still, she couldn't help but wonder what it would be like in real life, not just in a dream of the soulscape.

She also wondered what the colt's name was. No doubt he had one, and it would be impertinent of her to try to saddle him with another.

"Snowfire?" she said experimentally, and he turned to glare at her down his long, gleaming nose. "Precious? All right, all right. You'll tell me when you're ready."

By now, it was afternoon.

Jame took a handful of oats from her knapsack and went to lie on her back in the long grass. Stems tickled her ears and insects crawled over her out-flung arms. The sun beat on her face, turning her shut eyelids into red-veined curtains. Her skin began to glow. She remembered with unease that there were now only four days until the longest of the year, the summer solstice, but pushed the thought away.

She was almost asleep when she heard the cautious approach of hooves, then teeth tearing nearby grass. Through narrowed lids, she saw the Whinno-hir.

"I'm sorry I frightened you," she murmured, barely moving her lips. The sound of grazing stopped, but while the hooves shifted uneasily, they didn't move away. "What my uncle did to you was unforgivable, and I may turn out to be more like him than like my great-grandmother Kinzi. Truly, though, I'm trying not to. Will you help me, for her sake? Can we at least start over?"

She let her fingers uncurl. After a long moment, velvet lips brushed her palm to scoop up the grain.

# IV

THAT NIGHT, JAME woke to Jorin's low growl and lay still, holding him, her senses at full stretch. The crickets and night birds had fallen silent. She thought she had heard…no, smelled…something too, before she was fully awake, something that had darkened her last dreams with the shades of smoldering nightmare. Burnt fur. That was it.

She scanned the meadow and trees or what she could see of them, which was virtually nothing. The moon had long since set, and a haze shrouded the stars. No wind stirred the grass. Even the stream seemed oddly muted. She rose to add more wood to her campfire, moving slowly, deliberately.

*Show no fear.*

Why had that thought suddenly leaped into her mind?

*Because he can smell fear, and guilt.*

Out in the darkness, Chumley squealed and bolted, ponderous hooves thudding away.

*Shouldn't have feigned lameness. Bet you're sorry now.*

A swift rush through the grass and Bel-tairi appeared on the edge of the firelight. There she stood, poised for further flight with one fore-hoof raised, looking back over her shoulder into the darkness. Then, still looking back, she edged sideways in so close to the fire that she trod on its outer branches and jumped as they snapped.

A moment later, the rathorn colt joined her, taking the outer position of guard. Both ignored Jame, but through the colt's senses as well as through Jorin's she now heard the slow tread of great paws and smelled, much stronger than before, that peculiar, acrid stench of burnt hair. There, beyond the firelight, the Dark Judge paced. The equines turned with him, Jame now circling between them and the intruder with Jorin so close on her inner heel that he threatened to trip her.

*…bloody, stupid Merikit…*

The great cat's mutter rumbled through flesh and shuddered in the bone. Not just that: the earth itself shook. To the north, in the dark, rose a column of smoke, its dimensions defined by inner flickering tongues of lightning, its sullen mutter rolling down the valley.

It seemed closer than it had by day unless (alarming thought) this was another mountain. What if the entire range erupted?

*...think they can fool us, do they? Not again. Never again.*

Us? thought Jame. *Who is "us"?*

By now she could make out the prowling hulk of the blind Arrin-ken, always so much larger than one expected. It seemed to flow around the margin of the camp, a net of fiery cracks cast over darkness, opening into it. The fire-bugs had left the field and swarmed about a dark, upright shape that walked silently at the great cat's side. When the insects touched the second figure, they flared briefly and fell so that its passage was marked by a thousand tiny deaths.

*...burn, burn, burn them all, as we were burned.*

The mutter deepened to a growl, under-laid with hunger and a terrible, gloating eagerness.

*Eat away weakness. Consume sin. Devour guilt. You!*

His massive head swung toward Jame as the earth shuddered again. His companion also turned. Dying fire-bugs flared in the latter's eye-sockets, giving a brief glimpse of a charred, ravaged face that had once been human.

*Come to justice, little nemesis. Be purified in our flame for your holy purpose.*

"No."

He was frightening Bel, and that angered her.

"I will judge myself, as I always have, and will accept no more mercy than I am prepared to give. Now go away, you pompous bully; you've upset m'lady."

*Huh!*

His contemptuous snort blew her campfire apart. To the north, a second dark, roiling cloud arose, defined by the hot cinders swirling in it and the forked lightning at its heart. A distant boom rolled down the valley like thunder, and the earth shook again.

Mare and colt both screamed. The next moment, the rathorn had charged the intruders, who dissolved into a shower of sparks before him. Jame caught the mare and made her stand, trembling, as she plucked burning embers out of her mane and tail.

"Death's-head!" she shouted after the colt. "Come back, you fool!"

Eventually he did, having made sure the others had really gone.

"Death's-head," Jame repeated, watching him solicitously lick a scorched patch on the mare's shoulder. "Are you sure you want that for a name?" He bared his fangs at her over Bel's back and hissed, reminding her of the Randir's adder. "All right, all right. After all, that's what you are. Death's-head and Nemesis it is. For the element of surprise, though, I would have preferred Snowball and Buttercup."

# V

RECOVERING CHUMLEY TOOK most of the next day, during which Jame came to the reluctant conclusion that she was nowhere near the randon college.

For one thing, the more she saw of those ruins on the opposite bank, the more like Kithorn they looked.

For another, she was fairly sure she would have noticed a smoking mountain in the immediate vicinity. Poor as she was at guessing distances on such a scale, she was fairly sure it couldn't be more than five miles away, although the previous day it had seemed more distant.

That morning the grass had been lightly dusted with ash, and the ground now trembled almost continually. What was more, behind a screen of smoke the mountain top seemed to be growing some sort of spine or protrusion like nothing she had ever seen before—a plug of half-cooled lava, perhaps, forced upward by titanic pressure from beneath. If the mountain should pop its cork, well, the thought did not encourage hope for a quiet life in the near future.

One disaster at a time, though. First, find Chumley.

In the beginning, the trail was clear: A near-ton of panicking horse-flesh tends to leave its mark. However, rough terrain intervened, and then Jorin ran into a patch of deadman's-breath that left him rolling on the ground, trying to escape his own nose.

Jame was about to give up when she heard Bel calling. She followed the sound to a deep ravine. The Whinno-hir stood at the brink and there at the bottom was the gelding, up to his withers in brambles, looking unhurt but deeply embarrassed. He whickered plaintively up at her.

"All right," she said. "Hold your horses…er…that is, hold still."

She had brought her grapnel rope, which was hardly strong enough to haul up such a weight by brute force, even if she had had the strength to try. This would only work if Chumley stopped waiting to be rescued and started helping himself. Jame looped the rope twice around a smooth-barked tree and scrambled down. Luckily, the gelding still wore his halter. She secured the rope to it and encouraged him to climb, but kept sliding back herself.

Frustrated, she grabbed a handful of his flaxen mane, pulled herself up onto his broad back, and dug her heels into his sides. When he only shifted uneasily, she unsheathed her claws. Their use resulted in a surge upward. When he faltered, Jame flicked loose the slackened rope from around the tree and again pulled it taut, preventing him from sliding back down unless he wanted his neck to stretch like taffy. Thus by fits and starts they finally lurched up the slope and out of the ravine.

At the top, Jame slid down onto shaking legs and leaned against the gelding's sweat-stained side. Chumley was also trembling, but didn't draw away from her, which improved her opinion of his good sense, or at least of his good nature.

When they finally got back to the meadow, she cleaned the scratches on his neck and gave him a thorough grooming. Brushes, combs, and a hoof-pick had also been among her knapsack stash, on the advice of a bemused horse-master who couldn't imagine what a confirmed equinophobe like Jame wanted with them. However, she had had plenty of experience putting up her mounts after lessons, and even more when sharing her ten's various punishment duties.

The gelding leaned into the curry brush with a groan of pleasure. Remnants of his rough, winter coat came off in felt-like mats on the bristles and dried mud crumbled to dust. Then there were his hooves to pick, once one found them under all that heavy feathering, and his mane and tail to comb, tangled as they were with burrs and bracken.

As she worked, Jame wondered if in future she should hobble him. No, she decided. If he had to run again, better that he not trip and break his neck. Anyway, after the first shock of sharing pasture with a carnivorous rathorn, he had settled down remarkably fast. Rathorns used scent to communicate. Jame suspected that the colt could change the way he smelled to soothe potential prey just as he could to terrorize enemies. Bel enjoyed company as she grazed; therefore, Chumley had been made to feel welcome and seemed disinclined to stray, even after the previous night's visitors.

The Dark Judge and the Burnt Man, the worst (or least the most unstable and dangerous) of both worlds, Kencyrath and Rathillien. Now, there was trouble beyond the scope of her imagination, and only three days to go until the solstice.

The gelding took a long time, leaving Jame hot, sweaty, and plastered with loose horse hairs. Set free, he stretched like an overgrown cat, yawned hugely, and ambled off for a nice roll in the mud.

"Huh!" said Jame, dropping the brushes in disgust as she watched him undo all her hard work. Then she went to wash in the stream. She was considering a swim when the Whinno-hir's reflection appeared in the water behind her own and a soft nose nudged her shoulder.

Oh well, she thought. This too had been part of her plan.

As Kinzi's mount, Bel must have been groomed lovingly and often. Her body remembered it as the brushes slid over her coat even as she trembled, no doubt also remembering the last time she had been touched by human hands.

One usually began with the head. However, when the mare flinched away, Jame smoothed her mane to the right and started on the left side. At the withers, she paused to probe tense shoulder muscles with her finger tips, then knead them with her knuckles until Bel relaxed, sighing, hip-shot. With brush and touch, Jame moved down the mare's body. Dull, dead hair lifted from creamy new growth; white dapples emerged on back and flanks. The white tail seemed to lengthen as she combed it until half of it trailed on the ground. The mane also proved surprisingly long, reaching below the mare's knees. However, not until Jame reached Bel's hooves did she realize what was happening.

As she held one in her hand, about to pick it clean, she noted how long it was in the toe. In fact, it grew as she watched, becoming wavy and turning up at the end like a dandy's slipper. Forty-odd years in the Earth Wife's lodge were catching up with the mare all at once. No wonder her hair was suddenly so long. If she had been a normal horse, not a potentially immortal Whinno-hir, she probably would have dropped dead of extreme old age on the spot, just when she had had been brought at last to accept life.

Bel shook free her foot and placed it gingerly on the ground. All four hooves now looked like curved skids and were obviously painful.

The rathorn's teeth closed on Jame's collar. He lifted her off her feet, gave her a hard shake, and let her drop, with a menacing snort down the back of her neck.

"Look," she said, on bruised knees, glowering up over her shoulder at him. "This isn't my fault. And no, I didn't think to bring farrier's tools, supposing I'd know what to do with them if I had them. D'you want me to float her back teeth too?"

It occurred to her even as she spoke that that too would probably be required, as it was with horses. Barbs grew on the outer edge of their teeth, designed to keep hay from falling out of their mouths as they chewed. However, unless these hooks were periodically filed down, they could rasp the inner cheek raw. If that was true, as with her hooves and hair, the Whinno-hir would now also have trouble eating. Of the four of them, that only left Jorin with a decent appetite, as long as he stayed away from pretty bugs.

A spill of white mane between the ears fell like a curtain over the mare's features. Jame parted it, slowly, carefully, unveiling a mystery.

A woman gazed steadily back at her out of one large, liquid eye set in half a flawless face. A savage scar seamed the other eye shut before curving off down her cheek to the rim of her nose. Jame traced it with a finger, overwhelmed with pity and rage. Nothing was bad enough for the man who had done this, never mind that he was long dead. She was Nemesis, dammit, or soon would be. Who said that vengeance stopped with the pyre?

A light touch brought her back to herself. As she examined Bel's scars, so Bel had been studying hers. The other's cool, slim hands slid up to cradle her face, lifting black hair as Jame's did white.

*We are sisters of the brand*, her voice murmured in Jame's mind. *We are stronger than what has been done to us. So my lady told me. So, thanks to you, I now understand. Be at rest in your strength, Kinzi-kin, as I now am in mine.*

She kissed Jame lightly on the lips, then let the black hair swing back over her face. By the time Jame had scooped it clear, the mare had moving gingerly away on her overgrown hooves, shaking each in turn before she stepped on it like a cat who has accidentally trod in something unpleasant. In her place, the rathorn stood glowering.

"What's the matter?" Jame twisted up her hair and clapped her cap back over it. "Haven't you ever seen two girls sharing secrets?" She retrieved a brush. "Your turn."

But the colt only gave a snort and trotted off.

# VI

THAT NIGHT JAME sat by the fire combing her damp hair with her claws, trying to decide if she really needed any dinner. Jorin had already gone off to hunt his own.

Rescuing Chumley, not to mention grooming him and the mare, had been surprisingly hard work, and a swim in the chilly stream afterward had only restored her in part.

*Face it*, she thought glumly, teasing out a snarl. *You're starting to draw on reserves that you don't have. After all, there are reasons why people eat regular meals.*

The rathorn hadn't eaten yet either...in how many days? And he was a growing boy, if usually a bloodthirsty one. His anger at her had faded somewhat, unless he remembered to keep it fueled. Now, more than anything else, he was being stubborn.

*I won't eat and you can't make me.*

Idiot.

And so, of course, was she as well, for getting them all into this fix.

"I ought to have a sign nailed to my back," she muttered, getting her nails caught in her hair and impatiently yanking a dozen strands out by the roots. "'Unsafe for man or beast.'"

"How about women and children?"

The gruff voice made Jame start.

On the other side of the fire, just beyond its light, sat a large, lumpy figure that might have been a hillock rising out of the grass. Jame could barely make out a shaggy head and hands with fingers like thick, knobby twigs. Click, click, click...it was knitting, and what it knitted was alive.

"Quip?" said the work, flexing on the long, thin needles that were its bones. Bright eyes in a fox-like face caught the firelight. "Quip!"

"Almost done, my sweetling. Patience."

"Some day," said Jame, "will you teach me how to knit? I'm hopeless with needle and thread, but that looks...well, restful. Most of the time."

The foxkin was flapping his one finished wing frantically, trying to escape. The Earth Wife wrestled him down. "Wait till I cast off, dumpling. D'you want to unravel in midair?" She examined the limb more closely and clucked in disapproval. "I've made a right mess of this. Too much on my mind. Hold still, pumpkin. This won't hurt…much."

"QUEEE!"

Jame winced as powerful fingers slid the work in question off the bone and ripped it out back to the shoulder.

The Earth Wife glared at her, eyes reflecting flames. Fire-bugs nestled in her wild hair, illuminating patches of its tangle and stray quadrants of her lumpy face. "Should I let it go a cripple? Here. You try." She tossed the living bundle to Jame, who nearly dropped it into the fire. "First, take off those stupid gloves. Then put the stitches back on the needle."

Jame hastily stripped off her gloves as the creature crawled about in her lap, making small, busy sounds to itself as if taking notes. Its body was quite solid, furry, and about twice the size of a bat's, but the wing stubs ended in a frill of loops. She picked up the latter one by one, sliding them onto a slender, white needle. The foxkin hooked his hind claws over the bone and hung upside down from it, regarding her inquisitively.

"Quip?"

"Now what?" Jame asked, holding the needle and its burden away from her face.

"Take the other needle in your left hand and slip its point through the first stitch from front to back. Now loop the yarn over the left needle, draw one stitch through the other, and lift the new stitch off to the left. Careful. Don't accidentally knit in his claws or he can't use 'um."

"Squeee!"

"And not so tight. Let it ride loose on the bone. I hear you had company last night, and the night before that—yes, through the big ears of that *imu* in your pocket. So the Burnt Man won't be fooled any longer, will he?"

"So the Dark Judge said." Jame focused on capturing the next stitch. How could someone so nimble-fingered at picking locks be so clumsy with any sort of needlework? "Is that bad?"

Mother Ragga snorted. The sound turned into a truly seismic belch that shook the ground and dislodged burning branches in the campfire in a shower of sparks. To the north, the volcano rumbled as if in sullen reply. Fire glowered at the base of the spine at its top, sending veins of incandescent scarlet upward. The clouds above reflected back a ruddy, smoldering glow. In the darkened meadow, Chumley neighed uneasily. Much more of this, and there would be another stampede.

"'Is that bad?'" Mother Ragga repeated in what might have been a mincing imitation of Jame's voice. "By stock and stone, girl, I can't make out if you're innocent, ignorant, or just plain stupid. I told you in the Moon Garden: there are rules. If the Burnt Man wasn't fooled before, at least he pretended to be, and so the seasons rolled on. Where are we now, if death won't yield to life? Somehow, that great, bloody burnt cat of yours is mucking things up. Got it in for you, has he? Why?"

Jame gave an uncomfortable shrug and dropped a stitch. "Damn. I'm apparently half way to becoming That-Which-Destroys, whether I like it or not. If I have a correspondence to any of the Four, it would probably be to fire. The burnt cat shares that link, but he has his own ideas about what should be destroyed."

"Huh. Namely everything. That's where you confuse me, girl. Granted, you can be lethal. What you did to the colt, now, that was nasty, but here you are, trying help him, and the mare too. How does that fit with this three faced god-thingie of yours?"

"I've been asked that before." Jame probed for the lost stitch and accidentally poked the foxkin, who squealed in protest and nipped all the way around her fingertip with his sharp teeth, luckily without breaking the skin. "Sorry. It's a hard question. If the priests know…well, I'm not going to ask those bastards anything. There's honor, of course, but also responsibility and kindness. Good teachers taught me that. They also taught me to try to balance myself, not that I always succeed. Some things need to be broken. Others don't. I try to make distinctions and act accordingly. Then again, I'm not the Third Face of God yet and may never be, if the other two don't show up. But if I should become Regonereth, the Ivory Knife incarnate, destroying everything I touch, everything I love—well, I'll do what I was born to do, break what needs to be broken, and then break myself."

She hadn't quite thought it through before, but there it was, with a nice, solid thud. Such power without responsibility would pervert everything she had ever tried to accomplish and dishonor her

Senethari, at least one of whom had died for her sake. The least she could do was back her word with her life.

The Earth Wife eyed her askance. "Huh. Give that back. I should have started you on something easy. Like a tube-worm."

Jame returned the incomplete foxkin, surprised at her own reluctance. Knitting might not always be restful, but she suspected that it was addictive, assuming the work in progress could be persuaded not to eat one's fingers.

She looked again at the glowering mountain. How close it now seemed, blotting out half the night sky, its fire-veined tip thrust, pulsing, up into the dark.

"Is it my imagination, or is that thing trying to creep up on us?"

"Schist, girl. You're in sacred space now. Sometimes it surprises even me."

"Oh." Jame considered this. On the whole, it was not reassuring. She glanced up again at the throbbing tip. "Impressive."

The shadowy figure gave a rumbling chuckle. "Aye, that he is. A hot lover to warm an old woman's bed. Too hot for those damn fool Merikit. Chingetai has gotten into the habit of underestimating us. Thinks he can trot in wearing the Burnt Man's soot and do what he likes."

"He wasn't there for most of the Summer's Eve rite," said Jame soberly. "He didn't see it from inside sacred space, the way I did, when the Four unmasked and turned a mummery into the real thing.

"That is Kithorn over there, isn't it? How in Perimal's name did I get here?"

"You asked, I answered: 'Take me where you will, wherever he waits.' The land folds at my biding, doesn't it?"

"Yes, but I thought that if I brought Kencyr steel, even horse tack, over the Merikit border, some sort of alarm went off."

"So it should have, but now, thanks to that silly bugger Chingetai, all his borders are down, including those to the north, and there are tribes up there near the Barrier all too friendly with the shadows."

"I didn't know that," said Jame, startled.

"Har-*rumph*! Who d'you think guards the northern end of the Riverland, or should if he was paying attention? The Silver is a natural concourse to the heart of Rathillien. Last year, didn't you people stop a thrust up from the south? First bit of useful work you've done since you got here. Chingetai should have made his northern border secure at Summer's Eve, but instead he makes a grab for the entire Riverland and gets his fingers burned for his pains. Your doing, that, I hear tell."

"It wasn't deliberate. How was I to know that pocketing a Burnt Man's bone would spoil his plan? Er…does he know that I'm here?"

"The man's a fool, but not an idiot. On his door-step, aren't you? Of course he knows. Thanks to him, you're my Favorite, and so I brought you here to play your part. But Chingetai doesn't want you showing what a mess he's made of things, so he means to use a substitute."

"But now the Burnt Man says he won't be fooled."

"Aye. Troubling, that, although he might just as well have meant getting a stick of a girl presented to him as his son instead of the strapping boy he expects." She burped again, hawked raucously like a mountain clearing its throat, and spat a gob of flame into the dying fire. "G'ah. Heartburn. Earth and fire don't mix well. I don't see how this is going to play out, and that's a fact. On top of it all, if there's a bloody big bang, we need the Tishooo to blow the ash northward over the Barrier, and he's home sulking. Thinks he should have a bigger part in the midsummer festival. Huh! Every year we get this nonsense. Mind you, I can protect the Merikit, little as they deserve it, and it might be a good thing in the long run to bury you lot up to your eyebrows in hot ash, but I don't half like this northern wind. It reeks of the shadows."

To Jame, it simply reeked, mostly of sulfur. She hadn't considered how a major eruption might affect the Riverland. When the mountain had been a mere smoking bump on the horizon, it hadn't seemed to matter much. Perhaps, in real space, that's where it still was, too far away to be a threat. On the other hand, what did she know about volcanoes, other than that they tended inconveniently to explode?

Ah." The Earth Wife's mirror-fire eyes shifted to something behind Jame and her crooked mouth twitched into something like a smile, red light from within a jagged line between her lips. "Here's someone come to call. Hold still."

Even with the warning, Jame started as a pair of slim, white hands appeared over her shoulders. She thought they were going for her face but instead, as she held herself rigidly still, they gathered up her loose hair and smoothed it back.

"Soft," said a voice behind her, odd and husky as if it hadn't spoken in a long time, and it spoke in High Kens. Fingers took up combing out her tangled locks where she had left off. When she tried to turn, however, a firm hand on the top of her head prevented her.

"Who is it?" she hissed at the Earth Wife, even as the glimmer of an answer occurred to her. After all, how many people had she encountered since her arrival here, and how many Kencyr Highborn wandered the wilds, as free as the wind through the trees?

"You should know. He's one of you lot. The Merikit call him Mer-kanti."

Jame thought she could put a different name to the stranger, but not here, where the very sound of it might draw those enemies sworn to his destruction. Meanwhile, his deft fingers slide through her hair, smoothing, separating, gently tugging.

"That feels good," she murmured, surrendering to his touch.

The Earth wife laughed. "You folk are peculiar. D'you have to go into the wilderness to give and take pleasure freely? Mind you, Mer-kanti's passions are obscure. He finds company in stacked stones, a painted mare, and the flight of crown jewel-jaws. We feel him glide through our seasons. Earth, air, wind, and fire are all one to him, although daylight hurts his eyes. Look for him in shadow and darkness, or where the red blood flows."

"And those who hunt him?"

"The Merikit gave up long ago. Their quarrel with your kind was none of his making, and he spares where he might easily kill. Others come, sometimes, from the south, but they leave their bodies to richen my soil."

Although she held herself as still as still, Jame felt the pulse in her throat quickly under that light, caressing touch. "Their blood too?"

"Ah." She thought she heard the hint of smile in the other's voice. "That's his business, isn't it? But enough of that. I foresee fire and ash, a peculiar dawn and darkness at noon. What happens next depends in part on which way the wind blows, and I mistrust anything that comes from the north. Best you were gone, girl. After all, the solstice is tomorrow."

"What? It can't be...or did I somehow miss a day?"

"Yes, getting here. Sometimes folding the land takes time. By the way, I like your big horse. Not many are up to my weight. Fare you well. *Hic!*"

She tried to stifle it, but the belched flame erupted like a geyser from her mouth and set her straw thatch of hair on fire.

Jame leaped to her feet, meaning to push her into the stream to extinguish her, but Mother Ragga's blazing figure crumbled at her touch. Out of it sprang the terrified, singed foxkin, landing in Jame's arms and scuttling inside her jacket for shelter. Mer-kanti had disappeared. In the distance, the mountain grumbled and spat.

Jame sighed. *Life is strange*, she thought, and went to bed with a half-knit foxkin curled up under her chin.

# Chapter XVIII: Solstice

## Summer 66

## I

JAME WOKE THE next morning, disoriented.

Surely it had all been a dream, and not a very good one at that. The Burnt Man and the Dark Judge, the Earth Wife and the creeping mountain, a green mare and a half-knit foxkin…

"…quip…" said something furry under her chin, and snuggled down again with a sleepy kneading of claws.

All right. She would grant the foxkin.

And the mountain. It was rather hard to miss in that it now loomed overhead, taking up most of the northern sky. If it had looked any closer, she would have been under it. Around that ridiculous spine at its top it was smoking like a chimney, assuming anyone would want to burn brimstone and rotten eggs. The ground under her head rumbled steadily—rock's equivalent of a warning growl: Just you wait.

Then she remembered. The wait was almost over. This was the summer solstice. That also rattled her, coming as it did a day before she had expected it, again like a bad dream.

But I'm not ready.

A sudden blare of horns made her jump and the foxkin dig in its claws. Distorted by hill and mountain, the ruckus presumably came from the Merikit village hidden by a turn farther up the Silver. A cloud of ash-laden vapor drifted eastward toward it from the volcano's peak, some settling to darken the summit snow, some lifting back into the air to distort the sunrise before the prevailing north wind caught and pushed it south. The solar rim had just appeared between two eastern peaks, a bow of improbable sharp blue spiked with turquoise rays in turn edged with shimmering green. So began the longest day of the year, in a haze of smoke, a discordant blat of horns, and a stench of sulfur.

For a moment, Jame wished that she had acceded to Index's demand and brought the old scrollsman with her. He might have had some idea what she should expect, at least from the Merikit.

She felt like someone on the edge of a great pageant, knowing that she had an important role in it and fretting that she wasn't there. At the same time, no one would thank her for stepping forward to claim her part. The Earth Wife had as good as told her to leave. If she had any sense, she would have saddled Chumley last night and ridden away as fast as his great, galumphing hooves would take her.

She rose and began in a distracted way to break up camp as the foxkin rummaged, chittering, in a saddle-bag, looking for breakfast. Over the past few days, Jame had forced herself to eat a bit of this or that—hard bread, a crust of cheese, some withered apples, even the squishy little sprout heads, although those had come back up faster than they had gone down. Not much remained. However, the foxkin's busy quest reminded her of the other bag of provisions, still sunk in the icy water. She waded out to retrieve it.

The contents were, of course, wet and cold, but also well-preserved. Jame extracted the roast chicken and sniffed at it suspiciously. To her surprise, it smelled good. Since when had anything done that? She tore off a leg and was about to take a ginger nibble when the rathorn's head snaked over her shoulder and snatched it out of her hand.

Jame sprang to her feet, aghast. She tried to grab it back before he swallowed any bone splinters, but the colt backed away, raising his head out of reach like a horse refusing the bit. Then he spat out a mouthful of intact bones, gulped down the meat, and made another dive at the carcass. Both suddenly ravenous, they wrestled over it briefly before it tore apart. Jame tumbled over backward, clutching a pair of wings. The colt retreated, snorting, with the rest.

Gnawing on her prize, she watched him pin his to the ground with a dew-spur and frantically rasp flesh from bone with his tongue. The latter must be barbed, as with some large hunting cats. All this time, she had only needed the proper treat to break his stubborn resistance, but how could she have guessed that he had a passion for cooked meat? For that matter, it seemed to have surprised him as much as it had her; after all, there weren't many roast chickens running about loose in the wild.

The last scrap gone, he shoved his nose into the wet saddle back looking for more, then jerked it back with the foxkin clinging to his nasal horn. As he backed in a circle, trying to shake the creature loose, Jame gathered the chicken bones before Jorin could get at them and threw the lot into the stream. It too was beginning to steam and stink; ground water as well as run-off must contribute to it. She had retrieved the saddle-bag none too soon. Meanwhile, Chumley, the painted mare (where had she come from?), Bel, and Jorin were lined up, accidentally according to height, watching the rathorn's wild gyrations with wary fascination.

As the foxkin scuttled over his ivory mask, the colt's red eyes crossed, trying to follow it.

"Quip!" it said, popping up between his ears and sticking its sharp, inquisitive nose into one of them.

The colt squealed, reared, and went over backward, scattering his audience but not shaking his tormenter. He lurched back to his feet and careened off, bucking, across the meadow.

Meanwhile, Jame had dumped the contents of the bag onto the ground. Was there anything left to tempt the colt or, for that matter, herself? Ah. Some beef jerky and a few slabs of smoked ham, perfect for a picnic under an active volcano.

Before she could decide what to eat and what to offer, the sun lifted clear of the mountains and drums in the Merikit village greeted its ascent.

"BOOM-Wah-wah…BOOM-Wah-wah…"

The sound was approaching, gaining definition as the procession cleared intervening hills, but she couldn't see it from the meadow. Nor was there any reason why she had to, Jame told herself. She couldn't do any good although, given her nature, she might inadvertently do harm. Still, the drums called.

"BOOM-Wah-wah-BOOM!"

She stuffed a greasy slab of meat into a pocket and set off at a trot down the meadow. By the time she reached the bottom and dove among the ferns under the shadow of overhanging boughs, she was running. Before her, the stream leaping over a cliff into the torrent below. On the other side of the Silver's chasm rose sandstone bluffs, still deep in shadow, with the ruins of Kithorn on their summit. Could she snag her grapnel on the opposite heights and swing over? *No. Too far. Then climb.*

Of the trees offered to her, a black walnut some two hundred feet downstream loomed the tallest. She stripped off her gloves and tucked them into her belt, wishing for the first time that she had clawed toes as well as fingers. The corrugated bark gave good handholds, though, as did sturdy boughs. Her hands soon stank of the bruised leaves' distinctive, astringent scent. The trunk bifurcated, once, twice, and again into a limb stretching over the Silver. Jame crawled out on it.

*A good thing I'm not afraid of heights*, she thought, then froze as the branch dipped, groaning, under her weight. From below rose the thunder of water and mist that wrapped the tree in wet, slippery moss. She was a long, long way up.

At least from here she could see over the broken wall and tower, which her brother had accidentally burned down the previous fall. How strange, as it were, to be looking into Marc's past. After all, he had grown up in the shattered keep now spread out below her. Like a score of minor keeps dotting the edges of Rathillien, all but forgotten, Kithorn had kept watch on the Barrier with Perimal Darkling according to the Kencyrath's ancient trust. Yes, she had been here before, but too close really to see how small a place it was, how desperate its defiance against the dark must have been.

In the center of its inner court was a wide well-mouth, rimmed with serpentine marble, the relic of a time long before Hathir and Bashti had laid their arrogant claims to this ancient land. All the Riverland keeps were built on the sites of Bashtiri or Hathiri fortresses, but these in turn had been raised over the ruins of still older hill forts. However, none of the latter were more potent than this one.

From her perch, Jame couldn't quite see over the well's lip down to the ring of teeth within or the muscular red throat below that, but she knew they were there. After all, on Summer's Eve she had been dropped down it and had had to climb back up, fast, for this was the mouth of the River Snake whose vast length ran beneath the Silver from one end to the other, whose restless stirrings could throw the land into convulsions.

Although Marc's lord had allowed the Merikit private access for their rituals, he had not known what they were doing until he had accidentally learned, in a year of violent quakes, that they meant to throw a hero down the well to fight the snake. This he had forbidden. Afraid that their world was about to be shaken apart, the Merikit had tried to take the garrison hostage to prevent its interference, but someone had panicked, ending with the slaughter of every Kencyr there except for Marc, who had been off by himself, hunting. And so the hills had been closed.

If the Earth Wife had spoken true, the terrible irony was that the Kencyr and the Merikit shared a charge to maintain the Barrier against Perimal Darkling here at the Riverland's northern end. Instead, the Merikit cut Kencyr throats and the Kencyr—at least in Lord Caineron's case—spread flayed Merikit skins on their floors as trophies of the hunt. *What a waste on both sides,* thought Jame, *and what a potentially fatal error.*

The drums stopped. A number of Merikit were already in the courtyard, hanging back around the edges, but all attention focused on the four bizarre, gnarled figures who now entered. Ash-smeared, with goat-udders swaying under their long, unbound hair, the shamans trotted around a square drawn in charcoal on the flagstones, at whose center was the well-mouth. Jame couldn't hear them over the water, but she knew that the bells strapped to their ankles were going chink-chink-chink in unison with each step. Interspersed between them were three other Merikit made up to represent Earth Wife, Falling Man, and the Eaten One—earth, air, and water. Last of all came fire, the Burnt Man, muffled in a cloak. That, undoubtedly, was the chief, Chingetai, pretending to be invisible until his time came to take center stage.

He entered the square with the rest of the Four, each at his own corner, and the shamans prepared to close it. That left two, the Favorite and the Challenger, the first in red britches, the second in green.

It seemed that Chingetai meant to enact the entire solstice fertility rite, just as if he hadn't already done so, prematurely, on Summer's Eve, and gotten saddled with her, Jame, as the Earth Wife's current Favorite and his presumed heir. Jame recognized the substitute Favorite as the former Challenger—the one who had jammed the victor's ivy crown on her head and shoved her into the square in his place. He didn't look any happier in red than he had in green. His opponent also seemed reluctant to enter the square, only doing so when poked from behind with a spear.

*Bloody, stupid Merikit,* the Dark Judge had said. *Think they can fool us, do they? Not again. Never again.*

The hillmen had good reason to be nervous. In trying to change the rules, Chingetai was literally playing with fire, and with their lives.

Tied to the smithy door was a goat, who would hardly have looked so bored if it had known what role it was about to play. At least the loser wasn't going to share Sonny's fate, which had almost been Jame's own.

Now should come the closing of the square and the opening of sacred space, but nothing happened.

*Of course,* thought Jame. They were already in sacred space, or what passed for it this time around.

The shaman in Chingetai's corner—probably Tungit, Index's old friend—tried to build a bone-fire, but it kept falling apart. He spoke urgently over his shoulder to the chief, but a sharp gesture silenced him. Jame suddenly wondered if, like his dead son, Chingetai couldn't see the changed landscape around him. Some people were like that, psychically blind. Perhaps, to him, the smoking mountain was still a bump in the distance. Perhaps that would even save him if it exploded. She guessed, though, that both Tungit and the substitute Favorite could see all too clearly what loomed above, and that it made them very, very nervous.

When the Challenger glanced away for a moment, the Favorite snatched off his ivy crown, popped it onto the other's head, and threw himself on the ground. He had deliberately forfeited without a fight. Again.

A moment's stunned pause, and then Chingetai surged out of his corner, roaring with rage. The Burnt Man's bone-fire scattered before him.

WHOOP.

The earth leaped, throwing everyone off their feet.

Jame's tree shook as if hit solidly in the trunk by something massive. She scrabbled to maintain her grip in a hail of falling leaves and unripe nuts, slipped, and found herself hanging upside down by her knees, cap gone, hair tumbling free. Through the quivering canopy overhead, she saw snatches of the mountain top as it exploded. The spine disintegrated into a black, billowing cloud, out of which shot chunks of red-hot rock, trailing fire.

A trick of the wind brought a crash and a horrified shout from Kithorn. Twisting around, still upside-down, Jame saw that a boulder half the size of the smithy had smashed into the square beside the well. There was Red Britches, still curled up like a hedgehog, and Chingetai, and Tungit, but where was Green Britches, the new Favorite? Silly question. Smashed to bloody pulp under the boulder, of course. What very bad luck, or what very good aim.

A whistling sound made her look up.

"Oh schist," she said, as another flaming rock punched through the upper branches.

It struck the limb from which she dangled and smashed it. She fell, snatching at leaf and stem, twig and branch, until a sturdy bough seemed to leap up at her. It hit her in the side, or rather she hit it, and there she hung for a moment, stunned and breathless. A huge splash and a jet of steam up through the leaves marked the fire-ball's plunge into the river. Would she follow it? River or ground, broken neck or back?

Neither.

She slid off the bough and fell again, into someone's arms. For a moment, dazed, she looked up into the pale, hooded face of the man whom the Merikit called Mer-kanti.

"Run," he said, in a voice rusty with disuse, and dropped her.

More fiery stones fell, incandescent against a lime-green rain of leaves and unripe walnuts. Jame lurched to her feet, trying to gather her wits; even for her, that had been a jarring fall——three of them, in fact, in rapid succession. She limped toward the meadow, met by Jorin as he bounded toward her through the ferns, chirping in alarm.

They emerged down-meadow from the stream, to a sight that stopped her in her tracks. A huge, black cloud towered above the shattered mountain top. Vivid pink lightning snapped within it, its crack almost swallowed by the volcano's roar. As the cloud rose, flattened, and spread, the morning light dimmed to a murky yellow. Underfoot, the ground shuddered continuously.

Jorin pressed against her leg, his terror as clear as speech. Time to leave. Now.

"Not yet," she told him.

She set off slantwise across the field, going as fast as she could with a hand pressed against a savage stitch in her side. Please Trinity she hadn't broken a rib. Or two. Or three. Something white drew her. There stood the Whinno-hir Bel-tairi, trembling, with one foot barely touching the ground. She must have tried to run with her overgrown hooves and pulled up lame. Yes, dammit. Drawing closer, Jame saw the bulge between knee and pastern of a bowed tendon.

A white-haired boy, stood at her head, trying to coax her forward. As Jame approached, he turned a stricken, desperate face toward her and mouthed a plea for help that came out as a half-strangled bleat.

Jame knelt and ran her hand down the mare's leg. It was already hot and swollen, unusable without the risk of permanent damage. Now what?

She shot a glance over her shoulder at the mountain. Perhaps the worst was over. However, black clouds still billowed from the ragged heights and sections of the upper slope were giving way in massive landslides of melted snow and mud. Trinity, Jame thought, watching two hundred-foot tall ironwoods topple like pins. How clear and close it all seemed. If the Merikit village was anywhere near the foot of that monster, it would be swallowed whole, yet the Earth Wife had said that she could protect it. How?

The answer came from high up on the southwest flank of the volcano. There, a broad area bulged outward, then split open in an even greater explosion than the first. For a moment, molded in shifting chaos, Jame saw the Earth Wife's face, mouth hugely agape, vomiting fire. Ten seconds, fifteen…

BOOM!

The concussion made her stagger and Jorin skitter sideways, while mare and colt cried out as if with one terrified voice.

Gray and white debris boiled out of the cleft mountain and rolled down the face opposite the Merikit village with a rumble that shook the earth. Unlike the first eruption's storm cloud, this was a dirty, spreading avalanche. Both, however, seemed to move slowly—a trick, perhaps, of distance. After all, despite how close the mountain appeared, it had taken that massive concussion some time to reach her. Mother Ragga had turned the major eruption away from the Merikit. Perhaps those in the meadow were also safe, but somehow Jame doubted it. The Burnt Man had been thwarted once. He would not be again, if he could help it, especially not with the Dark Judge muttering vengeance in his charred stub of an ear.

"Bel can't run," she said to the boy, "but perhaps she can ride."

Understanding lit his face. In a moment, he had reverted to the equine—if, in fact, his quasi-human appearance had been real at all—and Bel sank down on the grass with a cry of pain. Jame caught her cold, white hands.

"Lady, please. You must."

She helped her rise, and was very relieved to find that she was as light for a woman as she had been for a horse. It still took an effort to lift her onto the rathorn's back against the savage throb in her side.

The colt lunged away as soon as he felt his rider's weight, but then he swerved to circle Jame. She felt his confusion as he cantered past, just out of reach. His instincts were screaming at him to run, to escape, to save what he valued most. Under that like bile lay long cherished hatred. If he couldn't kill his dam's slayer outright, he could leave her to her fate, except that the bond between them held as strongly as the chain that had trapped him in the riverbed. Under that in turn was something else, something new, furiously denied but still there.

No time to explore that now.

"Go," she told him. "Get m'lady away from here, as far as you can." When he hesitated, she told him again, unwilling to force her command on him but ready to do so if she must. "I'll find another way. Go!"

He tossed his head—*Huh. If you insist*—and was gone, a swift, pale shadow across the darkening grass.

Jame turned back to the stream. It surprised her how much she wished she gone with Bel—not just to escape, either, but to race the wind on that splendid creature. To ride a rathorn might be madness, but what divine folly, worth any cost. Well, not quite. She feared that the colt's legs weren't strong enough to carry two, at least as far and fast as necessary. Besides, there by the water stood Chumley, whose great hooves could still surely take her to safety.

More rocks fell, trailing smoke and fire. Most were no bigger than a clenched fist, but some roaring past overhead were huge, and shattered on impact, leaving great craters in the soft ground. At least their fall now seemed random and they were easy to dodge if one kept an eye on their flight.

As she neared the river bank, Jame saw that Chumley wasn't half screened by grass as she had thought but by the painted mare. Mer-kanti stood between the two horses with a hand on each, steadying them. Several paces in front of him was a large, smothering boulder, half-buried in the stream's gravel margin. Jame slowed, staring, then approached cautiously. The rock's crust was laced with fiery cracks, and some pieces has fallen away like unusually thick bits of shell from a gigantic, boiled egg. Out of one crack protruded a scrap of burnt material. In its filigree of ash, clearly preserved, were the loops and whorls of knit-work.

Jame fell to her knees beside the boulder, close enough to feel the waves of heat rolling off of it.

"Mother Ragga? Earth Wife? Are you in there?"

Another bit of lava-shell fell, hissing, onto the wet river pebbles. The thing was hollow. Inside, something moved, and coughed.

"Well, what are you waiting for?" said a thin, peevish voice. "Get me out of here."

Jame incautiously grabbed a patch of shell to pull it loose, and her gloves burst into fire. She plunged them into the steaming stream, then sat down abruptly on the stony bank with her scorched hands jammed into her arm-pits, and swore while Jorin slunk around her, chirping urgently. Dammit, that had been her last pair of gloves.

"What are you staring at?" she demanded over her shoulder. "Can't you help?"

The hooded man lifted a hand from Chumley's shoulder, then quickly dropped it again to stop the enormous horse from bolting. The message was clear: if he lost physical contact with either beast, instinct would throw it into blind flight. Presumably they needed both if he, Jame, and the Earth Wife all must flee.

"…water…waaater…"

The odd, gargling voice came from the stream. There, dead trout floated past, silver bellies up, but one particularly large fish had caught on the rocks broadside to the swift current. Its back was steel blue speckled with black, its eyes already glazed and turning white as the water boiled it alive. From its gaping mouth came again that desperate plea:

"…waaaater…!"

All right. A talking fish. This was, after all, still sacred space, home also to the Eaten One.

"I can't make the stream run clean again, or cool it down," Jame said, exasperated. "I can't save you. Sweet Trinity, who do you think I am?"

"Water." This time the croaked word came from Mer-kanti, and he nodded toward the lava-shell.

"Oh," said Jame.

She grabbed the empty saddle bag, dipped it into the stream, and dumped its contents on the hot shell, which exploded, knocking her over backward. She heard Chumley scream and through the steam saw him rear above her, looming higher than the mountain, it seemed, all flared nostrils, bared yellow teeth, and eyes rolling white with terror. Mer-kanti's thin, strong hand slid up the chestnut neck as far as it could reach and the gelding came down again with a snort, enormous hooves crashing to earth on either side of Jame's head. Belatedly, she yelped and scrambled clear.

The top had blown off the hollow rock, leaving a rough bowl full of something at first impossible to identify. Then a bony hand rose from a pale welter of flesh, clutched the edge of the bowl, and raised a thin arm drooping with loose skin. A face turned upward, and what a face. Sagging flesh hung off the skull except where eyes, nose, and mouth pinned it in place. Only by those ancient, gummy eyes did Jame recognize the Earth Wife's formerly plump features. The lava's heat had made her fat run like melting wax within her skin, settling to swell the lowest points. She stared at her wasted arm, festooned in rolls of hanging skin, and her toothless mouth gaped in a wail.

"Just look at me! Damn you, Burnie, was this fair? Was this right? Oh, bury me quick! I want to die!"

She dropped her face back into the folds of her flesh. Steeling herself, Jame reached in, rummaged about, and pulled the Earth Wife's head up again by its thin, gray braid.

"You can't die," she said. "You're Rathillien, or one quarter of it, anyway. Pull yourself together!"

"I'm blind!" Mother Ragga howled, and indeed at the moment she was: the tension on her hair had caused her skull to sink within its sack of skin and her eyes with it to the bottom of deep, indrawn dimples.

Jame could have shaken her, but was afraid that she would slosh.

Hot ash stung her face. It had started to descend unnoticed, as a fine dust growing rapidly thicker. This would be fall-out from the first eruption. The roiling clouds of the second still churned down the mountain side—closer, it seemed, and picking up speed.

"Listen," she said desperately. "You like my horse, don't you? I'll give him to you."

"Present?" said the sunken mouth, suddenly hopeful. Nothing, it seemed, could quell the Earth Wife's greed for gifts.

"Yes, but you've got to accept him *now*. Come on. D'you want...er...Burnie to win?"

She left go of the braid and Mother Ragga's skull rose to meet its features. She stared avidly at Chumley who stared back at her, ears pricked, fascinated by this strange creature with the peep-a-boo face.

"Nice horse," she crooned. "Big horse. *My* horse."

Mer-kanti slid his hand up to the gelding's withers and pressed down. Chumley sank ponderously to his knees.

When the Earth Wife rose and leaned, reaching eagerly for him, she looked like a skeleton wearing a half-collapsed tent of skin, and a small skeleton at that, coming barely to Jame's chin. It might have belonged to a child, weighed down by an old woman's mortality, anchored by it, too: liquefied fat had settled in her legs and feet, swelling them to grotesque proportions. Jame struggled to lift one leg from the lava shell. It squished in her grasp like a thin boot full of mud. Raising the White Lady had been hard. This was like trying to shift the foundations of the earth.

She heaved, the shell tipped, and Mother Ragga spilled out on top of her. Jame found herself buried under folds of hot, sweaty skin, inside of which anonymous organs oozed, gurgling. G'ah, what a smell, like all the old women in the world baked in a pie. She struggled to her knees. Sharp bones dug into her back. After an agonized, fumbling moment, the mass lifted and she could breathe again.

"Next time…" she gasped, staggering to her feet, "bring your own…damn mounting block."

Mother Ragga had indeed gotten one leg over Chumley's broad back. Now she was slowly toppling off the other side. Up came her near foot, a bloated bag of skin with thick, yellow nails half-sunken at one end. Jame grabbed it and pulled down to center the ungainly rider. As she did so, the sudden stab of sore ribs caught her in the side like a dagger thrust.

She found herself back on aching knees, trying to catch her breath. The world had gone gray for a moment, more likely for several. She thought she remembered Chumley lurching to his feet with a squeal and the Earth Wife's shriek trailing off into the distance. Yes, they were gone. Her claws were out and bloodied. Without meaning to, she had raked the gelding's side, trying to stop her fall. No wonder he had bolted.

So had the painted mare.

Jame looked up just in time to see her plunge away across the
meadow with Mer-kanti on foot beside her, gripping her mane.
How beautifully he moved, barely touching the grass, wind-blowing
Senethari at its finest. Just before both vanished into the deepening
twilight, he swung up onto the mare's back.

Jame shook off her dazed wonder. "Wait!" she cried, struggling to her feet. "Come back!"

But he too was gone.

The world was still gray, and growing darker by the second. Ash fell thickly now, like a hot, dirty snowstorm stinking
of sulfur. Jame shrugged off her jacket and draped it over her
head. The improvised hood protected her eyes as did the curtain of her loose hair, but it was now impossible to see more
than a few feet ahead. Then for a dazzling moment lightning
shattered the sky, followed by a crack of thunder. In the stunned
blindness that followed, panic reached her through senses not
her own.

"Jorin!" she cried, and without thinking took a deep breath of
the ash-laden air to call again. When her convulsive coughing
stopped, she reached out to the ounce with her senses, but there
was no answer.

Lost. Gone.

That meant nothing, she told herself. The link between them
often broke at the most inconvenient times. But what would he do
in this thickening nightmare? Curl up in an ash bank and wait for her
to find him or for the storm to pass? Small chance of the former,
unless she tripped over him. If the latter, he would die. Worse was
coming. She knew it.

*It's all your fault.*

Insidious whisper, borne on an uneasy, shifting wind. Who or
what spoke, if not her own guilt?

*You destroy everyone who trusts you, everyone whom you love.*

"No," she said, denial ash-bitter in her mouth, parching her throat.

But what if it were true?

As if called, the dead came to her on the swirling breath of
distant fire: Dally, dragging his flayed skin behind him; Prince
Odallian, melting into a puddle of flesh corrupt through no sin of
his own; Tirandys, smiling on his pyre. Ash they had all become,
because of her. As ash they returned.

"If I become Regonereth, the Ivory Knife incarnate," she had told the Earth Wife, "I'll do what I was born to do, break what needs to be broken, and then break myself."

*Then break and die.*

"No," she said again. Blink hard, and they were gone. A trick of the mind. Besides, as much as she regretted their deaths, none of them had been her fault.

*Or were they? Think.*

Between the stab and crack of lightning, the gray world was unnervingly quiet, the ash a blanket that muffled the senses. In that dead silence there was far too much time for thought.

True. However good her intentions, around her things happened. Even her most innocent action could become a pebble cast into the pool of events, with ripples far beyond her control. Then too, not all her actions had been inconsequential in themselves, as witnessed by the string of ruins that she had left in her wake.

Still, buildings didn't necessarily fall down or burn up whenever she walk into them, as she had told Timmon.

No, just most of the time. And how much worse it would surely become as her god-cursed nature worked its way to the surface like a festering wound.

*Then lance it and die. You know you are poison.*

Why else had everyone abandoned her, not once but over and over again? Why should they stay, sensing what she was?

*G'ah*, she thought, giving herself a shake that was half a shudder. *Horses bolt and death sweeps people away, whether they wish it to or not. Am I to blame for that?*

*For everything*, breathed the gray wind. *Someone must be.*

That brought her up short. "Now wait just a minute."

*No. Behold those who would judge you.*

Lightning flickered across the sky, illuminating it in quick jabs that made the intervals of darkness between all the more intense. A shape formed within the dance of ash, gaining definition with each flash and drawing closer without seeming to move. It was slim and elegant with a pale face under an unruly shock of black hair threaded with white. Silver-gray eyes caught each lightning flare and held it in the dark that followed. Jame couldn't clearly see his hands, but she knew them to be as fine-boned as his face and gloved in a lacework of scars. Her sudden longing for their touch was so sharp that it hurt. Here at last was someone who, surely, would not abandon her.

Then he saw her, and turned away.

*It's only a trick*, part of her mind insisted, but it hurt too much to ignore.

"Torisen!" she cried after him. "Brother, don't leave me!"

"Why not?" He paused to answer her but askance, not meeting her eyes. "What can you be to me but my destruction?"

"But I love you!"

"Destruction begins with love. So our father taught us. So our mother taught him. So he was doomed to dust and bitter death, all honor spent. Would you likewise doom me?"

"No! Never! How can you say so?"

"Because I know what you are."

His features shifted, his voice as well, growing harsh with anger and bewildered pain.

"Filthy Shanir." Her father turned to glare at her, as gray with ash as his name. Death had hollowed his face to dry patches of skin clinging to the skull, but his silver eyes blazed. "How dare you look so much like your mother and not be her? Tricked. Betrayed. Poison fruit of a tainted tree, where is my sword, my ring, my life?"

Before that cry of pain Jame recoiled a step, but only one. Once his rage had thrown her into panic-stricken flight. It could still make her flinch. But she remembered what she had heard at Tentir about a cadet humiliated by his lord father, tormented by his lordan brother, driven out prey to passions at which she could only guess.

There was the crux. She didn't yet know what had happened to her father that night in the lordan's quarters. Perhaps neither did who or whatever now challenged her.

"Father," she said, "if that's who you are, tell me: that night, in that hot, stinking room, what broke you? I want to understand. Please tell me."

He stared at her. What flickered through those dead eyes—surprise, chagrin, anger? Then he threw back his head and howled. He didn't want to be understood, much less pitied. What was he, after all, without his mantle of rage? Already he was changing. Gone, the patched, gray coat worn thin by years of bitter exile and the prematurely gray hair; gone, that thin, haunted face.

Sleek and smug, Greshan smiled at her, and twitched straight his exquisitely embroidered jacket with a coarse hand.

Jame's fists clenched, nails biting palms. Was this how her father had learned to live with himself, by becoming the thing that had marred him?

"No," she said to that smirking face. "He made mistakes. He hurt a lot of people, including me. But he never put hot iron to the face of an innocent, nor tormented little boys for fun. He didn't become you."

The other's smile twisted and slipped. She wanted to rip it off his face altogether, and that foul coat off his back.

"What happened in your apartment, uncle?" she demanded, both pleased and annoyed that he seemed to drift away as she advanced on him. Lightning and darkness flickered back and forth to a muffled shout of thunder. "What did you do, or try to do, that left your Randir friend nailed to the floor with a knife through his guts, your servant in flames, and you fouling yourself in a corner? Brave man. Great warrior. Daddy's boy. How did you die, and why did your death cause a man like Hallik Hard-hand to turn the White Knife on himself? Answer, dammit!"

She tried to pin him with her rage, but he slipped away, dissolving into darkness.

Again came that flicker of doubt. What was all this anyway—guilt, hallucination, or something else altogether? Who was it that must have someone to blame, who kept trying to push her in directions she didn't want to go? That had happened before, at least twice recently.

Then she knew.

"All right," she told the chaos that seethed around her. "Enough fun and games. Show yourself."

*Ahhhhhhh*...breathed the storm, and the air grew ominously still. Murky yellow light filtered down from above, gray motes afloat in it. Ash no longer fell on Jame but circled in a dark storm wall of which she was the eye. Although it was still sweltering hot, she resumed her jacket and defiantly shook out her hair; the better to face whatever was coming to face her.

A huge shape moved in the shifting darkness, ill-defined by clots and flowing streamers of ash. Here was the bulge of a great shoulder; there, the cavernous socket of an eye; and all the time gigantic paws soundless in themselves kept pace with the shuddering earth.

Jame turned with it. This was the third time in recent days that she and the blind Arrin-ken had danced around each other, if one counted the first when she had been flat on her back, half dead from blood loss and scared half out of her wits. On some level, she was still afraid—how not, faced with such a creature?—but she was also angry.

*Be* angry, whispered her Shanir blood. Be strong. Be like your father.

"Now that I have your attention," she said, hardly knowing if fear or rage shook her voice, "I have a question. You are a judge. Trinity knows, the Kencyrath needs justice. So why don't you go after bastards like Lord Caineron, who would corrupt all that we are, or that lying priest Ishtier? Where were you when the Witch of Wilden made her pact with the Shadow Guild to slaughter my family or when my dear uncle Greshan played his filthy game with Bel?"

A flame-savaged face turned toward her, baring its fangs.

*The innocent are not my concern.* She flinched involuntarily as his voice snarled in her head, like teeth scraping the inside of her skull. *I judge only those of the Old Blood with destruction ripening in their veins, if their own kind are too cowardly to judge them first. Such as you. Dare you call yourself innocent? Dancer's daughter, you were born guilty.*

"That I deny, nor am I yet damned."

*Liar!*

His terrible face snapped at her out of shifting shadows, itself a shadow but ravaged with such hunger that it seemed ready to devour itself for want of other food.

A surge of near-berserker rage made Jame stumble. *Careful,* she thought, fighting to regain both control and balance. *Fall now and you fall forever...like your father. But you know who you are and what you may become.*

"Liar?" she repeated as levelly as she could, hearing her voice quiver, catching it. Without thinking, she began to move in the kantirs of the Senethari, wind-blowing with a touch of water-flowing, gliding around the savage eddies of his anger. "That too I deny."

The dance imposed its own discipline. Move the hand just so to cup the wind. Dip and sway around an errant coil of ash as hot as thwarted vengeance, as cold as lost hope. Such self-devouring anger! Such despair! Here were fires that might consume the world, yet hunger for more. Ah, gently, gently. Feel the cool flow of water over scorched skin. Spill the wind through spread fingers and comb it with the heavy silk of black hair until all flowed smooth. There. Let it go.

"I am not like you, burnt cat, blind judge. I came from the darkness, but I do not embrace it. What is there in the Master's House but dust and ashes? You were burned there, so you make yourself a fire to burn others. Does their pain ease your own?"

*Yes!*

Such deadly vehemence, causing even ash to flare in fiery motes, but the dance threaded through it, catching him unawares. God's claws, this was dangerous. Don't think. Dance.

The great head, half-seen, swung...in assent, denial, confusion?

*No. If I hurt, if I burn, it is to make me what I am, to do what I must. What other reason can there be?*

"Must everything have a reason?"

*YES! How else are we to endure such misery if in the end there is no one to punish for it?*

What did one say to that? If you can't live with a run of bad luck, stop whining and die? Or was he right? Cause and effect. One understood that. But effect without cause? What if, after all, the world was nothing but random chance, without justice or sense? Better madness than to believe that.

Never mind. He was answering questions despite himself. Ask more.

"You say you judge those Shanir allied with the Third Face of God, That-Which-Destroys. Whom *have* you judged?"

*Arrrr...not Greshan. He would have been my meat, ripe and rich, but his own kind judged him first.*

Jame blinked. What?

*The Brandan matriarch, Brenwyr, a maledight and matricide. Despite that, however, she is still innocent. Soon, soon may she fall. You have pushed her hard, little nemesis. Already she totters on the edge of her doom. The Witch, ah, the Witch. I will have her in the end, when she uncloaks and her defenses at last fall. But they are nothing, nothing, while the Master lives and so does his servant Keral, who burned out my eyes.*

"There you name true evil," said Jame, and heard her voice begin to purr with the seductive power of the dance.

Ah. That was better. Her ribs no longer hurt, nor did she feel the weight of her own body. Doubts, too, began to fall away. Why have such power if not to use it?

"You name your failures, Lord Cat. What have you accomplished in this great crusade of yours? What are you but a stinking shadow to frighten children if you cannot strike at evil's root, there, under shadow's eaves?"

He howled and raked at his own flesh as if to punish it. The air thickened with flakes of charred skin.

*Do you think I have not tried? Year after bitter year, I have prowled the Barrier, seeking a way through, but no Arrin-ken may enter Perimal Darkling until the coming of the Tyr-ridan, and that is never, because our god has forsaken us.*

If he and the Kencyrath managed to kill off every destructive Shanir, they guaranteed that failure. Jame suspected she wasn't the first potential Nemesis, only quite possibly the last. She was about to say as much, but the great cat still spoke as if under bitter compulsion, and his words stunned her.

*Once, only once, he came within reach. I felt him cross into this world, into a garden of white flowers, but by the time I arrived he was gone, leaving yet another marred innocent. I would have judged her, punished her, but she had license for what she did. She showed me. The one I should have judged, the one who had doomed her, was then long dead, and he her own father! All things end, light, hope, and life. All come to judgment—except the guilty.*

Trinity.

The dance flew out of Jame's mind, and its power spiraled away. Up to that moment, she hadn't realized that she was air-borne on its wings.

*Dammit,* she thought, spitting out grass and trying to catch the breath that surprise and the ground had slammed out of her. *I've got to stop falling from great heights. It's unhealthy. But* what *did he say?*

Fire and ash roared up in a shape that towered above her, an awakened holocaust with flame raging in its jaws and the deep pits of its eyes.

*Child of darkness, Dancer's daughter, you dare play your filthy games with ME?*

Clearly, the dance had released him too. What had she been trying to do, anyway? Not reap his soul. Not quite. But the dark thrill remained of searching an Arrin-ken for weakness as for cracks of bitter honey in his soul, like Rawneth in Brenwyr's soul-image.

*I could have shattered him,* she thought, amazed, appalled. *He almost came apart in my hands.*

Did that, finally, make her guilty and thus subject to his judgment? But he hadn't broken, and neither had she.

The ash storm ignited into a hurricane of fire that ringed her, roaring with his voice. Green grass withered and kindled; strands of her hair, lifting, sizzled and stank. Her face stung. He would burn her alive through sheer mindless fury, justice be damned, and in doing so he would damn himself.

"Lord!" she cried. Heat had almost closed her throat. Was that feeble croak her voice? "A judgment! Am I fallen? If not, are the innocent now your meat?"

The great cat sprang at her, and the flames rose with him.

*This is my pyre,* she thought, staring up as the fiery wave crested above her. Incandescent orange and glowing red, laced with gold and a deep, luminous blue...*How beautiful.*

At the top of his leap, a blast of scorching wind caught him. He fought it, howling, but it shredded him. Jame fell flat on the ground, claws out to anchor her against the gale. What in Perimal's name...? In a lull of sorts, she raised her head and saw that the Arrin-ken had vanished, but what was coming in his place?

The wind had whipped away most of the low-level ash, leaving the newly-risen sun a pallid smudge in the sky. Movement to the north caught Jame's eye. Very, very close, boiling clouds from the second eruption rose from the valley that converged just below Kithorn with the Silver. The head of the avalanche had momentarily disappeared behind a high bluff, but now it rolled back into sight at the northern end of the meadow. Its vanguard appeared to be not clouds but huge, tumbling figures, gray, black and white, veined with fire. A raised, baleful head, the stump of a foot, a hand with charred stubs for fingers, reaching, then over it would go as another took its place and another after that in a seething, eager muddle.

"*Wha, wha, wha?*" came their questing cry.

Then they saw her.

"*HA!*"

Jame had leaped up. Their booming, triumphant shout and a second tempest blast struck her almost simultaneously, bowling her over. She rolled to her feet and fled, all but flying before the wind with the Burning Ones hot on her heels.

There was no way that she could outrun them. Belatedly, she remembered the cliff over the waterfall, high enough perhaps to take her above their reach, but that lay behind her now. When she turned her head to gauge how far, the wind smacked her hard in the face. Through a blur of stinging tears, she saw the Burnt Man's host roar across the stream, which exploded into stream at their touch.

Run, run, run...

Immediately in front of her stood a door, surrounded by the seared meadow, half sunk into it. Serpentine forms and gap-mouthed *imus* rioted over its wooden posts and lintel. It hadn't been there before.

Jame couldn't have stopped if she had wanted to. She crashed into it and it gave way, spilling her down a step onto the dirt floor of the Earth Wife's lodge. A large shape took up one entire end of the room—Chumley, whickering in alarm and hitting his head against the low ceiling. The room was full of animals, sleepily growling, squawking, and squeaking in protest at her sudden arrival. Jorin pounced her in delight before she had stopped rolling. On the other side of a smoky fire sat Mother Ragga herself, lumpen in her chair with the half-knit foxkin bright-eyed in her lap.

"Well?" she said, sounding petulant. "If you're staying, shut the door."

Jame did.

# Chapter XIX: Darkness at Noon

## Summer 66

## I

BELOW GOTHREGOR, THE Silver bent to the east before resuming its southward course. Long ago, the low-lying ground within
this angle had been cleared and enclosed along the edge by an earthen
dike. Every spring part of the snow-swollen river was diverted into
the resulting three hundred acre meadow and then drained out its
lower end, leaving a new, rich layer of silt through which the early
grass soon shot vivid green blades. On the far side, where the land
rose to meet the Snowthorn's foothills, long terraces supported bright
ribbons of flax, barley, rye, oats, and wheat, all ripening toward the
Great Harvest at the end of summer. At midsummer, though, attention fixed on the lower meadow and the haying, which took
every hand that the Knorth could muster to bring in the harvest
before the weather turned.

First came a line of reapers with a hiss and flash of scythes, the
hay falling in swathes at their feet. The next line of workers turned
over these sheaves with rakes to loosen them for proper drying.
Twenty great wains, drawn by horse or oxen, lumbered behind them
between the rows. Onto these the hay was pitched under the expert
eye of the load-masters. When a wain was full, it pulled aside to one
of the growing stacks. The hayricks themselves were meticulously
constructed and, in their way, things of beauty. Each sat on a stone
foundation which in turn was covered with a deep layer of green
bracken, both to raise the hay off the damp ground and to protect
it from rats, which could no more chew through the tough branches
than through horse hair. Set on top of that was a wooden structure
in the shape of an open-sided pyramid, against which the hay was
stacked, again under careful supervision.

All in all, the Lesser Harvest progressed smoothly, well oiled by
centuries of practice.

Torisen worked with the reapers, hot, sweaty, and not as smoothly
as he would have liked. In past years, he had either been with the
Southern Host or saddled with other duties, making this his first

season in the field. He knew his Kendar would prefer that he stayed aloof, pretending to oversee—after all, what would their enemies say if they saw the Knorth lord slaving away beside the least of his house? However, Torisen didn't care. At least he had mastered the long-armed scythe well enough not to cut off anyone's foot; and if his row was less orderly than those of more experienced mowers, well, he could learn. After all, there were his hands, both of them, moving at his will. The bandages and splints had come off weeks ago, but his relief remained, as sharp and clear as the moment he had first flexed his mended fingers and known that he wouldn't be a cripple after all.

Besides, it was pleasant to be under orders again, even those of someone as ill-tempered as the harvest-master. The man was behind him now, shouting at a raker in a voice as raspy and irritating as the chaff that worked itself into everything.

"Here now, you cow-handed cadet! Turn those swathes and loosen 'em properly. What, you've never heard of tight-packed hay heating 'til it bursts into flames?"

The cadet Vant stifled a derisive snort. *Who are you*, it said, *to be telling me anything?* As a ten-commander, he had already made it clear that he resented playing such a menial role in the harvest, never mind that everyone from senior randon to the highlord himself labored beside him.

"You think that's funny?" The harvest-master must be almost in the cadet's face, up on his toes to bring their eyes level. "Well, I've seen it happen, boy, a whole field of burning ricks, pale tongues of fire in the summer sun, and that winter the cattle lowing with hunger so loud that no one could sleep. So shut up and do your work properly!"

Torisen felt those hard, impatient eyes turn to fix on his back. *I dare you*, he thought.

"Huh!" said the master, and stomped off to shout at someone else.

Marc and Brier Iron-thorn worked side by side down the line, two tall, strong figures swinging their blades in identical, effortless arcs. The girl's hair glowed sullen red, swaying back and forth as she moved. The man's beard was a thick, white bush with some lingering touches of fox, his head sunburned and peeling under its crown of thinning, reddish hair. Someone was always hiding his hat for a joke; this time he apparently hadn't found it yet. He said something to his companion and she laughed, white teeth ablaze in that dark face which seemed bred into some Southron Kendar. Torisen had never heard Brier Iron-thorn laugh before, or even seen her smile.

He wondered again why Marc—ever so gently, as if not wanting to cause pain—had turned down his offer of a permanent place with the Knorth. Anyone else in the Kendar's position would surely have jumped at the chance. For that matter, any decent lord should have been glad to have him. True, in his mid-nineties he was past his fighting prime, but he had so much else to offer for those who valued kindness and inherent decency, not to mention his growing skill as an artisan. The man was waiting, but for what? In the meantime, ironically, in part because of his refusal to accept Knorth service, his was one of the few names that Torisen was absolutely sure he would never forget.

Not that he had misplaced anyone since the unfortunate Mullen. His people wouldn't let him. In his presence, everyone had pointedly called each other by name until he had demanded that they stop as it gave him a headache. Dammit, didn't they trust him?

*Don't answer that.*

Kindrie had also declined a place in his service. At the time Torisen had been both surprised and relieved, if puzzled. According to the Matriarchs, an illegitimate Highborn was kin to no one, but that didn't change the fact that Kindrie was the son of Torisen's unfortunate aunt Tieri—a first cousin. And the Shanir was desperate for a home. Why, then, had he turned away at the last minute?

For that matter, Torisen hadn't formally bound his sister Jamethiel. It had never occurred to him to try, nor had she seemed either to expect or want it.

There was another sore spot, dimming his pleasure in the day: Jame's ten-command had come to help with the harvest, but without her. The Min-drear cadet Rue had said that his sister had unfinished business in the hills. What, for Ancestors' sake? Surely she couldn't be mad enough to try to pick up with the Merikit where she had left off at Kithorn on Summer's Eve. He remembered now, uneasily, that she hadn't agreed with him that such a thing was out of the question. Her quiet independence alarmed him, as if she only submitted to authority when she wanted to.

*Am I losing control?* he wondered, not for the first time. *Of my sister, of my people, of myself? Was I wrong to assume my father's title with his curse hanging over me? Can the disowned inherit power anymore than the illegitimate?*

But he had seen how close the Kencyrath was to falling apart. As he had sensed Ganth's death, so had others, if less clearly. Some Highborn, soon, would have claimed the Highlord's seat. Caineron, probably. Or Ardeth. Or Randir. Then there would have been civil war and slaughter enough to make the White Hills pale by comparison. Those seeds of destruction were also part of his father's legacy.

*No matter what I do,* Torisen thought, swinging his scythe with untoward force, making the Kendar next to him hastily step aside, *I stand in his shadow.*

"Rest!" bellowed the harvest-master.

Reapers grounded their tools and reached for the water bottles hanging from their belts. Some sat down, drew out cheese and onion wrapped in black bread, and began to munch on it. A ripple of talk and laughter passed down the line, some of it directed at the workers behind them whose failure to keep up had caused this welcome halt. As it was, they had almost reached the bottom of the meadow. Tubs of oil and sand were brought forward along with the hones to whet the blades for the final assault.

Harn trudged up, an eight-foot pitchfork cocked like an ungainly spear over his shoulder.

"Hot work," he said, offering Torisen a swig from his bottle, which turned out to contain hard cider. He squinted up at the hazy sky and at the sun, which was ringed by a halo. "Odd light, odd weather. D'you suppose it's going to storm?"

Rain was coming, thought Torisen. He could feel it in his new-knit bones. And something else, somehow connected to his delinquent sister...but to think that was ridiculous. All natural disasters weren't Jame's fault—maybe just the unnatural ones.

There had been several jolts around dawn, enough to crumble some already damaged walls and to stir fears of another earthquake like the one that spring, whose marks could still be seen up and down the Riverland. Torisen looked northward. Early that morning, from window of his turret quarters, he had seen a plume of smoke on the horizon. Now clouds were coming—strange, lobed ones white against a darkening sky. The air stirred, laced with a hint of...what? Rotten eggs? Birds flew overhead, all going south.

Someone shouted a warning as a herd of deer bounded across the field between and sometimes over harvesters, who threw themselves flat to avoid the flying hooves. At a stag's heels, snapping, ran a white streak. The wolver pup Yce had grown over the summer, although not as much as a wolf cub would have, and she chased anything that fled her. Deer, cows, sheep, people...

"Just wait until she gets big enough to make her first kill," Harn said grimly, watching. "One taste of fresh blood, and there'll be no stopping her."

Yce gave up pursuit and loped back to Torisen, as usual stopping just out of reach.

"What am I going to do with you?" he asked her, "and what in Perimal's name do you want of me?"

No answer but that unnerving, ice-blue stare.

More than ever, she reminded him of his sister. Both seemed to be challenging him in ways he couldn't understand, or perhaps didn't want to.

Again came that sick sense of lost control, like tumbling down an abyss by stages with no bottom in sight.

...*Daddy's boy, run, hide*...

Words spoken in delirium. Ridiculous that they should have struck so deep, that they continued to hurt. She hadn't known what she was saying, of course.

He still didn't know how his sister had come to be injured. Apparently no one did, although Torisen sensed that the Caineron Gorbel knew more than he would admit. Something odd was going on between the two lordans, if by "odd" one meant anything besides the inevitable house rivalries, which in the past had bordered on the lethal. And then there was the Ardeth Timmon as well. Peredon's son. Adric's favorite. What had he to do with Jame, and why did both of them keep edging into his most intimate dreams?

*G'ah, think of something else.* But he couldn't.

After half a lifetime his twin sister had returned, but she kept slipping away again into one outlandish situation after another. She was younger than he now, but sometimes she seemed older, with eyes that hinted at experiences beyond his comprehension and at a certain rising irritation: *You might at least* try *to understand.*

On top of all that, she was now a cadet at Tentir, where he had longed with all his heart to go.

*She is gaining strength, boy*, murmured the voice in his head, behind the locked door. *Even your war-leader Harn speaks well of her. The randon like a fighter, and she is becoming one of them. What if, eventually, they prefer her to you?*

Madness. Don't listen.

Besides, not everyone at Tentir wanted her there. The cadet Vant, although an ass in other respects, had said as much. To many, she was a freak, her mere presence at the college an insult to all randon past and present. Vant had also hinted that no one expected her actually to stay the course. M'lord shouldn't worry. His people at Tentir knew his mind.

*Ha,* thought Torisen. He wished that he knew it himself.

Harn nudged him. "Company."

Two riders were coming down the New Road, one a randon guard, the other...damn. A lady. Torisen mopped his sweaty face, silently cursing.

He had thought that, here in the middle of a hay field, he would be safe from the Matriarchs. As Rowan had predicted, their schemes had grown subtler since the farce of the first few days, but they were far from giving up. Over the past few weeks he had been presented with everything from an unhappy bald girl, her head newly shaven (someone must have noticed his strong reaction to long, black hair, but taken it the wrong way), to the wide-eyed seven-year-old who had first asked him to marry her outside Adiraina's quarters.

Occasionally, on the sly, he visited the Jaran Matriarch Trishien to reassure himself that all Highborn women weren't mad; and if she should have news of Jame by way of Kirien, all the better, although he took care never to ask directly.

Rowan's suggestion floated in the back of his mind. If nothing else, it would be sweet to confound them all by taking his sister as his consort—only for show, of course.

Torisen slipped back on the black jacket that he had discarded in the heat. One should show one's enemies respect, and wear whatever protection was available.

"Hello!"

He straightened, surprised at the hail. Decorum kept most of his would-be consorts silent, except for the seven-year-old whose naive, highly improper stream of questions no one had been able either to stop or to divert.

Then he recognized the newcomer as Lyra, Caineron's young daughter, and relaxed. It was hard to feel threatened by a girl nicknamed "Lack-wit." Besides, at Kithorn she had stopped her sister Kallystine from slapping him with the same razor ring that his former consort had used to slash Jame's face. Even if the girl's interference had been an accident, as she claimed, he owed her for it.

Not waiting for help, Lyra tumbled off her pony in a swirl of flame red velvet and plunged across the rough meadow toward him. Bemused Kendar drew aside to let her pass. From the freedom with which she moved, Torisen guessed that she had left her tight underskirt back in the Women's Halls. Then she saw Marc and threw herself into his arms with a squeal of delight.

"I saw you in the courtyard, working with all those pretty bits of glass, but they wouldn't let me go out to say hello. Hello!"

Marc laughed, gently returning her enthusiastic hug. The top of her head only came up to the lower edge of his rib cage. "I saw you too, lady, at an upper window waving and, I think, shouting. Then someone pulled you away."

"That was the sewing mistress. It's so funny when she gets hysterical. Just ask, 'Why?' and off she goes. Young ladies aren't supposed to ask questions, you see, which I think is stupid, so I ask them all the time."

"You must be very popular with your teachers," said Torisen, amused. "I didn't realize that you knew Marcarn."

"Oh yes!" She turned to beam at him—quite a pretty girl, actually, from what one could see behind her deceptively demure half-mask; and no fool either, despite her nickname and manner. "Marc rescued us from the palace at Karkinaroth. That was after it caught fire and before it fell down, of course. In between, poor Prince Odallian died." Her pert face dimmed at the memory, a cloud crossing the sun, but immediately brightened again. "Then we three rode a barge down the Tardy to Hurlen, along with that darling ounce Jorin. That was fun. Such exciting things happen when your sister is around!"

"I've noticed," he said, with a smile that was half grimace. "But she's not here now. To what do we owe the honor of your presence, lady? Surely the Matriarchs didn't send you."

"Oh no," she said blithely. "They threw a bucket of water over the sewing mistress, just when she was getting interesting, and sent me to my room to practice knot stitches, but that's so boring! Nearly everything is, in the Women's Halls. I'd ask to go home, but Kallystine would probably kill me. Anyway, I just had to get out of the Halls for a while. I would have come alone, except Marrow here spotted me and besides I needed help with the basket. I thought I'd bring you a picnic lunch. It *is* almost noon, you know."

Torisen had noticed the wicker hamper that the cadet guard Marrow carried self-consciously slung over her arm. He also noted that harried look on her face of someone rushed into something without time to think it through. No doubt her captain would give her seven kinds of hell over this later.

Lyra spread a white garment over the hummocky stubble—so she hadn't left her underskirt behind after all—and dumped the contents of the basket onto it.

"There!" she said. "I brought some of everything that I like to eat."

Torisen accepted a purple sugarplum scrolled with cream frosting. Marzipan, chocolate rolled in crumbled walnut, snails encased in ginger shells...the Caineron larder was obviously much better stocked with luxuries than the Knorth, and probably with everything else as well.

"So you know our kitten as well as our Marcarn." Harn popped something bright green into his mouth, made a face, and swallowed it whole. "I think that one was still alive."

"Well, you wouldn't want to eat a *dead* candied cockroach, would you? Oh yes, Jame and I are like sisters. After Hurlen, though, we didn't see each other again until she showed up at Restormir just before the weirdingstrom. *You* know," she added, turning to Brier. "You were there too."

"I've heard something about that," said Harn. He eyed the rest of Lyra's offerings, but didn't take any. Around them Kendar were settling down to their more mundane repasts, pretending not to listen. "What *did* happen, cadet?"

The rest of Brier's ten in the second row stared at her with ill-concealed horror. Vant, down the line, went white under his peeling sunburn. The story was by now well known in the barracks at Tentir, with many unintended embellishments gained by repetition. So far, though, no senior randon had gotten around to asking for a formal account of it, probably afraid of what they would hear.

Brier gave her report in a voice so flat that one could have rolled a marble across it. They had encountered the lordan while on patrol. She had stated that her servant Graykin was Lord Caineron's prisoner and that she was honor bound to rescue him. They had helped her accomplish this.

Everyone waited for the Southron to go on, but she had come to a full stop. Vant sighed with relief.

"Oh, you don't know how to tell a story at all!" said Lyra impatiently. "Listen. Everyone was up in the Crown—that's Restormir's tower—getting beastly drunk and making a row. I was with Gran in her rooftop garden, but she sent me down to fetch some food from the kitchen, and who do you think I ran into there? Jame and a bunch of cadets, chasing a chicken. No, that's not quite right. My uncles and cousins and brothers were chasing it to make soup— Father's drinking had made all our servants sick, you see, so we had to fend for ourselves—and it (the chicken) ran into the pantry where we were hiding. That's when Jame told me why she was there. Gricki—that is, Graykin—used to be my servant at Karkinaroth. He's also my half-brother by some Southron kitchen maid. Anyway, Father was mad at him for changing houses and so he jabbed all these red-hot hooks through his skin."

Lyra paused, remembering, suddenly sober. "He screamed," she said. "A lot. No one should have to scream like that.

"Anyway, then Father attached wires and swung him out into the Crown's central shaft. For a while he made him dance like a puppet. Then he got bored and left, thinking that the hooks would eventually tear through Gricki's skin and that he would fall all the way down to the Pit."

"That's a good two hundred feet," one Kendar muttered to another. Both had turned pale at the thought of dangling from such a height. Others also looked sick.

"But he didn't fall," Lyra continued. "We reeled him in...well, I helped a bit...and unhooked him. By then, though, Father was coming. I ran. Then Father caught you."

She looked up at Brier, a bit uncertainly.

"He said something about binding you by the seed, whatever that means, and ordered you to kneel. It scares me when he uses that voice. Somehow, there's no disobeying it. I was back on top in Gran's garden by then, kneeling on the edge, so I couldn't see anything, but I could hear. Jame said, 'BOO!' and Father said, 'HIC!' and the next thing I know, he bobs out over the rail, into the shaft, floating upside down with his pants undone and flapping in his face."

"Sweet Trinity," breathed Harn. "Sheth said something at the Cataracts about Caineron 'not quite feeling in touch with things.' What in Perimal's name did our kitten do to him?"

"I don't know," said Lyra, "but he's terrified of her. Then she said, 'Make sport of decent Kendar, will you? Play God almighty in your high tower, huh? Well, the next time the urge takes you, remember me. And this. And keep looking down.'

"Then he started to scream.

"Brier, you said, 'You don't know what you've done.'

"And she said, 'I seldom do, but I do it anyway. This is what I am, Brier Iron-thorn. Remember that.'

"And neither of us ever will forget, will we? Because she said it in a voice just like Father's."

# II

FOR A MOMENT, no one spoke.

The wind shifted to and fro between them, swirling eddies of chaff like ghosts trying to rise from the shorn field, then slumping back among the rows. Vanguards of the north wind and of the tardy Tishooo from the south skirmished in the upper air.

Harn shot Torisen a look under his heavy brows. "Remind me later to tell you about something else that's happened. At Tentir. Concerning Caineron's councilor Corrudin."

Torisen didn't want to hear it. He had heard too much already.

Lyra's recitation had left her looking frightened, as if she hadn't realized what she was going to say until she had said it. Now she jumped and squealed as a dead bird plummeted to earth beside her. They were falling all over the field. So was a light fall of what at first appeared to be dirty snow. The clouds were almost upon them, growling with muffled thunder, pulling a shroud over the sun.

Marc tasted a flake that had fallen on his hand and spat it out. "Ash," he said. "I was afraid of this. Some mountain to the north has blown its top."

The harvest-master bustled up, scowling. "That hasn't happened in my lifetime," he said, as if to assert that it wasn't possible now. "Say you're right, though, we're way to the south. How much of the damn stuff could we possibly get?"

"Anywhere from a dusting to several feet." Marc looked apologetic. "Usually Old Man Tishooo blows the worst of it northward over the Barrier, but this time he seems to have been slow off the mark. It may also rain."

The master stared at him, then cast a wild glance at the upper terraces where cat's-paws of wind tossed the ripening grain in its gleaming bands. Golden brown barley bowed to shine silver gold. Wheat bent more stiffly, its beards of grain barely open.

"We might gather some," he muttered. "A few bushels of early wheat, at least, or rye, or oats, just in case…"

Torisen glanced at Marc, who shook his head. There wasn't time. "We must save what we can here in the water meadow," he said, "and hope for the best."

The master looked stricken. Just as hay was vital to the beasts' winter survival, so the Greater Harvest at summer's end was to anything on two legs.

But it wasn't famine that scared the Kendar, Tori realized. He was afraid that if supplies ran short, his lord would send most of his people south while he himself stayed to hold the keep with a token garrison. As weak as the Highlord had recently shown himself to be, to leave Gothregor unguarded was to risk having it seized by a stronger house. On the other hand, of those he sent away, how many would he forget? Mullen had flayed himself alive to escape such a fate.

All the weight of his position fell back on his shoulders, no longer to be escaped, harder than ever to bear. *They depend on me. I gave them that right when I assumed my father's place.*

He touched the Kendar's shoulder.

"It will be all right, Stav." *Somehow.* "Carry on."

The harvest-master blinked at the sound of his own name, and that sudden flare of panic faded from his eyes. He gave his lord a brusque, awkward nod and turned to the assembled troops. "Forget the last standing grass. Get those hayricks covered. Move!"

As Kendar sprang into action all over the field, Marc picked up a frightened Lyra, set her on her pony's back, and handed the reins to the already mounted cadet guard. "Ride for Gothregor," he said. "Fast. Tell them to bring in the livestock, hood the wells, close all chimney dampers, secure the shutters, and stuff as many cracks as possible with rags. At the very least, this is going to be messy." Lyra yelped as lightning split the sky and her pony shied. "Go. We'll follow as quickly as we can. And don't lock us out!" he bellowed after them.

At the bottom of their loads, all wains carried mats woven of wiry rye stalks. Kendar now hauled these out and started to pitch them over the hayricks. It took four to cover each stack. Frantic hands laced together the edges with wisps of straw and bound them to iron rings set in the stone foundations. Before some mats could be secured, they tore free to flap and flail while swearing Kendar fought to control them.

The winds were picking up, and they came from both directions. The Tishooo and the northern wind clashed overhead, warm and cold, clear and ash-laden, roiling together, with sudden cracks of blue sky between them and sharper cracks of lightning. Wrestling funnels dipped and swayed above the field, lashing it with their tails. Chaff flew. Horses screamed. Then the stack which Torisen was trying to cover exploded in his face.

Nearby, a Kendar cried out as the wind drove sharp straws like needles into her eyes.

Torisen found himself flat on his back, staring up at an ascending maelstrom of hay. It seemed to take shape as it rose, assuming the nebulous form of something huge with wings that spanned the entire valley. There might or might not have been the figure riding it, an old man whose beard streamed behind him. Against him came the clouds of ash, and they too had gained both form and voice.

"*Wha, wha, wha?*" howled the roiling, black figures of the Burning Ones. "*Tha!*

They dove at Torisen.

*My father's curse*, he thought, watching them come. *My own weakness. I deserve this.*

The wolver pup Yce was suddenly crouching over him with her oversized paws heavy on his chest and her white teeth bared at the falling sky. The thing of hay and wind swooped, every straw pricked to the attack, but what good is chaff against fire? Torisen threw his arms around the pup and rolled to protect her as flaming debris rained down on them. He found himself holding a small body shaken by its own pounding heart. Small hands, short fingered, long nailed, clutched his shirt. A child looked up at him with terrified blue eyes set in a mask of creamy fur, then buried her face against his chest. He tightened his grip.

*Me, you can have; her, never.*

The field burned around them, but the flames cast curiously little light. Falling ash had clamped a tight, black bowl over the earth. In the outer darkness, things fought with muffled bellows of thunder, but not even the lightning stroke of their blows penetrated the gloom. Then the sky split open and the deluge descended like a cataract.

The fires hissed out.

The world filled with noise and hard driven water.

Torisen stumbled to his feet, still clutching the child who was also a wolf, and nearly fell again. Mixed ash and mud slithered under foot, in a blinding rain. It had also turned surprisingly cold.

Would the other ricks stand, or had they already lost the Lesser Harvest? Where was everyone? Please Trinity someone had pulled the injured Kendar to safety and tended her wounds. It was a terrible thing to be maimed. Kindrie could help her, but he wasn't here. Because of Torisen. Because of something the healer had seen or felt in that moment when their hands had touched, his cringing at the mere thought of accepting a Shanir, the other's thin and cool and suddenly withdrawn.

*"My lord, I can't do it."*

Why? What corruption in him could repel one already tainted by the Old Blood? What, but a father's curse?

*I am doomed and damned*, he thought. *That too perhaps I deserve, but not my people as well!*

A vertical crack of light opened in the chaos and widened slightly. As it did so, faint horizontal lines joined it above and below. Trinity. It was a door, in the middle of a field. As he stood gaping at it, a familiar voice spoke from inside:

"Well? Don't you know enough to come in out of the rain?"

# III

TORISEN DECIDED THAT he was dreaming, or had finally gone barking mad. Either seemed more likely that that the destroyed haystack had been built around such a large, stone hut, or rather a full-sized lodge. Down several steps was an earthen floor covered with lumpy forms. Opposite, a small fire smoked and flared on a sunken hearth, its light picking out low rafters from which hung an odd assortment of shapes. Most appeared to be drowsy bats and foxkin but one, larger, rustled leathery wings and glared sleepily at him with obsidian eyes set in a wizened, almost human face.

"Watch out for that one," said Jame behind him, closing the door. "It blew north with the weirdingstrom, and I don't think it's had a decent meal since."

As his eyes adjusted to the gloom, Torisen saw that the room was full of sleeping creatures. Hawks and sparrows, side by side, perched one-legged on the mantle, chair backs, and the enormous antlers of a snoring moose. Badgers and otters rolled up together for warmth under a table. That huge mound by the door was a cave bear, covered by a living coat of ermine which rose and fell with his stentorian breathing. As for the cauldron of water beside him, surreptitiously seething…

Stiff whiskers broke the surface, then a wide, gaping mouth and a pair of round, knowing eyes.

"Bloop," said the catfish solemnly, and sank back out of sight.

"What *is* all this?" Torisen asked, more convinced than ever that he had fallen into some insane dream.

"They're refugees, of course."

Jame picked her way across the room to a chair next to the fire. "Not everyone could get to shelter when the ash-flow came…"

She removed a hedgehog from the seat and settling it in a basket of knit-work on the floor.

"Quip!" said the knitting in drowsy protest.

"…but a lot did. It must have been a madhouse in here before Mother Ragga told them all to shut up and go to sleep."

She stepped up onto the chair, balancing carefully on its arms as it creaked under her, and began to do something to the upper end of an unusually large bundle suspended from the rafters.

The wolver pup wriggled out of Torisen's arms and bounded toward the hearth, where a cat rose, hissing, to meet him. It was a surprisingly big cat, Torisen noted, as its arched back rose higher and higher. Flames surrounded it in a nimbus of red-gold, bristling fur and its eyes reflected only fire.

"You'd better call off your friend," said Jame. "Jorin is in no mood for games, and I haven't the time. Who is she, anyway?"

"Yce, an orphan from the Deep Weald, or so Grimly tells me."

"Ice?"

"Close enough. It's a wolver term for a frozen crust over deep snow. The name seemed appropriate."

Pup and ounce met on the hearth. After a moment's hostile posing for honor's sake, they settled down side by side, not touching and studiously ignoring each other, to watch the fire.

"This is a very strange place," said Torisen, wiping rain out of his eyes the better to see it. "Where are we?"

"Inside the Earth Wife's lodge, which in turn could be anywhere. It moves around a lot. I found it in a meadow near Kithorn, just before a volcano caught up with me. Now I'm guessing we're closer to Gothregor, or were when you came through the door. But I'm forgetting my manners. Mother Ragga, this is my brother Torisen, Highlord of the Kencyrath. Tori, this is Mother Ragga, also known as the Earth Wife."

The lower edge of the bundle stirred. Knobby hands lifted what turned out to be the hem of an inverted outer skirt and a florid, upside-down face peered out, like a pudding hanging in a sack.

"Highlord, eh? About time we met. Welcome to my house, if not necessarily to my world."

The features started to rotate sickeningly, as if for a better look, but Jame gave her a warning slap.

"Stop that. D'you want to get stuck with your head on the wrong way?"

Torisen saw that the upper end of the bundle was a much patched underskirt held up, as was the whole body, by a rope around the ankles. Above that, close to the supporting beam, were a pair of enormously swollen feet. Jame resumed squeezing the sausage-like toes as if trying to milk an upside-down cow.

"That tickles!" protested Mother Ragga.

"I told you, this isn't my sort of job."

"What," asked Torisen, bemused, "hanging old women up by their heels?"

"That either. But Kindrie is the healer, not me—not that he could probably do any better. Y'see, the volcano melted all the fat in her body and it settled to what was then the lowest point. I'm trying to work it back into place before it cools and hardens where it is. This was her idea, by the way, and it seems to be working, if slowly."

The bundle twitched irritably. "Well, hurry up! I'm getting dizzy." Then she yelped as she was suddenly jerked up, her feet jamming hard against the underside of the rafter. Dislodged dust drifted down.

"Chumley!" Jame called into the darkness at the end of the room. "Stand still, you great lummox!"

Torisen traced the taut line of rope over the beam and down into the gloom. Beyond the mounds of sleeping animals, he could just make out an enormous pair of hindquarters with a flaxen tail swishing complacently between them. The rope appeared to be secured to the beast's other end.

"There's horse in the corner," he said. "Also, I think, a meadow."

He could see now that the room had no far wall. Where it should have been, there was a sea of grass lit only by the dance of fireflies and a few reluctant stars low on the horizon. Night, and no mountains. They were no longer in the Riverland, or at least that side of the lodge wasn't. Unconcerned, the big horse continued to graze.

"This is madness," he said.

"Oh, for Ancestors' sake." Jame stopped squeezing the Earth Wife's toes and began vigorously to knead her calves through the patched underskirt, ignoring muffled squawks of pain and a certain amount of thrashing below. "You must have seen as many strange things as I have—well, almost as many. Neither of us has led an exactly normal life. Things happen to us. Powers seek us out. You know that, although you seem Perimal-bent on denying it. How can either of us be sure what's sane and what isn't?"

Torisen started to protest then stopped, considering his words. "We are a house noted for our madness, or so everyone says. Are they wrong? What about our father?"

His sister paused, frowning. "There's more to his story than we were ever told—if not enough to forgive him, perhaps enough to understand and take warning. Tori, since Summer Eve, have you had any strange dreams?"

He stiffened, remembering a flurry of them, some of which he had no intention of repeating to his sister. "All dreams are strange. What about it?"

She also looked acutely ill at ease, but determined. "I had one that first night at Tentir and another, later. Do you remember dreaming that you were a cadet at the college, and being summoned up to the lordan's quarters late one night?"

He did. Twice. Trinity, that second time...

"Do you remember who you were, and who waited for you on the hearth, wearing a particular coat?"

His mouth felt dry. "It was beautiful, all the colors of creation, but the man wearing it..."

"...was Greshan, our uncle. A monster. It was also me, somewhere inside him, only able to watch through his foul eyes. And you were there too, inside a young Ganth, our father."

He remembered, as hard as he had tried to forget. "So? It was only a dream." After all, he had been cured, mysteriously, miraculously, of those nightmares that had driven him to the edge of madness—or had he only been relieved of the foresight that had led him to try so hard to fight them off?

She sighed. "Perhaps they are only nightmares, frightening but harmless. I hope you're right. If not, though, I have to warn you: there will be at least one more, maybe several, in that room, before that hearth, and the last will be worse than all the others rolled up together. Something terrible happened to our father there. No one alive today knows what it was, but something at Tentir seems to be trying to show me, to show us.

"Tori, listen: There have been schemes within schemes, enemies behind enemies, treachery, murder, bloody betrayal. What happened to our house was no accident. I'm sure of that, although I don't yet understand it all. But what started then isn't over yet, however strange its course has been. Some of the answers lie at Tentir."

She gave him a quick, almost feral smile, all white teeth and a flash of inhuman, silver eyes.

"Trust me in this at least: I'm good at hunting down hidden enemies."

He believed her, and it frightened him.

She had turned back to contemplate the Earth Wife's swaying feet. "Y'know, I think that bump did more to shift things than all my prodding has. Chumley, again."

Obligingly, the massive horse shifted back and forth where he stood, with each forward surge reaching farther for fresh tufts of grass. Thud, thud, thud went the soles of the swollen feet against the rafter, to accompanying yelps from below.

"Oh, stop complaining, you big baby. You did ask me to hurry up. This is my revenge," she murmured aside to Torisen, "for a good many frights and indignities. No doubt she'll get her own back later, by the bucketful, and I'll be lucky to survive it."

The prospect, however, didn't seem to alarm her. What kind of a life had she led, to take such things so casually?

*Don't ask.*

Instead, he regarded her intently, seeking reassurance. They were, after all, twins. How different could they be?

Both had always been slight and fine-boned, even for Highborn, but quick and agile. If he was stronger, she made up for it by constantly surprising him. She did so now, stepping up onto the chair's back and balancing there as it teetered, apparently for a closer look at the thumping progress. She moved like a dancer or a fighter, with easy balance and a chilling disregard for personal safety. Like her, he took far too many unnecessary risks, or so Harn kept telling him.

Torisen also didn't think much about his own appearance. If his servant Burr caught him at a weak moment, he might consent to wear the Highlord's finery, but otherwise why bother? Plain, simple, and black suited him best. Maybe that was why in part he hadn't thought to supply his sister with garments befitting her rank. For that matter, she hadn't asked for them. She didn't seem to care much about what she wore either, given some of the clothes he had seen her in—that outlandish dress at the Cataracts, for example, formerly the property of an overweight Hurlen streetwalker. Given a preference, though, she also seemed to favor plain and black, like that oddly cut jacket slung aside on the floor.

Was she handsome?

People kept telling him that they both had the classic Knorth features. For that matter, several times she had been mistaken for him on the battlefield—something which he found profoundly disturbing.

Was she beautiful?

Not by the standards of Kallystine's voluptuous charms that had drawn him despite his better judgment. His former consort had been adept at intoxicating the senses, but with an after-taste that had made him both loathe and mistrust his own passion. One of the Highborn subsequently thrown at him, a ridiculously young Ardeth girl, had seen enough to suggest that Kallystine had used potions to entrap him.

Women.

He would trust his life and honor to most Kendar, but to few Highborn. Kirien and the Matriarch Trishien, maybe, but Jame?

Did he trust his own sister?

*No!* said the voice in the back of his mind. *Never!*

Yet he felt drawn to that lithe body with its clean, spare lines and to that wry smile as to a cool breath in an overheated room. If Kallystine had been poison, perhaps here was the antidote.

Then, for the first time, he realized that Jame wasn't wearing gloves. Even with their nails sheathed, those long, slim fingers made him shiver, threat and promise in one touch.

Her face also looked oddly bare, and not for the lack of a mask.

"What happened to your eyebrows?"

She touched her forehead, annoyed. "I got too close to a fire. So did you, apparently. Your jacket may be soaked, but it's also scorched and still smoldering."

Torisen shrugged it off and dropped it on a pile of snow-footed ferrets, who woke briefly to quarrel among themselves before settling back to sleep under the reeking cloth.

Now that he looked, he saw that her clothes were also charred in patches and hanging in long strips, as if fiery claws had tried but failed to catch her. The heavy fall of her long black hair covered her better than the tattered remains of her shirt, although both slid away from delicate curves as she moved. Had the Burning Ones been after her too? If so, why? She had her own secrets, he reminded himself, years' worth of them between the time when their father had driven her out and when he had taken her back in.

As he studied her, so she did him.

"There were strands of white in your hair the last time I saw you," she said. "Now they're gone. So are your scars."

Torisen stared at his unmarked hands. He had grown so used to the phantom pain of the Karnids' red-hot gloves that only now, when it was gone, did he miss it.

"For the first time since we were children," she said slowly, giving voice to his sudden dread, "I think that we're the same age."

They regarded each other, she (infuriatingly) amused, he on the verge of panic.

"For how long?"

"Probably only while we're in the Earth Wife's lodge. Mother Ragga, is this your idea of a joke?"

Between grunts as her horny soles hit the rafter, something like a stifled chuckle emerged from the inverted skirt. "...seemed only fair. Taking advantage..."

"I was not!" Torisen burst out, and then, to his horror, found himself blushing as he hadn't since his youth. Trinity, was he about to be thrown back to those long-gone, miserable days? On the whole he would rather drop dead, here and now, than live through them again. Maybe Jame would too.

*Had* he taken unfair advantage of the years he had gained on her? After all, they were twins and always would been, however strangely their lives had diverged. He wasn't even sure which one of them had been born first. But that didn't matter. As the male, he would always come first and she be his inferior—but that wasn't how it felt. Did he need to be older, to feel that he had control over her, and why was that so important anyway?

*Because destruction begins with love, and you love her.*

"No," he said out loud. When in doubt, attack. "Lyra tells me that you ordered her father to step off a balcony two hundred feet up, and he did."

"You disapprove?"

"No. I mean, yes! Who are you to order the lord of any house to do something like that, and what did you do to Caldane at the Cataracts anyway?"

"Finally, you ask! He held me prisoner in his tent, and I had to escape to bring you Father's ring and sword. I slipped him a powder I had picked up on my travels, not knowing that it would do to him, at that point not really caring." She suddenly grinned. "If you ever want to get an...er...rise out of m'lord Caldane, just startle him into an attack of the hiccups."

"Harn said something about Caineron's advisor, Corrudin." He didn't want to know, but could no more prevent himself from asking than he had from fretting endlessly about his bandaged hand. "What did you do to him?"

"That filthy man." Her abrupt, deep anger made the room's temperature drop. Rumbling, sleepy complaints rose from all sides. "He tried to make me order Brier Iron-thorn to lick the mud off my boots. I told him to back off and he did, right out a third story window. I wish he had broken his neck."

"'This is what I am,'" Torisen quoted, teeth chattering, breath hanging on the air. "'Remember that.'"

"Yes. Sorry. Corrudin and I both abused our power, which probably makes me no better than he is, at least in Brier's eyes. I do care what she thinks, you know, and Marc, too. If they disapprove, then I've still gotten it wrong somehow. It's so hard to find a balance. Sweet Trinity, haven't you ever made someone do something he or she didn't want to?"

"Not like that!"

Even as he spoke, however, he remembered forcing the Ardeth Matriarch Adiraina to tell him what had happened to his sister in the Women's Halls that winter. Afterward, Grimly had called it "a good trick," and he had nearly snapped the Wolver's head off for suggesting that he had done anything unusual. It wasn't the same, though. It couldn't be. He certainly didn't feel that power in himself now. On the other hand, this young body didn't know that the man who had sired it was dead. In this strange house, in this displaced moment, that authority hadn't yet passed to him.

Then again, perhaps it never had, and never would.

*"Damn you, boy, for deserting me. Faithless, honorless...I curse you and cast you out. Blood and bone, you are no son of mine..."*

Words spoken in searing bitterness by a dying man. By his father. How could any curse be more terrible?

To his horror, he felt himself growing younger, smaller, while the edges of the Earth Wife's lodge dimmed around him into the dusty corners of the Haunted Lands keep where he had grown up, which he never seemed able entirely to escape.

"Tori, stop it!"

She had jumped down from the chair and crossed the room to seize him. As her nails bit into his shoulders, the keep faded.

Something crunched, and the wolver pup backed off, shaking her head. Seeing him apparently under attack, she had bitten his sister's leg, or tried to. Something white and hard showed through Jame's torn pants at shin level.

"Oh no, child," she said to Yce. "You don't want to taste my blood, or my brother's either." And Torisen knew, somehow, that the pup would never try to again.

"What's happening to you?" he demanded. While he could clearly see the fine lines of her face, simultaneously it wore a sketchy half-mask of ivory, more like a rudimentary helm than any frivolous product of the Women's World. Then the ivory faded as had the shadows of the keep, although he sensed that neither had gone far.

"This lodge exists in Rathillien's sacred space. From there, it seems to be a short step to the Kencyr soulscape. I don't entirely understand that. It may be as the Earth Wife wills, or as our needs demand. My soul-image is changing. They can, you know. You should try it. Get away from that foul keep, from that voice of madness, before it's too late!"

"'Daddy's boy. Run. Hide.'"

"Er...sorry. I didn't mean it quite like that, and I don't think I told you to hide. Oh, Perimal. You can't leave, can you? Not while that door stays locked with half of what you are on the other side."

This time he grabbed her, hard. "What are you talking about? Filthy Shanir, what have you done to me?"

She didn't flinch, but her gaze was stricken. "Now you sound like Father. I've gotten it wrong again, haven't I? Kindrie told me as much. But I was only trying to help, to buy you some time. You weren't ready then to open that door. Are you now?"

Involuntarily, he glanced over his shoulder at what was some-how the door both to the Earth Wife's lodge and to the ramparts of the Haunted Lands' keep.

Someone knocked on it.

Without thinking, the twins found themselves in each other's arms. Torisen held his sister tight, his face buried in the glorious richness of her hair as if to hide in it. Her breasts pressed against him in odd, soft contrast to the firm, boyish lines of her body beneath his hands. Gray eyes met gray, mirroring each other. Her lips tasted like wild honey, sweet and bitter at once.

"Stay," she murmured. "I will stay with you."

*Thump, thump, thump,* fists on the door, feet on the rafters, his heart against his ribs...

On the keep stairs, heavy footsteps descended. Two children huddled together in bed, terrified. They had heard him in the room above, smashing Mother's things, raving. *"Betrayed, betrayed, whore, slut, love...oh, return to me, return!"* Now he was coming for them, the last vestige of her that he possessed, the last bit that he could still hurt, and if he found them together...

Torisen thrust his sister away in sudden panic. "I can't stay. I won't."

He had to get out. Better anywhere than here.

The door flew open as he threw himself at it and he fell out, face first. The wolver pup landed on his back and bounded off again, driving him yet deeper into the mud.

"Well," said Harn's voice over him, hoarse with exasperation and relief. "There you are at last."

# IV

JAME STARED AT the door. It had swung shut in her face, but not before she had glimpsed the gray, sodden hay field beyond and recognized Gothregor's outline against a leaden northern sky. At least Tori was safely home. Just the same...

"Damn, damn, damn," she muttered, touching her lips where his lips had touched them. Her whole body tingled from that unexpected contact, which had been almost as much an assault as a kiss. But if so, who had attacked whom, and why did she long for a rematch?

She turned, and the bat-thing from the south lunged at her, all gaping mouth and teeth, hissing. She punched it in the face. Its nose flattened with a faint crunch of cartilage, and its red eyes crossed.

"Oh, go suck an egg," she told it as it slunk, whimpering, into a corner.

Then she went to let Mother Ragga down before all the fat went to her head.

# Chapter XX:  The Bear Pit

## Summer 68 - 90

### I

EVERYONE AGREED AFTERWARD that it had been the most eventful Minor Harvest in living memory.

All the northern keeps received at least a dusting of ash and a day of darkness, reeking of sulfur, not unlike the end of the world. Beasts ran mad in the fields, the Silver seethed white with debris, and scrollsmen gleefully collected samples from the ramparts of Mount Alban.  Later, one swore that he had recreated a miniature volcano, but as the glass globe containing it immediately exploded, his claim went unrecorded—and no, colleagues said, the chaos to which his room had been reduced proved nothing, unless he wanted to credit the college kitchen with similar feats of spontaneous creation on a daily basis.

Gothregor suffered the worst of ash, wind, and rain, due to the clash of the north wind and the Tishooo directly overhead.  Half a dozen hay ricks were torn apart or burnt down, but the rest stood firm under their hoods of woven rye while their stone foundations raised them above the subsequent torrent of ash-laden mud.

The stepped fields above, however, were utterly destroyed, and their precious crops with them.

The only good thing was that a day later the Highlord had suddenly reappeared, face down and dazed but otherwise unhurt, in the middle of the ruined field.

The day after that, his sister the lordan Jameth limped back into Tentir by a side door, apparently hoping that her return would escape immediate notice.  It didn't.

Vant stopped short in the doorway of the Knorth barracks, staring at this dirty, singed apparition with its clothes hanging off it in rags and its eyebrows gone.

"Lady, what in Perimal's name happened to you?"

"Don't ask," she snarled, echoed by the ounce at her heels. "Just tell Rue to get me hot water, fresh clothes, and food.  Lots of it.  I'm starved."

# II

THE RANDON COLLEGE quickly settled back into its routine, with a growing sense of urgency. All too soon would come the autumn cull and the end of many hopes.

Jame in particular had cause to worry. After a slow start, she had lost more training time than any other cadet due to various mishaps, and now she was hindered by severely bruised if not broken ribs. Her ten-command began to look worried and Vant increasingly smug.

It disturbed her to learn, by accident, that the cull would not be like the summer testing, as she had assumed.

She and Timmon were on their way down from sword practice on the second floor of Old Tentir. Jame, as usual, had been disarmed with unnerving speed. This time the blade had spun straight out the window, to be caught below by the Commandant and returned with a polite request that in future the Knorth Lordan was, please, not to substitute disemboweling her instructors for driving them insane.

*Huh*, thought Jame sourly. Sheth hadn't even had to ask whose escaped weapon it was.

"That's another black stone for you, for sure," said Timmon cheerfully. "Maybe you'll break the college record and get all eleven of them. You know," he added, seeing her puzzled expression. "Black stone, white stone, leave or stay."

"I *don't* know. What are you talking about?"

"I keep forgetting. You weren't raised in the randon tradition, were you? See, each member of the Randon Council has one black stone and one white. That's..."

"Eighteen in all. I can count, you know."

"Actually, it's twenty-two, because the Highlord's war leader— Ran Harn, in this case—and the Commandant each get an extra black and white to play with. You look confused. Now, attend, child, while I teach you the facts of life."

He sat down on the steps, obliging her to do the same and other cadets to swerve, cursing, around them.

Jame gritted her teeth. She hated it when Timmon went all superior on her or forced her to follow his lead. Even more, though, she feared these sudden gulfs of ignorance that kept opening up under her feet, threatening to swallow her whole.

"Did you notice that rather severe Ardeth randon watching us at play just now, when you threw your sword out the window? Remember his gray silk scarf? That's the mark of a randon council member, one of nine, each a former commandant of Tentir except for the one currently wearing the white scarf."

"Sheth Sharp-tongue."

"Indeed. You may also have noticed other gray scarves wandering around the college recently. Even Harn Grip-hard had dug up some ratty bit of gray cloth to mark his rank—honestly, your house and its clothes! Anyway, they're taking note of the best and the worst of us. Sometime before Autumn Eve, they meet in the college Map Room to cast the stones.

"Imagine the scene: It's nightfall. The room is lit with a thousand candles, illuminating the murals of all our greatest battles. The Council sits in a circle on the floor. Behind each stands a sargent of his or her house. Also there's a scrollsman tucked away in a corner somewhere to keep score.

"So. Starting with the Highlord's house, the attendant randon calls out the name of each cadet in turn. As lordan, you'll come either first or last, as I will for the Ardeth. If no one casts a stone, you're in. The same goes for one or more unchallenged whites. Get only black, though, and you're out."

His blithe tone began to make Jame feel queasy. Of his own success, he apparently had no doubt. It was that stress on the second-person pronoun "you" that twisted her guts.

"Yes," she said, "but what if there's a mix of black and white stones?"

"Ah, then it gets interesting. In the second round, get at least six white stones and you're in, or at least six black and you're out. If it's four or five either way, though, they consider it too close to call, so on to round three, where Harn's and Sheth's extra stones come into play. There, simple majority rules."

"Enough," she said, standing up. "You're making my head hurt."

"Ah, don't fret." He also rose, with a laugh. "If you do get thrown out, you can always try a contract with me. Trust me, it would be fun. We could practice tonight, to see if we suit each other."

Just then, an Ardeth girl brushed past them on the way down the stairs, ramming her elbow into Jame's sore ribs as if by accident. Timmon caught her as she lurched sideways and nearly fell.

"Narsa!" he shouted after the descending Kendar. "Stop that!"

Jame caught her breath and drew herself upright, out of his embrace. She had recognized Timmon's one night conquest from so many weeks ago before he had given up trying to make her jealous.

"Still after you, is she?"

Timmon looked exasperated. "I keep telling her that it's over. Why won't she believe me?"

"You, my boy, have been a bit too free with your glamour, and don't look at me like that: You know what I mean."

"There was never a problem with it until you came along," he muttered, no longer meeting her eyes.

"None that you deigned to notice, anyway, and from now on stay out of my dreams. One of these nights, you're going to get hurt."

They had reached the great hall and stopped to watch the Danior cadet Tarn wrestling with a Molocar pup. Young as it was, all bumbling paws and flopping dewlaps, it easily bowled him over and sat on his chest, licking his face.

"The Caineron Lordan gave him to me," he explained, trying to escape its great, sloppy tongue. "We haven't bonded yet, and of course nothing can replace Torvo—Turvie, stop that!—but still..."

He laughed as the pup rolled onto its back, grinning idiotically, and presented its belly to be rubbed.

Jame pressed her hand to her forehead in sudden pain. "Ouch."

"Now what?" Timmon demanded, half solicitous, half exasperated.

"Nothing. Someone I've been expecting has just arrived." She flinched again. "Quit it! I hear you. I'm coming. Excuse me," she said to Timmon. "I've got to find the horse-master."

On the ramp down to the underground stable, she met Gorbel and the other four Highborn of his ten-command, on their way up from their last lesson of the day. The Caineron Lordan grunted when he saw her and would have limped past without speaking.

"It was kind of you to give Tarn that puppy," she said, stopping him.

"Huh." His eyes, bloodshot and sullen, refused to meet her own. Obviously his willow-infected foot still hurt despite Kindrie's best efforts. "Runt of the litter, wasn't it? Either that or throw it to the direhounds."

One of the Caineron made a low comment to another, and both snickered. Gorbel had come back from Restormir with a new set of Highborn "friends" or, more likely, spies for his father. Jame wondered how they could rank as cadets, arriving this late in the season, long past the tests. The Commandant hadn't said anything, but then neither had he about Gorbel.

At a guess, the Caineron Lordan had also gotten an earful from Caldane about fraternizing with the hated Knorth, however accidentally. Jame sighed. It looked as if they were going to be enemies again, not that they had ever had much of a chance at friendship. A shame, that: Gorbel was better than most of his house, when his father left him alone. She stepped aside and let him go.

The horse-master stood at the door of the tack-room, watching with disapproval as the five Kendar Caineron cleaned up after the Highborn whom they served.

"You ride it, you care for it," he muttered aside to Jame. "M'lord Gorbel knows that. What cause has he suddenly to go all high and mighty?"

"I think his father is riding him. Hard. And his foot hurts, which is partly my fault. Master, I need your help."

He raised bushy eyebrows at her. "*Now* what have you done, stampeded the herd off to Hurlen?"

"No, they're quite close," she said, somewhat distractedly, adding as if to the air, "*Stop* that, or d'you want me to start shouting back?"

"Here now, lady, are you all right?"

"Oh, I'm not the one hurt…much. Please, master, come with me, and bring your tools."

"Which? What for?"

"Overgrown hooves, back teeth that need floating, a bowed tendon, and a roast chicken. No, sorry, I'm supposed to bring that last one. Meet you at the north gate."

Some fifteen minutes later Jame emerged from Tentir with a soggy bundle hidden under her jacket, leaking grease onto her shirt. The horse-master waited, a bulging leather work-bag slung over his shoulder.

"I think," he said, "that you three lordan have run mad. That fool Timmon just tried to charm his way into coming too."

Of course his curiosity would have been piqued, thought Jame, looking anxiously about for the Ardeth's grinning face.

"No, no. I set him to cleaning tack—a proper punishment for all the times he's left his own mount in a muck sweat. The last I saw, the Caineron were jamming the tack-room door, pretending to be deaf and pointedly polishing spurs, with him boxed inside. Ha. Let him practice his guiles on that lot. Now, which way?"

Jame paused to check her mental compass. "West, above the college."

He grunted and set off. Like most of his charges, the horse-master had four gaits: walk, trot, canter, and bolt. Their brisk pace soon had Jame clutching a stitch in her side. They passed between the trees, climbing toward where the lower slopes of the Snowthorns were strewn with enormous, fallen boulders, like so many snaggle-teeth set in a giant's lower jaw. Most of them still had drifts of volcanic ash piled against their western sides where the pounding rain had failed to wash them completely away.

Rounding a huge rock, they came on a pale lady with long, white hair, sitting on a stone. She leaped up with a frightened cry, swayed, and became a Whinno-hir standing on three feet with the fourth raised, delicate hoof trembling.

The horse-master had stopped dead, staring. "M'lady? Bel-tairi? I thought you were dead!" He dropped his bag with a muffled, complicated crash and threw his arms around her neck. The mare suppressed a start, then bent her head gently to return the embrace.

A sharp clatter of hooves, and there was the rathorn colt, ears flat, crest rising all down his spine.

"It's all right!" Jame hastily stepped between them. "I told you: what do I know about these things? But he can help. Here." She tossed the soggy bag at the colt's feet. He ripped it open and began to tear at the roast fowl, all the time keeping a wary eye on the two Kencyr.

"Seems you've been busy, lady," said the horse-master to Jame. He blew his nose on his sleeve and reached for his tools. "Ancestors know, you're the last person on Rathillien I would expect to be keeping such company, nor yet a Whinno-hir with a rathorn, for that matter. How did it happen, and where's m'lady Bel been these forty years past, while we all mourned her as dead?"

While he bound the bowed tendon back into place and trimmed the mare's hooves, Jame tried to explain, if not the whole story, at least as much as applied to the two equines. It was, perforce, a narrative full of holes.

"Let's see if I've got this straight," said the horse-master at last, as he lifted one of Bel's rear hoofs and began to rasp it flat. "M'lady here gets branded by that bastard Greshan, then chased to the top of a mountain path where she finds a stone door opening into…what? Oh, right: the lodge of the Earth Wife, whoever that might be. There she falls asleep for the next forty-odd years until she hears Lady Kinzi's death banner calling to her. Once she's found that, she comes looking for you. At that point, four decades' worth of teeth and toenails all catch up with her at once."

"Er, yes, more or less." She noted that he had skipped over the mystery of Greshan's death, if indeed it was a mystery and not simply a hunting accident as Hallik Hard-hand had reported, before killing himself. On the other hand, how many would know the truth, besides those who had been there? "You believe me?"

"I'm not about to call the Highlord's sister a liar. Besides, here Bel-tairi is." He started gently to brush her mane away from the ruined side of her face, but let it alone when she flinched. Instead, he turned his attention to the overgrown sweep of her tail, tangled with briers but still magnificent. "A pity to cut that. Braid it, maybe, but later." He drew a long file out of his sack. "Open wide, m'lady."

When the Whinno-hir did, looking nervous, he unceremoniously slid his hand into her mouth, seized her tongue, and drew it out to one side.

"Here, make yourself useful. Hang on to this, firm but gentle. Don't pull it."

Jame found herself gripping that surprisingly thick, muscular organ. It twitched. The mare's eye rolled with alarm as the master slid the file between her back teeth and her raw, inner cheek, but Jame's hold immobilized her as he began to rasp away the barbs. The sound was awful.

A hot, menacingly snort blasted down the back of Jame's neck.

"Don't give me that look," she told the rathorn over her shoulder. "This is apparently how it's done, and it doesn't seem to hurt her."

"Not if done right," said the master briskly. "Change sides. Hold. And that's that. A few weeks for the mouth to heal, a bit longer for the tendon, decent forage with plenty of oats, and all will be right again."

"Except for her poor face," said Jame, watching the mare wander off, gingerly working her jaw.

"Well, yes. No helping that, worse luck, but one can live with scars, as well you know." He bent to clean and stow his tools. "About the rathorn, now. You say he's gotten himself blood-bound to you—a damn fool thing to do, but there it is. How d'you mean to handle that?"

Jame sat down on a rock and considered. The colt crouched some distance away like a great cat, pinning his prey with a dew-spur, occasionally raising his head to spit a bone at her.

How indeed?

So far, he had communicated with her mostly in blasts of raw emotion, usually rage or fear. He was intelligent, though, with a complex language of his own comprised, as far as she could tell, largely of scents and images. No doubt he already understood her better than she did him, although she suspected that he would pretend to misunderstand whenever it suited him. They hadn't come yet to a true test of wills.

*Just you try*, said those red, red eyes, with a glint of unholy anticipation.

Jame sighed. Sooner or later, she would have to. In the meantime, ancestors help them, they were stuck with each other.

The master stood and shouldered his bag. "You're going to need help," he said flatly.

Jame had been hoping for just such an offer, but now she hesitated. This was clearly a job as much for a dragon-tamer as for a horse-trainer; and while the bond between them prevented the colt from deliberately killing her, she sensed that he would cheerfully slaughter anyone else who annoyed him.

"I think," she said, "that he and I should get better acquainted first. I'm right, aren't I, that he's still too young to put under saddle?"

"By half a year at least, if he were a horse. With a rathorn, who knows?" He shook his head—in exasperation or amusement, it was hard to tell. "Mad, the pair of you. No, I won't speak of this to anyone, nor of m'lady Bel's return. Yet. Small blame to her, poor thing, but Trinity only knows what ancient stink her reappearance may stir up."

On the point of leaving, he paused and looked back at them with a sudden lop-sided smile under his flattened nose.

"Ah, but what a thing that will be, someday, to ride a rathorn—assuming he doesn't have you for breakfast first."

# III

THREE WEEKS PASSED.

By now Jame's ribs had healed, although the bruise on her side remained a wonder to behold, if anyone had been there to see it. On her return that first night, Graykin had announced that he had found lodgings more to his taste and had departed, meager possessions in hand. Jame wondered where he had gone and what he found, day after day, to occupy himself, but was too pleased at her sudden privacy to ask questions on the increasingly rare occasions when he reported to her. She hadn't realized until then how much she had grown to dislike his nightly, disapproving presence. God's claws, if she didn't care how she looked, why should he?

On the other hand, Harn had finally exerted his authority during her absence to repair the barracks roof. She supposed the work had to be done sometime. Still, it irked her not to see the stars at night slowly wheeling overhead or to wake in the morning with dew on her face.

*...rootless and roofless...*

Huh. Maybe she just didn't like roofs.

Worse, though, with the attic enclosed, for the first time she became aware of the stale reek of the lordan's quarters below, seeping up through the floor-boards. The smell gave her bad dreams, or rather the same dream over and over, in which she sat drunk beside a roaring hearth, listening with a terrible, gloating anticipation to hesitant steps as they approached on the outer stair. Then the door would open and she would see her brother's bewildered eyes set in their father's incongruously young, terrified face.

One night, the door opened and Timmon stood on the threshold, his smirk melting into dismay.

"Eek!" he said.

"You have the most uncomfortable dreams," he informed her the next day. "Just once, why can't I find you frolicking naked in a meadow or something?"

"I frolic poorly, and I did warn you. That dream is particularly dangerous. Stay out of it."

She certainly wished that she could, but some sly, malignant force seemed to be behind it, pushing. Sooner or later, as she had warned Tori, they would both have to see it through, but not just yet.

In the meantime, partly to escape it, partly to keep Bel and the rathorn company, she took to sleeping up among the boulders, sometimes waking in the early dawn to find herself bracketed by their warm bodies. Whenever that happened, the colt always lurched to his feet with a snort of disgust as if to say, *How dare you sneak up on me?*

Often, though, she woke to the arrival of the horse-master, come to apply fresh poultices and to re-bandage the mare's leg. A bowed tendon, obviously, was not to be taken lightly. As night turned to pallid dawn, he often stood with her by the hour in a mountain stream, up to their respective knees in icy water and his flat nose running with the cold. Meanwhile, a diet of oats and lush summer grass began to fill in the flesh between her ribs and to restore the gloss to her coat.

The colt foraged for himself, although he still complained bitterly whenever Jame forgot to bring him treats or anything other than his beloved roast fowl.

"So learn how to catch and cook them yourself," she told his retreating back as he stalked away from an offering of (admittedly) rather tough stewed kidneys.

She emptied the sack on the ground in case he changed his mind and tucked her hands under her armpits to warm them. It might be summer, but mornings on the mountain were cold. She missed her gloves, the last pair having gone up in flames while rescuing the Earth Wife. Rue could knit her mittens by the dozen, but was struggling with bits of soft leather to make acceptable alternatives with fingers.

The horse-master came back with the Whinno-hir limping after him. "Fifteen minutes' walk twice a day," he said. "Slow and sure. Not to fret, lass: she's getting there, although things would go much faster with a few leaves of comfrey and yarrow from your grandmother's moon garden. That in a mash of linseed oil and mangle-wart would do wonders."

He paused. "A word of warning: sleeping up here is all well and good, and I daresay that colt won't let anything happen to you, however foul his temper, but be careful. The hill-tribes have started raiding southward earlier than usual, and coming in larger numbers. There's already been trouble at Restormir and Valantir with their outlying herds. I dunno what's gotten into old Chingetai. He must realize that if his folk start killing ours, there'll be Perimal to pay."

Jame wondered too. The Merikit had made a proper mess of their midsummer rites and were lucky as a result not to have been buried up to their necks in volcanic ash or mud slides, if not molten lava. Could the chief's power be so undermined that he had to prove himself with these dangerous raids or—here was a thought— what about the tribes living farther north, near the Barrier, whom the Earth Wife had mentioned? Thanks to Chingetai's earlier scheme, the Merikits' territory now lay open and unguarded in all directions.

Below in New Tentir, the morning horn sounded.

*Late again,* Jame thought, dashing breathless into the square with Jorin on her heels. Rue slipped a chunk of bread into her hand as she passed. At least she had managed to enforce her order that the rest of the Knorth eat breakfast whether she was there or not, despite Vant's protests. No doubt he had taken his complaint to higher authorities. Having heard nothing back, Jame only hoped that no one was keeping a secret ledger against her, full of black stones.

As she took her place before her house, twitching grass-stained clothes straight, the master sargent on duty stepped forward to announce the day's assignments. For Jame's ten, this amounted to field maneuvers and archery before lunch, the Sene and composition afterward, partnered respectively with ten-commands from the Coman, Danior, Edirr, and Jaran. Only the last caused a murmur of dismay among the Knorth: according to rumor, the scholarly Jaran were taught their letters before they learned how to walk. Now, how unnatural and unfair was that?

Nonetheless, Jame enjoyed her classes. Maneuvers involved not just formation work but directed attacks, each member of the ten responding to her gestures like the fingers of a hand. They were learning to work well together, knowing each other's strengths and weaknesses, trusting that however unorthodox her orders, they usually got results. There were, Jame supposed, some advantages in coming to such work with no preconceived ideas, assuming that one didn't confuse one's own command more than one did the enemy. In the meantime, it was rather fun to see how often she could make Brier blink with otherwise well-concealed surprise.

During archery practice, as an experiment, they blindfolded Erim and spun him around until he wobbled like a drunkard. His subsequent shots hit a half-inch sapling, a rabbit hole, and the sargent's hat. He could hit anything, he admitted afterward, somewhat shamefaced, as long as it wasn't alive.

After lunch, they practiced the Sene with the Edirr, who could be trusted to bring imagination and enthusiasm to any endeavor. It took skill to shift from Senetha to Senethar in time to the flute, which played for one but not for the other, stopping and starting at the player's whim. Dance to fight, fight to dance, the forms flowed together and apart. At one point, Jame found herself part of a line of Knorth dancers all moving as one, met by an Edirr row that mirrored their actions. At such a moment, it felt as if the world itself was finally coming into balance, the same thrill running down every nerve.

Then the instructor clapped to end the lesson.

Jame and her Edirr opposite relaxed and saluted each other with a mutual sigh of appreciation:

*Ah, that was nice.*

On the way to the last class, an unfamiliar sargent pulled Jame aside and directed her to follow him into a section of Old Tentir where she had never been before. There, he showed her into an interior room some thirty feet square, its wooden walls deeply gouged and prickly with splinters. Even more unusual, a wide circle had been cut in the ceiling so that it opened into the room above. A waist-high wall surrounded the hole and several dark figures lined it, back-lit by torches. The glimmers of a white scarf and of a pale gray one marked the presence of two randon council members.

The sargent handed Jame a padded jacket and a leather hood with a metal grill over the face, then withdrew. So, she thought, shrugging on the heavy coat and buckling it. This was the infamous fight pit, where the Arrin-thar was taught and cadets were thrown to the monster. After the last lesson, it felt like a sudden plunge into the dark heart of the Kencyrath, where secrets were sealed with spilt blood and tied up with entrails.

She wasn't surprised when the door opposite opened and Bear shambled in.

He was every bit as large as she remembered, barefoot, and as shabbily dressed. Tangled gray hair tumbled into the horrible cleft in his skull. He yawned, rubbed his eyes, then saw her and uttered a grunt of mingled surprise and interest.

She made herself stand still as he lumbered over to her, his personal miasma rolling forward with him. Trinity, didn't anyone ever provide the poor man with bath water? Then again, he might simply drink it. He touched her hair—since she had lost her last cap, she had taken to braiding it—and sniffed its scent on his fingertips. His claws were huge, more overgrown than the last time she had seen him and beginning to curve in on themselves, as did his toenails to the extent that walking must surely be painful. He took her hands, turned them over, and pressed the palms to make her own much smaller claws extend.

"Huh," he said, satisfied, letting them go.

She pulled on the hood and mask. He had none. Did the watchers think she would never break through his guard, or didn't they care?

*"We gave him a White Knife,"* Harn had said. *"He picked his toenails with it. Some would poison his food or rush him with spears like a cornered boar, but God curse anyone who takes the life of such a man without a fair fight."*

They saluted each other, formal on her part, sketchy on his as if he only half remembered how. For that matter, she recalled precious little of her one lesson with the clawed gloves. At the time, she had been too shocked by the instructor's matter-of-fact acceptance that she had the real things. He had said then that she would need special training. Well, here it was.

She imitated Bear's pose, hands up, claws out, weight balanced between one foot advanced and the other withdrawn. He began a series of movements, slowly, so that she could mirror them. These must be the practice kantirs of the Arrin-thar, similar to those of the Senethar or the Sene but darker and deeper.

*Here we reach the hidden nature,* she thought. *Here is the secret compact with our god, who has made us his champions and his monsters. Remember, you have five razors on each hand—you, who don't even like knives. But you are no one's prey, and no one can disarm you without destroying what you are.*

After a lifetime of concealment, the change in focus felt very strange, and almost exhilarating.

Bear's actions became faster and surer as his body remembered what his mind had forgotten. His claws raked the air in slashes that could tear out a throat or rip off a face. Strike lower to disembowel.

He clapped.

Jame stopped, startled, then surrendered her hands to his so that he might shape them properly. Of course: her nails, like his, curved, although not as much. A straight, fire-leaping spear-strike wouldn't work. She must angle the blow, so, to penetrate the muscle wall and scoop out the vitals within. Huh. Just what she needed: something to make her more dangerous. Never mind. One used what one was given.

Faster now.

They no longer mirrored each other but struck and countered, advancing, retreating. He was nearly three times her size and weight, his enormous hands surprisingly fast, but his half-crippled feet less so. Use that. She must play agile ounce to his massive Arrin-ken. Slip under his swing, slash at his side in passing…damn, why hadn't they given him armor? He turned, nearly catching her. A huge grin split his bearded face. She wouldn't trick him that way again.

For some time, there had been a growing disturbance on the balcony, erupting suddenly into a scuffle.

"…told you this was too dangerous!" someone was shouting. It sounded like Harn. "Stop them!"

Despite herself, Jame glanced up. At that moment, Bear's open palm strike caught her in the face guard and smashed her back against the wall. He had, of course, expected her to block or dodge. All she could see, and that not very clearly because they were so close, were his claws driven through and entangled in the metal mesh.

A roar. A thud that shook the floor. Harn must have jumped down into the pit and be coming at them. Bear swung around to face him, perforce swinging her with him, nearly off her feet. He shook his hand to free it, only managing to shake her as she gripped his wrist until she thought her neck would snap. If she was lucky, only the hood would rip off.

"Er…" she said, aware that probably no one could hear her. "Help?"

Then she remembered, and clapped her hands.

Bear stopped immediately. Harn did too, if only because several randon had grabbed him by the arms and were holding him.

"Child?" Sheth spoke mildly, somewhere behind her, also from the pit floor. For a moment there, it must have rained randon. "Are you all right?"

"In a minute." To herself, she sounded muffled and half-strangled, which was close to the case. "Can someone please get this hood off of me?"

She felt strong fingers unlace the cords behind her head and at last was able to wriggle free, wincing as caught strands of hair pulled out at the root. Her head at least still seemed to be attached, as she discovered by gingerly rotating it.

Bear had stepped back, one huge hand still tangled in the mask, the other absently scratching himself. That filthy lair of his must breed fleas by the dynasty. He also needed new clothes even worse than she did, especially pants.

"You know," Sheth was saying gently to Harn, "you nearly got your lordan killed. Bear was under control. You weren't."

The burly randon stared at him, then shook off his captors and blundered away. As Timmon had noted, he was indeed wearing what looked like a gray rag around his neck, probably the closest thing to a council scarf that he could find. Jame started after him, but Sheth stopped her. "Let him go. He needs to think about this."

"Ran, does it help or hurt him that I'm here?"

The Commandant considered this. "A good question, but then I don't know the answer, for any of us. We will just have to see, won't we?"

He had turned to go when she spoke again, on impulse: "Commandant, Bear is your older brother, isn't he? You were the one who pulled him out of the pyre, there, in the White Hills, when he had been left for dead."

He paused, a dark elegant shape in the door way, head bowed, face averted. "Ah, yes. And did that help or hurt? I don't know the answer to that question either."

Then he was gone.

# Chapter XXI:  Loyalty or Honor

**Summer 90 - 110**

# I

JAME TRACKED BEAR back to his den by his bloody footprints. After the guards had locked him in, the Commandant stood for some time, motionless, brooding outside the door. Then he turned in a swirl of his black coat and left. When all footsteps had faded away, Jame slithered inside through the food-flap.

The apartment was much as she remembered it, dark, hot, and airless, but she had time now to see that otherwise it was fairly comfortable with solid furniture, lively (if hard to make out) tapestries, and toys such as the little wooden warriors strewn enticingly about the floor. The Commandant had done the best he could for his brother. Unfortunately, Bear was in no shape to keep it clean, and any walls will close in when one can't escape them.

The big randon had subsided into his tattered chair before the fireplace and was slowly dismantling the guard mask still entangled in his claws. *He must have kept it,* Jame thought, *to play with like a puzzle,* as good a distraction as any for so damaged a brain. He grunted when he saw her but didn't rise. Considering the state of his bare feet, she wasn't surprised. The toenails were much worse than she had realized: several of them curled all the way under until the sharp points pierced the heavily calloused soles of his feet. That he could walk at all, much less fight, amazed her.

To one side was a table with fresh food and drink set out on it. Beside that, she found a small shaft set into the wall that allowed one to haul water up from the springs beneath Old Tentir. This she heated in a basin over the fire and finally got Bear to put his feet in it. The water immediately turned black with dirt. Several basins later, with his toes clean and beginning to wrinkle, she drew out a huge, hairy foot, braced it on her thigh, and began to pry an embedded claw out of the calloused sole. Bear nearly kicked her into the fireplace. It hadn't occurred to her that the big man might be ticklish.

"What I really need," she said to him, picking herself up, "is a nail clipper from the kennel. And maybe a file."

For the moment, however, she must make do with her knife. Finally, she worked out the first claw, rather like digging a nail out of a board, and trimmed off its needle point. Another came out red at the tip, with a sluggish ooze of blood and a faint whiff of corruption. Kendar don't infect easily. Nonetheless, Bear was very lucky not to have suffered worse damage than this. It occurred to her, as she whittled down lethal, overgrown tips, that perhaps this was what Bear had been trying to do when they handed him the White Knife. Life was too strong in him to cut it short, but no one should have to suffer perennially sore feet. Such a simple thing—perhaps too simple for anyone but another Arrin-thari to have noticed.

"There," she said, sitting back on her heels. "The next time, I'll bring the proper tools and do a proper job, on your hands too. These nails are still going to need a lot of filing."

"G-g-g-g-g…"

"Good?"

"G-g-g-g-g…"

"Girl?"

He leaned forward and patted her clumsily on the head. Unfortunately, the hand he used was still spiky with wire so it took awhile, again, to disentangle her hair without tearing out patches of skin with it.

*Maybe I should ask Rue to make me a new cap as well as gloves*, Jame thought as she wriggled out into the hallway. Long, lovely locks were all very well, but not if people kept nearly scalping her…and be damned if she was going to crop it short, however much Harn grumbled.

# II

OTHER LESSONS WITH Bear followed, none as dramatic as the first but all invaluable.

Harn stayed away, for which Jame was sorry. Although their situations were very different, she wished Harn could see that Bear wasn't a monstrosity so that, by extension, he might feel less like one himself. She certainly felt more at ease at least with that aspect of her Shanir nature than she had since childhood—not that she appreciated being born one of her god's pet monsters. Surely, though, it was better to have such weapons than to face life without them. After all, whatever her heritage, what mattered was what she did with it—or did it? Whenever her thoughts reached that point, she still felt confused. Had she free will in these matters, or did her blood damn her, whatever she did? But to accept the latter was to surrender responsibility for her own fate as Bane had done, and look where that had led him.

At any rate, it was impossible for her to deal with Bear without seeing him as Marc so easily could have been, under similar circumstances.

And Bear had taken that terrible injury fighting a useless battle led by her father. There, if you please, lay the true madness, sprung from her own blood, nurtured in the broken world it had created.

She was sure that exercise helped both Bear's temper and health and would gladly have taken him on midnight rambles or down to one of the hot water pits in the fire timber hall for a proper bath. However, his was a door fitted with a lock that for once she couldn't pick, perhaps because it was Kendar work, and Bear certainly couldn't squeeze through the flap. At least she was able to get his clothes washed and repaired, once she induced him to shed them—an operation that left him huddled naked as far under his cot as he could get, scarlet with embarrassment, probably wishing somewhere in his befuddled brain that this mad Knorth female with her fetish for clean clothes had never come into his life.

Jorin usually stayed in the outer hallway. Occasionally through him, Jame caught the hint of an amused presence outside, but when she flipped up the panel to look, no one was there but the ounce, sometimes batting around an exotic fruit or a new toy soldier for Bear.

# III

THE DAYS OF high summer passed, divided for Jame between lessons and barracks duty, rathorn colt and Whinno-hir mare, Bear and a changing assortment of gray scarved senior randon, who always seemed to be there, watching, at the worst possible moments.

On the good side, Bel-tairi was healing rapidly.

"Soon she'll be fit to ride," the horse-master said, with a sidelong glance at Jame.

However, Jame had no idea if the mare would permit such a liberty. Bel was still bound to her great-grandmother, as far as she could tell, or at least to the blood that bound Kinzi's soul to her death banner. Death was proving to be at least as complicated as life.

The colt continued to run wild. With Bel for company, however, he didn't plague the remount herd so, except for random sightings, only Jame and the horse-master knew that he still haunted the area. Sometimes the master brought out harnesses and lunge lines, but on the rare occasions when the colt allowed them to be strapped on, it was only for the pleasure of tearing them apart. Normal training for him, obviously, was out of the question.

"Never mind," said the master with a sigh, watching the colt prance off flinging aside snapped leather straps and broken rope. "I'll think of something."

Jame hoped so. She had an odd feeling that they would never be complete without each other, but how was she to ride such a creature when she still could barely stay on the quietest lesson horse? Forget the bridle bit. As with the Whinno-hir, she sensed that the colt would never submit to one. A halter, maybe, for appearance's sake. At the very least, though, she was going to need a tightly girthed saddle and stirrups.

Still, he was young, and so was she. There was time.

More worrying were reports that hill tribes had begun to raid farther south, and more aggressively. A Caineron flock had been slaughtered in the high fields, the carcasses left to rot, and the Kendar herders flayed alive. Worse, not only were their skins taken but their raw flesh was smeared with sheep fat so that, when found, they were still alive, in agony, begging for the White Knife. Perhaps one shouldn't wonder at such barbarity, given Caldane's practices, but it still didn't sound right to Jame. From what little she knew of the Merikit, they weren't given to wasteful, wanton cruelty. Nonetheless, Caldane now regularly hunted them, pushing farther and farther into northern lands once closed to him, thwarted only by the mysterious folds in the land from striking at the heart of Merikit territory.

She could only guess what the scrollsman Index felt after his years of study and friendship with the Merikit. He had given up demanding that she take him with her up into the hills, which was ominous in itself. She hoped he wasn't going to do something stupid, while simultaneously feeling guilty that she hadn't come up with a plan of her own. She was, after all, still the Earth Wife's Favorite and, technically, Chingetai's heir.

*And the Burnt Man's son*, she reminded herself.

Trinity knew, she had no desire to face that nightmare again, Burnt Man and Dark Judge combined, ready to pass judgment on such an errant darkling as herself. To them, she must represent the worst of both worlds, much as they did to her.

Then there was Torisen. She heard nothing more about her brother's problem in remembering the names of those Kendar bound to him. Sometimes, though, she felt a shiver ripple through the fabric of her house and for days after that, everyone would call each other by name in her presence. She wasn't sure what good it would do, but she began to learn every Knorth name she could, alive or dead, until her head hurt.

# IV

ONE NIGHT LATE in the barracks dining room, Jame dawdled over a cup of cider, listening to Vant set the next day's duty roster with the other ten-commanders of their house. As this was one of his chores, she didn't have to be there, but it amused her how his eyes kept sliding toward her and how at such times he lost focus on the matter at hand.

Just then, a sort of muffled rumpus broke out overhead, punctuated by Graykin's sharp voice raised in protest.

Jame rose. "Carry on," she said to the ten-commanders. "The roster sounds fine, Vant, except that you have cadet Cherry cooking dinner and cleaning the latrine simultaneously. What goes in does come out, but usually not that fast, unless Cherry is a much worse cook than I realized."

With that, she went quickly up the stair with Jorin on her heels. The second story dorm was quiet. Above, however, feet tramped back and forth between the front common room and the lordan's quarters to the back.

From the landing, Jame saw that the latter's anteroom door stood wide open, as did that of the larger, inner chamber. Flames leaped in the oversized fireplace. She fell back a step before the heat, feeling for a moment as if she had suddenly walked into her as yet unresolved, recurrent nightmare. The floor was even strewn with clothes.

Inside, Rue was directing the dismantlement of the northern wall of chests, while Graykin stood before the southern ramparts as if ready to defend them with his life.

"What's going on?" Jame asked the assembly at large.

Rue set a pugnacious jaw.

"Well, lady, you keep coming back clad in naught but rags, if that. It isn't proper."

What she meant was *Consider our pride, if not your own*, and Jame knew it. Clothes weren't that important to her, but the other houses were beginning to laugh at the increasingly shabby Knorth lordan.

She glanced at her servant, who glared back at her defiantly.

"There's plenty dumped out on the floor already," he said. "Tell them to leave this side alone."

Besides his normal, dusty gear, he wore an elegant if filthy scarf woven of silvery silk, embroidered along the borders in peacock blue with animals engaged in enthusiastic if highly improbable frolics. No doubt he had pilfered it from one of the chests. Well, she had told him to take whatever he wanted. She also suspected that he had wormed through the southern barrier to set up his new lodgings in the deserted rooms beyond. It was easy to forget that the lordan's suite extended in both directions down the length of the western wall.

"Leave the south side of the room intact for the time being," she told Rue. "Trinity knows, there's enough here already for me to wear a different set of clothes every day for a year."

Rue wrinkled her pug nose at the armful she had scooped up. "But not all of it is salvageable." She tossed the lot into the flames, which snatched it and roared up the chimney. "Ugh, that stink!"

Jame regarded the room's north wall. "Let's have it all down," she said abruptly. "I want to see what's behind it."

Cadets stared at her for a moment, then Rue gave a whoop of delight and practically threw herself at the barrier. Jame backed out of the way as the others leaped to help. It hadn't occurred to her that they had been itching to reclaim the lost rooms—more like to exorcise them. It had to happen sooner or later.

*But am I ready?* she asked herself, and didn't know the answer.

Not all the chests contained clothes. Some held ornate weapons more for show than use, pretty baubles, broken musical instruments, scrolls with many interesting illustrations along the lines of the scarf, and enough ointments, unguents, and cosmetics to have kept the courtesans of Tai-tastigon in business for a year.

There were also cracked kegs leaking a gooey, amber substance and crates of corked bottles of every size, shape, and color.

Beyond that was a door.

When Rue stepped forward to open it, however, Jame stopped her.

"After all," she said, bracing herself, "he was my uncle."

It was unlocked, but its rusty hinges ground like iron teeth and all was dark within. Dar ran to fetch lights. As she waited, Jame tested the stale air both with her own senses and with Jorin's. Here and now, though, the attic smelled worse than the darkness before her. When Rue handed her a lit candle, she entered cautiously, to find dust, small empty rooms, smaller windows in the outer wall, and at the end of the hall, a kitchen. These were the servants' quarters.

Looking back down the long, dusty hall, she saw Graykin still in the central room, glowering back at her, guarding the unseen master chambers behind him that he had claimed as his own.

He was welcome to them.

Jame sighed for the lost, airy freedom of her attic.

"If those rooms were cleaned up," she said as they left the dreary wing, "I suppose I could live there. It will certainly be warmer than the attic, come winter. Rue, ask Ran Harn if we can knock out some walls to make larger spaces, and maybe enlarge some windows. Cold be damned. I hate feeling shut in."

Rue agreed with such enthusiasm that Jame realized her odd choice of living quarters had been as much a source of embarrassment to her house as her sparse wardrobe. Speaking of which...

"As a council member, Ran Harn needs a proper scarf. Graykin, give me that, please. Consider it rent," she added as he hesitated to surrender his prize. "Rue, wash it and do something about that border. We can't have the Knorth war leader sporting hounds in heat, or hopping hares, or whatever these beasties are supposed to be."

In the common room across the landing, cadets both female and male were busily sorting, cutting, and sewing. Dusk had fallen. Candles cast pools of light through which needle and knife flashed like silvery fish. The cadets might be serving their own pride as much as her need, but the cheerful babble of their voices and the sacrifice of their scant free time touched Jame.

"Use most of this to make new clothes for the cadets," she told Rue. "Truly, I only need a serviceable wardrobe, not an enormous or fancy one, and some of us are even shabbier than I am. Remember, we're a poor house. I'll wear whatever you can salvage for me—within reason—but not that damned jacket."

The Lordan's Coat sprawled on a chair in the corner, as if sent there in punishment like a naughty child. Even untenanted, it had an air of indolent, stupid malice to it as faint but persistent as its reek, and just as personal.

Rue made a face. "Beautiful needlework it may be, but a foul thing nonetheless. You wouldn't think that one man could leave such a taint."

"Master Gerridon did," said Jame grimly, not adding that he, too, had been her uncle.

The smell reminded her that she had only reclaimed a few, dusty rooms. Greshan's personal quarters and the nightmare he had left behind had not yet been exorcized. In that, the coat seemed to mock her, the past overshadowing the present and threatening the future. For that matter, if she failed the autumn cull, all here would sink back into obscurity; and she knew, perhaps better than anyone, what malignant strength that darkness held.

Given that, it was a comfort to pass through the candle-glow of the common room, greeting those cadets whom she knew by name, learning the names of others. As master ten of the entire barracks she should have done this long ago, except for distractions and a lingering fear that many (like Vant) wished that she would just go away. Their cheerful welcome on this particular evening warmed her. Had she really, somehow, come to be accepted?

But at the door, watching, stood Brier Iron-thorn, as wooden faced as ever, judgment reserved.

No, thought Jame sadly, slipping past the big Southron and down the stair with Jorin on her heels. She wasn't home yet.

# V

THE REMAINS OF an incredible sunset hung over the black bulk of the western mountains, smears and whorls of red, orange, and yellow, lurid and smoldering, as if the entire sky were a great fire dying down to ash. Such spectacles had become common since the eruption, and the light on cloudy days was often an odd, murky yellow tinged with olive green shadows. The wind picked up. Dust rattled in the practice square and the tin roof of the surrounding arcade flexed with a hollow boom like imitation thunder. Warm light spilled from barracks' doors and windows. Supper over, cadets and randon alike were settling down to their favorite evening pursuits before bed.

Jame walked south, then east around the square, bound for Old Tentir—not the most direct route, but she preferred to stay clear of the Caineron and Randir quarters when by herself. After all, why ask for trouble?

She wondered, looking across at them: where did one draw the line between house and college loyalties? Just before their oath-taking, the Commandant had said, "While you attend this college, it is your home and all within it are your family, wherever you were born, whomever you call 'enemy' outside these walls. Here we are all blood-kin."

So far, it hadn't quite worked out that way...or had it? There were rivalries between barracks, of course, that turned many lessons into fierce competitions; but that was nothing, and good in its way. Here, everyone competed all the time, enthusiastically.

However, you didn't tie blood-kin to a tree as bait for a rathorn, or try to feed them to a poor, mad monster in his lair, or drop poisonous snakes on them as they slept.

As for the first, though, Gorbel probably hadn't meant to harm her, intending to get the rathorn before it got her.

The Randir had indeed tossed her into Bear's den, but that was before she had formally become a cadet.

True, she still had no idea who had introduced her to Addy the gilded swamp adder so informally.

Then there was the Randir Tempter…but presumably, whether the Witch watched through the randon's eyes or not, she was only doing her job. She and the Commandant both tested weaknesses and exposed flaws—valuable work, as far as that went. Jame had certainly learned more about self-control here in a half a season than in years outside the college walls.

Yes, but if so why had no one tested Greshan…unless that role had fallen to the unfortunate Roane? Was Roane the Randir also a tempter? If so, how far had he intended to go before he passed judgment on the Knorth lordan? Too far, it seemed, as Roane had ended up dead, warping her father's life forever in the process. How far were the current tempter and commandant prepared to go?

Could one be at Tentir, but not of it?

Clearly, her uncle Greshan hadn't belonged here, only attending because that was what the Knorth lordan was supposed to do. From what she had heard, he had made no attempt to fulfill a cadet's duties. Did Gorbel belong? Did Timmon? Did she? The Commandant had said that the college had its own rules, its own justice, and that by the end she would know for sure whether or not she had succeeded. Getting out alive would be a good start. Ah, but winning one's randon collar would be even better.

Jorin's ears flicked as something stirred on the other side of the square. The lower story of the Randir barracks was dark, the main door almost invisible in the arcade's shadow, but figures were slipping out of it and moving quickly, silently, toward Old Tentir. Some seemed to be carrying bows.

What in Perimal's name…?

Keeping to the shadows herself, Jame entered the great hall by its southernmost door. On the other side was the ramp leading down to the stables. That was where they were going. She had been bound there herself, to ask the horse-master some minor question about Bel. If those were bows, who or what were the Randir hunting with such stealth in such an unlikely place at this time of night? Should she tell someone or find out first, if she could, what was going on? The latter appealed more. She crossed the hall and descended, moving briskly and openly, as if nothing were wrong.

Most of the subterranean stable was dark, its inmates fed and settled for the night. Here and there for light, candles floated in pans of water, open flame being a serious danger when surrounded by so much dry wood and hay.  As she passed, Jame glimpsed pale, hooded faces drawing back into the dark and heard the restless movements of horses.  Jorin growled, until a soft word from her quieted him.  But he had caught a familiar scent, and they followed it, down again into the fire-timber hall, where giant upright trunks of iron-wood smoldered in their pits, fifty feet from brick floor to ceiling.  Here among other facilities was the farrier's forge, glowing red.

A gray mare stood patiently in cross-ties, waiting to be fitted with new shoes.  The horse-master himself manned bellows, tongs, and hammer, his bald head shining with sweat that ran freely down his face, unimpeded by his flattened nose.  When he saw Jame, his eyebrows rose but he continued as if a visit by the Knorth Lordan at such an hour was nothing unusual.

"What a beautiful animal," said Jame, running a hand down the mare's neck.

Encircling it was a thin leather band.  All traces of paint had been washed away, but between the band and those mild, leaf-green eyes, the creature was unmistakable.  Jame was greatly relieved that Mer-kanti had outrun the volcano; she had been worried about him.  But what was either he or his mare doing here?

"Her name is Mirah."  He lifted a fore-hoof to check it against the shoe.  Jame bent as if to examine his work.  "Her master is in danger," he breathed, lips barely moving.  "The bastards have set an ambush.  You've got to warn him."

"Where is he?"

"Probably in Ran Harn's apartment."

Jame straightened with a casual "Good night, then," hoping that her sudden departure would take the lurkers off guard.  She hadn't spotted any in the fire timber hall, but three surrounded her at the top of the ramp, bows drawn.

"Now what?" she asked them.

Coming up behind, farrier's hammer in hand, the horse-master dropped one with an arm-shattering blow.  An arrow flew wild, and in the stable's darkness a horse screamed.  Confused, the second archer wavered between two targets, and Jame took him down with a fire-leaping kick.  Turning, she found that the third had melted back into the shadows.

"Run," said the horse-master.

Jame did, with Jorin bounding ahead. From behind came the master's defiant war-cry, a hawk's jeering shriek, cut short. She hadn't known that he was Edirr.

The stable was awake now, nervous horses bugling, hooves ringing on wood, great flanks crashing into slat walls and boards cracking. Dark figures flitted through the chaos, on the hunt. The hunted fled, dodging down aisles, around corners, through stalls, under hooves. The ramp up to the great hall would surely be guarded.

Jorin's nose twitched at a sharp, well-remembered smell. Bales of hay hid the back wall, but behind them was the hole that the wyrm had eaten through solid stone that first night at Tentir, which now seemed so long ago. Jame scrambled through it and up the steep, slippery stairs on all fours, toward a faint line of light. Yes, here was the secret door, still ajar, and beyond it the charred ruins of the Knorth guest quarters. The weakened floor groaned under her feet and clouds of stale dust made Jorin sneeze.

Had anyone heard? Were they being followed?

Out into the hall. Now, which way?

The maze of Old Tentir had proved harder to master even than the labyrinth that was Tai-tastigon. Someone either expert at misdirection or mentally unhinged had designed it so that one never quite knew where one was, at least within the public halls. Jame guessed that east lay to the left and set off in that direction, only to find herself in a room with many doors, one of which opened on a blank wall, another on a sheer drop, and a third on a flight of stairs going up. She climbed. At the top, fading light met her through the arched windows of the eastern third story. Down the corridor to the left was the base of Harn's tower.

At the foot of the tight, spiral stair, the ounce paused and Jame with him, panting, catching through his senses the smell of fresh blood. She sprinted up the steps two at a time, only to trip over Jorin at the top and fall flat on her face at Harn's feet.

"Well," he said, looking down at her. "Look what the cat dragged in."

By dusk, the small room was pleasant and homey. Its windows stood open to the north and south so that the evening breeze blew in one and out the other. A fire played in the grate, its light dancing on the two large chairs drawn up on either side of it. A platter on the table held the remains of...what? In shape it looked vaguely like a roast bustard, but it was covered with brown and white fluttering wings. These suddenly took flight, circled the room, and settled upon the occupant of the chair turned toward the stair-head. Those who landed on his face, hair, and hands turned white, the others a mossy green veined with gold to match his hunting leathers. Mer-kanti smiled at Jame through the restless mask of their wings.

"Soft," he said, greeting her in his rusty voice.

Jame rose, thoroughly rattled. "I thought jewel-jaws were blue," she said, no doubt sounding as stupid as she felt.

"The common ones are." Harn poured a glass of wine and handed it to her. "Drink this. It's said to be good for out-of-breath idiots. These 'jaws could be blue too, if they wanted, but they're a species called crown jewels that can match almost any background. They still do like blood, though."

Mer-kanti put a hand over his goblet to ward off questing feelers. The glass' content, a dark, opaque red, clearly wasn't wine. Jame noted that Harn wore a bandage around his wrist.

"When we were both cadets here," Harn said, "he could still eat raw meat. Now only blood and milk will stay down. Honey too, but it hurts his teeth. Mine too, for that matter. Still, this"—he nodded at his wrist—"at least makes a difference from horse blood."

Jame remembered the band and plug on Mirah's neck, the permanently open wound. The thought made her a little queasy, but it didn't seem to bother the mare.

"And the...er...crown jewel-jaws?"

"He migrates south with 'em. The Riverland is no place for man or insect, come winter."

"Harn, you're forgetting your manners," said the Commandant from the other chair, whose back was turned to Jame. "I believe these two know each other, but not formally."

"Huh. Lady Jameth, Lordan of the Knorth, meet Lord Randiroc, Lordan of the Randir—yes, yes, Wilden's so-called missing heir, although not as lost as some would like."

Jame felt as if someone had jabbed her in the ribs. "Mer-kanti—that is, Lord Randiroc, they've set an ambush for you in the stable. A trap. I think Mirah is the bait."

The Randir rose so quickly that he left a shell of himself in glimmering wings.

"Surely they wouldn't hurt her," said Harn, distressed, "and who d'you mean by 'they' anyhow?"

"They hurt the horse-master," said Jame grimly. "I heard him cry out. And 'they' came from the Randir barracks, or at least seemed to."

Harn caught the Randir's arm as the latter started for the door. "Wait a minute. No need to charge in by the front door. We can slip down the private stair in the Knorth guest quarters."

"That's how I came up," said Jame. "They'll be watching it."

"Well, there are other hidden ways. Your gray sneak isn't the only one who knows Tentir's secret passages."

"As many at least as you can fit through, and there are fewer of those each year."

The Commandant's words were light but not his expression. He rose, seeming to fill the small room with his dark presence. "We are not 'sneaking' anywhere. This is Tentir, and they mean to pollute its honor by spilling innocent blood."

"These are also probably cadets, however misguided. Let me at least sound the alarm. That may bring them to their senses."

Jame had never heard Harn use that tone before, much less beg for anything.

"You always were too soft on others, and too hard on yourself," said the Commandant in a quiet voice that yet rasped like drawn steel. "We may live in a world of shifting values, but some lines can not be crossed." When Harn still blocked his way, he put him gently aside. "My old friend, you should understand. Tonight, I am Tentir."

Some slight noise below caught Jame's attention. She ran down the stairs and at their foot collided with someone. They fought briefly, soundlessly, until Jame drove her opponent back against the wall hard enough to knock the wind out of her. It was the Randir cadet Shade.

The Commandant and Harn descended the stairs, the latter still arguing, the former as silent as death. Jame pushed her adversary back into the shadows and held her there, a hand over her mouth, as they passed.

*Trinity*, she thought. *Don't bite me. Please.*

Then came the Randir Lordan, in a mantle of fluttering jewel-jaws. He paused and looked at them. A surprisingly sweet smile crossed his pale face.

"Nightshade, my cousin," he said.

Jame dropped her hand. Shade looked stunned.

"Randiroc," she said, hoarsely. "My lord."

The two cadets stumbled after the randon, Jame supporting the Randir. "Cousin" could mean almost any relation within the bonds of blood-kinship. "My lord" was less ambiguous, especially the way that Shade had said it. She had probably never met this man before, her natural lord, whom she had been taught from childhood to hate.

The Commandant meant to approach the stables without stealth, by public ways. Jame knew another, faster route, and hustled Shade along it. As they went, both felt the Commandant's silent call go out to all the college's Shanir. No wonder he was taking his time, allowing them to respond. Whatever happened, there would be witnesses.

Below in the hay-sweet darkness, she depended on Jorin's nose and ears to slip past the hidden assassins, whoever they were. Would the Randir really be this blatant, here of all places? Despite all that she had seen, like Harn she didn't want to believe it. Tentir should mean so much more than that.

They hid behind one of the massive pillars that surrounded the underground arena. The stable had quieted somewhat, although hooves still shifted uneasily on straw. Mirah stood alone in the center of the torch-lit space, head drooping, hip-shot. She might have been asleep on her feet, shoeing done, awaiting her master's return.

However, the leather band around her neck hung low, unbuckled. In its place was something thicker, something golden, something that bent sinuously to lap at the thin stream of blood that trickled down the mare's neck.

Shade's breath caught. "That's Addy," she said. "I left her in the barracks. I never thought…"

Jame grabbed her arm. "Wait. Has she bitten Mirah?"

"No, or the mare would be dead. Addy likes warm blood. When she only nips her prey, her saliva paralyzes it. She can live off a stunned rat for days before she eats it, but she will strike if alarmed."

She started forward again, and again Jame held her back.

"If either one flinches, both, eventually, will die. D'you think they will spare a horse-slayer? But I know both of them. Who else at Tentir can say the same? Let me try."

The Randir shivered under her hands, wide eyes on the golden band. Unconsciously, the tip of her tongue slid over teeth which, for the first time, Jame realized, were not filed.

"Go then," she said hoarsely. "Now."

Jame had also heard feet on the ramp, Harn's voice still raised in protest. From farther away, through Jorin's senses, came puzzled calls and questions as the Shanir responded to the Commandant's summons. She stepped out into the open and walked toward the mare. The faint groan of drawn bows almost made her stop. How many? Twenty, at least. She might not be their target of choice, but she was there, in the way, and if these were indeed Randir, they bore her no love.

Glancing behind her, she saw Shade on her knees, arms clasped tight around Jorin to restrain him. Knorth and Randir they might be, but here at least they understood each other perfectly.

"Hush," she said softly to Mirah, running a hand down the mare's sleek back. "Are you half-asleep, dreaming? Dream on, a moment longer."

The adder had raised her head and flicked a black, forked tongue, tasting the air.

"Yes, you too know my scent. Your lady awaits. Be still while I return you to her."

She slid her hand under the serpent's head and lifted her away from the trickle of blood. The adder loosed her grip on the mare's neck and curled her thick body trustingly around Jame's arm.

"There. Good girl."

The Commandant stood at the arena's side, watching. He waited until Jame had retreated—not too fast, not too slow—then strolled forward with Harn and Randiroc on his heels. The former stumped, scowling, daring anything to happen. The latter moved with his usual seemingly weightless stride. When he stopped beside the mare, apparitions of him drifted on in the uncertain light, defined by a flutter of wings. He slid the leather band into place and fastened it. The dribble of blood stopped. Mirah leaned against him with a sigh and closed her green eyes.

Meanwhile, the Commandant paced slowly around them, his long, black coat swishing with each stride. Again, Jame was re-minded of an Arrin-ken, but not of that charred, stalking menace that was the Dark Judge, warped by pain and hate. Here too was judgment incarnate, but cool and precise, wearing the mantle of power as he did his white scarf of office—with negligent grace, but not to be taken lightly.

"So," he said to the shadows. "Here we are. You will perhaps recall that I once spoke to you of the special contract that you enter when you take the cadet's oath. As I said then, whatever your house, whomever your enemies there, within these walls we are all blood-kin."

As he spoke, the Shanir arrived: the Falconer; the horse-master, looking rather dazed, with a lump rising on his bald head; Tarn with his Molocar pup; Gari with a humming halo of bees; Timmon, faintly luminous; Gorbel, his hair in cow-licks, clad in a glorious, untied dressing robe with nothing on underneath—cadets, sargents, officers.

"*We are many*," the Randir Tempter had said, "*and we are proud.*"

There, even, was Bear, his claws ragged and bloody with splinters from ripping apart the door of his prison in answer to his brother's call. He joined the others in watchful silence at the foot of the ramp and waited, shifting his great weight from foot to foot. Among them too was the senior Randir officer, a raw-boned, gray-scarved woman named Awl. Sheth acknowledged her with a nod. Other members of the Randon Council stood in the background. As most, like Harn, were pure Kendar, not all could be Shanir; some other instinct or message must have brought them. All nine were present, Jame realized, for the first time all summer. The autumn cull must be near, even tonight, but at the moment that hardly seemed to matter.

"You may also recall," said the Commandant to those other hidden watchers, "that I spoke of honor, and nothing about honor has ever been easy. So, ask yourselves and answer truthfully: here and now, which is more important to you, loyalty to your house or to your oath of fellowship to Tentir? Those who choose their house, come forth."

A blank moment followed. Then a score of Randir cadets stumbled out into the open, bows at the slack. Shade started forward too, but stopped when Jame touched her shoulder and spun around, glaring.

"Think," said Jame.

She didn't know how far the Randir had been in this plot, but she hadn't been carrying a bow.

"Stay. Please."

Shade gave her a brooding look, then a curt, reluctant nod.

Sheth regarded the other cadets, not without compassion. They looked very young and stricken, as if suddenly awakened from a nightmare only to find that it was real. "I release you from the college," he said, "without prejudice. You were tempted and you fell. The politics of your house are…complex, if not torturous, but they have no place here. Apply again a year hence, when you have had time to think, if you still wish to become randon."

The senior Randir gave a slight, stiff nod, accepting his judgment. Whether her lord or lady would be as understanding was another matter.

Sheth's hawk eyes swept back to the shadows. "You have also made your choice. Do you hold to it?"

An arrow flashed out of the shadows. Randiroc caught it in mid-flight, snapped it in two, and dropped the pieces. He was, after all, in addition to everything else, a weapons-master.

"I see," said the Commandant.

*The rest will slip away*, thought Jame. *What have we done here but unmask a few weak souls?*

But then she felt another presence in the shadows and remembered the oath ceremony in the great hall under the house banners, when she had suddenly known that someone was swearing falsely. Over that lay a second memory, like one stink on top of another, of a much different hall and a far stranger banner, where black stitches crawled like maggots into the semblance of a smile.

*My name is legion, as are my forms and the eyes through which I see.*

The worm was back in the weave.

Jame found herself walking out into the arena, her Shanir senses questing. Everyone was staring at her, but that didn't matter. She would find the wrong thing and she would break it. Again. And again. And again. Until it stayed broken forever.

*This is what I am. This is what I do.*

As she drew parallel to the Commandant, another arrow hissed out of the darkness. He thrust her aside, then made a faint sound and rocked back on his heels.

"Now that," he said mildly, "was uncalled for."

The shaft had gone through high on his right shoulder, taking his scarf of office with it. White silk began to turn red.

Jame was vaguely aware of a struggle as many hands gripped Bear to restrain him. She stepped forward on the Commandant's right, and Gorbel on his left. Their voices caught each other's pitch perfectly and launched it with all the strength of their outrage into the shadows:

"COME OUT."

The Randir Tempter stumbled into the open, her bow falling from palsied hands. She clawed away her half-mask. The lower half of her face was a shredded ruin, and she spat red through a full set of sharpened, bleeding teeth. Gorbel fell back, staring. No one else moved.

"Damned Knorth." That voice, however mangled, was not her own, nor was the soul that glared out of her eyes. "Again and again and again, you thwart me, even when such is not your intent. Worthless chit. Damaged goods."

"Not half as damaged as the woman whom you now ride."

The Witch laughed through her servant's mask of pain, a wet, ragged sound. "My people obey me willingly. Child of a fallen house, what do you know of such devotion, such sacrifice, such worship?"

"Only what I have seen of their results. They aren't pretty."

They were circling each other now, so close that Jame could see her own reflection in those wide, black eyes, in pupils with barely a rim. She felt her anger grow, a cold, balanced thing, a weapon poised to strike. Their breath hung between them on the suddenly chill air and the floor under their feet rimed with ice.

"The cadet Simmel gave his life for you, lady, but you left him to die alone."

"Not quite alone. You were there. In fact, I believe that you killed him. Did you enjoy it, Kinzi-kin? Was his death sweet?"

"Dust and bloody teeth scattered in the dirt. I took no pleasure in it, snake-heart, nor in what you are doing to your servant now, enemy of my house that she is."

The Tempter bared her sharp teeth, or perhaps the Witch did, twitching the other's raw sinews like some ghastly puppeteer. "You Knorth, hypocrites from first to last. The Old Blood runs strong in you. You savor it, girl, don't you? Did your father, the night that he slew my dear cousin Roane? Well, did he?"

Jame stared at her. "You don't know what really happened, do you? Your lover Greshan wouldn't tell you, for all your wiles, and that still galls you, after all these years."

"Just as it does you, dear child." She raised a hand as if to caress Jame's hair, but Jame slid away from it. "Something changed your father. Several things. And this was one of the first. His blood is yours, and your brother's as well. Is his final madness also your joint inheritance? How much easier it is to hate than to understand, but can either of you truly know yourself until you understand him? Little girl, dare you try?"

The Witch knew something about the haunted room, about the lordan's coat, about nightmares faced or fled. Such things weren't spoken of outside the Knorth barracks, but they were hardly secrets either.

Her black eyes turned to sweep contemptuously over the silent, watching randon.

"And you, Tentir, such noble talk of honor when my darling Greshan's blood is still wet upon your hands. What are decades to such guilt as that? Be assured: he will yet have his revenge, and soon."

She swung back to smile almost playfully at Jame. "But first, dear child, I think I will finish Kallystine's work and rip off your face."

Her hands curled into claws and her ruined mouth gaped, wide, then wider, all sharp teeth bared to bite, to tear.

"Steady," murmured someone. It sounded like the Commandant, but his voice was strangely blurred, as if with the hum of wings. "Wait, wait..."

Jame smiled into that terrible face, without humor, without mercy.

"I told you once, as the Randir Tempter, never to touch me again and now, in her form, you can't. But I can touch you."

She extended a claw and drew it delicately in a swooping curve down the woman's face from the forehead, across the bridge of the nose, down to circle that ghastly mouth. Her finger tip left a thin, red line.

"There. The first stroke of the rathorn brand. Of course, when your dear Greshan did this to the Whinno-hir Bel-tairi, he used searing iron. What is it about innocence that drives you to destroy it?"

She traced a second red curve from one nostril up around a sharp cheekbone. "The lesser horn. Slayer of innocents, you ordered the assassination of all my female blood-kin, didn't you? Why? What did you and Kinzi quarrel about that it should lead to such slaughter?

"The line of the greater horn, you know," she added, conversationally, "will cut across your eye, as it did across Bel's."

Then Jame heard it under the other's voice, the deep temptation that had been there all along:

*Give up. Give in. Become the monster that you know you are.*

The Randir began to laugh, half-choking on the ruins of her tongue. "Oh, child of darkness. Tempt me to speak, would you? But I am older than you, and stronger. How you betray yourself! Tricked. Trapped. Here, before all those whose opinions you value most. Cut deeper, then, and prove me right."

Silver eyes reflected back from the gloating, obsidian stare. Behind them both, the angry, frustrated thrum of wings grew.

Jame's smile grew. "So be it."

She cupped the woman's face in her hands, claws extending, and kissed her on the lips. "Tempter, victim of a greater temptation, randon, sister, farewell. I'm sorry." Then she drove her thumbs into the other's mouth, back to the hinges, forcing her jaws open.

"Gari, now!"

The bee swarm roared over Jame's shoulders, around her head, and down the Randir's throat. Eyes widened in shock as they began to sting and to die, inside her, yet more came, and more. They crawled down Jame's arms in a furry, furious pelt, down her hands, down into that seething mouth. The Randir began to gag and thrash, but she couldn't touch the one who held her. When she fell, Jame went down with her, straddling her body as it bucked and convulsed under her.

"This is your servant!" she shouted into those bulging eyes, at the alien presence within. "Keep faith with her and stay to honor her death!" But the black pupils were already contracting as the Witch fled.

Jame let go and sat back heavily on the floor.

"Damn you," she muttered, close to tears. "Witch, bitch, worm, damn you to the Gray Lands and there let the dead have their way with you forever."

She had no wish to witness those final, terrible death throes, but it seemed as if someone should. At last the body lay still, except where dying bees crawled beneath its clothes, their entrails torn out with their stingers. Then came a bright flutter of carrion jewel-jaws that settled, eagerly, on whatever exposed flesh they could find.

Timmon leaned against a pillar, throwing up his dinner.

"I just told them to go," Gari was saying, again and again. "I didn't tell them to do that. I didn't...I didn't..."

Sheth put his uninjured arm around the boy, and the cadet clung to him, sobbing. "Of course you didn't," the Commandant said gently.

"Huh." Gorbel nudged the body with his foot, only just not kicking it in case some of the bees were still alive and armed. "You do come up with interesting ways to kill people, Knorth."

"Oh, shut up," said Jame.

She considered vomiting too, but decided it wouldn't make her feel any better. Nothing she could think of would. But here was Jorin, anxiously nuzzling her ear, trying to crawl into her lap where he hadn't fit since he was a kitten. She held him, surprised to find that she was both chilled and shivering.

The Commandant stood over her. "All right, child?"

She gave a laugh that was half a sob. "You keep asking me that, ran."

"With you, the question continually arises."

"Er...you do know that you still have an arrow stuck through your shoulder, don't you?"

"I had noticed," he said dryly.

Harn snapped off the head and pulled out the shaft, which had punched Sheth's silk scarf of office through the wound from entry to exit. "No splinters there," he said. "Finally, the damned thing has served a purpose."

Jame climbed to her feet, trying to pull herself together. She thought distractedly that she must give Harn the silver silk scarf as soon as possible, cavorting beasties be damned. It seemed a lifetime since she had first seen it wrapped around Graykin's dirty neck.

"I'm curious," said the Commandant to her. "What did the Tempter mean about you killing Simmel? That young man's fate has always puzzled me. All we ever found were his clothes and a pile of teeth."

"Well, ran, I did hit him in the head with a rock, but that's not why he crumbled to dust."

"I see. Or rather, I don't. Perhaps, at some future date, you will enlighten me."

By now, the others who had lain in ambush had slipped away. Making no fuss about it, the hunt-master gave a lymer the scent from the feathers of the arrow that Randiroc had snapped in two. When the tracker had found the scent and sped up the ramp in pursuit, he loosed a direhound after it.

"This has not been one of Tentir's better days," remarked the Commandant. "It might, however, have been worse."

He turned aside to speak with the Randir Lordan. Mirah had sunk to the ground asleep, legs folded neatly under her, head cradled in her master's arms. Clearly, she would not be fit to travel at least until morning.

Harn stared down at the Randir's body. "Trinity, girl, Blackie would never..."

"No, ran, I don't suppose he would; but I am not my brother."

The big Kendar regarded her soberly for a moment, chewing on the inside of his cheek. "It will be Autumn's Eve in ten days," he said. "Blackie hasn't asked for you, but tomorrow you should leave for Gothregor to stand by him on the night. I think he's going to need you."

His eyes were still on her, hesitant but heavy with judgment.

"Tonight we cast the stones for the autumn cull. I'm sorry, but I don't think you will be coming back."

# VI

JAME LEFT THE stable, feeling numb.

The college was still in the process of rousing; the departure of its Shanir, without a general alarm, had been too sudden to create more than an initial stir, but now word was filtering back to the barracks that something startling if not terrible had happened. Lights flared in rooms among groggy sleepers. Those who hadn't yet gone to bed stood in their barracks doorways, bootless, calling questions to which there were few if any answers. Jame slipped by them as if invisible.

Outside her own barracks, she stopped to lean on the rail. Across the practice square, on the second floor of Old Tentir, candlelight glowed through the peach-colored screens of the Map Room and spilled out onto the Commandant's balcony. There, tonight, the casting of the stones, the autumn cull, would take place, but probably not for awhile yet: the Commandant would need to have his shoulder properly patched up, and then there was that mess below to sort out. She wondered what they would do with the Tempter's body. On her way out, she had heard Sheth say something about putting it outside the walls, to be claimed by whomever cared to take the trouble. If not, he had said, let Randiroc's jewel-jaws have it.

Was that fair? Was it right? She didn't know.

Almost at her feet, on the other side of the low wall and in its moon-cast shadow, the direhound raised its black head and snarled up at her over its prey. Front paws on the rail, Jorin growled back. The white lymer crouched to one side, its tracking done, patiently waiting for its reward of fresh entrails.

"I know the hunt-master doesn't starve you," she told them both. "Return to him." The hound bared bloody fangs and crouched to spring. "Go."

As one, they flattened and went, slinking.

Huddled as the body was, she could only guess that the Randir cadet was male. Given the great pool of blood in which he lay, he was most certainly dead. So. Those were the fingers that had smoothed the arrow's feathers, set its notch to the string, and loosed it at a man whom this cadet had been told was a mortal enemy of his house.

"I'm afraid," she said to him, "that you've been both gulled and culled. Perhaps I have been and will be too, soon."

Maybe Harn was right. Maybe she didn't belong at Tentir and should be cast out. On the simple level of skill, except in a few areas she still trailed far behind the rest of her class. There was still a huge gap between their experience and hers. And she was dangerous—but would she be any less so elsewhere? Sending her back to Gothregor for anything longer than a visit was chancy, to say the least. What did one do with a nemesis between catastrophes, anyway?

"I have *got* to learn how to knit," Jame muttered to herself. "What's the worst I can do with a ball of yarn and a pair of needles? No, don't answer that."

"I've been looking for you," said a grim voice, and there was Shade, with Addy draped around her neck like a thick, golden collar. She glanced over the railing. "Quirl. He always was a fool. Then again, I wasn't so bloody smart this evening either. Why did you do it?"

"Do what, or rather, which? It's been a busy night."

The other snorted. "You might well say so. I mean, why did you stop me? I could be packing now too, or more likely looking for a White Knife. My lady grand-dam does not like failure."

Jame had forgotten that Shade was Rawneth's half-Kendar grand-daughter and that Lord Kenan was her father, not that either seemed to count for much among the Randir.

"Would you have done it? Shot a fellow randon from ambush in the heart of Tentir?"

Shade scowled. "I don't know what I was going to do. Listening to the Tempter, it sounded right: kill the enemy of our house; accomplish what even the dread Shadow Assassins have failed to do, these forty years past; protect our blood. Then I followed you, and spoke to him, and suddenly nothing was simple anymore." She shook her head. "It was always so clear before. Us against you. That's the way I was raised. No questions. No hesitation. Tentir is changing that, and so are you. I don't like it. It makes my head hurt." She shot Jame a look askance. "I was there, you know, in the stable. That devil hound went for me first because I was closest, but he veered off."

"Why not? You hands were clean."

"Is that why you stopped me from stepping forward?"

"I suppose. Also, I like your snake." Jame looked up at the Map Room where shadows were beginning to move against the peach-colored screens. "Tonight, for me too, there were moments of such blinding clarity, when I knew exactly what I had to do and how to do it."

She rubbed her mouth, as if to wipe away the cold touch of the Tempter's lips: *Victim of a greater temptation, randon, sister, farewell.* Somehow, she had known that the swarm was coming, and why, and how to open the way for it. No doubt. No hesitation. No question, even now. Only guilt.

Jame sighed. "Now so much is murky again. Right and wrong, good and evil, honor and loyalty…"

"You sound more familiar with confusion than with certainty. I don't envy you." Shade nodded toward the body almost at their feet. "That's certain, at least."

"Death? I'm beginning to think that it's the most complicated thing of all, next to honor."

She straightened and stretched, feeling the strain of the day in all the muscles down her back, hearing her spine creak.

"The cull is about to begin, the stones to be cast. I wish you luck, Randir. For my part, this is probably my last night at the college, and I have one last thing to do while I still have the chance."

The other looked at her suspiciously. "What?"

Jame had started to turn toward the barracks door but hesitated, looking back. A wry smile twisted her face. "Why, sleep, of course. And dream."

# Chapter XXII:  Casting the Stones

## Summer 110

## I

RUE MET HER at the barracks door, with a startled glance after the retreating Randir, then another at the general stir along arcade.

"Lady, what's going on?"

Jame didn't feel like explaining, assuming she could, so she chose the simplest answer: "The autumn cull has begun."

The cadet shot an aghast look across the square at the lit windows of the Map Room.  "What, tonight?"

Other Knorth cadets crowded behind her in a rising babble of voices: "What did she say?" "They're casting the stones!" "But what's this about a pile of corpses in the stable?" "Never mind that. It's the cull!"

Jame recaptured Rue's attention with difficulty.

"Take the gray silk scarf to Ran Harn.  Hurry."

"B-but I haven't even had time to wash it, and as for the embroidery…"

"Never mind that.  He's about to cast the stones with what looks like a dirty sock tied around his neck.  Go."

She climbed the stairs against a swift tide of descending cadets. They had all known this was coming, of course, but to have it suddenly upon them was another thing altogether.  It didn't look as if anyone else would either want or get much sleep that night.

The Lordan's Coat still sprawled, ignobly abandoned, in the corner of the third floor common room.  Dragging it by the collar as if by the scruff of the neck, she entered the lordan's apartment and closed both doors behind her.  Jorin slipped through on her heels.

The inner room  was still a desolation of discarded clothes, empty chests, and tarnished trinkets, the tawdry remains of a worthless life and of a death largely unmourned.  Even the smell seemed old, a dusty, faint reek of mortality.  The door to the north wing servants' quarters stood ajar and a thin, cold breath of air moved through it like a long sigh.  Jame closed it.  Then, feeling a bit foolish, she balanced a chair against it so that it would topple if the door moved.

Somewhere behind all those other boxes against the south wall, there was another door, but she didn't care to dig it out. Either Graykin was asleep in whatever nest he had made there or, more likely, he was out earning his keep by spying on the Map Room. Whichever, what she had to do now was none of his business. With a certain grim amusement, she booby-trapped that side of the room too with an assortment of knickknacks and bottles sure to crunch or roll under the unwary foot.

*There. I warned you never to spy on me again.*

A few embers glowed on the hearth among heaps of smoldering rags. Jame tossed in the wreckage of a cedar chest to rouse the flames and held her hands up to them as they flared. She still felt very cold, and shaken, and not at all prepared for what came next.

For that matter, was it really necessary, or even wise? One couldn't be physically hurt in dreams as one could in the soulscape, or so she supposed, but if she had actually begun to dream true, nightmares of the past might tell her things that hurt far worse than any punch in the nose. Did she really want to know what had happened in this room to her father so long ago? The old days held so many dark things, some perhaps best left undisturbed.

Ah, but the past wasn't dead, only asleep, waiting to rise again and to strike. She had the Witch's promise of that.

"*Something changed your father*," Rawneth had said through the Tempter's bleeding lips. "*His blood is yours, and your brother's as well. Is his final madness also your joint inheritance? Can either of you truly know yourself until you understand him?*"

So much for any choice in the matter. This concerned Tori as much as it did her. Besides, in her experience if you turned your back on a problem, it tended to bite you in the ass.

Here was a pile of not too musty clothing, perhaps dropped by Rue in her rush downstairs. Jame heaped them on the raised hearth in a rough bed, lay down, still fully clothed, and tried to make herself comfortable. The fire warmed her back and Jorin crept into her arms, but she continued to shiver.

From the shadows by the door where she had let it fall, the Lordan's Coat smirked at her. There was no other word for the expression conveyed by those peaked folds of stitch-thickened cloth, too heavy to crumple even when unceremoniously dropped. With a sigh, over Jorin's protest at being disturbed, she rose to fetch it. After all, why else had she brought the damn thing in here with her? Rue had cleaned it as best she could and darned the ripped lining, but at the least movement the old stench seeped out of it, as strong, personal, and offensive as ever. As Jame returned to the hearth with it, she considered throwing it on the fire. Heirloom or not, Greshan had surely tainted it past repair. But if it had become the flayed skin of old nightmares, she still needed to learn its secrets.

With a smug reek, the coat settled over her in an unwelcome embrace. Wrinkles in the garments upon which she lay creased her flesh and Jorin grumbled as she shifted restlessly. The fire snarled over its wooden prey. From outside came the muted stir of the barracks.

Never in her life had she felt less like falling asleep.

# II

"WHAT ARE YOU grinning at?"

Harn Grip-hard glared at the senior Edirr randon, sitting cross-legged third to his right around the circle, beyond the haughty Ardeth and a Danior who seemed far too young to be here, in such august company. As in the hall below, the Randon Council kept to the order of their house banners, but in a circle without head or foot.

"Oh, nothing, nothing," said the Edirr hastily, and turned to speak to the grave Brandan on his right.

Harn tugged at the silk scarf. Pretty it might be, but slippery; he had had to knot it around his thick neck to keep it from slithering off. Now, however, he felt as if it was trying to strangle him. Either that, or guilt: The cadet Rue had intercepted him just outside the Map Room with a quick, hissed message that the Knorth Lordan had said he should wear it—this, when Jameth must know that he was about to betray her.

He squinted surreptitiously at the embroidered border that seemed to amuse the Edirr so much. Seen upside down, it looked like an abstract pattern, peacock blue thread on shimmering gray. Nothing to laugh at there, or anywhere else tonight that he could see.

The Tempter's grisly fate didn't bother him—much: clearly, the woman had crossed any number of lines, putting an arrow through Sheth Sharp-tongue being the least of them.

But that boy in the square with his throat torn out...such a pitiful, little heap he had made, his eyes and mouth agape with frozen horror. Harn remembered him alive, small for his age with a thin, intent face, struggling to keep up. A child. The Tempter would have used that: *Here is your chance to prove yourself, to be blooded in your lady's service.*

Blood. The ground had been soaked with it. His own hands felt wet and greasy—only with sweat, he told himself; but when he closed his eyes, all he saw was red.

*What's happening to us, Blackie? How can such a thing occur, here of all places? Have we failed in honor, or has honor failed us?*

He rolled two stones in his palm—one white quartz, the other black limestone, both polished smooth by a mountain stream and warming to his touch. Two more of each lay before him. Like the rest of the Council, he had spent the last few weeks making up his mind which stone each cadet had earned, white or black, in or out. Some of the choices hadn't been easy. One was getting harder by the minute. Perhaps he should ask for a delay. After such a night, were any of them fit to judge wisely?

The senior Randir Awl sat across from him, her back roughly to the east wall as his was to the balcony and the west. Murals flickered by candlelight all around them, each the bloody chaos of battle resolved into clean lines and glowing color. There on the north wall was the newest: the Cataracts. Awl had done fine service at the Lower Huddles and on many other so-called fields of honor, often by his side. A good woman. A good randon. Tonight, though, she looked like the unburnt dead. At her left hand was a knobby bone, the vertebra of a large snake; at her right, a black...thing, compact but convoluted, as if tightly wound, with an oily sheen—both no doubt the choice of her lady the Witch. Harn was angry for his colleague's sake. What had happened tonight wasn't her fault. Why did clean hands such as hers have to touch such things?

But she hadn't asked to delay the cull.

The Commandant sat to his left, beyond the Jaran. Candle-glow picked out the hawk-sharp lines of his face and a fresh, white scarf serving as a sling. His shoulder must throb with every heartbeat, but he showed no sign of it except perhaps for the gathering shadows under his eyes.

He hadn't asked for a delay either.

Harn sighed. If Sheth could do this with a bloody hole punched through him, so could he. Oh, but it was hard.

"We know why we are here." The Commandant's voice was flat. *This is our sworn duty*, its inflection said, *and we may not turn from it.* "The college cannot support its current population over the coming winter. More important, only the best belong here, and we have now had time to determine who they are. A score have already departed this night."

Awl's thin lips tightened, but she didn't speak nor did anyone look at her.

"We need to cull at least a hundred more. Are we agreed? Then let the stones fall—for the good of our randon fellowship, for our houses, for the Kencyrath as a whole, and for our personal honor, tonight so grievously wounded. May duty heal us all."

# III

*THIS IS RIDICULOUS*, thought Jame, still fidgeting on the hearth.

Never patient where his comfort was concerned, Jorin had long since retreated to a quiet corner. She herself had slept sound in stranger places than this. So, why not tonight?

Earlier, she had wished she had some of Kindrie's foul tincture of hemlock. That in turn had reminded her of the bottles Rue had unearthed and, rising, she had found one still marginally drinkable, in a square green bottle sealed with wax and soft lead. Tubain had kept a similar jar behind the counter at the Res aB'tyrr in Tai-tastigon, until Cleppetty had made him empty it into the gutter. Jame remembered the curbstones smoking. But Highborn, she reminded herself, were very hard to poison. Anise, tansy, wormwood, and a kick like a cart horse. One swallow had numbed her mouth and made her eyes sting; but that, apparently, was all.

Oh, why couldn't she sleep?

"Because you will always fail," said the Tempter's voice, filtered through a hum of insects.

She hawked to clear her throat. An ejected bee tumbled out onto the floor, its guts ripped out with its stinger. It righted itself, unsteadily, and bumbled into the fire where flames kindled its wings. The Randir herself stood in shadow, her form still yet strangely a-seethe.

"You haven't the focus," she said. "Lover of confusion, of chaos, of destruction."

"I am not! I just don't see things as simply as you Randir do. Poor Shade. I made her head hurt. Mine is throbbing now too."

"Serves yuh right." Simmel balanced on the wobbly chair set against the side door, gumming his words without teeth. Grains of dust trickled out of his ears and empty eye sockets, *tick, tick, tick*, onto the floor. "Look at m' poor head, all s-smashed an' hollow."

"Thank your lady for that," Jame snapped. "She's the one who emptied your skull, not me, and you let her. The world is *not* black and white."

"It is tonight," said the Tempter, with a ghastly, toothy smile full of mangled, wriggling bees. "White stone, in; black stone, out."

Jame felt warmth against her back. She thought it was the fire, until it stirred restlessly.

"I'm going to fail," murmured her brother. "So many faces, so many names…how can I remember them all?"

They might have been children again in the keep in the Haunted Lands, huddled together in bed for comfort, for protection.

"Mullen. Marc. I will never forget them, but one is dead and the other refused my bond. Father said I was weak, and I am. I am. I am."

*All right,* Jame thought. *I'm asleep after all, but is this my dream or his?*

"I'm going to fail…"

She tried to turn, but the lordan's jacket fought her. How many arms did the thing have anyway, and why couldn't it keep them to itself?

"Tori, let me help you. Dammit"—this in a sputter to the coat, as it wrapped a boneless sleeve around her face and tried to stuff itself down her throat—"Ummph…let me go! Tori!"

Could he hear her? Was he even there anymore?

With a great effort she flung off the coat and scrambled to her feet, to find by the draft that she had shed all her other clothing as well. Simmel snickered from the shadows.

"Oh, shut up," she snarled at him. "You're not so pretty yourself."

"Remember me!" dry voices cried from the ashes of the past, from the crack and greedy hiss of the pyre. "Remember me! I brought your grandfather word of his son's death, and for that he cursed me." "I honored seven contracts, at last dying in childbirth far from home." "I fought beside your father in the White Hills, and died at the hands of my own mate for the sake of our unborn child." "I saved Tentir's honor at the point of the White Knife or thought that I did, but all in vain…"

She could almost see them now in the arc of the fireplace, a vast, gray host crowding around her brother, reaching out to him with unraveling hands. How many there were, all the past Highborn and Kendar of their house whose blood, like Kinzi's and Aerulan's, trapped their souls in the weave of their death.

Torisen held out his beautiful, scarred hands—to embrace or to ward them off?

"Yes, yes, I know my duty and am honor bound to it, but so many names, so many faces—how can I remember you all?"

That last gray shape who had spoken of honor, Tentir, and the White Knife…he had been a big Kendar with large hands and a broad, almost familiar face.

*I know him*, thought Jame. *I know* him!

"Tori!" she called over the wasteland of ashen heads, of gray faces turning slowly toward her even as they crumbled to ruin. "That's Hallik Hard-hand, Harn's father! And that other must be Sere, Winter's mate. Don't you remember his face painted on the walls of our parents' bedroom? I know others as well, dead and alive. Let me help!"

But could he hear her? The cries had grown shrill, demanding: "Me!" "Me!" "Take me!"

Banners unraveled and rewove to clothe the living. Highborn ladies swarmed around Torisen in a swirl of stolen funereal finery, clawing strips off each other to reach him. What are the claims of the dead compared to the ravenous hunger of the living?

"Take me!" "Me!" "Me!"

What was this, a feeding frenzy?

Jame plunged in among them, naked and thoroughly exasperated. They scattered before her with faint, horrified shrieks at her unmasked face. No doubt about it: This was Tori's nightmare, asleep and awake. If even a fraction of it was true, the Women's World had lost its mind, or at least its head. No wonder Tori was running scared. But where was he, or rather where were they?

She had followed him to a cold, dark place which, surely, she should know by that thin, sour smell, but it was so very, very dark, and it felt safer somehow not to know, or to be noticed. Voices muttered, rising and falling, woven together with the dense texture of an argument that never ends but only repeats with endless variations.

"…hands, hands, hands," Torisen was saying. He sounded much younger than he had a moment ago, and his voice cracked with helpless exhaustion. "How they clutch and cling! They will drag me down, but I swore never to fail another as I did Mullen. I s-swore!"

A hoarse, muffled voice answered him, an insidious murmur from within. "We all swear. Many swore to me, and all swore false. I have lost thousands. I lost you, my only son. What is one man compared to that?"

"He was just that, a man, and he trusted me. They all do."

"All who trust are fools. I trusted you. Trust no one."

"But she's my s-sister, my twin, my other half. Why can't I trust her and accept her help?"

It was the voice of a child, pleading against the dark. Jame wanted to shout at it, "Oh, grow up! Don't ask. Tell him!" But her own voice caught in her throat.

"Because, boy, she is Shanir."

"Is - is that really so bad?"

Now she was truly struck dumb. When had Tori begun to question that, the bedrock of their early training?

"Anar taught us the old stories. Mother sang them to us in the dark, before she went away. Once, those of the Old Blood did great things…"

"Terrible things."

"That too. Yet everything else in life is gray. Why is only this black and white?"

*…white stone, black stone, in or out…*

"You ask me that, again and again and again. Do you think, if you whine long enough, I can change night to day? Weak, foolish, faithless boy. Shall I tell you, again, what that filthy Shanir, my brother Greshan, did to me as a child, no older than you are now? Shall I show you?"

*No!* Jame wanted to shout. *Leave him alone, you bully!* But fear swallowed her voice.

"See. Hear. Learn," said that loathsome voice, gloating over each word. "Just a drop of his blood on the knife's tip, not strong enough to bind for more than an hour or two, just long enough to make the game more interesting. Dear little Gangrene. You went crying to Father the last time, but he didn't believe you, and he never will. Not against me. You're a worthless, sniveling liar, and everyone knows it. Now open wide like a good little boy or I'll break your teeth—again—with the blade. There. Now, come to me."

And Jame woke on the cold hearth, with the iron taste of blood in her mouth from her own bitten tongue and her brother's cry of horror echoing in her mind.

# IV

THE FIRST ROUND of the cull went much as expected, although with a few surprises. Naturally, the Highlord's house began, and the first name called by the sargent standing behind Harn Grip-hard was that of the Knorth Lordan.

For a long moment, no one moved except for Harn, tugging again at his gray silk scarf. No stone cast, black or white, meant that Jameth was in. Then the senior Jaran leaned forward and rolled an ivory ball carved with lesser runes into the circle. Harn felt the room swim. Must he be the one after all to cast the black? But the Randir spared him. Whether on her own judgment or by order of her lady, she let drop her black ball. It neither bounced nor rolled, but fell with a plop and lay there, twitching slightly.

Again, everyone waited, but no one moved. Then Jaran and Randir scooped up their markers and the next name was called.

Harn let his breath out in a loud *whoosh*, causing the Commandant to shoot him an amused glance. Jameth's fate would not be decided until the second round, or possibly the third and last.

Judgment was also suspended on the Caineron and Ardeth lordans. Politics aside, some felt that the former was too clumsy and the latter too casual to make good randon. Brier Iron-Thorn also received one white and one black stone. No one doubted her ability, but several were still wary of her sudden change of houses. Such things rarely happened, and caused great suspicion when they did. At the end of the first round, the fates of some two hundred cadets remained undecided.

By now, it was well into the night, the thick candles banded with the hours half burnt.

"At this rate," murmured the young Danior to the Brandan in the pause between rounds, "we won't be done until dawn. D'you think the Commandant will last that long?"

The Brandan gave a short, mirthless laugh. "I've seen Sheth Sharp-tongue direct a battle, aye, and fight in it for three days running, with a thigh slashed two inches deep. We only found out about it at the end, when he dismounted and collapsed from loss of blood. Awl worries me more. Every time she touches that damn, black ball, something goes out of her."

"And Harn?"

"You sit closer to him than I do. Keep watch. I don't like his color, or the way he keeps tightening that blasted scarf; and I don't trust the Ardeth to help, although he sits closer still."

They both glanced at the senior Ardeth who stood aside, sipping amber wine from a crystal glass. He and the Jaran were the only pure Highborn currently on the Randon Council, although otherwise they were as different from each other as fine leather and rough silk.

"So Lord Ardeth still isn't speaking to Blackie."

"Not directly." The Brandan took a swig of watered cider. Only Harn was drinking his neat, and hard. "We hear rumors that he's trying to get at the Highlord through his matriarch, Adiraina. Our own matriarch hasn't been near Gothregor since she returned the Knorth death banner."

Tactfully, the Danior didn't comment on this. Everyone knew that Brenwyr was unwell and that her lord brother worried about her, but whatever ailed her belonged to the impenetrable, no doubt trivial mysteries of the Women's World.

The Commandant returned to the circle and sank into his place on the floor, followed soon after with some cracking of stiff joints by the rest of the Council. The second round of the cull was about to begin.

# V

GETTING BACK TO sleep required several more pulls on the green bottle, taken reluctantly: Jame remembered all too clearly how helpless she had felt when Kindrie had dosed her with hemlock. Dreams were tricky enough as it was, she thought as she dropped back into her noisome nest on the hearth, head and stomach roiling.

As it was, she no longer knew who was dreaming what. Had that last been a dream at all, or had she descended far enough to eavesdrop on Tori at the bolted door in his soul-image? Even then, it had been strange, that slip from her father's voice to her uncle's. Greshan, a blood-binder? It didn't surprise her much, nor that his Shanir powers should have proved so much weaker than her father's, considering that the older boy had only been able to bind the younger for short periods of time. It certainly helped to explain Ganth's hatred of the Old Blood, without forcing him to realize that he possessed it himself.

What a miserable childhood he must have had, almost as bad as her own. What had it been like, to live under the shadow of such alternating cruelty and neglect? Her mind drifted toward sleep, trying to imagine the boy her father had been.

It was Autumn's Eve.

The boy wandered in his grandmother's Moon Garden, between banks of tall, pale comfrey and lacy yarrow, between primrose and arching fern. He had the slight build of his house and the fine, strong bones just emerging from childhood, but undercut by an anxious air like that of a beaten puppy. All around were healing herbs, but none to cure the emptiness within, the echoing sense of worthlessness so carefully nurtured by his older brother, the Knorth Lordan.

Another walked beside him in his moon-cast shadow: daughter-to-be, child of his ruined future. *If he thinks so little of you*, it asked, *why does he bother to torment you at all?*

The boy didn't know. All he asked was to be left alone. Somehow, though, he was like a secret itch that his brother felt compelled to scratch until it bled.

He glanced unhappily up at a dark window set high in the garden's northern wall. Only with his grandmother Kinzi did he feel safe, but the Knorth Matriarch was visiting her friend Adiraina in the Women's Halls. He would wait here until she came home. Then he would go up to say good night and hear a kind word in return.

He turned, and found that he was no longer alone. The door to the outer halls had silently opened. Just inside it stood a slim, masked girl clad in black, white, and silver, her eyes fixed, greedily, on that dark, upper window.

Jame half-woke with a sick start.

*That's Rawneth*, she thought, gulping down green nausea. *Young, beautiful, and oh, so hungry. But for what?*

Now they were in Kinzi's apartment, and Rawneth was looking through the Matriarch's possessions

*This is wrong. Why did you bring her here?*

She had been so kind to him in the garden, so sympathetic. Why hadn't he gone with his father on this Autumn's Eve to remember the Knorth dead? The Highlord hadn't asked him? Oh. Well, perhaps Lord Gerraint thought that he would be bored and it was, really, such a long, dull ceremony. Anyway, it was the Lordan's duty to attend his father tonight. What, Greshan hadn't gone either? He was out hunting? How curious.

He reminded himself that she was only sixteen, a bare three years his senior, but so poised that they might have belonged to different generations. The lower third of her full skirt, her arms, and her mask were black, her bodice white, tight laced with silver—the markings of an elegant direhound.

She had always wanted to see the Knorth quarters, especially those of the Knorth Matriarch. Would he show her? How her dark eyes glittered behind her mask, how red those thin lips against that white skin. Her fingertips, long nailed, caressed his cheek and he shuddered, torn between desire and repulsion, hardly knowing which stirred him more. Show me. Please?

Now he stood back watching, increasingly uncomfortable, as her pretense of delicate curiosity fell away and she began to paw through Kinzi's things like a dog on the scent, digging avidly for dirt. What she found was a square of fine linen, covered with tiny knot-stitches.

"Well, well, well."

Greshan lounged in the doorway. He reeked of the hunt, of sweat, blood, and offal, a filthy, gorgeously embroidered coat draped over one shoulder. Tunic laces hung loose, half undone, at his throat.

"What have you brought me, Gander? Will I enjoy it?"

They circled each other beside Kinzi's bed. Her long, black hair stirred and rose about her as if in an updraft, although the room was close and still. Her fingertips brushed against his bare chest, leaving faint red lines. He slid his hand through her shining hair, then suddenly gripped it and jerked her face up to his. She stifled a cry, but tears of pain glittered in her pale cheeks. He bent his head, licked them off, and shuddered.

"Bitter," he said thickly. "And potent. Is the magic in your blood as strong?"

"Taste it and see."

The tendrils of black hair that had wound about his hand slowly relaxed into a caress. She gave a husky laugh.

"You should meet my cousin Roane. He likes to play games too."

"Later. Gangray, get out."

She eyed Ganth askance over Greshan's shoulder, black eyes glittering half in mockery, half in challenge. "Oh, let the little boy watch...unless he wishes to join us and become a man."

Then everything stopped.

Kinzi stood in the doorway. The Knorth Matriarch was a tiny, neat, old woman with a crown of tightly plaited white hair which, unbound, would have brushed the floor; but all one really saw, in that froze moment, were her eyes, as hard, bright, and cold as burnished silver.

"Leave," she said to her older grandson. "Now."

Greshan goggled at her, made a choking sound, and reeled past, out of the room.

Knorth and Randir faced each other.

"So. You would bind the Highlord's heir if you could."

"Do you think it beyond me, Matriarch?"

"I think you believe that very little is."

They were circling each other now, gliding, the tall, elegant girl and the tiny, old woman. The boy, forgotten, backed into the corner, as far away as he could get. It seemed to him as if the room was tilting this way and that, twisted by the clash of their wills; but there was no question who was the stronger.

Kinzi held out her small hand. "Give me that."

All this time, Rawneth had been clutching the embroidery with its fine pattern of knot work. Now she tried instinctively to hide it behind her back, but Kinzi's hand was still out. Step by grudging step, she drew the younger woman to her and took the cloth from her.

"If I were to tell the Highlord what those knots say…" Rawneth began defiantly.

"Would you indeed, and betray the very heart of the Women's World? What Adiraina writes in the love-knots of this old letter is meant for me alone."

"If I told…"

"You would be excluded forever from the solace of sisterkinship—if, indeed, anyone should ever want you. As it is, I cast you out from the Women's Halls. Never come back. And leave my grandson alone. He may be a fool, but he is not for the likes of you, nor do you want him for anything but his bloodlines. I smell your ambition, girl, rank as a whore's lust."

The Randir drew herself up, trembling with rage.

"Do you think you Knorth will rule the Kencyrath forever," she spat, "you, who are already so few? And who will come next, when your oh-so-pure blood is finally spent? Do you think about that, old woman, in the long nights? You should. Change is coming. I have foreseen it. I am part of it."

"Not today. Not while I live. Go, snake-heart. Now."

And Rawneth went, out of the room, out of the Knorth quarters, out of Gothregor.

Kinzi sank onto her bed and dropped her head into her trembling hands. She looked suddenly smaller and more vulnerable than the boy had ever seen her. It frightened him.

She looked up. "Ah, child. You shouldn't have seen that. Forget."

His eyes went blank and he stood swaying like one asleep on his feet. Clearly, he had indeed forgotten.

Her gaze shifted to the watcher who stood in his shadow. "Perhaps that was wrong of me. I never made him face what he was, or knew what his brother had done to him as a child until it was too late, the harm already done, and he grown out of reach. I made so many mistakes. We all did. And now you live with the consequences."

*Lady…*

It was hard to speak as a dream within a dream, to a past in which she did not exist. Her voice sounded to her like the thin whine of the winter wind under a door.

*Rawneth. The Witch. I see how your quarrel started, but why did it end like that, in such slaughter?*

Kinzi seemed about to answer, but then her look sharpened, and her voice as well. "Child, you have company. Wake up."

"W-w-wha…?"

Jame lurched out of sleep, thoroughly disoriented. Where was she…and why was someone scrabbling at the jacket, trying to get at her throat? She freed a hand with difficulty from the coat's embrace, caught the other by the wrist, and stopped the knife's descent. Along its fire-lit edge, she met a young Kendar's furious glare.

"Narsa, what in Perimal's name…"

"I told you: Timmon is mine."

The Ardeth cadet bore down on the steel until the point touched the hollow of her throat, but then Jame gathered her wits and kicked her off. Both rolled off the raised hearth and onto their feet, one surprised to find that, as in her dream, she was naked. And unarmed. And furious.

"Dammit, I was finally about to get some answers, and you come busting in with your stupid jealousy! Oh." The floor seemed to lurch; no, that had been her own unsteady legs. The square bottle was striking back.

*Wonderful,* she thought. *I'm about to fight for my life while half-drunk.*

"I told you…"

"And I'm telling you: he's not mine." Jame sat down on the hearth, to make a virtue of necessity. "Take him if you can get him, with my blessings, or find someone better."

"Y-you've bewitched him!" The knife wove before the Ardeth, but her eyes spilled over with such tears that it seemed unlikely she could strike true with it. Her thin face was already blotched and swollen with weeping. "He can't talk about anyone but you, especially tonight. Jameth this, Jameth that, on and on and on…"

"You're the one who put Addy in my bed," said Jame, suddenly enlightened. "You did me a good turn there, but you've got to stop sneaking up on me while I'm asleep. Someone could get hurt."

"Witch!" Narsa threw the knife at her, missed, and fled, wailing.

As Jame fished in the ashes of the dying fire for the blade, Jorin ambled out of the shadows, yawning.

"Some guardian you are," she told him.

How was she supposed to dream true with all these interruptions? For that matter, how did one tell the true from the false in such matters? That last dream had felt painfully real. How like Greshan, and Rawneth, and—here came a pause—that poor boy, who would one day become her father. But nowhere had she caught so much as a glimpse of her brother, Tori.

Jame sighed. Painful or not, it hadn't been the dream she was after. She would have to try again.

Whatever was in the green bottle seemed to help, even if it made waking more a nightmare than sleep. She picked it up, feeling by its heft that it was still half full, with a solid residue at the bottom.

A warning sounded in the back of her mind: *The more you drink, the less control you will have.* Under that came a more urgent whisper: *Think. The Witch's taunt has set you on this path: Little girl, dare you try?*

She wasn't thinking clearly and she knew it; but the taunt galled, as it was meant to. Caution be damned.

*Yes, I dare.*

She upended the bottle and, half choking, drained it.

# VI

THE SECOND ROUND of the cull slowly drew to its close. This time, the Council had reversed the order so that the Knorth came last. Before that, the stones were cast again and again, settling the fate of cadet after cadet. Three black and six white, in. Six black and three white, out.

The Danior sniffed. "Do you smell something burning?"

A sargent went to investigate. On his return, he bent to whisper in the Commandant's ear, then resumed his station.

"Well?" demanded the Ardeth.

Sheth dismissed the matter with an incautious shrug, followed by a suppressed wince. "There has been a small fire in the stable, but it is under control. Proceed."

Finally, only one cadet remained in doubt: the Knorth Lordan, Jameth.

The Randir and Jaran cast as they had at first, the former against, the latter for. The Ardeth also tossed an obsidian sphere into the circle: even if it hadn't suited M'lord Adric that the Knorth girl should escape his schemes, the senior randon of his house didn't approve of her being at Tentir on general principles. The Danior, defiantly, cast white, as did the Edirr, with a mischievous grin. Coman, black. Brandan, white.

"That's four white and three black," murmured the Commandant. He fingered a stone, then sighed and cast it.

Black.

"Why?" burst out the Danior. "I thought you liked her."

"So I do."

"What, then? Did M'lord Caldane order you to vote against her?"

"Of course."

"And you agreed?"

The Danior's voice cracked slightly. He wasn't asking as much for one cadet, even a lordan, as for Tentir. The others stirred uneasily. All knew that politics played a role at this level, but none cared to admit it, especially when it ran counter to their own instincts. If the best among them surrendered his judgment to his lord's will, what case could the rest make for following their conscience rather than orders?

"I take my lord's wishes into consideration," said Sheth levelly, "but only that. As for the Knorth Jameth, as we all know by now, she has great power and is learning—for the most part—how to control it. As for skills, her Senethar is excellent. Although she might still learn something from Randiroc about wind-blowing, I doubt if anyone in generations has seen a purer style."

"Yes." The Coman leaned forward, as pugnacious as his young lord. "But where did she learn it, eh? Who was her Senethari?"

This, indeed, still caused debate in the officers' mess hall. In Jameth, they seemed to have an effect without a cause, a pupil without a teacher. If she had belonged to any other house, they could have shrugged it off as chance, however unlikely. With the Knorth, however, one had to wonder.

"Well, whoever it was," the Brandan said, "we are her teachers now. Her weapons' mastery is less than satisfactory…"

"Flying swords," murmured the Ardeth. "A new form of combat, perhaps? I seem to remember that her brother once favored throwing knives."

"…however, it isn't hopeless. She can learn. The same goes for leadership."

"But don't forget," interposed the Randir, startling the others because she had spoken so little that evening, "we aren't talking about an ordinary cadet here. She is the Highlord's heir and his possible successor."

Several members of the Council snorted.

"Blackie will never carry through with that," said the Coman. "We all know that he's just buying time. I've even heard that he's considering taking her as his consort when she fails here."

"If she fails."

"When, you mean."

"No, if!"

"No, dammit, when! Remember, none of us thought she would get even this far."

"D'you really think Blackie might contract for her?" the Danior asked Harn undercover of the general uproar, leaning past a disdainful Ardeth who pretended not to hear him. "After all, that was the Knorth way with powerful Shanir before the Fall, and it's not as if he has to ask anyone's permission now."

Harn grunted. "How should I know? Nobody tells me anything."

"Gently, gently." Sheth eased his arm in its sling with a faint grimace. As the candles had waned, the shadows under his eyes had grown. "You begin to sound like a conclave of scrollsmen. No offense, Jurien."

The Jaran Highborn shrugged. He sat on that council as well and might one day, when he retired as a randon, become its director. "Why should I take offense at the truth? Academia has made squabbling a fine art. You, my dear friends, are mere novices by comparison. For that matter, Mount Alban would be pleased to offer the Knorth Lordan a place, if Tentir is fool enough to toss her out. With her brother's permission, of course. She has a mind, that girl. I suggest that we dismiss it at our peril. Anyway, she needn't graduate from Tentir to become Highlord. Ganth didn't. Torisen didn't."

"And here she is vulnerable."

Everyone turned to the Commandant. After all, so far he had only listed reasons why the Knorth Lordan should stay.

"There are the usual risks, of course, but so far she has proved equal to them. If anything, we have been in more danger from her than she from us."

Somebody laughed. Others glared.

"However, this is the Highlord's heir, subject to special judgment. If she passes this cull, the next may prove far more deadly. Come summer, do you really think that she will pass unchallenged, or must she suffer the fate of her uncle? Yes, I both like and value her, too well to want her blood on my hands."

"Nor on mine." Harn let fall his black stone to lie beside Sheth's. He tugged at his already tight scarf, turning an alarming shade of purple in the process. "My house brought death and bitter shame on Tentir once. Never again."

That seemed to take his last breath. As he strained, gaping, to draw another, the Danior made a dive for him across the Ardeth. However, the sargent standing behind Harn reached him first, slipping a knife under the scarf, as if to cut his throat, but instead slicing free the silk.

"I think," said the Commandant, as Harn sat gasping, his face slowly changing from purple to mottled red, "that a short recess is in order."

Four white, five black.

It was nearly dawn. Soon would come the third and last round of the cull when Commandant and Knorth war-leader must cast their extra votes, with only one cadet in question.

# VII

JAME SAT SHIVERING on the ledge of the raised hearth, the Lordan's Coat draped over her shoulders, staring at Narsa's knife which had been driven deep into the floor at the center of the old blood stain. New blood spread out around it and welled up through cracks as if the very wood bled.

Trinity, what a terrible dream.

She had suddenly found herself straddling the hips of a prone Timmon, both of them naked. He had looked as surprised as she had felt, but then he had smiled.

"At last!"

The smile twitched and faded from unease to dawning alarm.

"I think," he had said uncertainly, "that I'm going to throw up again."

"Not on me, you aren't. I told you this dream was dangerous."

Then she had looked down and realized that she was gripping not what she had thought but the hilt of the knife as it jutted obscenely out of Timmon's stomach. Her fingers were still cramped with the effort that it had taken to drive the steel through him, and his blood spilled out over her hands.

With that, she had started awake on the hearth and hastily leaned over its edge to vomit green slime onto the floor, where it was now eating a hole in the wood. Oh, for a drink of cold, clean water. A river. An ocean. But those were passing thoughts.

She also hoped that Timmon was all right. Huh. If nothing else, maybe this would teach him to stay out of her dreams, even when summoned.

What appalled her most, however, was that that had only been the end of the nightmare. In the shock of waking, she had forgotten the rest.

At least she had stopped shivering. The fire roared at her back, fed with more shattered crates, warming her through the heavy, embroidered coat. She had the odd sensation of expanding to fill it. A warmth also filled her stomach, replacing the previous clammy nausea. There was a cup of wine in her hand. She sipped it, and felt the glow within increase.

*That's funny*, she thought, and heard someone chuckle thickly—herself, but not in her voice.

A soft laugh echoed her from the other side of the hearth, from a dark Randir face. Who...oh.

"M'dear friend, Roane."

That slurred voice again. Not hers. His. Greshan's.

"Well, of course," it said. "After all, I *am* the Knorth Lordan."

"Of course you are," murmured the Randir, and touched his glass to his lips without drinking.

The Knorth knew vaguely that he had had far more wine tonight than his companion.

*Can't hold his liquor and knows it. Not like me.*

He took another gulp and started to say something so clever that he burst out laughing at the mere thought of it. Wine spurted out his nose like blood onto his white shirt. That, too, struck him as exquisitely funny.

Behind Roane, in the shadows, stood two figures, watching. He squinted at them. One had a strangely shaped head, as if it had been smashed flat on one side; the other seemed to be chewing on something that squirmed and faintly buzzed. More Randir. Roane had strange servants. Well, damn them all with their superior, knowing airs. He would show them something that they wouldn't soon forget. The best joke yet.

"No, truly," he heard himself cry, "such games we used to play, my brother and I. The things I made him do!"

"Did he enjoy them?"

"Now, if he had, where would have been the fun? Once the poor little fool even tried to tell Father, who called him a liar to his face for his pains."

He was leaning forward now, supporting himself with a hand heavy with glittering golden rings, the gifts of a doting parent.

*Wrap the old fool 'round m'little finger. Be done with him soon. Then we'll see how a true highlord can rule.*

In the meantime, there was this damned Randir with his knowing smirk, as if he knew how much Greshan's younger brother vexed him, and how much it irked him that he *was* vexed.

"Killed our mother, didn't he? Giving birth. Father hates him for that. So do I."

*Saying too much. Stop it.*

He dropped his voice conspiratorially. "Listen. This very minute, he sleeps below in his virtuous cot. Dear little Gangrene, all grown up and come to play soldier. Shall we summon him, eh? See if he remembers our old midnight game?"

"Why not? It might be...amusing. Permit me."

Roane's misshapen servant stepped forward in response to a languid gesture and silently left the room.

Greshan licked his lips, feeling a sudden flush of anticipation. It had been a long time. Not that the real pleasure came from the act, but from the control, the sense of superiority. No one stood up for Ganth Grayling but their grandmother Kinzi, and he was sure that the little bastard hadn't told her anything. He had that much pride at least. Too much pride. To think that dear little Gander had actually come here, as if to make something of himself. What arrogance. Clearly, he hadn't yet learned his place, which was to be, always and forever, infinitely his brother's inferior.

The door opened. On the threshold stood a slim figure, backed by the odd clot that was Roane's servant. The latter shoved the former inside and closed the door after them. The lock snicked. At a push, the boy stumbled forward through a welter of discarded clothes and came into the light.

Jame looked into Torisen's wary eyes.

*We have been here before, haven't we?* they seemed to ask.

*Yes. Now we are here again.*

The others' voices became a distant mutter. Greshan was telling his brother Ganth to take off his clothes. Fingers fumbling numbly, the thin boy with the strangely familiar face removed his tunic. Knorth and Randir laughed at his slight build.

"Now the pants," said Greshan.

*Tori, remember in the Earth Wife's lodge? I warned you this was coming. Fight him! Resist!*

When the boy didn't move, the ruin that was Simmel grabbed one of his arms and the Tempter, coming out of the shadows, seized the other. Her ruined lips moved, dribbling insectile fragments, as she whispered honeyed poison in his ear. Roane sauntered toward him, turning a familiar knife in his hands. Now he was behind the young cadet who was, simultaneously, Ganth Grayling in the past and Torisen Black Lord in the present.

Jame shivered. She had wanted to learn what had happened to her father, not to force Tori to relive it; but she had also wanted him to see, to understand. Was this all her fault?

She felt her ears clear, as if water had drained out of them.

"Little boys should do as they are told," Roane was saying softly.

He teased the knife point under the captive's waist band and, with a flick of the wrist, cut it.

"In your grandfather Gerraint's day, your house was soft, rotting from within. There sits the sodden proof on the hearth."

The blade slid neatly down first one leg, then the other. *Snick, snick.* Clothes fell away.

"Such a one I could have molded to my purpose, or so I believed."

He was speaking directly to Torisen now, a dead voice out of the dead past, yet with a familiar under-note. Simmel snickered. The Tempter broke into her ghastly grin. Both pressed in on their prisoner who stood rigid between them. This was the boy whom Jame had met in the Earth Wife's lodge, her twin brother as he should always have been, her age, her peer, but now so terribly vulnerable. Granted, being stripped naked didn't help.

Simmel leaned in, mumbling through a mouthful of dust. "You're weak, and y'know it."

From the other side came the Tempter's insidious, buzzing whisper: "Your people trust you and you fail them. How many more will slip through your fingers?"

Torisen's hands clenched into fists. They had been unmarked in the Earth Wife's lodge, but now the hint of white scars rose on them. The Randirs' words had hurt. Sinews flexed up his arms as he tested the grip in which he was held. For someone so slight, he had wiry muscles and balance, but not yet the experience he would gain with age.

*I'm sorry*, Jame tried to tell him.

The corner of his mouth almost twitched in response: *You would be.*

Roane followed his gaze. "You see her in his eyes, don't you? Your sister. The Shanir freak from nowhere. She will fail you too, or worse. See how alike they are, uncle and niece, monsters both."

*We are not!*

"Monsters, or alike?"

Snarling, Jame struggled to free herself. *Just you wait.*

Although she could see and hear clearly, Greshan's essence still enfolded her like the rank folds of his coat. This might be her dream, but she no longer felt in control of it.

A trap. A trick. But whose, and how?

"Witch." Her voice was his, thick, hard to manage. "You planned this."

Roane smiled, mockingly, askance, teeth white and sharp, eyes obsidian. "I hoped, and the liquor helped. Dear, dead Greshan. How else was I to learn what you would never tell me?"

"Don't…"

Jame felt his dull alarm, like the noxious gas of corruption rising through mud.

"Ah, but why not? We might have savored this together. Lover, how we would have laughed! But the past has weight. Set in motion, it must follow its course." Long-nailed fingers caressed the captive's cheek. Torisen stiffened. "Now be a good little boy," purred that two-toned voice, Roane and Rawneth together. "Submit."

As the Randir moved behind him, his gaze becoming remote and stony. So he must have looked when the Karnid torturers had presented him with their gloves of white-hot wire. Now as then, he would endure and survive; but oh, the pain and the scars, the branded memory…

Jame felt something inside her snap.

*Be angry. Be strong.*

"You will not hurt my brother," she said, and she spoke from the clutch of cold hands, over her shoulder to a man dead these forty years.

Her hands twisted in their clammy grasp and gripped them in turn. She sent Simmel floundering, suddenly boneless, into the figure on the hearth and the Tempter headfirst into the fire. The knife's point skittered across her hip, drawing its own hot line of pain. As Roane's wrist shot past, she grabbed it, pulled, and bent. They were on the floor now, she on top, Narsa's blade between them. Firelight shifted across their faces as the Tempter staggered about the room, wrapped in flames. Flakes of charred cloth and skin whirled away. Then a swarm of blazing bees erupted from her and she fell.

Jame looked down into the Randir's wide, obsidian eyes, and smiled. "The past does have weight," she said. "Let's see how you like it." And she drove the knife into his belly. Down it went with all her cold fury behind it through muscle walls, scrapping against the spine, into the floor. Blood welled up over her hands. Then, slowly, she screwed the blade home.

Something shadowy blundered away from the hearth with a faint cry of horror and the fading stink of voided bowels. Her brother stood in its place, a black silhouette against the flames.

"This is what happened," she told him, breathing hard, trying to collect herself. "Our father's berserker nature saved him, but he couldn't face what he was or what he had done, so he left Tentir that night. Tori? Do you hear me?"

But he was gone.

Jame looked down at a knife stuck in the floor, in the middle of the old stain, and at her own bloody hands, the palms cut on the blade's edge.

"Oh, schist," she said, then bent over to retch painfully from the bottom of her soul.

# Chapter XXIII: Touchstone

## Summer 111

## I

AN HOUR OR so before dawn, the horse-master emerged from Old Tentir into the training square. There he paused, rubbing his hands together for warmth against the early morning chill, noting the unusual but subdued stir in the barracks. Some cadets still kept vigil, perhaps playing gen to stay awake. Others probably dozed on benches or the floor, waiting for word of the cull's outcome. Only the most phlegmatic or exhausted would be in bed.

Where had he been, some fifty years ago, on this night? For a moment he couldn't remember and felt mildly alarmed. Had that Randir bash to the skull scrambled his few remaining wits? After all, it wasn't as if he had any hair left to cushion the odd blow. Then to his relief it came back to him: He had been in the stable. With the dun mare. Waiting for her to foal. Of course, she had waited until he turned his back. They always did. A fine colt that had been— three white socks twinkling in the dusk as if they ran by themselves. Odd to think that the mare and all her babies were long dead, although their blood still ran strong in the herd. Wild Ginger and steady Brownie, foolish Knicker who spooked at everything and naughty Marne with that sly, side-long look before she kicked...

Come Autumn's Eve, he would walk between the stalls naming all their occupants, past and present, perhaps pausing by an empty box to listen to a mare suckle a newborn foal, fifty years ago.

Above, the Map Room windows glowed softly. The Council was still hard at it. The horse-master had guessed that they would have a long session, if only because of one particular cadet. Being who and what he was, he worried more about the fate of two unlikely equines. Still, it was a pity that such a fog of distractions surrounded the Knorth Lordan. With any other cadet...ah, well, there it was: she wasn't just a cadet but a lordan, and Knorth, and female. Too many complications, too much to make the Council nervous, especially these days. Things were much simpler in the stable—usually.

He applied his flatten nose to his sleeve, sniffed, and made a face at the stench that clung to it. *You've lived to see strange times, old man.*

Shouldering his leather work bag, he left the college by its northern gate and headed west along its outer wall, toward the hills above.

It was still dark with a freckling of stars overhead and a waning gibbous moon perched atop the western peaks, about to roll down the far side. The air was crisp and still, his breath a haze through which he walked. He thought about winter fodder, and bedding, and the stable fit to burst with horses on the coldest days when all must be brought in or risk lung infection. The Commandant would probably allow him to use the great hall for the over flow or for quarantine if the winter cough broke out again. Some Highborn might complain—what, a manure pile under our precious house banners?—but Sheth Sharp-tongue was too sensible to listen to such nonsense. If he weren't also so moody, he would have made a good horse. That, from the master, was the highest form of praise.

At last here was the jumble of massive, pale boulders, glimmering in the dark. Among them, he came suddenly on the White Lady seated on a rock by the stream. With a flash of white limbs, she leaped to her feet, all four of them, a human cry turning half way through into a mare's frightened whinny.

"Now, now..." he said, to soothe her, but from behind came a hasty step.

The master turned, swinging his heavy bag, clouting the rathorn on the nose.

"Behave, you," he told the colt as it retreated with an outraged snort, shaking its head. "Sorry, lady. I didn't mean to frighten you."

Then it was his turn to start. With a splash and a gasp, the Knorth Jameth sat up in the stream and clawed wet hair out of her eyes.

"If you're trying to drown yourself," he told her, "the water is too shallow."

"I have a headache. Or maybe a hangover."

"You aren't sure?"

"I've only been drunk once before."

She rose, wobbling in the swift current as smooth river stones shifted underfoot. Long, black hair clung to her like a sleek pelt, leaving slim, white arms and legs incongruously bare except for rising goose-bumps.

"Cold water helped, the last time. At least now I don't feel like turning my stomach inside out."

He handed her a cloth as she waded ashore. "Here. Rub yourself down."

While she wrung out her hair and then hastily dressed to a chill clatter of teeth, he unwrapped the mare's leg and felt it. No heat. The tendon had settled firmly back into place and the swelling had at last subsided.

"Good as new," he said, pleased. "Still, we'll keep it bandaged for a few days more to be sure."

"Master, what's that smell? You reek like a pyre."

He paused, remembering. "Well, now, that was a strange thing. We'd put the Tempter's body in an empty stall, hoping that the Commandant would change his mind about exposing it outside the walls. After all, the woman was a randon. Then I heard horses cry out and smelt that greasy smoke. No mistaking it. Her body had burst into flames as if someone had spoken the pyric rune over her, but nobody was there. It burned down to ash, all but the hands, feet, and skull, which split open in the heat. The straw beneath was scorched, but nothing else. Very strange indeed."

"Yes," said the Knorth. "Very strange."

From her tone, he might almost have thought that she knew more about it than he did, but that was silly.

"Randi..."

He stopped himself. Best not to say that name in the open. Such were the days in which they lived, where the innocent suffered rather than the guilty and the past threatened to overshadow the present. Without thinking, he slid his hand up the Whinno-hir's leg to pat her shoulder. Greshan had paid for what he had done to her but, in the master's opinion, not enough.

"That's to say, Mer-kanti is saddling Mirah. Huh. Actually, he was in the stable with her all night, keeping watch and playing artist. If you're traveling with him and that cadet as far as Gothregor, you should go."

"I take it that Gari passed the cull."

"Yes." He had heard that much, at least, before the fire. "On the first round, without a challenge."

"Good."

She was standing over him now, absently braiding the mare's silky white forelock and mane to cover the marred half of her face.

The Whinno-hir leaned into her with a sigh, cheek to cheek, scar to scar. Sisters of the brand.

"Master, you've been at the college a long time, haven't you?"

So long that he had almost forgotten his own name, his own house. So long that all the family he cared to claim ran on four legs.

"Were you here when my father was a cadet?"

"Yes." What next?

"He never really had a chance, did he?"

"No."

"I didn't think so. Still, in the end, he found his strength and fought back. For that, if nothing else, I accept the consequences." She gave a strange little laugh, with a catch in it. "I once called Tori 'daddy's boy,' but in this I am truly my father's daughter, and my uncle's niece. Who would have thought that I had so much in common with either of them. Nonetheless, Tentir gave me my chance. Thank you, master."

*For what?* he wondered, hearing her turn to depart, wishing there was something he could do or say. He knew where he was with horses. With people, though, especially Highborn fillies...

When in doubt, groom.

He picked up a brush, but the mare stepped away from him. She was following the Knorth.

Jameth turned, frowning. Behind her, the eastern sky blushed with dawn.

"Bel, are you sure?" Her eyes sought his. "Master, are *you* sure that she's sound?"

He scooped up his tools and thrust them back into the sack. An idea had sparked in his mind. "She can bear your weight, if that's what you mean, assuming you take it easy. Nine days to reach Gothregor at eight or nine miles per day. Yes. The exercise would do her good."

Still she hesitated. "Well, if you think so..."

"I do."

"All right. Thank you, Bel-tairi. I would be honored."

The colt followed them anxiously. At the gate, as clear as speech, the mare told him to wait. Then they entered the training square.

The master dropped his sack. "Finish grooming her here," he said briskly. "I'll find suitable tack and bring it up."

She cast an uneasy glance around the surrounding barracks, then up at the Map Room's balcony. "This is awfully public. You said once that Bel's return might raise all sorts of ancient stink."

"None worse than what we've already smelt tonight. Carry on."

With that, he left at a trot for Old Tentir and the stable. *We'll see,* he thought, grinning as he went. *Oh yes, we'll just see!*

# II

THE COMMANDANT STOOD by the balcony, watching the western peaks above the college slowly emerge as the eastern sky lightened. It had been a long night. His shoulder throbbed in time to the beat of his heart, but he thought little of that. A randon's life was full of such minor pains. Worse was his sense of failure. He had hoped that fulfilling their duty would restore the Council's sense of honor, but how could it when even he felt compelled to compromise?

*Oh, I knew you were trouble*, he thought wryly of the last cadet whose fate remained undecided. *From the moment you rode into Tentir and tumbled off your horse practically at my feet. You test us, more than we test you. Your house always has. Against you words ring hollow, the form but not the substance of honor. Black stone, white stone, touchstone.*

Behind him, except for the Knorth, the Council was drifting toward the circle. Even those such as the Ardeth who had shown no hesitation before now seemed strangely reluctant. No doubt they told themselves that this was a small matter, easily decided, foolish, even. Trivial. However, it wasn't.

*What were you thinking, Torisen Black Lord, when you handed us this dilemma? Did you even know yourself? You are not one of us, but this girl will be, if she survives Tentir's judgment.*

Meanwhile, Harn had literally backed himself into a corner and stood there twisting the slashed scarf in his thick hands as if trying to figure out how to hang himself with it. The Commandant almost smiled. It had been an interesting challenge, over the years, keeping his old classmate alive and more or less sane. He knew how deeply flawed Harn believed himself to be, but he also understood the man's value. In his own rough way, Harn was also a touchstone, and a test. One reason the Commandant had suspended judgment on Torisen as highlord was that he had seen, from the start, how the boy had helped Harn keep his mental balance.

So too, unexpectedly, had the girl Jameth.

The Ardeth seemed to think that her very presence at the college would ultimately destroy it.

The Commandant considered this. She might, if sufficiently annoyed. Then too, as she had once said to him with that odd, almost embarrassed air of defiance, "Some things need to be broken."

Indeed.

*We have been playing with fire*, he thought. *Fire destroys, but it also purifies, and we are in desperate need of that too. Over the years, too many secrets have festered here. Yet now Harn and I are about to compromise our judgment, because we have seen too many Knorth die. Because we are sick of death. The others won't let her survive Tentir. They dare not. The last Knorth lady, her brother the last Knorth Highlord. Change is coming, one way or another. Will it strengthen or destroy us? Where does one stand in such a time, if not on honor, but what if honor means the death of another innocent?*

Hoof-beats sounded below. The horse-master had entered the square from the north gate, followed by the Knorth Lordan and a small, cream-colored mare with white mane, tail, and stockings, dappled with more white across the rump. No, not just a mare. A Whinno-hir. And not just any one at that.

The master dropped his bag of tools and darted away. The Knorth looked around again, nervous, not seeing the watcher above. Then, puzzled but obedient, she draw a brush from the bag and began to ply it against the mare's already shining coat.

Sheth slowly straightened.

"Well?" said the Ardeth behind him, impatient. "Let's be done."

"I think," said the Commandant, "that you should see this first."

Cadets began to emerge from the barracks in a trickle, then in a tide as word spread. Some stumbled, half-asleep; others didn't understand the excitement.

"So?" grumbled one of Gorbel's Highborn ten-command, kneading his eyes and yawning. "It's the Knorth freak and a white pony."

"Shut up," said Gorbel, his frog-face scrunched into a hard stare.

The horse-master returned with the tack. He placed a pad on the mare's back, then tossed a saddle over it. Meanwhile, Jame slid the bridle over Bel's head, noting as she did so that the bit had been removed. Rue ran out of the Knorth barracks with a packed saddle bag, Jorin trotting on her heels. Jame spotted Timmon at the rail. Seeing that she had seen him, he advanced with a sulky air to meet her.

"Are you all right?" she asked, voice pitched low in the presence of so many interested witnesses.

He rubbed his stomach and grimaced. "I've got a dirty, big bruise, if that's what you mean."

"Sorry. Somehow, I ended up on top of three different people last night, and none of it was any fun."

The corner of his mouth twitched despite him. "Then you weren't doing it right."

There was a stir on the balcony and a groan from its wooden supports as Council members crowded forward, staring down: "Is that...?" "It can't be. She's dead." "I tell you, it *is*." "Bel-tairi!"

The mare regarded them askance, ears flickering nervously, one hoof pawing the ground. She seemed on the verge of flight. Laying a hand on her shoulder, Jame glared up at the swarm of gaping faces. Her uncle might have committed the original sin against Bel, but damn them all for trying to consummate his evil against a true innocent.

*Cowards*, she thought. *Lack-faiths, toadies. Cursed be*...no, not that. Harn's father, Hallik Hard-hand, had paid the price...but for what, exactly?

Quivering muscles stilled under her touch. With ears pinned and teeth bared, the Whinno-hir gave a defiant cry that rang off the stones of Old Tentir like a bugle blast fit to wake the dead from their ashes.

*Yes. Me*, it seemed to say. *I'm back.*

From inside the Map Room came what seemed to be an answering shout of alarm. Like a released spring, the Randir's black "stone" had uncoiled into a host of frantic, fleeing snake-lets. Awl pinned one under her boot by the head as its whip-thin body frantically lashed her. She considered for a moment, then, deliberately, brought her weight down on it with a muffled crunch.

A band of tension seemed to snap in the room.

Sargents pursued the rest of the swarm as it slithered for cover. The senior Edirr and Danior gleefully joined in the hunt, the Brandan and Coman more sedately, while the Jaran tried without success to capture one alive for study. Meanwhile, with an air of supreme distain, the Ardeth stepped up onto the table, as if the better to look down his nose at such unseemly proceedings.

In the confusion, by chance or design, a white stone rolled into the circle, then another and another.

The Commandant sighed. To no one in particular, he said, "I give up. Come what may, who dares to vote against the cadet who has redeemed the Shame of Tentir?"

And he cast his two white markers into the circle, to join nine others. Only Harn hadn't remembered to vote: he was too busy jumping up and down on a bloody smear that had been a Randir snake, in imminent danger of smashing both it and himself through the floor.

The Commandant began to clap softly in time to his colleague's stomping feet. He stepped out onto the balcony and looked down, still striking sound hand against injured, ignoring the jarring pain to his shoulder. The Knorth cadets took it up, led by Rue, then the Jaran, the Brandan, the Danior, and the Edirr. Reluctantly, the Ardeth joined in, then the Caineron, following their lordan's slow, heavy lead. A few Randir cadets clapped, but then self-consciously fell as silent as their officers. Standing to the front with Addy a golden loop around her neck, Shade tapped the rail with a fingertip.

All of this commotion reminded the mare where she was, surrounded by those who had once been her enemies. Jame swung up into the saddle, half to reassure Bel, half because she didn't trust her ability to mount if the Whinno-hir spooked again. Trinity, how little control one had without a bit. Moreover, there had been no time to tighten the girth or adjust the stirrup leathers. The whole world seemed to reel. Above, shadows lurched across the Map Room curtains as if the Council has spontaneously broken into a wild, noisy dance.

"What's going on?" she asked Timmon, clutching Bel's mane

He grinned up at her, his bruise forgotten. "Congratulations. You've survived the cull. Travel safe and return soon."

With that, he slapped Bel on the rump and she sprang forward with Jame nearly out of the saddle. They careened through the great hall of Old Tentir, joined at the stable ramp by Gari on a raw-boned bay and a golden-green mare with rider. Luckily, the outer doors were open. Out they burst into the morning sun, down to the New Road, then south toward Gothregor. An ounce streaked at their heels, and above among the trees a pale, horned shadow kept pace.

Jame managed to hang on to the bolting mare until Tentir was out of sight around the road's curve. Then she fell off.

# GLOSSARY

ADIRAINA—blind Matriarch of the Ardeth, beloved of Kinzi; a Shanir who can determine bloodlines by touch

ADRIC—Lord Ardeth of Omiroth, Torisen's former mentorr

AERULAN—female cousin to Torisen, beloved of Brenwyr, slain in the Massacre of the Knorth women

ANAR—a scrollsman who taught Torisen and Jame in the Haunted Lands keep when they were children

ANARCHIES—a forest on the western slopes of the Ebonbane mountain range, where the Builders disturbed Rathillien's native powers and were destroyed by them

ARON—an Ardeth sargent at Tentir

ARRIN-KEN—huge, immortal, cat-like creatures; third of the three people who make up the Kencyrath along with the Highborn and the Kendar; judges

ARRIN-THAR—a rare form of armed combat using clawed gantlets

ASHE—a haunt singer

AWL—a senior Randir officer

BANE—guards The Book Bound in Pale Leather and the Ivory Knife; half-brother to Jame; may be alive or dead

BARRIER, THE—a wall of mist between Rathillien and Perimal Darkling

BASHTI—an ancient kingdom paired with Hathir on either side of the River Silver

BEAR—a randon who was brain-damaged by an axe during the battle of the White Hills; Commandant Sheth's older brother

BEL-TAIRI—Kinzi's Whinno-hir mare, sister to Brithany, also called the White Lady and the Shame of Tentir

BENDER—brother of Tirandys

BLOOD-BINDER—a Shanir able to control anyone who tastes his or her blood

BONE-KIN—distant kin, as opposed to blood-kin

BOOK BOUND IN PALE LEATHER, THE—a compendium of runes; one of the three objects of power lost during the Fall

BRANT—Lord Brandan of Falkirr

BREAKNECK ROCK—a rock jutting out over Tentir's favorite swimming hole

BRENWYR—sister of Brant; the Brandon Matriarch, also known as the Iron Matriarch; a maledight

BRIER IRON-THORN—a Kendar cadet, formerly Caineron, now Knorth; second in command (or Five) of Jame's ten

BRITHANY—a Whinno-hir and matriarch of the herd; Adric's mount, grand-dam of Torisen's warhorse Storm

BUILDERS, THE—a mysterious, now extinct race of architects who built temples for the Three-faced God on threshold worlds

BURNT MAN, THE—one of the Four who present Rathillien; an avenger linked to fire

BURR—Kendar friend and servant of Torisen

CALDANE—Lord Caineron of Restormir

CATARACTS, THE—site of a great battle between the Kencyr Host and the Waster Horde

CHAIN OF CREATION—a series of over-lapping worlds, each the threshold to a different dimension

CHAOS SERPENTS—vast serpents under the earth whose writhing creates earthquakes

CHANGERS—Kencyr who fell with the Master and, through mating with the shadows of Perimal Darkling, have gained the ability to shape-shift

CHERRY—an Edirr cadet

CHINGETAI—the Merikit chief

CLEPPETTY—a friend of Jame's in Tai-tastigon; housekeeper at an inn called the Res aB'tyrr

CLOUD—Commandant Sheth's warhorse

CORRUDIN—Lord Caldane's uncle and chief advisor

DALLY—a young male friend of Jame in Tai-tastigon

DAR—a Knorth cadet, one of Jame's ten-command

DARK JUDGE—an Arrin-ken allied to the Third Face of God, That-Which-Destroys, also to the Burnt Man

DARKLING CRAWLER—a wyrm, or very large creepy-crawly with a poisonous bite

DARKWYR SIGN—a gesture made to avert evil

DEATH BANNERS—tapestry portraits of the dead woven of threads taken from the clothes in which they died.

DEATH'S-HEAD—a rogue rathorn, also the name adopted by the rathorn colt whose mother Jame killed

D'HEN—a knife-fighter's jacket, with one tight sleeve and one full, reinforced with steel mesh, to turn attacker's blade

DIREHOUNDS—savage hunting dogs with black legs and head, white body

DREAMSCAPE—as with the soulscape, Kencyr dreams can touch, even overlap. However, on this superficial level one can only observe and sometimes communicate, not act.

DWAR—a forced sleep that promotes healing

EARTH WIFE, THE—also known as Mother Ragga; fertility goddess representing the earth

EARTH WIFE'S FAVORITE—a role in a Merikit rite, usually undertaken by a young man who acts as the Earth Wife's lover while pretending to be her son.

EAST KENSHOLD—a Kencyr border keep on the Eastern Sea

EBONBANE, THE—the mountain range that separates the Eastern Lands from the Central Lands

ERIM—a Knorth cadet; one of Jame's ten-command

ESCARPMENT, THE—three hundred foot tall cliffs on the northern edge of the Southern Wastes

FAITH-BREAKERS, THE—Knorth Kendar who refused to follow Ganth into exile and subsequently found places in other houses.

FALCONER, THE—the blind master of hawks at Tentir, who also teaches all Shanir with the ability to bond to other creatures

FALL, THE—some 3000 years ago, the current Highlord, Gerridon, betrayed his people when promised immortality by Perimal Darkling. This caused the Kencyrath's flight to Rathillien

FOUR, THE—Rathillien's elemental powers, represented by the Eaten One (water), the Falling Man (air), the Earth Wife (earth), and the Burnt Man (fire)—real people who suddenly at the point of death found themselves gods due to the activation of the Kencyr temples

GANTH GRAY LORD—the former Highlord; Jame and Torisen's father

GARI—a Coman cadet, bonded to insects

GEN—a game

GERRAINT—father of Ganth

GERRIDON—twin of Jamethiel Dream-weaver, also known as the Master, who as Highlord betrayed the Kencyrath to Perimal Darkling in return for immortality; see the Fall

GORBEL—present Caineron lordan

GRAY LANDS—where the unburnt Kencyr dead walk

GRAYKIN—Jame's servant; Caldane's Southron, bastard half-cast son

GRESHAN GREED-HEART—Knorth Lordan before Jame, uncle to Jame, brother to Ganth

GRIMLY HOLT, THE—wood on the edge of the Great Weald where Grimly's pack lives

HALLICK HARD-HAND—Knorth commander during time of Greshan; father of Harn

HARN GRIP-HARD—Torisen's randon friend and war-leader, a former commandant of Tentir, also a berserker who fears that he is losing control

HATHIR—an ancient kingdom paired with Bashti on either side of River Silver

HAUNTED LANDS, THE—land north of Tai-tastigon, under the influence of Perimal Darkling, where Jame and Torisen were born during their father's exile

HAUNTS—anything that has been tainted by the Haunted Lands and is therefore neither quite dead nor quite alive; usually mindless

HAWTHORN—a Brandan captain at Tentir

HEART OF THE WOODS—a place of ancient power, near where the battle of the Cataracts took place

HIGH KEEP—the Min-drear border keep far to the north, home of Rue

HIGH KENS—a highly formal and archaic version of the Kencyr language

HIGHLORD—leader of the Kencryath, always (at least until now) a Knorth

HOLLENS—Lord Danior of Shadow Rock, also known as Holly

HONOR'S PARADOX—where does honor lie, in obedience to one's lord or to oneself?

HURLEN—a town of wooden towers on islets at the convergence of the Silver and Tardy Rivers

IMMALAI—an Arrin-ken of the Ebonbane

IMU—a little clay face, dedicated to Mother Ragga

INDEX—a scrollsman herbalist who studied the Merikit

IRON-JAW—Ganth's warhorse, now a haunt

ISHTIER—a renegade priest of the Priests' College

IVORY KNIFE, THE—one of the three lost objects of power whose least scratch is fatal, now guarded by Bane

JAME—also called Jamethiel Priest's-bane and (incorrectly) Jameth; Torisen's twin sister, but ten years his junior

JAMETHIEL DREAM-WEAVER—caused the Fall, twin sister of Gerridon and mother of the twins Jame and Tori

JEWEL-JAWS—a type of carnivorous insect

KIRIEN—a scrollswoman and the Jaran lordan

JORIN—a blind, Royal Gold hunting ounce, bound to Jame

JURIEN—Jaran Highborn and Randon Council member

KALLYSTINE—Caineron's daughter, Torisen's consort for a time, who slashed Jame's face

KARIDIA—the Coman Matriarch

KARNID—religious fanatics who live in the Southern Wastes. Their torture permanently scarred Torisen's hands.

KENAN—Lord Randir of Wilden, father of Shade, son of Rawneth

Kencyr Houses: [see chart]

KENCYRATH—The Three People, chosen by the Three-faced God to fight Perimal Darkling

KENDAR—one of the Three People, usually servant class

KERAL—a darkling changer

KEST—a Knorth cadet; one of Jame's ten-command

KILLY—a Knorth cadet; one of Jame's ten-command

KINDRIE SOUL-WALKER—a Shanir healer, first cousin to Jame and Torisen

KIN-SLAYER—sword belonging to Torisen

KINZI—great-grandmother to Torisen

KITHORN—northernmost of the Riverland keeps, now on Merikit land. Marc's former home

KOREY—Lord Coman of Kraggen

KOTHIFIR—a city on the edge of the Southern Wastes, called the Cruel

LAWFUL LIE—Kencyr singers (and some diplomats) are allowed a certain poetic license with the truth

LORDAN—a lord's designed heir, male or female

LOWER HUDDLES—a field near Hurlen where battle of Cataracts took place

LYMERS—hounds, scent trackers

LYRA LACK-WIT—Lord Caineron's young daughter, sister to Kallystine

MALEDIGHT—a Shanir who can kill with a curse

MARC, MARCARN—Kendar friend of Jameth, seven foot tall, ninety-five years old, a former warrior

MARROW—cadet guard, Knorth

MASSACRE, THE—nearly thirty years ago, Shadow Assassins killed all the Knorth ladies except for Tieri; no one knows why, but Jame has her suspicions

MASTER, THE—Gerridon

MASTER'S HOUSE, THE—where Jame went when her father drove her out; the House extends back down the Chain of Creation from fallen world to world, stopping just short of Rathillien

MERIKIT—a native hill tribe, living north of Kithorn

MER-KANTI—the Merkits' name for Randiroc

MIN-DREAR—a minor Kencyr house

MINT—a Knorth cadet, one of Jame's ten-command

MIRAH—a gray mare painted green and ridden by Mer-kanti

MOLOCAR—an enormous war hound

MOON GARDEN, THE—Kinzi's secret courtyard at Gothregor, where Kindrie was born and which still serves as his soul-image

MOTHER RAGGA—also known as the Earth Wife; one of the Merikit's four elemental gods

MOUNT ALBAN—home of the Scrollsmen's College

NARSA—a female Ardeth cadet, in love with Timmon

NEW ROAD—flanks the Silver River on the western side

NEW TENTIR—the hollow square of barracks behind Old Tentir where the cadets live

NIALL—a Knorth cadet, replacement for Kest; survivor/veteran of the Cataracts

OLD BLOOD, THE—see Shanir

OLD TENTIR—the original stone keep

PEACOCK GLOVES—stolen by Jame in Tai-tastigon

PENTILLA—a young Ardeth highborn woman

PEREDON—son of Ardeth, who supposedly died fighting the Waster Horde in the Southern Wastes; Timmon's father

PERIMAL DARKLING—a kind of shadow that is eating its way up the Chain of Creation from threshold world to world. Under it, the living and the dead, the past and the present become confused.

PRIEST'S COLLEGE, THE—located at Wilden

QUILL—a Knorth cadet, one of Jame's ten-command

QUIRL—a Randir cadet who died trying to assassinate Randiroc

RANDIROC—the so-called lost Randir Heir or Lordan, a randon and Shanir, hiding in the wilds from the Witch of Wilden who has set Shadow Assassins to kill him

RANDON—a military officer and graduate of Tentir

RANDON COLLEGE—where randon cadets are trained

RAN—a term of address to a randon, male or female

RATHILLLIEN—the planet's name

RATHORN—an ivory armored, carnivorous equine, usually with a bad temper

RAWNETH—the Randir Matriarch, also called the Witch of Wilden

REGONERETH—the third face of god, That-Which-Destroys

RES AB'TYRR—an inn in Tai-tastigon

RESTORMIR—the Caineron keep

RIVER ROAD—an ancient road on east side of Silver River

RIVER SILVER—runs down the Riverland, then between Hathir and Bashti to the Cataracts

RIVER SNAKE—the huge chaos serpent that stretches underground from one end of the Silver to the other, causing earthquakes if not fed

RIVERLAND, THE—a long, narrow strip of land ceded to the Kencyrath at the northern end of the Silver

ROANE—Randir, cousin of the Witch of Wilden, killed by Ganth

ROWAN—female friend of Torisen, randon and steward of Gothregor

RUE—randon cadet from Min-drear, one of Jame's ten-command

SARGENT—a sort of non-commissioned randon officer, almost always Kendar, addressed as "sar"

SCROLLSMEN'S COLLEGE—at Mount Alban across from Valantir; also home to the singers

SENETHA—dance form of the Senethar

SENETHAR—unarmed combat divided into four disciplines: water-flowing, earth-moving, fire-leaping, and wind- blowing

SENETHARI—a master and teacher of the Senethar

SEVEN KINGS OF THE CENTRAL LANDS—Bashti and Hathir have devolved into seven minor kingdoms who are always at war with each other, often using Kencyr mercenaries

SHADE—also known as Nightshade; a Randir cadet, bound to a golden swamp adder; half-Kendar bastard daughter of Lord Kenan of Randir, grand-daughter of the Randir Matriarch Rawneth

SHADOW ASSASSINS—a mysterious cult of assassins who make themselves invisible (and ultimately insane) with tattoos that cover every inch of their bodies

SHADOW ROCK—the Danior keep

SHANIR—sometimes referred to as the Old Blood; some Kencyr have odd powers such as the ability to blood-bind or to bond with animals, aligned to one of the Three Faces of God; to be Shanir, one must have at least some Highborn blood.

SHETH SHARP-TONGUE—Commandant of Tentir, Caineron, Caldane's war-leader

SIMMEL—a Randir cadet and crony of Gorbel

SISTER-KINSHIP—sometimes Highborn women of different houses form lasting bonds with each other, about which their lords know nothing.

SNOWTHORNS—the mountain range through which the Riverland runs

SOUL-IMAGES—each Kencyr sees his or her soul in terms of an image such as a house or a puzzle or a garden. A healer works with this image to promote physical and mental health.

SOULSCAPE—all soul images overlap at some point, forming an interwoven psychic landscape; the Kencyrath's collective subconscious

STAV—harvest-master at Gothregor

TAI-TASTIGON—a city in the Eastern Lands where Jame and Marc met

TARDY—a river that converges with the Silver

TARN—a Danior cadet, bound to an old Molocar named Torvo

TEN-COMMAND—the basic squad unit of cadets; its leader is referred to as Ten and the second-in-command as Five

THOSE-WHO-RETURNED—Knorth Kendar who were driven back by Ganth when they attempted to go into exile with him; most became yondri-gon

THREE PEOPLE, THE—Highborn, Kendar, and Arrin-ken, who together are the Kencyrath

TIERI—a highborn Knorth, Ganth's sister, mother of Kindrie and first cousin of Torisen, whose life was saved during the massacre by Aerulan

TIGON—a randon from Jame's youth

TIMMON—a cadet, also, the Ardeth Lordan; son of Peredon (Peri), grandson of Adric

TIRANDYS—male darkling changer, Jame's former Senethari or teacher, deceased

TISHOOO—the southern wind, also called the Falling Man

TORISEN BLACK LORD—High Lord of the Kencyrath, son of Ganth Gray Lord, who stopped the Waster horde at the Cataracts

TRISHIEN—the Jaran Matriarch, a scrollswoman

TROGS—rocks with teeth, given to infesting wells, dungeons, and latrines

TUBAIN—owner of the Res aB'yrr

TUNGIT—a Merikit shaman and old friend of Index

TYR-RIDAN—human vessels for the Three-faced God to manifest itself through in the final battle with Perimal Darkling.

UPPER MEADOWS—a field near Hurlen where the battle of Cataracts took place

URAKARN OF THE SOUTHERN WASTES—citadel of the Karnids

VALANTIR—Jaran fortress north of Tentir

VANT—an officious Knorth cadet

WASTER HORDE, THE—a vast, nomadic, cannibalistic collection of tribes who endlessly circle the Southern Wastes, preying on each other

WEALD, THE GREAT—a large forest in the Central Lands, home to the wolvers

WEIRDINGSTROM—a magical storm capable of transporting people and things instantaneously anywhere

WEIRD-WALKING—using the weirding mist to travel deliberately

WHITE HILLS, THE—south of the Riverland, where Ganth Gray Lord fought a great battle following the Massacre, lost, and was driven into exile.

WHITE KNIFE—suicide knife, an honorable death

WHITE LADY, THE—the Whinno-hir Bel-tairi

WILDEN—the Randir fortress

WILLOW—little sister of Marcarn, killed when Kithorn fell

WINTER—a Kendar randon, first nurse to Jame, killed by Ganth

WOLVER GRIMLY—shape-shifter, friend of Torison

WOLVERS—creatures who shift easily between human and lupine forms, expert singers, usually peaceful unless they come from the deep Weald

WOMEN'S WORLD—the Council of Matriarchs in Gothregor trains young highborn women and initiates them into sister-kinship

WYRM—also called a darkling crawler

YCE—an orphan wolver cub from the deep Weald, rescued by Torisen

YOLINDRA—Matriarch of the Edirr

YONDRI, YONDRI-GON—a Kendar who has lost his or her house and has been offered temporary shelter by another; sometimes called "threshold dwellers"

## MAJOR KENCYR HOUSES

| House | Lord | Matriarch | Lordan | Keeps | Emblem |
|-------|------|-----------|--------|-------|--------|
| Knorth | Torisen | | Jame | Gothregor | Rathorn |
| Caineron | Caldane | Cattila | Gorbel | Restormir | Serpent devouring its young |
| Ardeth | Adric | Adiraina | Timmon | Omiroth | Full moon |
| Jaran | Jedrak | Trishien | Kirien | Valantir | Stricken tree |
| Danior | Hollens | Dianthe | ? | Shadow Rock | Wolf's mask, snarling |
| Brandan | Brant | Brenwyr | ? | Falkir | Leaping flames |
| Coman | Korey | Karidia | ? | Kraggen | Double-edged sword |
| Randir | Kenan | Rawneth | ? | Wilden | Fist grasping the sun |
| Edirr | Essien and Essiar | Yolindra | ? | Kestrie | Stooping hawk |

# The Randon College

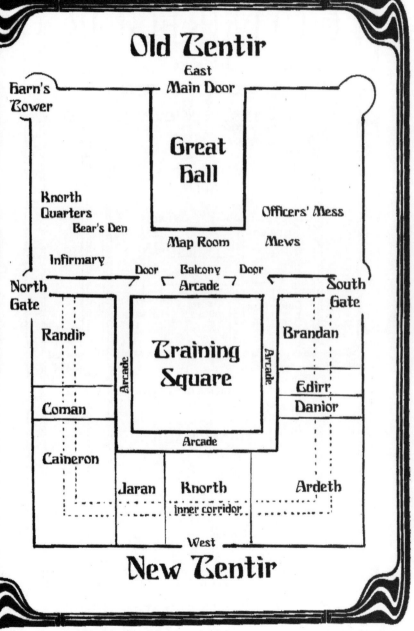

## Old Tentir

East
Main Door

Harn's
Tower

Great
Hall

Knorth
Quarters

Bear's Den

Officers' Mess

Infirmary

Map Room

Mews

Door

Balcony
Arcade

Door

North
Gate

South
Gate

Randir

Brandan

Arcade

Training
Square

Arcade

Coman

Edirr
Danior

Caineron

Arcade

Jaran

Knorth

Ardeth

inner corridor

West

## New Tentir

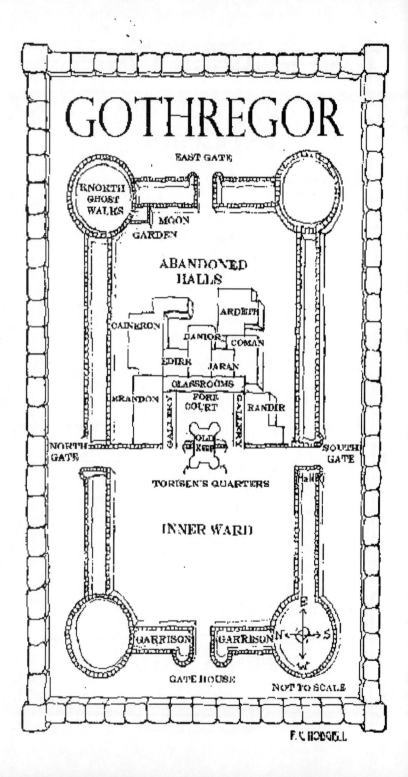

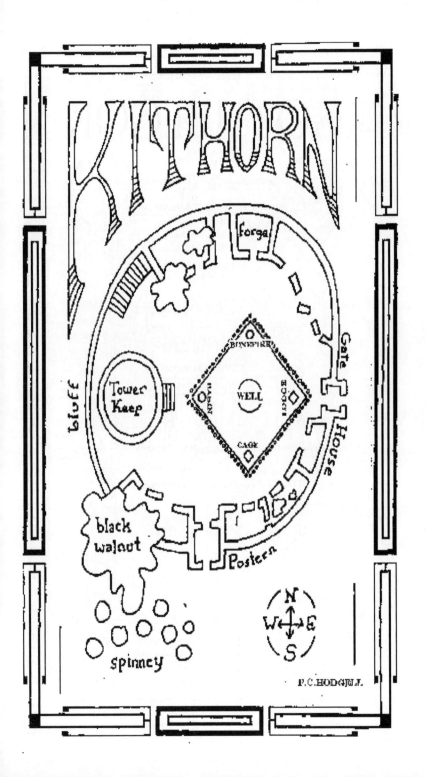

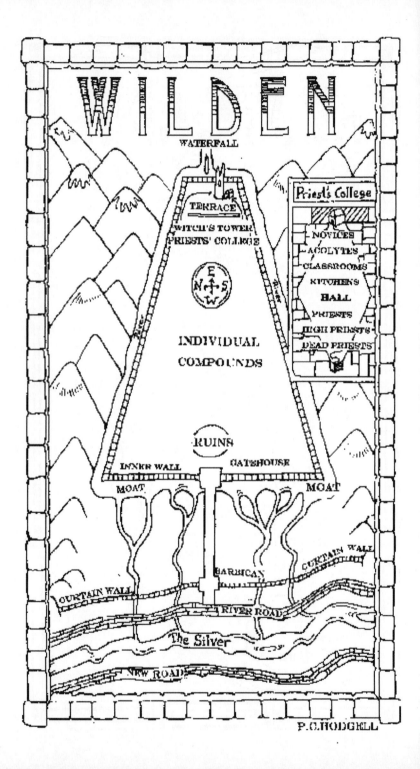

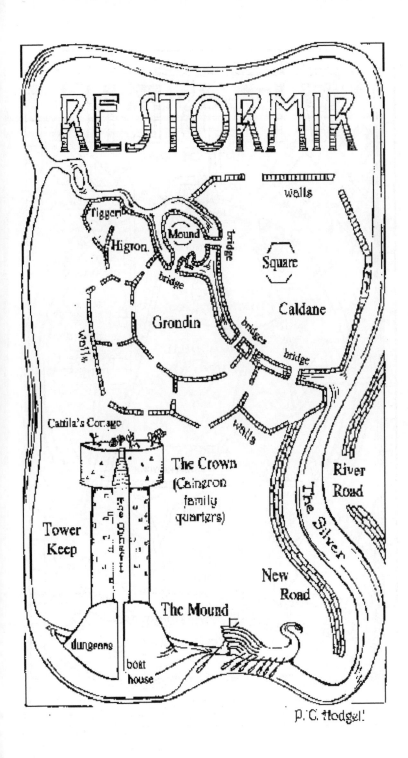

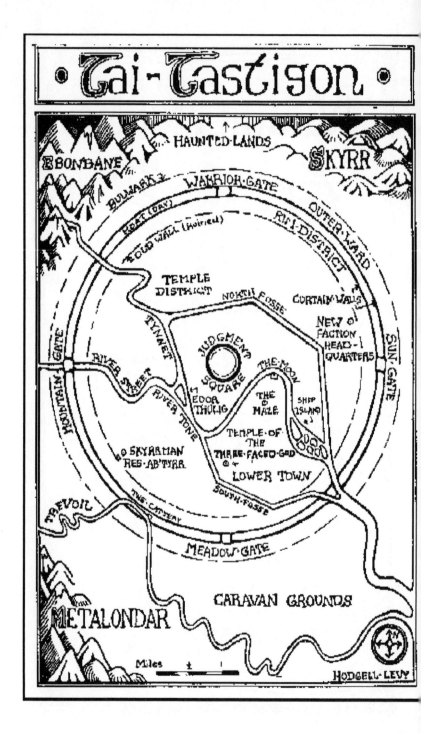

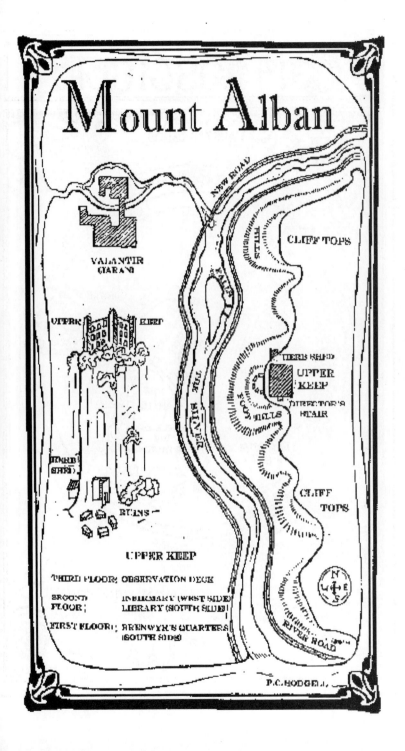

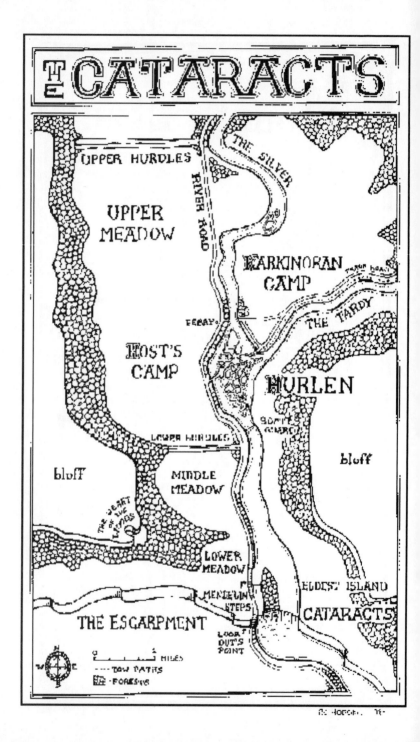